To papa,

here's happy
your birthday,

dots of love
and
Kisses,

Isabelle xxx.
(she of the acting
profession).

The Loves and Journeys of Revolving Jones

LESLIE THOMAS

The Loves and Journeys of Revolving Jones

METHUEN

'You Are My Sunshine', copyright MCMXL by Southern Music
Publishing Co. Inc., New York USA.
Southern Music Publishing Co. Ltd., 24 Denmark St, London wc2.
All rights reserved.

First published in Great Britain in 1991
by Methuen London, Michelin House,
81 Fulham Road, London sw3 6rb

Copyright © 1991 by Leslie Thomas

The author has asserted his moral rights

A CIP catalogue record for this book
is available from the British Library
isbn 0 413 63780 8

Printed and bound in Great Britain
by Clays Ltd., St Ives plc

To Dennis Jones,
with thanks for his generosity

'For man is a giddy thing . . .'

Much Ado About Nothing
William Shakespeare

BOOK ONE

One

According to the story I was conceived on the night of the great Armistice. Everyone was delirious with the celebrations; singing, drinking, wearing hats and jumping up and down, and it seems that my mother, Dora, did more jumping up and down than most. The ink was scarcely dry on the Treaty of Versailles before I was cawing in my cot.

Confusion was rife that night, many errors were made, and it appears that my mother made one of them with a soldier on the unforgiving wood of a church pew. It was St David's, Barry Dock, and David I was called.

Churches had flung open their doors so that people could thank God for the ending of the war, and apparently some were praying in the front pews while I was being briefly created at the back.

Uncertainty travels with us from the very spark of life, the seed dithering, turning this way for male or that for female, some never making the true distinction. My own uncertainty has taken the form of a lifetime of searching, with the roots of the quest very possibly in that November night. A psychologist might diagnose that I was really seeking myself, although at those times it appeared to me that what I sought were pleasant women and true love. Three times I have been married. Perhaps four.

My journeys as a sailor have landed me in many places: Cox's Bazaar, the Isles of the Bingo Sea, the State of Tonk, Dreamer's Creek and the Pongo Gorge up the Amazon. Before that the coast of my childhood spread level as a flat iron along our side of the Bristol Channel. On clear days some people with exceptional eyes boasted they could see England. Back into Wales the backdrop mountains sometimes showed a few green miles away. In Barry, coal dust covered much, gathering in the grass and gutters, lying like black icing on the tops of walls. Even snow turned black and there was often a sheen of coal dust on the sea. The company that owned the coal made a lot of money. In the space of a generation Barry, a village with an island and two beaches, had become one of the famous coaling ports of the world. A clever causeway was built across to the island enclosing and creating instantly a deep-water port. The railway hurried down from the mines. Streets grew like rows of beans on the small hillsides of the town; gas lamps guttered in gritty streets. Men's eyes glinted through black faces and women were dusty.

But I knew even before I was old enough to mutter multiplication at school, that it was a romantic place. One beach was wide and sandy, with coal dust at the hem of the water, frilled like black lace, and the other piled with ramparts of pebbles. In summer there was a funfair grinding out circular tunes.

From the beach, where my uncle used to take me on Saturdays, I would see the ships lying in the Channel, waiting for berths. In the roads, they used to say. Almost my first words were 'Barry Roads' or rather 'B-b-b-arry R-r-roads' because I was born with a stammer. To say my name under even the mildest stress – 'D ... D ... Davy' – was to cover everyone in the vicinity with embarrassment and often spit.

If everything was silent in the parlour room, a place like a little museum with hard velvet furniture and relics of the family, photographs and even pieces of hair in frames, and I was sitting, my aunt would sometimes ask casually but suddenly: 'And what did you say your name was?'

In that calm I could usually throw off 'David' quite well,

4

and she would reward me with a custard cake. Terror began, of course, when eventually I joined the others monkishly chanting tables in the school. I was often several reckonings adrift, stumbling to catch up, like a boy with a leg iron striving to run a race. We had a boy with a leg iron, actually, and he and I had a comradeship based on our infirmities, although he once told me he would rather have my stammer than his leg. Otherwise the matter was never discussed between us; we used to play together and the others understood. Once, however, a boy called Porky Morgan began to bait me by imitating my impediment and Pallister, the boy with the leg, swung it at him. The black iron support caught Morgan across his knee. It was a muffled impact, as though a cushion had been hit with an axe.

Miss Brangwyn, our teacher, had a puffy face and whiskers projecting each side like a cat. She played the piano with soft, bulging fingers and sang shakily. It was after one of these music lessons that she caught my arm kindly. The sun was drifting into the classroom, and shining along her whiskers as it shone on telegraph wires.

'David,' she said. 'You don't stammer when you sing, do you?'

'N . . . n . . . no, miss,' I said. 'The . . . the . . . there's no time.'

She said: 'If you *sang all the time* perhaps it would stop altogether. Sing instead of speaking.'

After that, for a long time, almost every conversation we had at home was in song, an unending oratorio. Uncle Griff and Auntie Blod entered into it with vigour. We sang about mundane things, about eating breakfast or cleaning my shoes. When I came in at four-thirty my aunt would lilt: 'And what did we do at school today?'

'We had playtime,' I would warble back. 'And ge-og-ra-phy.'

When Uncle Griff returned from the Tubal Cain Iron Foundry he too launched himself into this homely opera.

5

'Home, home, home at last,' he would sing in his reasonable tenor, flinging his arms wide. 'The bus was cr-ow-ded.'

'Would you like a cup of tea?' Blod's mouth was heart-shaped.

'I'd relish a cup of tea!' he soared splendidly. He had never refused in twenty-five years of homecomings. 'Two lumps of . . . sugar! Tra . . . la . . . la!'

Although the performances were for my benefit, I was often at a loss because I found myself reduced to the audience. But it did a lot for them. I would look from one bright face, one shaking mouth to another as they chorused. Sometimes they even cut across each other with a descant. And all the while my mouth hung hushed; no chance of getting a tune in edgeways.

Eventually my turn would come. Griff would sit at the blue-clothed table, loudly drink his tea and bite into his regular two thick slices of bread and butter. His singing being temporarily trapped by food, I took my opportunity to join in the recitative. Auntie Blod, who smoked in the evenings, would light a first cigarette and her contributions were accompanied by puffs from her pursed mouth as though she were signalling the words. Neighbours complained on occasions when the windows were open in summer, or we were standing close to the walls and singing very loudly at each other, but generally they were understanding. Anyway, they had always suffered because Griff and Blod were apt to sit up in bed and sing when they could not sleep, no matter what part of the night. Hymns, cantatas, popular marching songs from the First World War, and music hall ditties, all howled around those flowered walls.

My mother was scarcely missed, only appearing as a guest, at first from Cardiff and then, intriguingly, from London. After she went to London her visits became less frequent but more exciting. She dressed differently from Barry people and had an aroma that spiced the house for hours. She arrived grandly by taxi, although the station was only ten minutes' walk away. She had the bobbed hair, the beads and the

6

flighty skirts of those days, her mouth uncompromisingly vermilion, her eyes dazzling as her talk. She smoked a cigarette in a holder, and would trip around the small, cluttered home, changing course sharply as if she were used to much bigger rooms, chattering unceasingly. Sometimes I wondered if she knew who I was.

Her slim hands were flung about and fluttered as she told us of the wonders of London. I was left, narrow-eyed as an ambusher, waiting for my moment to speak, which often never came. I would not sing my feelings to her, nor did my aunt and uncle sing while she was there. Eventually, usually just when I had gathered myself to tell my parent something interesting about my life, she would finish her sherry and exclaim: 'I can hear my taxi,' and off she would flounce, with an exhibition kiss for me, and a final shot of her scent. The taxi driver would gallantly get out and bowingly open the door for her. Her stockinged legs looked like slender white feathers as she tucked them in after her. When she had gone we all used to sit silently, almost sadly, missing her and wondering about our lives, and then Blod would clear the glasses and peer into the empty sherry bottle and say: 'Well, that's Dora.'

'Aye, that's Dora,' Griff would confirm.

One day, just as the taxi was departing down the hill to Barry Dock Station, I singingly asked my aunt why my mother had to live in London and what she did there.

'She's in service,' she sang back sadly. Her eyes glistened. 'It's her destiny.'

The school Houdini was called Tosh Brindley; known for throwing himself in front of chance cars and hanging by his hands from railway bridges. His mother knew little of these stunts, although he was sometimes carried home semi-conscious and gushing blood. Mishaps did nothing to discourage him and he was soon back at school putting his mouth over an unlit but active gas mantle, diving head first into a water butt and – a difficult feat – getting out again. He revelled in

7

his reputation as the local young daredevil. He was nothing to look at, and his scars did not help, but the girls admired him and laughed at his escapades and bravery.

There was a lighthouse down at Porthcraddoc, and still is for that matter, with tourists puffing up its curling stairs, gazing at the long coast from the round windows and tottering down again. The guide tells them a tale about the lighthouse, a bit of legend; but not a mention, of course, of what happened to Tosh Brindley there.

There had been no light nor men in the lighthouse for years. There was no longer any mechanism in the top, just a bare room, and it was a great attraction to all children who were warned by adults to keep away. Boys would go over and stand around the lighthouse, sizing it up, walking around it, hands in pockets, and with frowns, like contractors commissioned to move it somewhere else. Nobody at that time had ever gone inside, however, because it had a front door like a fort, with stout wood and studs, and a massive tongue of a padlock. There was also a cottage where the man was a retired coastguard. If we circled the tower too long he would come out with his dog and a torch and shout at us.

Of course Tosh was lured by the lighthouse and often boasted that one day he would get in and reach the top. He had been basking in glory following his entombment in some disused pit workings, his rescue requiring the efforts of half the men in the district, prayers in chapel and the tears of his mother who nevertheless smacked his face when he was returned, grimy and grinning, to the crust of the earth. The drama got into the *Western Mail* and after that Tosh knew that all that was left was to attempt something bigger.

'Want to take some girls up the lighthouse?' he suggested to me, one day after school.

'Which ones?' I asked trying to be off-hand.

'Any girls,' he answered.

'It's locked.' I did not want to climb the lighthouse.

'There's a window-latch gone. I can get a ladder.'

My heart began to tremble. He was quite a small boy, with

deeply scarred knees and elbows, his black hair singed ginger at that time, I recall, from some abortive home chemistry experiment, and a dent in his forehead from trying to break a brick by butting it. There were stitches on his eyelids. He leaned towards me from the waist, like a skinny bird, and whispered: '*I* been in there.'

'I might be interested,' I lied, and for two nights I could not get to sleep for dreading the dark curling stairs. Putting my head below the blankets I earnestly asked God to take this thing away from me, and I thought He had responded positively because Tosh said nothing more for almost a week. Then he drifted sideways towards me in the playground, and slid the words out of the corner of his mouth: 'Tomorrow night. I got the girls.'

'Can't,' I hedged desperately. 'Scouts tomorrow.'

'Fuck the scouts,' he responded. He was the only boy I knew who said that word without fear of immediate death from God, although, as it happened, God was waiting for him, His patience running low. After what happened I never said 'fuck' again until I chopped the top off my thumb into the Magellan Strait.

'Right you are,' I said to Tosh. 'Fuck the scouts.' I had a fearful fleeting vision of the expressions on the faces of my Auntie Blod, Miss Barley, the scout mistress, and, not the least, God. 'Who are the girls?'

'Daft Hilda,' he said. Then with canny narrowness: 'Dolly Powell.'

He knew my weakness. Dolly was a junior beauty, eyes like bits of coal, ringly hair and swellings beneath her woolly. You could see her smile from the bottom of Barry Hill.

'Dolly?' I asked suspiciously. 'How did you get Dolly?'

'Charm, matey,' Tosh said. 'Easy.' He wiped his disjointed nose with the back of his hand and grinned with his deranged teeth.

'I'm not going with Daft Hilda,' I told him, still fending off the spectre of the lighthouse. 'Not up there.'

'*You* can have Dolly,' he said magnanimously. 'I'll have Daft Hilda. I don't mind.' He nudged me.

'What time?' I said. 'My auntie always comes looking for me after eight.'

'Seven then,' he replied. 'It's dark enough. The password's Geronimo.'

He was as anxious as I was fearful. He needed to show off.

I kept praying Tosh was only boasting. My belief then was that God never took notice of prayers unless they were clearly and audibly detailed; that, due to technical reasons, He failed to receive silent supplications, or turned a deaf ear to them. The thought of God having a deaf ear was strong with me. That day, sitting in the playground lavatory, eyes clenched, hands touching in front of my nose, I prayed as I piddled. But God did not listen.

It was already dark when I got there. Three small shadows stood against the high stem of the lighthouse. Along the coast the beam from a real lighthouse flicked like lightning. There was a semblance of a moon and a smudge of lamplight from the cottage of the former coastguard. Tosh took a couple of decisive paces towards me and said: 'Geronimo.'

'Geronimo,' I responded flatly. 'We'll never be able to get in.' I was wearing my scouts uniform and I was embarrassed.

He went around the tower base and reappeared with a short ladder. 'Watch,' he said. The girls' faces were towards him, the expression in Dolly's eyes, I feared, was admiration.

'This,' I said patting the curved wall, 'looks like a one-legged elephant.' But poetry was lost on girls. They preferred action. Tosh put the ladder against the flank of the tower and climbed up with his customary deftness to a tight window which he easily opened. I wanted the dog to bark so that we could run.

'Geronimo,' Tosh whispered as he heaved himself up and in head first.

His face, white as a coin, reappeared. 'Come on, Davy,' he said. 'Shove them up.'

'He's not shoving me,' argued Dolly.

'Shove her,' repeated Tosh.

The ladder vibrated. I was directly below Dolly's rump. 'No looking,' she warned.

Decently I obeyed, my eyelids falling as my hands reached up to her flannelette buttocks. I pushed. She shakily rose to the window level and disappeared dramaticaly over the sill.

'You next,' I turned dismally to Hilda.

'Shut your eyes then,' she said. She clumped up the ladder. It took all the efforts of all three of us to get her to topple in.

From the ladder I kept glancing at the dumb coastguard's cottage. Along the coast the flashes registered regularly and the moon was fuller. Tosh caught my arms and heaved me through the aperture.

We were in the ground floor chamber. It had once been whitewashed and the growing moon through the window gave it a dingy glimmer.

'We done it!' whispered Tosh.

'Can we go home now?' said Hilda.

'Should have brought a torch,' I said looking around.

'Don't need one,' Tosh replied with the air of a boy who regularly consulted moon tables. 'It's light as light.'

It was, too, and growing. The moon had shuffled clear of the ragged clouds.

We went up into the second room. There was a paned window and the moon shone powerfully through it, forming squares and oblongs on the floor. 'Play hopscotch,' said Dolly. Putting herself on one leg she began hopping from one square of light to the next. Hilda followed clumsily. 'Pack it in,' ordered Tosh.

They stopped and followed him to the next set of stone steps curling up within the wall. Dolly and Hilda were behind him and I came last, protecting the rear. We were all jammed together on the dark stairs. Up and up we climbed, stage by stage.

We reached the last stage below the room where the light had once been.

'I'll go up first,' I said decisively.

There was a trap door. I pushed it up with my hands and my head.

As though I had released a devil, a scream and a commotion came from the room. I let the trap go with a bang and I fell down on Tosh who knocked over the girls. We were all in a pile on the stairs.

'S . . . S . . . something's . . . uuuuup there!' I stammered.

'Seagulls,' said Tosh. Pushing me aside he climbed up to the trap and levered himself into the room. I could see his shape in the moonlight. 'Stinks of shit,' he called down.

Dolly and Hilda giggled. Tosh said the girls should climb up next. I helped them, the light Dolly and the breathless Hilda. Then I tried but failed. Tosh descended like a demon, swinging, landing on his toes. I climbed on his back and reached the edge of the trap door. The girls hauled me through. Then Tosh sprang and, with his hydraulic arms, pulled himself up.

There were gull droppings and feathers on the floor. One of the window panes was missing. There was only now a straightforward ladder to the light chamber. Tosh let me go first. I got to the top and climbed into the room, into the centre of a great circle of windows; through them poured the unchecked silver of a gleaming moon.

The others followed and we stood, a small quartet, casting shadows longer than ourselves across the dusty floor, each of us revolving slowly to take in the full amazing sight.

But Tosh was not one to waste time on beauty. He strode towards an iron-framed door set into the curve of the window, wrenched the handle down and the door opened. Sharp air came in. He turned with a sort of triumph and said: 'Let's have a look out here . . . Dolly.'

The bastard, I thought. Oh, the bastard.

'All right,' agreed Dolly brightly. She stepped towards the door. Her bare legs looked pale in the moon. As I turned to Hilda I saw my disappointment reflected.

Together we glanced at Tosh and Dolly standing, romantic

and unafraid, on the open gallery outside the huge curved window.

Hilda grunted and let me put my arm around her solid waist. I could feel her elastic.

'I like being up here with you,' I lied. My other arm completed the circle around her, and I attempted to revolve her towards me. 'You're my sort of woman,' I said, trying to sound like a picture house hero. She seemed pleased, and turned herself towards me so that we were chest to chest.

I put my lips to hers and bent her over dashingly. She toppled backwards and we fell together to the hard and dirty floor. I ended up astride of her, staring down at her shocked expression, eyes already welling moonlit tears. At that moment Dolly appeared at the door in the curved window and said flatly: 'Tosh just fell off. He's down the bottom.' She began to sob. Hilda and I got up, dust all over us, and stood without moving. 'Go and have a look,' Dolly said. 'You can see him.'

I made myself go towards the door, the girls behind me. I stepped out onto the narrow metal gallery. It was terrifying out there in space, cold air and blatant moonlight. Dolly followed me but Hilda hung around by the door. A few paces along the gallery one of the rusty iron rails had broken away. Part of it was still attached and hung like a finger pointing down. 'There,' snivelled Dolly. 'See him?'

Fearfully I peered over. Tosh was clearly visible, lying still, far below on the rocky grass. 'This time he's really done it,' I said.

He was lying on his face, his arms and legs spread out at his four corners. He looked like a star. Just like a little star.

Once I kept diaries, log books really, but they are disused now, dead as spent fireworks, old letters, or ancient flowers; or the clothes that someone you loved once wore.

They are kept, with other bits, in a trunk which bears the initials 'RH' in brass studs arched over the dome of the lid. Everything else has worn and rubbed away, but if you give the studs a polish they shine yellow, like the eyes of a cat. Robert Horncastle, the initials stand for. He went missing by intention, overboard in the Tasman Sea almost twenty years ago. A whole watch had elapsed before he was missed. Hooker Collins, tears rolling down his pink cheeks, rushed along the deck bawling, 'Man overboard!' Man overboard!' over and over, not to anyone in particular, not even to the skipper, but to the sea; shouting at it out there, dark and callous, accusing it. But the sea has no remorse. It shrugs. Hooker was Robert's old woman, as sailors say, and it was a tragic night for him. It emerged that Hooker had told Robert that he was giving up the life and going back to his Birkenhead wife and Robert, understandably upset, had gone over the side. In the fo'c'sle the night before we had been talking among ourselves about Davy Jones' Locker. They always joked about my name. A Saban fellow had said that it was really Daffy Jonah because the Caribbean sailors called a ghost a Daffy and that Jones was really Jonah, of the whale; so Davy Jones is Jonah's ghost.

Whether all this got Robert Horncastle thinking about his situation I do not know, pointing the way down, but I can imagine it. The skipper knew what he had to do under the laws. He put the ship in a Wilson turn, like a figure eight, the quickest way to turn a big vessel around, and went back for as many hours as Horncastle had been missing, which in his case was a whole watch. That is a long time to keep dog-paddling, even if you did not mean to be in the ocean in the first place, and there was no doubt in anybody's mind of Robert's intention, and by now it was night. The carpenter knocked up a cross of wood and we dropped it in the dark vicinity. He had left a list on his bunk and Hooker found it.

All his belongings had been bequeathed to his shipmates; Hooker got only his woolly slippers, and to me he left his trunk, which had been at sea with him from his youth. Some men wondered why he had left me this and only left Hooker his slippers. It may have been spite because Hooker had decided to go home to Birkenhead and his wife, but I believe he did it because I once saved his life in the Philippines when a dance hall fell down. Whatever the reason, he willed me the trunk and I have it still.

On 17 November 1932, when I was thirteen, I wrote in my diary: 'Inquest on T Brindley' followed by a report of the events of that dramatic day. Folded into the page is a cutting from the *Barry Herald*, brown as dust now, and another from the *Western Mail*. It was the second time Tosh had figured in its recent columns. Both headlines say: 'Boy Fell from Lighthouse'. The *Herald* adds: 'Tragic Death at Barry.'

Dolly was enthralled at having to tell her story, as eager as Tosh would have been for the limelight. Hilda was solid with apprehension. She had already had a beating from her father and another was faithfully promised once the inquest was over. She was forbidden to go near the sea, the lighthouse, or me, which was no loss.

For a week before I could scarcely sleep and such sleep as I had was hung with nightmares.

The coroner instructed me to tell what I had seen; how we broke into the lighthouse and went to the top and how Dolly had reported that Tosh had fallen over the rail. We had stumbled down the stairs and wriggled out of the lower window. The girls had sat on the ground, Hilda howling, Dolly looking pale and dull, while I set off down the slope, still fearing the old coastguard's dog. I pounded on the door of his house, and was answered by a long groan. The latch sounded and a chain, and the man appeared, his underpants sagging, both hands scratching his vest. He was drunk: a bottle raised defensively over his head. His dog, whistling through its teeth, was lying dormant across the rug inside the door.

'A boy's fallen off the lighthouse,' I reported. 'Tosh Brindley.'

'Is this boy dead?' the old coastguard inquired lucidly. He lowered the bottle.

'He's all spread out,' I said.

'Shouldn't be up there in the first place,' he grumbled. 'Falling out.'

He tried to rouse the dog, lifting up its head and bawling its name in its ear, but the head just flopped down to the rug again. 'Drunk,' he said. The man came out into the night with me, locking his door behind him. 'Where is he?' he inquired in an interested way. 'Let's have a look at him.'

It was a cold Welsh morning, the day of the inquest, the sort of wet-cold that creeps like winter along the coast, into the town docks and alleys and into everyone's bones. There was a gas fire in the chapel hall where the hearing was held but only one of its muttering jets was working.

I had sat in the same chair a few weeks before at the school concert, when Tosh had performed an act which had gone wrong and the headmaster had needed to rush out and stamp on the burning floor. Now the head was standing in the same spot. He said to the coroner: 'That scorchmark, that very mark, was caused by this same adventurous pupil attempting to perform as a fire-eater.' He shook his head as though he would never understand and added: 'Brindley did things.'

Tosh's mother, her eyes pink with crying, nodded in silent agreement. A policeman told of the many escapades in which Tosh had been injured or had required rescue. It was a long list and demonstrated the wide scope of his activities; an incident involving an ape at Bristol Zoo, a jump from a Cardiff train into a pile of flints, and the near-fatal sinking-in-the-mud on a day trip to Weston-Super-Mare.

My diary records: 'Dolly told them what happened. Hilda cried so much she could not speak. Everyone said I did well with my evidence.'

Dolly, her pale lower lip flickering, had whispered: 'We went out there. And he started to get hold of the railing around the top, like he was testing it. Then he pressed on it . . .'

The coroner held up a hand like bone and said: 'Show me how.'

Dolly began to enjoy herself. She found a prop, the back of

16

her chair, and turning it around she pressed down and stretched her slight body as though she were exercising on a bar. 'That's how,' she said.

'Then what happened?' he asked, leaning and smiling at her.

'He just pushed too hard, I s'pose,' she whispered. 'One minute he was there and the next he wasn't. It broke. He looked like he was flying. He always said he wanted to fly.'

When the usher called: 'David Jones,' I went forward and stood by Tosh's scorchmark.

Just as if it had been lying in wait for that moment my stammer returned. 'D . . . D . . . D . . . avid . . . Jo . . . o . . . n . . . es . . .' I said.

'Don't worry,' said the coroner kindly. 'Take it steady . . .'

'*Sing* it, Davy,' I heard my Auntie Blod croak. 'Sing it to the gentleman.'

I did:

> 'We went up the lighthouse,
> Up the inside, up the stairs,
> And we came to the top room,
> And Tosh . . . that is Trevor went
> out with Dolly Powell
> And fell off . . .'

There was no particular tune, just a warble to fit the words:

> 'Dolly Powell said he's fallen off
> the lighthouse . . .
> I went and got the man and we
> went to Tosh and the man turned
> him over. His eyes were open . . . staring . . .'

According to the *Western Mail* I began to sob. It was even in the London newspapers. 'Boy Sings Evidence at Inquest'. 'Boy Sings of Schoolfriend's Death'. I was quite famous.

After Tosh had been buried – and his friends could only stare at the coffin from behind front room curtains because

17

they did not allow us to go to the cemetery – we all went back to school.

One afternoon in December I was going home when Dolly Powell tiptoed up behind me and then walked along beside me, sliding her hand into mine. On the Christmas card she sent were the rounded words: 'I truly love you.' Nobody had ever said that to me before and very few have since.

Few things bring out the protective, and even the loving instinct, in women more powerfully than a stammer. This I have learned from experience and, I confess, on occasions when I have been lonely or at a loss, it has occurred to my advantage. But until the inquest on Tosh I had not realised its potential, only its shame.

It was Dolly who told me that it was my stumbling evidence, followed by my emotive singing and my appearance in the press (today I would doubtless be singing it on television), that caused her to realise in her thirteen-year-old heart that she truly loved me. Children are not sentimental. Tosh was forgotten.

Together we would walk from school, kissing behind the milk crates at the back of Thomas's Dairy, and making certain that we sat within fumbling distance on Saturday mornings at the Gem cinema. Sometimes on bland evenings, as the summer grew, we would go to the seashore, to the beach or the old jetty. The jetty was little used because the coaling port had grown around it and the tall stone causeway which had been built to dam and deepen the harbour had pushed it out of sight and significance. But some older men still kept boats there and one evening we came upon an unattended rowing boat, shiftily shifting, loitering, asking to be taken out. A pair of orange oars lay side by side like twins. I boasted that I could easily handle a boat like that, and Dolly, with her sharp, bright eyes, dared me to prove it.

'All right,' I responded firmly. It was as though Tosh were urging me on. 'You come too.' I scrambled to the bottom of the coal-coated bank. Dolly edged down the shining slope and I grandly took her hand and guided her into the boat. It jolted as though roused and pleased. Dolly sat, her knees almost to her chin, and watched me.

I threw off the mooring rope. The dinghy went with a kind of waddle across the skin of the water. It was a good evening for a voyage, the sky orange and pale blue, speckled with birds.

As I blundered with the oars Dolly leaned forward, her eyes daring. She pulled her dress over her round knees. I wobbled and coaxed the boat around until its nose was pointing out of the inlet and then, balancing tenuously, I sat and began to tug at the oars. One of my fly buttons came off and clattered like a coin into the bottom boards. Dolly laughed, picked it up and put it in the pocket of her dress.

As well as I could, I rowed, straightening the bow, pulling a sturdy face at each tug on the oars. Now we were moving towards the sea. Dolly was impressed.

As we left the shelter of the inlet the first swell of the open Channel lifted the boat like a hand. Dolly let out half-a-laugh, half-a-cry, and stumbled forward. I dug the oars in shouting: 'Hold on, Doll! We'll be all right!'

We bounced over the early waves close against the shore and then slid into wider water. The oncoming swell lifted us again and then we dropped into the trough beyond. 'Go on back!' she shouted.

Now she was frightened and so was I. I could not turn the boat until there was more room and by the time we had gained that leeway, forty yards from the rocks, the ebbing tide had caught hold of us and swiftly carried us further out. The last of the sun was crimson on the waves. A thin wind cut over the dimming surface. Frantically I pulled on one oar to turn the boat, and as I did the other oar, as if it knew what was best for it, slipped over the side.

Both of us began shouting, 'Help! Help!' Dolly was crying and I began to stammer. 'H . . . h . . . help!' Daylight was running away fast. We could see no lights upon the shore. Our shouts were against the wind. Dolly sobbed into her hands and stamped her feet. The current was now carrying us out and out, the boat spinning slowly as if it were dancing. Slaps of water came over the side and we were wet and shivering.

'It's all your bloody fault, Davy Jones!' she wept. My free arm went comfortingly towards her but she cried: 'Don't you touch me!' I stumbled back onto my seat and desperately tried again to manipulate the oar. But I was only stirring the sea. Her sudden vehemence had shocked me. We continued to drift out in slow darkening circles.

According to the *Western Mail* report (which I have still in my trunk) we were in that open boat for six hours, but we lost track of any time, knowing only that as it got darker and colder so we drifted further from land. I had a jersey and she had a cardigan, but the air grew stiffer and the long rollers lifted us and we slid down their backs only to be lifted again by the next. Water spilled over the side. We were wet, trembling and exhausted.

'We're going to die, bugger it,' forecast Dolly in a blunt whisper. 'All because of *you*.'

I told her to lie down on some canvas. I was trying not to cry. While the craft swirled again, I staggered over to her and lay down on top of her. I managed to pull some of the canvas over us. With the cutting wind, the water slopping over, and our boat heaving and revolving, I hugged her to give her warmth. She kept whimpering: 'All your fault. All your fault.' We drifted eventually into a shivery sleep, for hours it must have been, until we were shaken awake by the massive clamour of a ship's siren. The sharp end of a big black vessel was coming towards us like an executioner's axe.

Dolly began to shriek. Again I put my arms around her. Savagely she pushed me away and I fell onto the boards of the boat. 'I'm going to die!' she howled. Our boat gave a convulsive heave and we rose like a balloon, up and up and up. I forced myself to open my eyes as I lay across the seat. The black hull with its red portside light was rising over us like a fiery-eyed whale. I was shouting and our craft was flung across the rolling waves.

Now we were soaked and bruised and both crying. Above us was a great hat of darkness. 'Let's pray to God,' I suggested.

'Oh God save me!' she responded, throwing her arms wide.

'Oh God, please help us!' I cried, looking upwards. Cold spray stung my face.

The boat rose and tipped and dropped. I tried to clutch her again but she thrust me away. It was all my fault. All my fault. She could scarcely get the words through her chattering teeth. The lights of the ship were being swallowed by the night. Then they became constant, stationary.

'It's stopped,' I whispered, as if hearing me would have caused it to change its mind. 'Dolly . . . it's stopped . . .'

In mid-sob she levered her soaked body up until her face was clear of the side. 'Yes . . . yes. It's stopped,' she confirmed. 'I'll be saved.'

'They've seen us. They'll come back!'

We stumbled to our knees and began to wave and shout in the dark direction of the vessel. A slant of vivid light shot over the water. The searchlight touched the surface and swung like a white arm. Madly we shouted and waved. It flew across, blinding us. We covered our eyes. It swept away but at once came back. They had found us.

'God saved us!' I cried putting my arms around Dolly's shivering body. 'Thanks, God! Thanks very much!'

'Thanks, God,' she reiterated. Then she turned cruelly and said: 'I'm going to tell on you stealing this bloody boat, Davy Jones.'

I shouted back at her, 'Trust you to put the bloody blame on me!'

'And don't you swear at me,' she screeched. 'I'm a lady!'

When the rescuers arrived they found two children disputing like drunks in a small boat. The launch chugged around and they threw a line which I somehow caught and made fast to the ring on the bow. Then they towed us slowly, shouting encouragement, back towards their vessel. It was getting light. They manoeuvred us under the lee of the ship to a ladder and then took our hands and pulled us clear of the rowing boat, helping us up the side until we stumbled onto the deck in front of the captain and the crew. Everybody cheered and Dolly laughed bravely. I was almost crying.

There was a lot of trouble. The ship took us to Swansea, and there was a police car waiting on the dock to return us to Barry. Dolly's mother seemed more concerned with the disgrace of her daughter's name appearing in the *Western Mail* once more than anything else. Dolly was ordered never to associate with me again and she said it would be a pleasure.

She left the school. There was only flat-faced Hilda sitting at the desk. I waited by the milk crates behind Thomas's Dairy for three afternoons, but she did not appear. I wrote hopeless notes.

After two weeks of this emptiness I heard that Dolly was to go and live with her aunt at a place beyond the known horizon. In my diary I noted sadly that she was leaving on the Saturday, and all day I loitered at the Barry Bus Station. I have spent a lot of my life waiting for Dolly.

Late in the afternoon I had to go to the subterranean lavatory, then the pride of Barry. I was very dispirited and while I was peeing I was crying too. During the time I was there Dolly and her mother arrived and got on the bus. I ran out, doing up my buttons, but she was already aboard. She saw me from the window but turned her head away. I had prepared another note for her which I waved forlornly. The moment before the bus pulled out she glanced towards me, and I thought I saw her hand half-raised in a sort of semi-goodbye. Then her mother turned to the window and saw me. Her face was like iron. The bus snorted, started, and shuddered away, and I was left waving the note after it.

At the end of the hill it turned and vanished from sight. My eyes were full of tears. When would I see her again?

Two

The *SS Bournemouth and Boscombe* which had found us swirling in the Bristol Channel was hardly a ship; only two thousand tons, but when her bow was soaring over us, the black whale snout and the flaming eye of her port light, she had been a leviathan.

Never before had I trodden the deck of a sea-going vessel and, after the relief and excitement of our rescue, I began to look around, aware of oil and salt, and when we were once more under way, to feel the great breathing of the ship.

We had baths in the captain's tub, and we were given bunks in one cabin, wearing various oddments of crew's pyjamas. My jacket was decorated with teddy bears. They gave us cocoa spiced with something aromatic and hot egg sandwiches while they radioed the shore.

Once we were in the bunks Dolly fell into an exhausted sleep. I whispered, 'Goodnight Doll,' but she did not answer. I could see her chest rising and falling. Although I was weary also, my surroundings would not let me sleep at once. The white metallic walls of the cabin, the porthole made blind by the deadlight screwed over it, the blinking bulkhead bulb, the confined corner housing a table with sides like a tray and a chair bolted to the floor, the yellowed washbasin; the enclosed feeling of the place. The deep safeness, while outside was a rolling wind, a storm-black sky and a cold Channel.

From those moments I decided to become a mariner and although I have at times tried to escape the sea, it has never freed me. I can hear and feel it, even perhaps when I have been far inland, up in mountains even. On nights, even now,

23

I imagine that my bed is moving darkly with the voyaging roll of a ship. In my dreams I hear hooters, the clank of chains; I see foreign shores where women wave. Often I walk like a shorebound sailor, head down, hands behind back, four paces one way, turn, and four the other.

That night long ago I eventually slept deeply while the SS *Bournemouth and Boscombe* plugged on to Swansea, and once Dolly had gone, I believed forever, I concentrated my thoughts and ambitions on becoming a seafarer. Blod and Griff would have none of it. 'Nobody ever came to any good by going to foreign parts,' Blod said scornfully, blowing out her cheeks. 'Try the railway.'

'Sailors are no good,' said my uncle. 'They pray when they're drunk.'

I went to the free library and inquired about books on seamanship. I took two manuals home and concealed them under my bed, taking them out at night. I could not understand them, but it mattered little because from the confusion of charts and mysteries there emerged, like evening stars, the words and phrases that have been my life's guidance and its poetry. Ropes and spars, masting and rigging, the vagaries of winds and waterways, the finding of channels and Preble's directions on steam navigation, buoys and sea marks, lading and loading, the names and dispositions of heavenly constellations, women on board, mutiny, repairs at sea, flags and signals, the prospect of ports, the leaving of land, the world's names: Cox's Bazaar, Valparaiso, the Dungeon Deep, the Bay of Fundy, and Alice Town on Bimini. Reading by candlelight I was already shipping out with the morning tide to St Pierre et Miquelon, the Indies, the Lesser Antilles, and the Isles of the Bingo Sea. I wondered what the inhabitants of the Dampier Archipelago were doing at that moment.

Instead I went to work in the Barry coal office. At the age of fourteen in the 1930s there was no chance of setting sail for anywhere. More sailors were ashore than afloat. Every Friday they shuffled towards their dole, and when they had it they drank beer at the Shipwright's Arms, recalling captains, girls, landfalls.

But the coal office was adjacent to the sea, almost against the dock gates. You could hear the ships coming in and leaving and see their masts and sometimes their funnels moving behind the rooftops.

From a mere rowing-boat village in Victorian times Barry had, within a generation, become the famous coaling port. Everywhere were faces engrained black, eyes shining pink and sore. Working in the office was a distinction. The men would stumble in on Fridays for their wages, stamping their boots, their lizard red tongues licking the coal from their lips. Their necks were like ropes, dust fell out of their hair, their ears, their boots. Some of the boys I had known at school would be in the shuffling line, hands held out at the moment of money. Often I did not recognise them.

At the end of their shift the coalers would trudge up the hill, each of them carrying a bag of dust for their own fires. Yanto Humphries, whom I knew from school, came out of Pendry's Fresh Fish and Chips one evening, holding an open newspaper before him like a smoking sacrifice. His face was still grimed by his day in the coal bunkers. He picked a chip from the paper with two fingers like black talons and dropped it into the ruby hole of his mouth.

'Want to go to Parry's?' he munched. I was conscious of my unblackened face. His muscled arm swung like a beam engine, his elbow hitting my ribs meaningfully. 'You're a drinking man.'

I agreed I was.

'Tomorrow night,' he said. 'Bring money.'

'How much?' I was saving for a coat.

'Much as you can,' he answered as though it were obvious. 'Be here, half-past seven. And don't tell.'

That night I lay awake listening to a ship sounding her way up the Channel until she reached Barry Roads and became quiet. What went on at Parry's? I told Blod that I was going to see Boris Karloff at the Gem. 'Don't have nightmares,' she said as I went out. I felt ashamed because I was lying to her.

Yanto had washed his face but not his neck. He was wearing his best trousers. The cuffs of his coat were almost at his elbows.

Parry lived at the end of a high terrace battered by every nasty wind that came off the Bristol Channel. The council house looked punch-drunk, chimney askew, door crooked, the windows squinting. Jack Sneddon opened the door. He worked at the docks. Inside the small room were a dozen men, strangely furtive and abashed, some wearing their best suits.

It cost a shilling to enter and I had to pay for Yanto. Sneddon shut the door behind us, poured two glasses of thick black stout, and called: 'New member present.'

The men all turned and looked at me. Some smirked because they knew who I was. Parry came from the scullery and said: 'Can you keep your mouth shut, son?'

'I can,' I said.

'It's in the shed,' he said. He looked around. 'Everybody here?'

'All present,' said Sneddon.

The stout tasted foul. Yanto took my glass and Sneddon refilled both. 'Right,' he said looking around. 'Ready boys?'

'Ready,' they mumbled. I felt sick, from stout and excitement. *Something* secret was going to happen. Bill Parry went to the window and pulled its poor green curtain aside. 'The coast is clear,' he said like a smuggler.

We were ushered from the room and into the patch of back garden. The rough men hurried on tiptoes like elves to the door of a long garden shed and clustered against it until it was opened and they could all slide in.

Some clattered as we went into the shed. Sneddon hissed, 'Shush.' A solitary light bulb illuminated the men shuffling along wooden benches. They turned and shushed at those

26

still entering. When the last man was in, the door was shut emphatically.

Garden implements were hooked on the walls of the long shed, and there was a rabbit hunched in a hutch, its nose blinking through the wire. There was a rocking horse draped with an old blanket as if it had been sweating, a mangle and some buckets and spades. We were crushed together, shoulders against shoulders and knees against knees. It was strangely like Sunday School. You could smell the men; sweat, tobacco, coal.

More stout, in a bottle, was passed along the four benches, each man taking a swig. Choking, I accepted another mouthful. At the back Parry pushed a sheeted table forward and like a conjuror took away the cover, revealing a box with a brass snout. Sneddon unrolled a creased canvas screen from the ceiling. 'Ah, it's a magic lantern show,' I said to Yanto. The men began breathing heavily. The shed was airless.

Sneddon sat down, stood again and made a minute adjustment to the tatty screen, like a fashion designer adjusting a hem. From the back Parry said: 'Ready boys?'

A beam of yellow light, frantic with dust clouds, shot onto the screen. Yanto sat upright. The man on my other side began wheezing. There were mutterings.

On the screen appeared an indistinct, browned photograph of a woman in a petticoat. She was peeping around a looking glass which she held in one hand while hitching up her silk garment to the hip with the other, exposing a long curved stocking secured by a suspender. 'Jesus Christ,' breathed the man at my side.

Growls sounded around me, like dogs in the dark. The picture disappeared sideways and was replaced by another, the same model now free of the looking glass and using both hands to lift up the petticoat to expose a pair of ribboned drawers. Some of the men began moaning.

My chest was tight with the excitement; the close shed, the smell of the stout, the eroticism. Parry changed the slide. His

27

hand shook. The new girl was peeling down the top half of her bodice showing a fine swelling of bosom, stopping short of its centre.

You could tell that the viewers did not want her to go but were eager to see what came next. The suspense was thick. Another shameless lady appeared, a beauty, full-bosomed and blatantly displaying one nipple. A man in the row in front fell backwards off the bench. Amid protests he was pushed upright again. There was a low cry of recognition. 'Titty . . . oh titty!'

'We don't need *you* to tell us what it is, Emlyn Protheroe,' snarled a voice. 'We've *all* seen one before.'

Well I had not. I could not believe my eyes. It was round and lovely, sheened, and the nipple like a sleeping eye.

The shed was taut with rapture. Yanto was gasping. The man on my other side let his teeth slide from his mouth and clatter to the floor. Somebody laughed madly.

They knew what was coming next. A full double-bosom appeared and the man who had fallen backwards did so again. He was restored roughly to his seat by the hands of others, whose eyes never left the screen. A man lost his glasses and searched for them, cursing.

Bill Parry pulled the slide out and there were cries: 'Put them back!' 'More!' 'Let's see them again!' Parry shouted: 'They get hot, boys. They get hot.'

The blank of light slid in and out again and now, with nothing covered but her legs, sat a beautiful, brazen girl, in sepia, with a gleaming bare bosom and below her belly a fan of thick black hair. A man stood up and was roughly tugged down again; there were harsh cries, blows were struck. In a moment, with the naked lady still on the screen, the benches toppled and I was among a mass of fighting coal-heavers. Yanto was striking out at somebody dimly behind. Everybody but me was hitting somebody. Bill Parry opened the door and staggered back as in charged three policemen, their domed helmets symbolic accusations of our illicit pleasure. I realised I was going to appear, once more, in the columns of the press. And I was only fifteen.

After my appearance in court, where I was bound over to keep the peace, and the shame of once more appearing in the *Western Mail* and the *Barry Herald* (although blessedly my name was withheld on account of my age), my Uncle Griff and Auntie Blod accepted, to my unbounded delight, that the only thing for me was to go to sea. 'Where we will find a ship to take you, I don't know,' intoned Griff. 'But Sinbad found a ship and so will you. You will be cheap, anyway.'

Only a week later he took me, scrubbed as an angel, aboard a collier called *Myrtle Matthews* lying near the dock coal office. As we walked there, me trying to match Griff's strides, I was aware of the eyes that slanted from the coated window of the office and from the bitter faces of the coal-loaders. I waved but nobody waved back. I was escaping.

The vessel was nothing more than a caked tub, reeking of the coal she both carried and which provided her power. Yellow smoke dribbled from her funnel, her brasswork was oily, her deck carpeted with grit, and her wheelhouse leaned to one side like a poor garden shed. But the bow was as jaunty as a snub-nose to the brisk breeze, and a pennant like a dirty handkerchief rattled from her foremast. To me she looked as if she had sailed from Nineveh.

Griff climbed down onto the unkempt deck trying to give the impression he had been doing so for years. He stumbled on some rope at the bottom.

'Slapdash,' he muttered kicking the rope. It was thick and coiled, like a dead serpent, and abuse did not disturb it.

'A mess,' he said more loudly than I would have liked. He scowled around. 'Look at it. Like a Chinse kitchen.'

'She floats,' I said, still taking her in. The rigging sang like a harp.

'Just about, by the look of her,' he said.

Under the wheelhouse was what looked like a cupboard with a planked wooden door. On it was a dull brass plate which Griff rubbed with his coat elbow, revealing the word: 'Captain'.

From within came a fit of coughing. Then a splutter: 'Are you out there?'

'We are out here,' called my uncle.

'Push the door,' croaked the voice. 'Shove it.'

Griff did. The door first resisted then opened. Although Griff was not a tall man he needed to stoop under the door head before stepping down into the cabin. 'Don't fall,' he cautioned me over his shoulder.

'He'll topple a bit on this ship,' said the captain. He stood from behind a worm-eaten desk with brass handles, dulled to bronze, and a worn leather top. He was a dumpy man with a dull red face flayed with broken veins, his cheeks puffed, as if he played the trumpet regularly. His eyes were bloody around the edges and his gingery hair protruded in tufts and patches. 'Captain Corrie Bracklesham,' he announced, coughing as he shook our hands.

'Does he know about the sea?' he asked, eyeing me. He began to wheeze again and threw his arm like a contortionist over his back to strike himself between the shoulder blades with his fist.

My uncle said: 'He knows about coal.'

'I work in the coal office on the dock there,' I nodded.

Captain Bracklesham seemed pleased that I had spoken at last. His cabin was a confined but cosy place, with two photographs of small ships so askew they appeared to be going down; one by the stern, the other by the bow, and two portholes with a whale's tooth hanging between them. A sextant lay in its case on the shelf behind the desk together with a decorated tobacco jar and a picture of an Indian woman who was waving. A door led down to sleeping quarters, an unmade bed upon which was a peaked cap. At the extreme end of the cabin were wooden stairs, with a brass rail, leading up to the bridge.

'We don't want a coaler,' said Captain Bracklesham.

'What else can you do?' The red tufts of his hair rose. 'Can you sing?'

'He's a good singer,' said Griff swiftly.

The captain reached behind him. I thought he was going to bang himself on the back again but instead he picked up the tobacco jar. He put it on the desk and raised the lid. It was full of oddments: bootlaces, pencils, a ragged cigar. His fingers probed deeply into it. 'Have a lozenge,' he invited. 'If there's one left.' His red-haired fingers poked further. 'Ah, there is. Only one.'

The unwrapped sweet was furred and worn as if it might have been previously sucked and put aside for another day. To my relief he put it into his own mouth. 'What I need,' he said, 'is someone who can *sing*. Cheer the place up. And to do the messing. Can you cook?'

'Yes,' I said desperately just ahead of Griff's lie: 'Yes, he cooks. A bit.'

'Couldn't be as bad as the last cook,' muttered the skipper. 'Strained stew through his socks.'

Captain Bracklesham stared out of the porthole from his desk; his face began to crease as if he were trying to recall where we were. 'Barry,' he said eventually. 'Good old Barry Dock.' He had made up his mind. His rimmed eyes settled on me. 'Right you are,' he said. 'One pound a week. We sail Thursday, I think. On board by noon.'

My face warmed with happiness. I looked towards my uncle and then at the captain. 'Thank you, sir,' I croaked almost as deeply as he had done. 'I won't let you down.'

'Be difficult to let *anyone* down on this ship,' he sighed. 'Nobody expects much. As long as you can sing and cook.'

'Where . . . where are we sailing, sir?' I could scarcely get the words out.

'Swansea,' he said. He must have seen my disappointment because he made an effort: 'Then on to . . . somewhere,' he rumbled. 'France, somewhere.' He opened a drawer in the desk and took out several pieces of creased paper. 'Let's have a dekko.' His eyes squeezed. He held the papers like a fan.

31

'God knows,' he said hopelessly. 'My glasses are in my bunk. Here.' He handed one piece of paper across to me and began coughing again.

'It says Brest,' I said. 'France.'

'That's it,' said the captain. 'I knew it.' He seemed pleased, as if I had already proved myself useful. He went to the chart on the wall tapping it randomly. Then we all shook hands again. 'Cooking and singing,' he summarised. 'One quid a week. Sail Thursday. Noon.'

When we climbed on to the dockside there were two figures black as the dust they were sweeping into heaps. I was almost floating with happiness. Briefly their glistening eyes regarded me. They turned their faces back to the coal dust.

'You can't cook,' muttered Griff gloomily as we walked. 'Never boiled an egg.'

'I can learn,' I answered. At that moment I felt I could do anything. 'It's only Monday.'

The day I joined the *SS Myrtle Matthews* Griff came with me to the dockside and we wheeled between us a handcart which bore not only my new sea-bag, but an additional soiled but solid suitcase containing tinned meats and vegetables, soups, puddings, and concealed sealed basins holding as many dishes as my aunt could cook in three days and nights. In that same span I had learned to make gravy and custard, both of which Blod said covered a multitude of sins, and also to brew the heaviest tea.

She had cried as I left. 'Treat the stove as a friend,' she sobbed from the doorway. It was a low summer morning, wet grey clouds lying over the harbour. Again I had to run the gauntlet of the coaling office window and the eyes of the loaders along the dock. Someone shouted: 'Don't spew up to windward!' and they all laughed so much they ended up coughing over their spades.

A cowlick of smoke dangled forward of the funnel of the *Myrtle Matthews* and a tall, nervous man came up the gangplank, glancing up as though something might be threatening

32

to fall on his head. He said his name was Feeney and he was the engineer. He took my sea-bag, and flung it down onto the deck, fifteen feet below.

'Shortest distance between any two points . . .' he announced. We stood helplessly as he picked up the food-filled suitcase and flung it after the sea-bag. '. . . was always a straight line.' The case hit the grubby deck heavily. Its locks held.

Feeney continued along the dockside. 'That's torn it,' Griff mumbled looking down to the case on the deck. He handed me a white piece of paper which for a moment I thought might be a last message, but turned out to be a five pound note. I had never had so much money. Overwhelmed I thanked him and we said goodbye. He went off wheeling the empty handcart, staring solidly at the seaside clouds. Slowly I went down the gangplank. At the foot were two men, Jack and George, who were brothers. One told me he could play the concertina. I picked up the heavy suitcase. Something was moving around inside. I turned to retrieve the sea-bag.

'Two?' said Jack.

'In case the weather alters,' I said.

They nodded together as if they understood well and went to the fore-end of the ship where another man was casually chipping at rust. With two arms I picked up the case containing the food, carried it below and opened it. All the basins had broken, the pies and puddings were a mash with the cracked jam-jars of soup and tins of vegetables like flotsam on a clogged river.

I was in the fo'c'sle, a squat and pungent room containing a long fixed table with high sides for bad weather and a bench down each side. There was an opaque porthole with a gull flailing outside it. A hatch led into the galley, *my* galley, a soot and fat-caked hole with a cringing stove at one side, a tin sink with a single tap, some dented metal cupboards and an unkempt bunk.

A man with rheumy eyes came through the hatch and regarded me sorrowfully. 'Have you sinned?' he croaked.

'Now and again,' I admitted. I thought he might have heard of the court case.

'I am the mate of this vessel,' he said. 'Name of Wilberforce, same as the slave-trader. Such of you which is without sin, let him cast the first stone.'

He stared at me fiercely. 'Escape now. Go,' he advised. 'God is going to strike this ship.'

'We're sailing at noon,' I said.

'If the skipper remembers,' he grunted as he went out again.

I opened one of the cupboards and several tins and a bag of weevil-filled flour fell out. In the other cupboards there were numerous tins, soup, vegetables, some mouldy bread and a greasy tin of margarine. Carefully I retrieved the surviving bottles, jars and tins from my case, leaving the broken containers of Blod's accumulated pies and puddings.

There were movements on the deck, clamberings and clumps. There was a clock on the fo'c'sle. It was eleven-thirty. I went up into the daylight, walked up the gangplank and ran. As I was panting towards home the aroma of Pendry's Fresh Fish and Chips came to meet me. Slowing, I came abreast of it. I went in and, breaking into my uncle's five pounds, bought eight hot meat pies and five shillings worth of chips. The man stared at the money. 'Where's this from?' he asked, holding out the note at arm's length. 'It's mine,' I told him forcefully. With the bundle wrapped in clean newspaper under my arm, I ran back towards the dockside again to where I could see the smoke beckoning me from the funnel of the *SS Myrtle Matthews*.

We eventually sailed at two-fifteen on the afternoon tide. By the time we had located the harbour mouth and then searched out our direction in the Bristol Channel it was getting late.

Sailors, I soon came to know, are like children on the sea, prone to romance and uncanny beliefs, nagged by mishaps, riven with moods and tempers. Few men would have sailed with this crew. While the tide had reached its peak and began to ebb, Feeney, the engineer, remained stupified below, when he should have been coaxing the engines; the mate, Wilberforce, sulked in his bunk because it was the captain's turn, indeed, responsibility, to take the vessel to sea: the captain was ashore having his hair cut, and the three hands listlessly played cards on deck, sometimes gazing at the land as if wondering when it was going to move away.

We caught the last possible two feet of the tide. Heaving the meat pies and chips into the oily oven, I ran up to the deck to watch my home slip away on this, the first voyage of my life. 'Get back to the galley, boy!' bawled Captain Bracklesham from the wheelhouse. He had opened the glass to shout. It hung by one hinge. His scalp had been shaved almost naked like a Tartar. Wilberforce was standing moodily on the wingbridge holding up the palm of his hand to test the wind. The man on the wheel, Jack, of the two brothers, began vaguely wiping the wheelhouse screen, now closed again, with his sleeve. I retreated below.

Eventually I felt the long rolling of the Channel under my feet. After an hour, during which I had removed the pies and chips from the oven six times and replaced them seven, the mate appeared in the companionway above me. 'God shall cast all tears from their eyes,' he said. 'Bracklesham's really done it this time. The coastguard's gone mad.' He laughed. 'Your sin will find you out.' He regarded me as if I might argue.

'The food is ready,' I told him. 'It's hot now.'

'Five minutes, that's all,' he said, preparing to climb the steps again. 'Let us see if he has seen the light.' He paused. 'The one on the peninsular.'

Fifteen minutes later they were sitting at the tables, the captain at one end and two of the crew at the other. Wilberforce came down when the captain had completed wiping the plate with a piece of pie crust, and I had to take Feeney's meal below to the engine room where he ate with one hand amid the thudding of the pistons.

There were no complaints. The captain dropped two chips on the deck and retrieved them, brushing them off fastidiously before putting them in his mouth. I served strong tea in china mugs, each jealously decorated with the owner's name.

I had planned to hurry ashore at Swansea that evening to buy another consignment of chips, this time with fish, but we missed Swansea altogether the first time (there was an argument in the wheelhouse) and had to turn and go back. Once we were tied up and the engines stilled the captain went to bed and the rest, apart from the watchman, climbed onto the dock and strode towards Swansea. The watchman, George, of the brothers, waited until they had gone, looked in on the snoring skipper and left, telling me only that he knew a girl. I was left in charge.

At first I stood resolutely at the gangway looking up and down the deserted evening dock. There were two larger vessels alongside and I saw a man walking around on the upper deck of the nearest. After watching him in the late drifting light, I waved in a seafaring manner, but he ignored me.

It began to drizzle, coming out of the low underbelly of sky. Snores rattled from the captain's quarters, and I decided to make a run for the nearest chip shop. Swiftly I went along the quay. At the dock gates there was a watchman in a yellow-lit box and outside a woman in a mackintosh with a newspaper held over her head against the rain. 'Want to come home, lovely?' she asked me.

For a moment I thought she must be someone I knew but failed to recognise. 'I'm going for fish and chips,' I said.

'Fucking fish and chips,' she murmured softly as though stirred by some memory.

I began running again. Looking over my shoulder I saw that she was standing desolately observing my retreat, like someone who had, without warning, lost a friend.

The shop was only two streets away. It had damp tiled tables along one side, each with an oasis of salt, pepper, vinegar and bottled sauce. A man and a woman bearded by

36

steam sat, attentive as players in a game, selecting chips from a spread newspaper.

Above the gurgling vats there was a sere and fissured mirror, flanked by red, white and blue boxing posters. A previously concealed man rose like a slow jack-in-the-box from behind the counter. 'What's the order?' he said.

'Fish and chips for one,' I said. 'Three penn'orth of chips.' Behind me I could hear the couple munching.

'Your death, you'll get,' the woman said.

I turned. 'Out in the rain,' she said.

'And another six pieces of fish and five shillings' worth of chips,' I told the shop man. The couple were impressed.

'You must be hungry,' said the man, his mouth full.

'I'll have the fish and chips for one first,' I said over the counter. 'I'll take the others with me.'

The shop man took a miniature steel shovel and scooped out the chips, putting them on a plate; he then gripped a piece of battered fish with a pair of tongs and held it up for inspection. 'Can't see no light through that,' he boasted.

'The other order is for the rest of the crew,' I said as I sat down with my plate.

'Oh,' the man at the table looked up. 'Where you bound?'

'Just France,' I answered. 'Brest.'

'Brest,' he repeated. 'You're lucky.'

'*You've* been,' said the woman jabbing a wedge of batter at him. 'You *must* have.'

'Plenty of times,' he said. 'And Cape Town.'

He regarded me challengingly. 'Cape Town,' he repeated. 'On the Cape.'

'He can't get a ship now,' said the woman indicating her companion this time with a chip.

'There's not a ship big enough for me,' the man sniffed. He chewed his chips. 'Nowhere.'

'A bosun,' the woman nodded.

'Aye,' he confirmed. 'The best.'

They rose from the tiled table. The woman screwed up the

oily newspaper and wiped first her mouth and then, in a houseproud way, the table.

The fish shop man watched them leave through his vapour and said contemptuously: 'Cape Town!'

'All talk,' I agreed.

He was wrapping my order in swathes of newspaper. It was all one parcel like a bundle of laundry. I finished my meal. A friendlier light flickered in his eye. 'Here,' he said. 'Two free pickled onions.'

He wrapped them in a tiny separate parcel and I thanked him. Rain like celluloid was still veiling the street as I went towards the dock gates. The woman was still there and said: 'Give us a chip.'

Between us we unwrapped the big package to expose the great spread of chips. Hungrily she gazed at them but delicately selected only one. I told her to take a handful and she did so. 'It gets so cold,' she said. She regarded me, her face damp. 'You're a good boy,' she said.

There was no call for the fish and chips that night aboard the *Myrtle Matthews* because three of the crew came back drunk and three did not return at all. There were oaths and dark fumblings which I heard from my bunk in the galley, but nobody demanded food. Someone tripped on the deck and lay sobbing.

By morning the missing three were back. The mate came on deck in time for a consignment of old pitprops to be loaded. When the captain was roused, because once more we were in danger of missing the tide, it was noon and again we set out for the sea.

Once more, it was not easy to find. There were a good many dodgings and alterations to course, and disagreements on the bridge, before the *Myrtle Matthews* was clear of shoals, rocks and the general bulk of Wales. How we would ever detect France, let alone Brest, was worrying to a novice, although the vessel herself seemed to have a good nose for navigation.

The fish and chips I heated in the oil stove and served up

38

once we were at sea. No one seemed to notice they were stale, indeed they evoked contented grunts. Then a fierce argument over who should have the picked onions erupted as Captain Bracklesham ducked into the fo'c'sle. All three deckhands wanted the two delicacies, and Feeney, who had ascended from his engines, was insisting that he, of senior rank, should have them. The captain settled the matter by grabbing the two onions, putting them between his teeth and crunching them loudly. 'I'm in command here,' he said wiping his mouth.

He returned to the wheelhouse to see where we were. From the single porthole in my galley I looked out to find the sea moving by, level with my nose, the pale day streaked across it. Land had gone and the Bristol Channel lay rumpled and quiet.

That evening I took out the shattered pies and puddings, putting the dented pastry, the damaged meat and jam on the galley table and wondering what I could make with them. I separated the meat and crust from the preserves, put the former in a baking tin in the oven and waited in hope. Most of it turned a decent brown, although some, near the edges, became blackened due to the decrepitude of the stove. Then I boiled some potatoes the way that Blod had demonstrated, remembering the salt. When the first sitting of dinner was waiting, which meant everyone except the captain and the man on the wheel, I poured gravy – thick as tar – over the whole morass and marched hopefully in with it. I took a good portion on a plate with some potatoes for the skipper and carried it to his cabin. He was snoring in his bunk but he awoke when he smelled the gravy. I left it for him and returned to the fo'c'sle where all the men were delving ravenously into the food.

'What's it you call this, laddie?' asked the engineer.

'Bristol pie,' I said.

He hummed approval and the others joined in.

Back in the galley I had given the same treatment to the

jam and fruit pies. They were a touch charred but I covered them with heavy custard.

The crew said they had enjoyed their meal that night better than any they had eaten on board, and some said at home. Everyone drank beer and I was awarded a special whisky. I returned to the galley, ate some food that I had set aside and, weary from my first day at sea, I turned in and went at once to sleep to the creaking of the hull. But not before I had smiled deeply to myself, because now I was a sailor.

As we sailed, west and south, across the swaying sea, and night came down, they asked me to sing. Our small vessel was out there in the dark and the wind, and all but the man on the wheel gathered in the fo'c'sle. They were again contented with the meal, a medley of tinned meat and vegetables with the remainder of the wreckage of the broken pies as make-weight. They had drunk beer and Captain Bracklesham and Wilberforce, the mate, he having temporarily left religion, were sitting with a bottle of Scotch between them, the whisky wobbling with the ship and getting lower in the bottle, like water in a dry dock.

Jack got out his concertina, squeezed and tugged it, until Captain Bracklesham ordered him to stop and me to sing.

'D'you know "The Moon Shone on the Shithouse Door?"' inquired Feeney pleasantly.

The captain admonished him. 'He's a decent Welsh boy, Feeney.'

'It's a fine song,' insisted Feeney. He began to warble:

> 'The Moon shone on the shithouse door,
> The Candle had a fit . . .'

'Stop it, Feeney,' ordered the captain again, but more sharply. 'It's not suitable.'

Jack began re-flaying his concertina. 'Just giving him the note, Skipper,' he said as Bracklesham eyed him. 'By way of introduction.'

'God help us,' said the captain.

'God is ashore,' said Wilberforce as though to reassure himself. 'Out here there is no God. He is no sailor.' He eyed the waving whisky.

'The boy can introduce himself,' said Bracklesham. He poured another glass of Scotch, examined the bottle, and turned his stark eye on Wilberforce. 'You're on watch next, mister mate,' he warned.

'Aye, aye,' said Wilberforce heavily. Then he called: 'Hush, the boy is going to sing.'

They at once subsided, slumped in their various attitudes around the close fo'c'sle, and I sang 'The Ash Grove' followed by 'She'll Be Coming Round the Mountain'. The skipper requested me to sing the second song again because he liked the line about the lady wearing silk pyjamas and sang it with me, his eyes agleam.

I went through all I could remember: sacred and everyday compositions learned in chapel and at school. The sailors were not particular, glad of anything, although Feeney kept on asking for the song about the moon and the door. He offered to write out the words for me, then rested his head in his arms on the table and began to snore. Jack also had his ragged eyes closed although he still wheezed the concertina, as if to accompany a dream. George, his brother, sat attentively upright, trying to follow the words, desperate to join in, only to be thwarted by his own slowness and left to bang his beer mug in time.

The captain roused everyone for a final reprise of 'She'll Be Coming Round the Mountain' and then we stood to attention in the rolling room for 'God Save the King'.

'Good boy,' the skipper approved. 'Fine messing, fine singing.'

They went to their sleeping places. The helmsman was relieved by Jack who continued to squeeze the concertina with the movements of the wheel. Wilberforce had to be levered into the wheelhouse by the captain who then fell down the steps to his own bunk. After they had all gone, I went up to the wet and empty deck. The dark wind was soft, the sea lolling, and the lighthouse on the island of Ushant was swinging its illuminated arms. And I was happier than I had ever been.

At break of light I went up to the deck and saw my first foreign place; a threadbare morning, the sky shredded grey, the sea morose, the land almost black with a few pale lights. But there were houses, patches against the dark, the heads of trees and a village with curls of early smoke. A road came into view with a bus, its windows lit, containing *French* passengers, strangers from a land unknown to me.

A coaster, a few tons larger than us, was bowing her way south, and a big ship was making the opposite course.

'Blue Cross Line,' said the captain when I took his tea to the bridge. 'Bound for Middlesbrough.'

I went below, my culinary confidence now grown, and prepared bacon, eggs and fried bread for breakfast. The mate came down, took out and unrolled a stained chart, marked with lines and figures. 'There, y'see,' he said pointing along the drawn coast. 'The great port of Brest.' He wiped it with his hand. 'Unless it's a cobweb.'

By noon he and the captain were in the wheelhouse gazing perplexedly at the width of the estuary that opened to the port, pointing out possibilities to each other. It had begun to rain and there were many ships strung across the mouth: moving ships, smoking ships, ships at anchor, most of them naval vessels, almost merging with the grey rain.

'Where's the cursed pilot?' the captain cried.

His head and that of the mate appeared on opposite sides of the wheelhouse, staring out, necks stretched. We were wallowing in the oil swell. A French destroyer crept up on us abaft, surging by, hardly a dozen cables away, flags and smoke streaming, and with a contemptuous snort from her siren. Going to the rail of the wingbridge, our captain waved his fist. The warship cut a dirty white swathe in the leaden sea. 'Frog Bastard!' he bawled.

The destroyer's rolling wash sent us bucking like a horse. Captain Bracklesham was almost thrown over the side but hung onto the rail at the final grab. 'Frogs!' he cursed. 'Frogs!'

The *Myrtle Matthews* slackened and began to wallow sulkily in the estuary. A small, busy boat detached itself from the confused seascape ahead and came towards us, a moustache of foam at its bow. 'About time!' shouted the captain.

When the French pilot climbed aboard, bulky in oilskins, a man almost too cumbersome for his boat, the captain shook his hand unctuously. The Frenchman looked around our deck and blew out his cheeks in a gesture of resigned disgust. He clambered up to the wheelhouse and we began to inch towards Brest.

As the channel narrowed we sailed between ranks of warships lined against the quays. French sailors in their red pom-pom hats were drawn up in ranks along the deck of a cruiser. Captain Bracklesham strode out onto our tawdry wingbridge and stood at the salute as if they were parading for him.

The pilot coaxed us into a side-channel where several small merchant ships were lying and we berthed next to a Pole carrying fertiliser. The smell drifted potently. One of the Polish crew came to its stern, leaned insolently on the rail, and began to laugh at our ship. He called some of his compatriots and they all joined in as we edged clumsily into the berth. 'Scum!' our skipper howled at them shaking his fist while the rest of us stood, hurt, on the deck. They went off laughing still and the pilot shook hands with the captain and with a final gaze around our deck and a farewell blowing out of his cheeks, he went ashore. 'Frog,' muttered Captain Bracklesham.

A man with a gloomy accordian was playing French tunes in Le Chat Rouge, Brest, that night but the romantic music was lost on the clients. Against the bar the silhouettes of the customers were like rocks along a shore. The tables were full.

Women in breathless dresses laughed and pushed playfully at anxious men, accepting drinks, heaving bosoms and flashing legs and eyes.

Captain Bracklesham squatted at an adjacent table to the three members of the crew and the jovial women who had joined them. Mr Wilberforce had privately gone somewhere else, he said to pray. God was ashore. Mr Feeney ordered beers, wines and whiskies, his gestures extravagant as those of a blind man, and the captain protectively motioned me to sit at his table, pointing mutely to a chair. A man fell down unheeded at the bar, sliding to the floor like a flag going down a pole.

The skipper went out to the lavatory and Feeney, having ordered the drinks, had suffered one of his sudden fits of despair, and was resting his face in his arms. Francine appeared. She came towards me like a panther, sliding into the seat, her clothes tight, black and shiny, her face strong and colourless. Her scent reminded me of my mother's. Her bosom lolled out of her dress. There was cigarette ash on her breast and she brushed it delicately away. 'You are very pretty, *monsieur*,' she whispered potently. Her eyes searched me. I felt my face grow warm. Nailed to the chair, I glanced quickly towards the other members of the crew. I needed the separate reassurance that they were nearby at their table and that they would keep their distance. She elevated her hand. 'You are high, but not so high. You are strong and I like your face . . .' She leaned a little and touched my hair. Her touch went down my boy's body like a shock. '. . . And this, your hair. So dark.'

'I'm Welsh,' I explained inadequately. 'From Barry.'

She moved her white hands sideways and silently measured my shoulders. I felt myself glance to one shoulder then the other as if to make certain they were still there.

Her eyes came at me like steel rods. 'And you are so young,' she said.

'No, no.' I almost stammered for the first time in years. 'I'm fairly old.'

'Ah,' she sighed. 'To be so young.' She leaned forward, her

perfume and her bosom advancing on me, and said: 'I am Francine.' Her voice was low but clear in the din. 'What is your name?'

Certain that she would hear or see the thumping of my chest, I prayed that the skipper would remain long in the lavatory. 'Davy,' I told her. 'Davy Jones.'

'So beautiful,' she breathed. 'Davy Jones.'

She clapped her hands softly as though it had made her happy. Captain Bracklesham came back and said: 'Don't buy drinks for women.'

'She didn't ask,' I told him.

Francine pouted. 'Perhaps this older person will buy me a drink,' she suggested.

'All right,' he agreed sportingly. 'A glass of wine, perhaps.'

'Of champagne,' she amended and snapped her long fingers like a pistol shot.

The Poles from the fertiliser ship came in. Through the gloom and the smoke their aroma came before them, provoking howls and held noses, and before they were even halfway to the bar there was a scuffle which ignited to a battle. Francine jumped from the table and threw her arms protectively, engulfingly, around me, pressing my head into the bolster of her bosom. Captain Bracklesham was encouraging Feeney to his feet and pushing him into the uproar. At the bar the rank of perched drinkers toppled sideways striking each other domino fashion. The accordian was stretched like a jack-in-the-box across the room. A man fell face forward across our table, smashing the glass. Francine released me, heaved him effortlessly away, and caught me powerfully by the hand. 'Come, *chéri*,' she instructed. 'We leave.'

She tugged me through the fighting and out into the night. '*Toqués*,' she said pointing at the side of her head. 'Crazy people.' I briefly wondered where Captain Bracklesham had gone.

'Where are we going, Francine?' I asked. The lamps of the town were splashed on the wet cobbles. Careful of my manners I changed places so that I was walking on the outside. She giggled fruitily, looped her arm around my waist, and I put mine happily around hers. I could feel the hooks and eyes at the side of her dress. She had picked up a short coat which she now had over her shoulders. She sang fragments of a French song as we walked.

From the end of her street there was the smell of warm bread. Light fell out onto the pavement and passing shadows carrying trays were loading a horse-drawn van. Francine sniffed. Her eyes were bright.

She guided me into the shop. The white-hatted occupants greeted her, bowing and shaking her hand as if she had been a long time absent. She introduced me: '*Mon ami*, Davy Jones,' and they paused in their warm work to give me a short round of applause. Long loaves were being pushed along a counter to be loaded into baskets and trays. Francine selected one and thumbed its crust. She broke off a piece and put it into my mouth. I was very excited.

Calling '*Adieu!*' to the bakery workers she led me outside into the mist, holding my hand like a mother, coaxing me around the corner and to a door behind the bakery.

A flight of stairs took up all the narrow entrance. She pressed a light switch and in the low glow of a single bulb, I watched her legs sharp as pistons as they went up before me.

She lit an oil lamp in the room, turning up the wick, the rosy light widening silently around the walls. The lamp sharpened her face shadows. I stood waiting.

'Davy,' she said sweetly. She wiped the damp hair on her forehead. 'You must give me some money.'

'How much?'

'Show me your money.'

'I fumbled for my shore money. Deftly she stepped forward from the lamplight and took my hand from my pocket, replacing it with her own. *Her fingers were inside my trousers.* There were some franc notes in there, but she brought out a coin only.

'That's an English sixpence,' I mumbled gazing at it in embarrassment as it lay in her palm. 'That's not enough.'

46

'It shines,' she said. 'I will take it. It is like you, Davy Jones.'

She stood in the oil lamplight, her eyes never leaving my face. Then before my intoxicated and incredulous gaze she slowly began to undo the buttons at her bodice.

The following night saw a notable storm which roared up from the Bay of Biscay. Sailors talked of it for years; men were lost, ships wrecked, run ashore; there were famous winds and galloping seas. But it was at our backs and it blew us home.

The captain remained on the bridge all through it, staring straight out through the black and heaving night. Mr Wilberforce stood with him, praying and, at intervals, singing evangelical choruses. Mr Feeney stayed below coaxing his engines. It needed Jack and his brother George to steer. She began leaking like a watering can and I had to man the pumps. My God, I was sick. Down in the bilges I thought my first voyage would be my last. But I came through it. George came down to relieve me and sent me up to make coffee and to take a spell with Jack on the wheel. Holding the helm was like trying to hold a stallion. It took two of us to stop her turning side-on to the waves coming through the dark. I was grateful it was night and I could not see the whole storm.

Jack and I sang at the wheel. Francine was still so vivid in my imagination that the power of her vision carried me through the most dangerous hours of my young life. Oh, but it had been so wonderful with her. My face in her riotous hair, the immense wobbling of her breasts, her long hands guiding me ('Be still, *chéri*. I must do the work for us.'), my manhood growing with her every adept touch. As the *Myrtle Matthews* pitched and shied, plunged and reared, her hull groaning, Jack and I held the wheel and sang:

> 'Sons of the Sea,
> Bobbing up and down like this . . .'

As daylight slid over the ocean we saw how awesome the tempest was, and by that time it was beginning to abate. By ten o'clock in the forenoon watch we were merely rolling.

Mr Feeney appeared from below and sat, head in arms, on the deck. He said he would never go to sea again. The captain told me to get some sleep after I had made sandwiches and coffee. I slept without dreaming but only for five hours. When I came up onto the deck we were sailing jauntily up the Bristol Channel, the sea was reduced to long, prowling rollers, and I felt a surge of triumph because I had voyaged and survived, I had known a real woman, I had become a man, and now I was heading home. The evening hills of Wales were bathed in green sunshine.

Three

There were times when it appeared that the SS *Myrtle Matthews*, in which I made my first three trips, to Brest, Newcastle and Cork, was left to her own devices, finding her own way across tides and into harbours; but Captain Bracklesham had, even when asleep or incapacitated, an innate feel for the art of voyaging. It was as though he navigated and coaxed the ship with his big toe. We always arrived.

An instinct for sea passages is not something learned on a canal. In his earlier years he had been one of the famous Cape Horners who raced around the bottom of the world through blinding weather; in the days before the Panama Canal was built, before the dread Cape was left to grow old almost alone, its waves unseen, its winds unfelt.

On my second voyage a Chinese cook signed on, a man with a face like a lantern, and to him I handed over my messing duties and became a deckhand. 'Better for you up there than cooking,' said the captain. 'Fat gets into your lungs.'

He called me into his cabin: 'Every year,' he said, 'the Cape Horners have our grand dinner in Cardiff. It's a considerable night, believe me, men who have rounded the Horn.' He glanced up. 'In wooden ships.' He drew Tierra del Fuego with his fingernail on the dust of the desk. 'Good singing too, sailors' choir, although last year it was a woman; mouth like a cave. Now, you *can* sing, you're a fine singer, and this year you're going to sing for us. Practise your shanties.'

There was not much time. It was only two nights later that

the Cape Horners dined; white mess jackets, faces weathered red, voices used to shouting against gales. There was no coast nor corner they had not been and seen. They ate and drank in rows at long white tables, with the best glasses and cutlery, retelling of old voyages, long dead men and storms, and remembered vessels.

Great store was set by the singing. The choir came from many ships. The pianist was a bos'un who looped his arms over as he played, like a man swimming the crawl. I stepped up for my solo:

> 'One Friday morn, when we set sail
> And our ship not far from land,
> I there did espy a fair pretty maid,
> With a comb and a glass in her hand.'

They joined the chorus until the glasses shook:

> 'While the raging seas did roar,
> And the stormy winds did blow.
> And we, jolly sailor boys, were up and up aloft.
> And the landlubbers lying down below!'

Captain Bracklesham beckoned me. His face was like a coke fire, his eyes glimmering, and he had wine and whisky before him. He was with a man tall and thin as a mast with a nose like a gull.

'This, Jones,' the skipper announced, 'is Captain Kilpatrick.'

We shook hands and Captain Kilpatrick said I had sounded well.

'Captain Kilpatrick would like you aboard his ship,' said our skipper. He grinned. 'She's a ton or two bigger than the *Myrtle Matthews* and just as seaworthy. She's an ocean liner.'

Even now I can remember myself, a youth going to sea, on the platform of Bristol station in a mist of engines and people, sunlight falling in pillars through the girdered roof. 'Signing

50

on the *Orion*?' He had a sea-bag and he was looking down at mine. I said I was. 'First trip?' he said.

'On this ship,' I nodded. 'Been at sea. All over.'

His name was Kenny Boniface. He had a sad and fugitive look.

'What's she like?' I inquired. He sniffed: 'Almighty terrible. If you're a butcher, I mean. Blood's nasty stuff. Try holding a handful of offal in a force nine.'

I sympathised and he shrugged. 'It's all I know. My old man was one.' He grunted scornfully: 'A champion chicken-slitter. They just look at my discharge book and say: "You're a butcher. Got your own knives? Right, sign on".'

Once we were on the train he fell into sleep, snoring in a dry way, leaving me to watch the homely countryside, different from the landscapes in which I had grown up, the patched greens, the rivers and their valleys full of trees, the oat-coloured houses. Boniface roused himself at Salisbury, stared at the Cathedral spire, and moaned: 'Another hour.'

'It's a long journey,' I said uncertainly.

'Not long enough,' he said.

He relapsed into sleep and I studied the woe of his face, creased and tucked, too old for his age; his hands were raw. He looked as though nothing went right for him. He awoke finally as we were running into Southampton. 'One day,' he said like a promise, 'I'm going to cut a finger off.'

We travelled alongside the muddy water. I had never seen so many funnels, masts and decks. They stood against each other, close as a city.

'There she is,' said Boniface pointing to a hand of ugly stacks. My heart dropped. 'It can't be,' I said. I turned to see his sad, long face cracked in half by a grin. 'Got you then,' he chortled. 'That's the power station. The *Orion*'s over them roofs, see? Three red funnels, blue stripe.'

They looked so high and grand above the dockside sheds, that at the station I almost tumbled from the train.

'Easy does it,' advised Boniface. 'Tide's not till three.' I stepped onto the platform throwing my sea-bag on my shoulder as soon as I was striding. 'Easy,' Boniface repeated. 'She won't sail without us.'

Outside the station I could see the blazoned funnels more clearly, a signature of white smoke wriggling from the stack at the rear. 'You watch out for yourself,' warned my companion as we set off with our bags resting against the sides of our heads. His feet hurt. 'Chopping block fell on them,' he grumbled. The *RMS Orion* grew with every step.

'You watch out for yourself,' he repeated darkly. He humped his bag like a refugee who could see no end to the road. 'The sisters, for a start.'

'Sisters?'

'They ain't women,' he said, from the edge of his mouth. 'Not proper women. Or men.' He stopped on the pavement and moved his sea-bag from his shoulder to his chest where he hugged it and gave it a kiss. 'Bummers,' he summed up.

We began to plod on again. 'I'll watch out,' I said. 'They won't get near me.'

He sighed. 'I don't get touched, because nobody takes a fancy to me.'

At the dock gate we had to show our papers. 'There she is,' pointed the watchman as if we were likely to overlook a 25-thousand-ton ocean liner with a band playing at her gangway. 'What a row,' grumbled Boniface as he led me aft. A headiness filled me as I climbed the crew gangway. It was like going up the side of a smooth, white cliff.

My companion nodded at the hull. 'All that's got to be painted,' he oberved.

At the top of the gangway, on the enclosed deck, an officer and the chief steward sat behind separate desks, checking in the crew as they came aboard. 'It's Bonny,' said the chief steward when he saw Boniface. 'Nice to have somebody cheerful aboard.'

'Thanks, Mr Stone,' responded my shipmate solidly. He indicated me. 'Joining,' he said.

'What's your name, son?'

I told him. He checked down his list and whistled: 'What's this? Special recommendation from the captain.'

I was embarrassed. 'He's a friend of my last skipper. They're both Cape Horners.'

'Well, what's good enough for the captain . . . You can go in with Boniface, as you know him.'

'In the butcher's?' I said, horrified.

He laughed. 'Want your leg cut off? No, in his quarters. You're down to work in the linen room. We've got some cases on this ship, but down there they're only pillow cases. And you have to report to the Master-at-Arms, according to this. Looks like you're going to be protected.'

Boniface trooped off with his sea-bag and I followed. We descended successive decks, our boots clanging on the iron steps. 'Like a prison, ain't it,' complained Bonny over his shoulder.

We gained the lower deck, long passages switching direction like a maze, and down a further flight of narrow steps. 'It's just us and the bilge tanks down here,' mentioned Bonny. 'If she hits an iceberg we'll be swimming in muck.'

He knocked politely before opening the door of our quarters. The cabin was tight, room for two berths each side and just enough leeway to stand between them. Sea-bags were stowed under the lower bunks and there was a rail with coat hangers at the far end. A thin whine issued from a ventilation shaft and indifferent light from a double bulkhead lamp. It was too far down for a porthole.

A pillow, a single sheet and a blanket were folded at the end of each bunk, except for one which had a blue curtain fully draped around it. There was an undrawn curtain on each of the other berths.

'Who's in there?' inquired Bonny oddly knocking at the curtain. The draped bunk stood silent as a coffin.

'Bonny?' came a thick voice eventually. 'It's Killer.'

'What you up to, Killer?' He spoke close to the curtain.

''Aving some privacy.'

The curtain was opened from the inside, briskly but only

for a short distance. The head was red and whiskery, the eyes so watery I thought he was crying. ''Ome for ten days,' he groaned. 'Don't get a minute to yourself.'

I stowed my sea-bag and went along the decks to the linen room, a cave of shelves, warm-smelling like a draper's shop, overseen by a steward called Totty who had a dyed beard. He had been at sea thirty years but he was unsure where he had been. Hong Kong he called Kong Hong, Naples was Nipples, Bilbao, Balboa and Balboa Bilbao.

'Me, I hardly know where we're bound, only that we're on the way. And going home again. That's all,' he said.

'You don't go ashore?'

'No, get away with you. What's ashore for? That's for passengers. Sometimes I go on deck and make sure that the sea's still there.'

Craftily he surveyed his cosy kingdom. 'Since you're going to be down here,' he said with a hint of conspiracy, 'I'll tell you how to work it.' Going to the door he looked out, both ways, and then closed the steel hatch with a soft sound.

'The secret, son,' he confided, 'is to take your time. There's all the time in the world down here. Nobody wants to learn about it. Navigation they learn, but not linen. So they think there's more to it than there is. And there ain't.' He winked ponderously. 'You can build a wall of quilts, even towels, and settle down behind them, for a couple of hours' nap. Most restful place on the whole ship, this is.'

I told him I had to report to the Master-at-Arms. He looked impressed and worried. 'Not a word about what I just told you,' he warned. 'He's like the Chief of Police, you know. He could have us in irons.'

As I was going to the Master-at-Arms' office, I felt the ship shift. It was like a thrill. Two decks down I heard the muted shouts and the buffered hoot of our siren.

An officer apprentice who opened the door at my knock said: 'He won't be able to see you, Jones, until we're under way. Come back later.'

'Thank you,' I hesitated. He looked younger than me. He prompted: 'Sir.'

I said: 'Yes . . . sir.'

'All right then,' he said with two pink blush points on his cheeks. 'Dismiss.'

I went up to the area of aft deck permitted to the crew. A group of men stood looking at the shore. One man turned and went below waving an angry hand, shouting: 'Good riddance.' There remained three Indian deckmen and a puce-faced cook in his blue check trousers and white apron, his tall hat bent like a chimney pot in the Solent wind. He was crying copiously. He took his hat off and wiped his eyes with it but then began to weep again, staring towards the shore. The tears made his face look cold. He was several paces back from the rail so it seemed that the object of his grief was not on the dock from which the ship was drawing away, but at a distance. I stepped around a capstan and went to the side.

Over the years I have left a thousand ports; in meagre craft that crept away and quickly headed for sea as though escaping; in ugly, shapeless ships that have blown final, insulting raspberries; in bulky vessels pushed and pummelled by tugs. But in all these departures there has rarely been anyone to witness our leaving; perhaps a knot of white-faced wives up to their ankles in ropes, but usually only dockers who cast off hawsers and trudged away to their breakfasts without a backward glance at the ship heading for the ocean.

But each sailing of an ocean liner is unique. The dock was crowded with people calling, waving and trying to catch the red, white and blue streamers that shimmered through the air from the passenger decks. The lusty band played 'Rule Britannia' and gulls danced around the masts. Two tugs were pulling us clear of the berth and another was nudging abaft as close as a piglet feeding from a sow. I watched the scene with a novel wonder. Many of the crowd on the dockside were laughing and blowing kisses. They were the class of people who could be confident they would see their loved ones again; it was no final parting. Obedient motor cars were lined outside the dock gates, waiting to take the wellwishers home.

I watched the throng and waved but nobody was looking up at my deck. The Indian hands gazed out uncaring. They were not leaving anywhere that meant anything to them, nor were they going home. They were just sailing again, their life and their lot.

'Hell!' cried the cook. The ship was edging out now, thirty or forty feet from the land with the distance widening. The tugs were sounding off triumphantly. The shrill toot of the tug at the rear seemed to decide him. He flung down his tall white hat and made for the rail. 'I'm going!' he bawled at me and the Indians. 'I love her!'

The deckhands moved swiftly, as though not unfamiliar with desperate moments. They ran towards him as he got a foothold on the rail. I jumped forward and caught him by his thick arm. The three Indians clung to his legs and body. It was done without much noise, as if the celebrations must not, at any cost, be disturbed, something the cook seemed to appreciate himself because his curses and sobs came through gritted teeth. 'Don't be silly,' I said to him. 'You'll be drowned.'

He blinked at me as if I were the madman. 'That's what I want, you prat,' he wailed. But abruptly he relaxed his grip and his foothold on the rail, and the Indians manhandled him, crab-like, away from it.

I picked up his cook's hat which had blown across the deckboards and handed it to him. 'Thanks,' he sniffed.

The Indians now unfolded their grips and allowed him to go shakily to the companionway. He staggered down the steps, his hands and sobs resounding against the metal walls.

I remained there watching the gulf widen between the ship and the shore, thrilled by the blasts of our siren. The people became small, the sound of the band diminished. I felt a breeze. Out into the Solent the tugs eased us, into the seaway. Then we moved ahead. Westwards down the Channel.

I went below and reported again to the Master-at-Arms. The officer apprentice opened the door. I called him 'sir' again and he blushed. He led me to an inner office.

The Master-at-Arms was clasping his hands on his desk. His was the best uniform on the ship, splashes and sashes of red and a *sword* which he had worn for the departure and which now rested in front of him.

'You saw the drama on deck?' he said to my surprise.

'Yes sir.'

'He couldn't be allowed to jump,' he continued as though I was owed an explanation. 'Not in home port.'

He scowled. 'No end of trouble. Fishing him out, taking him to the hospital or the mortuary. Late sailing, and we're *never* late sailing. The owners don't like it.'

'No sir,' I replied. 'They wouldn't.'

'That's why I had the three deckhands up there,' he explained. I wondered why he was telling me. 'Keeping an eye.' He smiled without much warmth at me. 'But you lent a hand too. Well done.' He picked out a sheet of paper from a wooden tray on the side of which was carved: 'A Souvenir of the Titanic.'

'Now, let's see. Davy Jones.' He looked up. 'Not much of a name for a sailor.'

'No sir,' I said in a low voice.

'The captain says you've got to be looked after, and what the captain says goes for me. Let's see, you're working in the linen room. Well Totty's safe. He's a lazy old sod, sleeping behind the quilts, but he's past all that.' He consulted the paper once more. 'Berthing with . . . Boniface . . . that misery . . . and Peace. Killer Peace and Norris. Norris is Irish. He'll only *bore* the arse off you. I'm going to put the word about, though, just in case.' He looked me up and down. 'You,' he said emphatically, 'are a protected person.'

I retraced my way through the decks to the linen room.

'I'm a protected person,' I told Totty. 'According to the Master-at-Arms.'

He sighed like a mother. 'That's what they're saying,' he remarked. 'Did he have a long chat?'

'Yes . . . quite long.'

'He's got nobody to talk to,' said Totty. 'Nobody wants to know him.' He picked up a docket from his list-littered table and read it to himself. 'Now it's the padre wants to see you,' he sighed. 'Wish I was good-looking. We haven't had a furore like this, not in the linen room, since the sheets caught fire. Nineteen twenty-eight. You'd better go and see His Holiness. We're hardly in the Channel and all this going on.'

'The Master-at-Arms knows you take a sleep behind the quilts, Totty,' I said cautiously.

Totty lightly banged his fist on his table and gently ground his teeth. 'He won't *do* anything,' he quietly exclaimed. 'Wouldn't dare.' His lips thinned. 'He'd better not mix with me. I could bring this ship to a standstill.' He looked around at the towers of clean sheets. 'And he knows it. Go and see the padre. Listen to him squeak.'

'He's not . . . not one of the sisters?' I asked anxiously.

'Never asked him,' replied Totty. 'His name is Fields. Gracie Fields.'

I went along the decks and corridors until I came to a door decorated with a cross and the name in curly clerical lettering: 'The Reverend Simon Fields.'

He piped, 'Come in.' I went in. He looked very youthful, bright-faced, with disconcertingly unblinking eyes and long, flapping hands. Both his hands went around mine as if he were clasping a rope, and he beamed ecclesiastically.

'My boy,' he breathed. 'What denomination are you?'

'Male,' I said stoutly.

'Religious denomination.' There was a touch of pique.

'Oh, I see. Yes, well . . . Chapel.'

'Well, we have all sorts and conditions on board.' He became businesslike. 'Sundays we have an inter-denomination service and the captain says you sing. We have a choir.

If you sing in it you are excused duties on Sundays and choir practice nights. The result is we get all the slackers who can howl a few notes. But you can really sing, I understand. What is it, alto?' He regarded me with faint hope.

I replied: 'Baritone, sir.' The brightness in his eyes diminished like a gas lamp and he said briskly: 'You must read the lesson on Sunday. The captain likes to have the newest member of the crew to do it, those that can read. It's Philippians . . . Have you got a Bible?'

'Not with me.'

Shaking his head he took a Bible from his shelf. 'Well, borrow this. And I *mean* borrow. I never get them back. This is a ship of thieves.'

I carried the Bible back along the decks to the linen room. 'I've got to read the lesson on Sunday,' I said to Totty.

'Look at that,' he said slowly taking the Bible from my hand. 'He gave you a Bible.' He regarded me craftily. 'Forget to give it back if I was you. They fetch good money, Bibles, in some parts. Some black man in Africa would give a week's wages to have that.'

'We're not going to Africa, Totty,' I said.

'I know that,' he said amiably. 'America we're going. Straight on. But you could stow it. You'll be sailing for Africa sometime.'

Sailors, by the nature of their calling and their myth, are imagined as strong, alert, steadfast men confronting dangers and the elements with resourcefulness and a fearless eye. The truth is different. The seafarer is often prey to fogs and fevers, prone to poxes, and inclined to moods, drunkenness, and any number of manias. Enclosed in their villages of floating iron they become victims of winds and waters, many are fat and frail. Terrors haunt them, fear of marine ghosts, spectral ships, God, mermaids, sharks, stars, the moon and the dark. All fear the sea.

My three cabin companions were all subject to peculiarities. Boniface bred ailments deep in his chest and would appear coughing at the door, at four in the morning, as he came off his night duty, covered in fresh blood from the butcher's bench.

Charlie Peace was nicknamed 'Killer' because he had been called after the famous murderer. His thin frame was vividly illustrated with tattoos; 'Glory Is My Game' and 'I Die For Love', they said, but they were his only fierce aspects.

Norris was an Irishman with a catalogue of stories from County Sligo and interminable and, it often seemed, terminal toothache. The onset of toothache stopped the stories. It was difficult to know which was preferable. He could hum like a jew's-harp and was often called in to accompany the ship's choir.

The lesson I was to read at the Sunday service I rehearsed on deck, quoting the Bible to the unlistening sea. We were in the Atlantic. The air was wet, the ocean crumpled. Birds had been left behind, even the biggest gulls, and we were out there on our own.

On Sunday the members of the choir were dressed in white tunics buttoned to the neck. In the congregation the crew were bundled together at the back. Boniface, Peace and Norris, not required that week for his humming, sat among the religious deckhands. Their pale, staring heads peered over the passengers and officers as I went forward to read the lesson.

'Whatsoever things are true, whatsoever things are honest, whatsoever things are pure, whatsoever things are lovely,' I recited and at the conclusion, '. . . think on these things.' My cabin mates at the rear began to clap. Passengers and officers turned. The three sat down bashfully.

The following day I was summoned from the linen room by the purser. In his office was a bulky old lady wearing a striped pink dress and straw bonnet, sitting with log-like legs projecting.

'Ah, Jones . . .' said the purser quickly, checking my name

on a list of crew members. 'This is Mrs Brewing. Mrs Brewing was very impressed with your reading at the service.'

There was a pause. Then the purser said: 'Mrs Brewing would like you to read to her at bedtime.'

'My eyes are not terribly good,' the lady smiled apologetically.

'I'm sure Jones will,' the purser answered. He turned to me. 'Mrs Brewing is one of our regular passengers. You'll be released from other duties, Jones.' He thought again. 'On the late watch, that is.'

'*Every* night?' I said, surprised.

'I have lots of books,' said the old lady brightly. 'Lots. You don't read in French, I suppose? But English will do. Perhaps you could start tonight. Ten-thirty.'

I went away thinking how strange it was that my voice, that poor, lame, thing of my childhood, had brought me to being a storyteller on an ocean liner. At ten-thirty I timidly knocked at Mrs Brewing's cabin door. When I obeyed her call and entered she was already all pink in bed, fluffy stuff around her veined neck, a pat of cream on her forehead and two more under her eyes.

'I do look a sight, don't I,' the old lady said cheerfully as I went in. 'Pull up a stool by the bed, Davy, while I rub this rubbish into my face. I don't believe it helps at all, but one can only try. You must thank God you'll never have to be an old woman.' She pointed to the dressing table. 'There's the book: *The Pickwick Papers*. You might like to rehearse it a little first.'

I was wearing my uniform of sharp white trousers, a white jacket with stiff collar, bright buttons, the same as I had worn for the choir, and now sat by the old lady while she massaged the optimistic cream into her cheeks. 'Are you familiar with Dickens?' she inquired through the side of her mouth as she rubbed. Without waiting for my reply she forecast: 'You'll enjoy this one. Fun in London and Kent.' She wiped her hands on a little towel and then leaned back with a deep breath against her multiple pillows. 'Begin now, Davy, if you please.'

61

I began to read: '*There are in London several old inns, once the headquarters of celebrated coaches in the days when coaches performed their journeys in a graver and more solemn manner than they do in these times . . .*'

I read slowly at the outset, but then began to get used to it, to measure it out, and later to adopt different voices for the spoken words.

'*"Sam . . . number twenty-two wants his boots."*

"Ask number twenty-two whether he'll have them now, or wait till he gets 'em."'

This pleased her immensely. 'Very good,' she smiled. 'Excellent indeed.'

I enjoyed being with her. She laughed like a dinner bell. I read for half an hour until I looked up and saw she was asleep. Closing the book I returned it to the dressing table and crept to the door. Her steward was outside, a stooping man who whispered. 'She's gone off,' he said professionally. 'I'll tuck her in. I always tuck her in.'

The following night I returned and she asked me to read some poetry. 'This is nice,' she said as if it were a suggestion of mine. '*A Shropshire Lad*.' She glanced at me already on the stool. 'You're not a lad from Shropshire, are you?' she asked.

'I'm Welsh, Mrs Brewing,' I said.

'My husband was part Welsh.' She gave me a playful nudge from the bed. 'I never knew *which* part.'

We both laughed at her joke. 'Twenty years departed,' she said without sadness. 'Go on, Davy, please begin.'

I read the simple poem carefully. When I got to one verse she stopped me with her puffy hand and asked me to read it once more:

> 'Loveliest of trees, the cherry now
> Is hung with bloom along the bow,
> And stands about the woodland ride,
> Wearing white for Eastertide.'

She sighed in a happy way, patted my hand again and closed her eyes. They did not open again. I read on and read on and eventually stopped and looked at her carefully. 'Mrs Brewing?' I inquired. 'Mrs Brewing?' I felt my face change.

'Mrs Brewing . . . are you . . . ?'

She was not. I moved closer, peering at her nightdress for signs of breath. There was no rise of the silk. Her face had suddenly become younger. 'Oh, Mrs Brewing,' I whispered. 'You're dead.'

Although Mrs Brewing had booked to travel only as far as New York and the ship was afterwards sailing south, through the Panama Canal and up the West Coast to San Francisco, her executors decided that she should have her long-expressed wish to be buried at sea from the liner upon which she had spent so much time.

'I saw her today,' said Boniface smugly. 'Your Mrs Brewing.'

I did not believe him. 'How?' I said.

'She's in our freezer,' he boasted. 'They always put them in there.'

'They don't! Not Mrs Brewing!' Aghast, I could imagine her in her fluffy pink negligée, lying stiff among the legs of lamb.

It was arranged that her burial at sea would take place two days after sailing from New York, off The Carolinas. The padre said I was to read the lesson and he did not indicate which so I read the verse I had recited to her on the last evening of her life:

> 'Loveliest of trees, the cherry now
> Is hung with bloom, along the bow,
> And stands about the woodland ride,
> Wearing white for Eastertide.'

We were standing at the stern on a day of ghostly sunshine, everyone wrapped up, and Mrs Brewing in her coffin on the chute that would project her into the sea. I felt like crying. Then, after I had read the verse, one of the lady passengers, very elegant and beautiful, moved a few paces sideways along

63

the deck, and while everyone else sang 'Jerusalem' she whispered in American: 'I've heard about your reading. Would you come and read to me?'

Dumbly I nodded. She smiled and gracefully went back to her place among the other passengers. When the padre came to the final words committing Mrs Brewing to the deep, a sailor pulled a cord, and the coffin slid over the side and hit the slanting grey-green sea like a depth-charge.

It was supposed to sink. But it did not. Instead it began to jump on top of the waves like a little boat. 'God save us!' exclaimed the padre religiously. He looked towards the aghast captain. 'Mrs Brewing is floating.'

It was an unhappy sight, Mrs Brewing bobbing around like that, in her coffin on the sea. Fortunately the ship was on dead-slow ahead because of the burial service, hardly making way at all, and we could heave-to while boats were launched to recover Mrs Brewing.

The lead weights and lead lining from the coffin, guaranteed to make it sink, had been stolen by a conspiracy between one of the undertaker's men from New York and two of our crew. One man was supposed to replace the valuable lead with sandbags, but he swore in court that Mrs Brewing opened her eyes in her coffin and stared at him.

The day following the second of Mrs Brewing's burial services a cabin steward handed me a note in an envelope. 'Mrs Tingley sent it,' he muttered. It said: 'Please come and read to me tonight at eleven. This steward is to be trusted. He will guide you.'

The messenger read the note over my shoulder. 'Cabin A forty,' he whispered. 'I'll be in the pantry. Come up from the crew deck for'ard.'

I began to worry. Reciting to an elderly lady as part of the ship's facilities, and with the knowledge of the purser, was one thing, but creeping along the eleven o'clock decks to reach a female passenger's cabin was another.

Silently and anxiously I left the cabin. Only Norris was in his bunk, his snores ruffling the curtains drawn around it.

The lower deck used by the crew went almost the length of the ship. It was hot down there and it rocked as we went out from the Panama Canal into the Pacific Ocean. The forward companionway steps twisted through an aperture like a chimney. Watchfully I climbed to the next deck. Her steward was in his pantry. 'Got your reading glasses?' he inquired with a leer. He put his American comic down and rose from his stool adding: 'She said I've got to show you where it is.' I did not change my expression. He pointed. 'Third door along. I go off-duty in an hour. The night bloke's on then, and he don't know nothing about this. I'm not sharing with him. So finish the story before then.'

My chest taut I knocked on her door. 'Please enter,' she summoned gently. My legs shook. What was going to happen? I went in, afraid she would see my legs vibrating.

In all the years since, I don't think I have ever seen a sight like Mrs Helena Tingley in bed. It was as if she had been transported from a Hollywood musical, like the one shown in the crew's canteen that very evening; luscious-legged ladies swimming in formation, or lying on divans, singing love songs. There had been groans in the dark. It had excited me. Now here she was – a beauty from the picture show.

The cabin was bathed in a fluffy glow. A big brown radio standing on the floor played subdued dance music from California. Underfoot the carpet crumpled like moss, the silk furnishings dangled with tassels. There was an ample mirror at one side so that I had a double vision of Mrs Tingley sitting, smiling her welcome, from the voluminous bed.

'I've come to read to you,' I said tremulously. I was in my white uniform with the tight collar.

Her smile engulfed me. 'Welcome, Davy,' she sighed in her thrilling American voice. 'You wore your cute clothes. I'm so glad.'

Her slender finger was beckoning me. I closed the door behind me. 'Turn the key,' she suggested sweetly from the bed. 'We mustn't let anyone hear.' I turned to face her again. She was about thirty-five years of age.

'It's a nice uniform,' she said.

'I always wear it for reading . . . to people,' I responded nervously. 'I used to for Mrs Brewing.'

'Poor Mrs Brewing,' she echoed. 'Floating away like that.'

I was now standing a mere yard from her bed. Waiting. She was wearing a cream robe of shiny material folded around her front. Her hair was lying deeply over her shoulders and her face was soft with few shadows. 'Be comfortable, Davy,' she said. 'I'm going to. We're going to be really good friends. I know that. Please sit down. There, I put that stool right there for you.'

Once I sat on the stool I felt better, although her glow and her perfume were heady. Her eyes were so beautifully big that I wondered, as I often did when I thought about her later, if there was some operation available in miraculous America where eyes could be expanded like that. Her hands were lying on the quilt, fine and fawn with vivid red nails and glinting rings. I had to say something. 'How is Mr Tingley?' I blurted.

'Not very well,' she said as if she were glad I had inquired. 'In fact he's dead.'

'Oh, I'm sorry,' I stumbled. Her crimson-crowned fingers were reaching for a book on the bedside table. It was *Tom Sawyer*. She said: 'I married him young, I was young, that is, and he passed on last year. Heart. Seventy-eight.'

Quickly dismissing her memories she held the book towards me. 'Why don't you start, Davy?' she suggested. Her eyes lifted. I could not look at them. 'From page one.'

She and the pillows both sighed as she lay back. When she was settled I began to read. '*The Adventures of Tom Sawyer*. By Mark Twain,' I recited.

'Just beautiful,' she sighed. 'How old are you?'

'Seventeen, Mrs Tingley,' I answered. There was no choice. I looked up from Tom Sawyer. 'Nearly eighteen.'

'Wonderful.' Her eyes were travelling slowly over me. I wanted to go to the lavatory. 'Would you like me to go on?' I said.

'Oh, please. Of course. The first words again . . .'

'*The Adventures of Tom Sawyer*. By Mark Twain,' I repeated. It was not a book I had read. In fact I had read very few books until then. But I could act the words. She took on a look of interest and smiled in a small way at some of the things that happened in the first few pages, but soon she appeared to become bored. She let her blonde hair run through her hands.

'Davy,' she said eventually. 'I'm sure I've heard this before, some time. There's something else I want you to read to me.'

Transfixed, I watched her slide like a lovely silk snake from the bed. Her long nightdressed legs slithered over the edge together, her creamy fingers easing her robe about her, that embracing smile glowing upon me. Just like one of the lovelies in the film. I could not believe I was there with her.

'Can I get it for you, Mrs Tingley?' I stood up.

She hushed me. 'No, I'll get it. It's in my drawer right here.' She opened the drawer and took out the book. Back she came, her thighs pushing against the silk. Tentatively I reached out for the book.

'More adventures,' I said reading the spine. '*The Adventures of Fanny Hill.*'

Smiling, she slid into the bed. 'It's an old book, Davy,' she murmured. 'But famous.' It looked worn and furtive to me. I opened it and as I read it began to dawn on me that it was different from Tom Sawyer. Mrs Tingley's eyes never left my face. Each time I looked up there they were, until I was afraid to take mine from the page. As I read the first paragraphs she began to wriggle impatiently. 'Davy,' she said in her stealthy voice.

'Yes, Mrs Tingley?' There was nothing for it but to look up.

'Give me the book a moment, Davy. There's a part of it I really enjoy.'

Slowly I handed the book across. Her hand moved to meet it even more slowly and she kept her eyes drilled on me.

'That collar looks so tight,' she observed casually as she took it. I put my finger inside the stiff white top of the tunic. 'It gets a bit hot,' I agreed. Over came her long finger and it curled inside the collar, cool as ice against my neck. 'Let's undo it,' she said and flicked open the button.

I *really* wanted to go to the lavatory now. 'Mrs Tingley,' I asked wretchedly. 'Could I go to your lav?'

The human request took the intensity from her face and she laughed beautifully. 'But of course,' she pointed. 'It's right across there.' Awkwardly, I got up and trudged over the carpet to the door. 'I'll find that special page while you're away,' she promised. I could sense her still watching me.

The bathroom smelled like heaven. There were coloured soaps and luxurious sponges. The taps winked. It was the loudest visit to the toilet I had ever made. My water echoed and gurgled in the delicate pan. It went on for so long, too. I prayed that she could not hear. 'Hurry up,' I kept urging myself through my clenched teeth. '*Hurry* up, will you.'

The flush was a magic touch on a lever. I had to look around for it because I had never seen a lavatory without a chain before. And it *oozed* instead of gushed, taunting me for my rustic noise. I stared down at it. The water was pink. Everything was luxury. I buttoned up and returned to the cabin.

There she was, laying back in the bed, one silken knee pointing at the ceiling, the book open on my stool. She turned her great eyes. 'I missed you.'

'Sorry, Mrs Tingley, I couldn't find the chain,' I said.

Picking up the book I painstakingly cleared my throat and squatted on the stool. I began to read the page she had selected:

' . . . *a tenant's son just come out of the country, a very handsome young lad, scarce turned nineteen, fresh as a rose, well-shaped and clever-limbed, in short a very good excuse for any woman's liking* . . . '

I began to choke. Hardly daring to look up at her, I apologised and said: 'I've got a lump in my throat.'

'In your throat, Davy? That's too bad.' She smoothed

down the bed covers near her, right next to the contours caused by her long legs, one stretched out, one crooked at the knee. 'Come and sit here,' she suggested. 'It's so much more comfortable.'

Knowing now, almost for sure, what her plans were for me, I rose from the stool and timidly sat beside her on the coverlet. There were a few moments' silence between us. I pretended to search for the page in the book. Her perfume clouded my head.

'Do you have a little girlfriend, Davy?' she inquired softly.

'Yes . . . well no. Not now. Dolly . . . I had . . . that is she *was* my g . . . g . . . g . . . girl . . . f . . . f . . . friend.'

As my impediment returned to terrorise me so she began to undo the buttons on my tunic. 'You have a stammer,' she murmured.

'N . . . n . . . ot of . . . ten . . . It's . . . it's . . .'

'It's *very* sweet,' she soothed. 'A sweet stammer.' She had both hands on me. 'Let's get this heavy coat off you.'

'I've . . . only g . . . g . . . got . . . my v . . . v . . . vest underneath,' I blurted.

'Go on reading, Davy.'

It was as though she were moving through a dream. Sleepily she began to rub my chest below my vest. 'So your girlfriend left,' she sighed. 'That's too bad.'

'R . . . R . . . Really,' I said. I was saying anything now. Anything. 'R . . . r . . . really she liked Tosh . . . but he fell off the lighthouse.'

Her voice descended to a soft drone, like a bumble bee. 'Read some more, Davy,' she said. 'Please. For me.'

My fingers slipping, I opened the book again. It was upside down. I turned it.

> '. . . *catching gently hold of his shirt-sleeve, drew him towards me, blushing and almost trembling, for surely his extreme bashfulness and utter inexperience called for at least these advances to encourage him. His body was now conveniently inclined towards me, and justly softly chucking his smooth, beardless chin, I asked him if he was afraid of a lady? . . .*'

She had opened my white tunic fully and now I had to release the book one hand at a time while she took it from my back. 'It's a fine – er – vest you have here,' she assured me. 'Let's continue on down here. Keep reading. I'm agog.'

So was I. Those long red-tipped fingers were on my fly-buttons, flicking each of them open like someone counting coins. She kept saying nonsense things as she did it and I was doggedly reading:

'. . . I stole my hand upon his thighs, down one of which I could both see and feel a stiff hard body, confined by his breeches, and that my fingers could discover no end to . . .

I saw with wonder and surprise, what? Not the plaything of a boy, not the weapon of a man, but a maypole . . .'

It was impossible to go on when she got to the final button because with a noise like a she-bear finding honey she opened the front of my white trousers and plunged both hands into my underpants. My personal popped out right in front of my eyes. I began to apologise profusely but she hushed me with one finger while she tapped it tenderly with the fingers of the other hand as though she believed she might get a tune out of it. Then, to my intense dismay, she tucked it away again. 'Don't you like it, Mrs Tingley?' I croaked haplessly. Her slow, hanging eyes came up. 'Hurry, hurry. I'm always in a hurry,' she muttered.

'It's no use rushing,' I gabbled. 'Would you like me to come back another time?'

'Move from this cabin and I'll scream,' she threatened deeply. 'You'll be behind bars in the bilge or wherever it is.' She took the limp book from me and dropped it to the floor. 'It's no use sitting there half-dressed, Davy,' she said. Her voice had become instructive. 'Just get out of your things.' She pointed to the immediate carpet. 'Right here.'

So I undressed in front of her. Her eyes never moved from me. 'You're so handsome,' she muttered. 'And seventeen.'

'Nearly eighteen,' I corrected desperately. I was trying to hide my penis with my hand. She began easing away her nightdress, the straps flopping over her shoulders and then her elbows until her glossy breasts toppled out and displayed themselves before my boy's gaze.

'Do you like them, Davy?' she asked.

'Yes, Mrs Tingley.' My breath felt used up. 'They're lovely.'

'Would you like to touch them, Davy?'

'Yes please, Mrs Tingley.'

'Come. Come to me.'

My personal was standing out like a bowsprit. She enfolded it tenderly and tugged me towards her. My hands staggered to the flanks of those breasts, to their wonderful warmth and sheen. She began to moan. 'Kiss them, Davy,' she whispered. Her eyes had become shining slits. 'Kiss them, for God's sake.'

Putting my lips to the nearest nipple, I kissed it almost formally and then lay right across her to the other one. Her arms folded me into her bed and her body. 'Enter me now,' she said firmly. 'This moment, Davy. I cannot delay.'

I did as I was told and was at once engulfed by pleasure. So apparently was she. 'Fourteen,' she moaned. 'Fourteen.' It seemed important.

'Seventeen,' I amended in the midst of her. 'Nearly eighteen.'

'Oh yes,' she gasped. 'Oh yes.'

'July,' I cried against her juicy cheeks. 'The fourth.'

When we docked in San Francisco on the following afternoon I kept going up to the crew latrine on the deck above to see if I could catch sight of Mrs Tingley as she disembarked. Totty had gone briefly and unusually ashore and I was left in charge of the linen room, awaiting a fresh delivery for the tables and cabins of joining passengers, so it was simple to run up the steps every few minutes. It would have been sad but easy to miss her, but I was lucky. Standing on the lavatory seat and craning my neck around the curved rim of the porthole, I captured just a glimpse of her as she went ashore into the arms of a waiting gentleman who wore a big grey suit and a homburg and had a car. He gave her flowers and there were others there who were glad to see her, a group of a dozen or more, wearing hats and furs. She embraced them and seemed happy. As for me, I waved what must have looked like a ghostly hand from the porthole but I doubted whether she saw it. She was back in her life and I was back in mine. I was grateful to her and I thought perhaps she was to me.

She had asked me to sign her visitors' book, for special friends she said, and to write my address so that she could send me a Christmas card. As I signed I could not know what a strange thing would come from this so many years after.

When she had boarded her car, I walked slowly back to the linen room and, lonely again, I went to sleep behind a newly-arrived pile of folded tablecloths. Totty found me there when he came back from his sample of dry land, as he called it, and said I could go ashore for an hour. I had not been able to leave the ship in New York so I stepped for the first time on to the soil of the USA, land of Mrs Helena Tingley. After walking up and down a couple of harbour streets, full of thoughts and regrets that I would never see her again, I went back to the ship where I belonged. She had left an enevelope in the crew post for me. Inside was a twenty dollar note and a message which said: 'Thank you for *reading* to me.' I did not spend the money but put it away in my kit-bag. My memory of Mrs Tingley.

Four

In Marseille there used to be a place called Les Trois Frères and if I had not gone there with Boniface, Charlie Peace and Norris one night, my life might well have taken a different, more settled course. Today I might be recently retired after a lifetime in maritime linen rooms.

It was my fifth voyage on the *RMS Orion*; to the Mediterranean, a cruise that was destined for Istanbul. The ship had stopped at Lisbon on the way south and once we had turned the corner she had, like a large cautious dog, circled Spain. As we cruised outside the three-mile limit and the passengers were dancing on the deck, they could hear the guns of the civil war sounding from the hills.

In Marseille Totty gave up his entire shore leave, eight hours of it, so that I could sample the port he had seen many years before and did not want to see again.

Les Trois Frères was a dark bar run by the three brothers. There had been a fourth, but he had been horribly found in a drain and the name had been changed.

My three shipmates entered this place with a collective but assured swagger, solely for my benefit because they were really timid and pessimistic men, and in a way it was I who was taking them.

A pregnant woman came and sat down by me and asked me if I would like to go upstairs. I had been drinking pastis, that cloudy cough-mixture concoction that appears so harmlessly medicinal and tastes pleasantly of peppermint. When I pointed out that she really should not be taking men upstairs in her condition (even the steepness of the stairs seemed to be a risk) she laughed coarsely and shouted, telling the people among the smoke what I had said. There were hoots and rough comments, because her job was merely to conduct the customers to the upper floor and help them to choose a mate.

'Go on, Davy,' Boniface urged. He and the others clutched the backs of their chairs. 'Go on up.'

As I stood, I realised that pastis was not as childish as it tasted. With bravado I picked up the clouded glass, drank it at a throw and felt it go down like hot water. My legs had become bandy as I walked with the pregnant woman to the stairs, and there were more taunts and cheers.

Tentatively I climbed them, focusing on each one as I did. The mother-to-be helped me. She had strong hands and arms. At the top of the landing sat half-a-dozen dull and perspiring girls, fanning themselves, applying lipstick, squinting into little mirrors. They did not smile until my escort said something sharply whereupon they burst into giggles. I chose one and paid the pregnant lady five francs. The girl tried to look pleased, and even made a little curtsey. I recall little about her, except that she changed my life.

She beckoned me with a jagged fingernail. We went into a heavy-smelling room, more like a cubicle, draped in French flags. On the floor was an uncompromising mattress.

It was all so different from Francine and Mrs Tingley. Suddenly I no longer felt young. The pastis was causing me to sway in the tent-like space. She grimaced and bad-temperedly took off her blouse, flinging it aside. Because of the drink her face looked double to me, like twins. Petulently, she indicated that I should take off my shirt and my shoes. Since the bed took up almost all the floor, I was standing in a confined space, like a man with his feet in a hole. Clumsily I sat on the mattress and undid my laces.

As I was about to take off my shirt, there came from below a huge and wrathful howl followed by shouts and confusion. Alarm stiffened her features. 'Gaston!' She shot a look at me as if I must know him. '*Mon Dieu*, Gaston!' She rushed to put on her blouse, her eyes wide with fright. She bundled me from the cubicle. Attempting to pick up my shoes, I dropped one but she would not wait. 'Come! *Tout de suite!*' she urged. She grabbed me roughly, a grasp like a bony man, and thrust me out onto the landing.

A fierce giant was coming ominously up the stairs. He had a gun. Everyone below was watching. The pregnant woman tried to follow him and caught hold of his coat, but he shook her off and, without turning his head, pushed her so she stumbled and rolled back down to the onlookers who hardly gave her a passing glance. He continued up the stairs. 'Paulette,' he snarled. 'Paulette, *que diable . . . que diable . . .* '

The other girls had vanished. 'Paulette,' I mumbled, looking around for the girl I had been with. 'You're wanted.'

She was trying to hide behind a screen on the landing but her naked legs were showing below it. 'Paulette,' he snarled again. Trembling she came from behind the screen. '*Sauvez moi!*' she pleaded. She would have been hard to save even if I had known and liked her. Gaston's gun was pointed unerringly at my midriff.

I was still in my stockinged feet with one shoe over my right hand like a pointed boxing glove. Paulette, not content with cowering behind my shirt, had now begun to push me forward towards the enraged Gaston who came ferociously up the final stairs like a monster rising from a hole. The watchers were silent at the bottom; each of his powerful and separate footsteps sounded like a solemn drumbeat.

'It wasn't me,' I said.

The revelation of my Englishness seemed to double his rage. '*Un Anglais!*' he spat. '*Cochon.*' He was so close now I could look down the hole in his revolver. He cocked it with a frightening click. His black eyes were gurgling with tears and there was no doubt he would have shot me there and then. Where were my shipmates? As if he heard my prayer, Boniface called out from the frozen crowd below: 'Look out, Davy!'

This pathetic advice served to distract Gaston for a fraction and I brought up my shoe as though I were kicking him with my hand. It caught the hand which held the gun. As the weapon swung upwards he pulled the trigger, and the bullet went into the ceiling bringing down a great gob of plaster and whirling flakes which fell like ice. At that moment Paulette gave me a vicious push from behind and I fell on top of Gaston who was trying to aim his gun again through the whirling flakes of plaster. The hard metal of the weapon struck my groin as I collided with him. He roared, swayed under my body, and toppled back down the staircase. I clutched him as if he were a rescuer. His big body cushioned my descent. We tumbled, bounced and rolled down the stairs. There was uproar now, shouts and screams and oaths and above it all Paulette screeching: 'Gaston! Gaston! *Chéri!*'

When we were almost at the bottom Gaston's gun, which was still jammed between us, went off. I felt as though a hot hammer had hit me in the stomach but it was the Frenchman who howled. I rolled clear of him. Smoke rose from my trousers. I felt for my private regions. There was no blood. I half got to my feet, fell down, and stumbled up again. Gaston was lying with his great feet propped up the stairs, his head on the floor. His thick leather belt had been burst apart by the shot. There was blood, a whole lake of it on his stomach, and a crimson river running onto the floor.

'*Il est mort! Il est mort!*' howled Paulette, rushing down the stairs. '*Mon chéri est mort!*'

'Women,' muttered a flat voice close to my ear. It was Norris. 'Bonny thinks we ought to be going,' he mentioned. 'He's already gone. So's Charlie. They're getting a taxi.'

There was confusion everywhere in the bar. So much attention was being paid to Gaston and Paulette, who was now kneeling beside him passionately kissing his big peaceful face, that I was able to move away and head for the door.

'I wouldn't go in there again,' muttered Norris when we were outside. 'Not if I was you.'

There was no sign of Boniface or Peace. Then a taxi turned the corner and they were in it. At that moment the pregnant woman from the bar came out and pulled the taxi door open, directing a stream of French at the driver, and tugged both Boniface and Charlie Peace onto the pavement. 'You, *monsieur*,' she stabbed her finger at me. 'Taxi.' She thrust my missing shoe and the francs I had given her twenty minutes earlier into my hand '*A la gare!*' she ordered the driver. I fell into the back and we roared away.

As we drove through the city towards the station, two police cars, their bells ringing, passed us and an ambulance followed them. '*Voici la gare, monsieur,*' said the taxi driver without excitement. 'It is good you go.'

'It wasn't my fault!' I pleaded. 'Where? Where can I go?'

'The police, they will come to your ship,' he shrugged.

'I'm going to give myself up!' I shouted at him. 'I can't hide anywhere. They'll find me.'

'*En Espagne,*' he offered. 'The train goes to Spain. They will not find you there.'

I felt shocked. 'But there's a war in Spain.'

The shape of his capped head nodded. '*Exactement,*' he said.

It was almost as if the train had been timed to aid my escape. The taxi driver refused payment, saying his mother had liked the British and he was always ready to help someone avoid the police. He pointed to the round nose of the engine as it approached the station. '*Allez en Espagne,*' he repeated. '*Au revoir.*'

Gratefully I shook hands with him. But then, after he had gone, standing on the platform, my anxiety making me sweat, I began to believe that I ought to give myself up or, at least, return to the ship and tell the captain. Gaston was shot dead but who could blame me? There were witnesses.

On the other hand, I had heard that the French police, particularly the Marseille police, who were accustomed to sailors' crimes, took a long time to ask questions, sometimes months.

The train had come to the platform. The windows of its carriages were lit only by dim blue bulbs and inside I could see huddled shapes. Then, at the end of the station, a group of marching shadows materialised. At first, in fright, I thought it was the gendarmes but then I saw it was men with packs on their backs, singing 'The Red Flag'. There were not many, perhaps twenty. They were wild, I could see as they stamped by me, their eyes bright and ragged in the platform lights. Some had axes and wooden clubs. One had a Red Cross knapsack and another an empty bandolier. They sang lustily in French but I knew the tune. It was now or never. Singing the words I knew I joined on the rear of the rough column.

We boarded the foremost carriage. With only the blue bulbs for illumination, I could see there were sleeping shapes in all the compartments and others sprawled in the corridors. My comrades had to step across these men and their baggage because they did not move; they scarcely seemed to be alive. The men before me went through the corridors to the rear of the train and were still searching out spaces to sit or squat in when the engine hooted and gushed and began to roll.

There was a goods van which was not so crammed as the rest of the compartments because it was being shared with a hobbled mule which urinated hugely to greet me. It remained fixed as a statue as it did and no one else moved either. I sat on the strawed floor with half-a-dozen other lumpish figures, leaned my back against the side and let myself fill up with despair. Even as a boy I had not been given much to crying but now I wanted to cry and it was only the sleeping men around me which prevented me from doing so. As it was, I sat all through the rumbling night staring straight ahead into the darkness. The men grunted, the mule grunted. Every now and then we would stop at a siding or a station, and voices would sound. Eventually, the first splintered light showed at the cracks in the boarded walls of the wagon. An hour later we were at the border. I worried that every man's papers would be checked. All I had was my seaman's discharge book and that itself might be enough to reveal that I was a fugitive from justice. But there was only a short delay. They checked the engine driver as a token gesture and the frontier guards and customs men cheered as we rattled through. I was on my way to war.

As the daylight grew stronger through the cracks, one of the men sitting in the wagon got up and opened a hatch. The train curved round a bend and a strut of sunshine came in and prowled about like a searching light. One of the other men who had been sleeping opened eyes full of fright as it moved onto his face and threw up his arms in a gesture of surrender. He began to curse in a language I did not understand, and the man who had opened the hatch said something in the same language. The hobbled mule crapped a steaming heap, adding to the pyramid it had built throughout the night and then again urinated savagely. One green stream was coming towards me and I backed away from its liquid advance, but the others did not alter their positions. 'You'll get more than a river of piss in Spain,' grunted a spindle-faced youth on the far side of the wagon. His English accent was northern.

'Where are we heading?' I asked leaning towards him.

'Don't you know?' he answered hoarsely. 'Bloody Barcelona.'

'Oh, I just wondered,' I said. I was not sure of the exact location of Barcelona, although it had been enough on the wireless. 'I thought we might be going further.'

He regarded me suspiciously. ''Ow can you go further?' he said. 'Bloody Barcelona's surrounded.'

One of the other men stood and cautiously peered from the open hatch, like a soldier in a dangerously exposed dug-out. He did not look at the land level, only at the sky. Then he shut the hatch and sat down amid the straw and mule excrement.

'They bomb these trains,' said the northerner. 'Machine gun 'em. Them German stukas.'

I sat silent and frightened. The others were listening, trying to hear above the noise of the wheels. 'It's too late when you 'ear them,' said the northerner.

'Where are you from?' I asked him.

'Bloody Manchester,' he said. He picked up a piece of mule dung and threw it on the floor at his own feet. 'I came for adventure. I wish I 'adn't now.' He looked up and, shocked, I saw that he was on the edge of tears. 'What you doin' 'ere?'

'Adventure,' I lied.

'Unemployed?' he asked. 'That's why 'arf of them come to Spain. No work.' His ugly face was crumpled. 'But anyhow you don't get shot at. I shouldn't 'ave come.'

One of the other men said something savagely to him, but the man who had opened the hatch turned on this man and silenced him with a word. Then he turned and told me they came from Yugoslavia.

The train slowed; there was a smell of smoke. The man opened the hatch again and squinted through it. 'Barcelona,' he announced flatly. He had all his belongings in a small, torn suitcase and he made a performance of opening it as if to make sure that nothing had been taken in the night. He took out a photograph and put it in his shirt pocket. The mule broke wind.

As we neared the city the smoke became more acrid, the train slowed and then with a long squeal stopped. Men were moving all along the corridors. There were voices by the side of the line and the hatch was once again removed. We took turns to lean out. There were soldiers on the embankment, orderless soldiers, one with a red flag. They waved and shouted but with no laughter. 'You can see we're on the losers' side,' said Manchester. 'Trust us.'

I knew little about the war to which I had travelled. I knew that the Nationalists, with help from the Germans and Italians – the Fascists – were fighting the left-wing Republicans who were gradually being squeezed to defeat. It had already lasted almost three years. The Republicans held the country and the Catalan coast around Barcelona and a wedge from Madrid to the western coast.

As the train moved into Barcelona the men looking out of

the hatch began muttering. One of them pulled his head down and sat on the floor again, almost at the mule's front feet, his head dropping into his hands. Taking his place at the hatch I saw my first bombed city.

We were travelling by ruins, walls and chimneys like ghosts. There were few roofs and no windows anywhere, only spaces and holes letting through the mocking summer sunshine. I let Manchester have my vantage place. 'Bloody 'ell,' he said. He only swore, it seemed, before the name of a location. 'I want to go bloody 'ome.'

The station was just debris with the cleared track between. Bent-backed soldiers stood with silent civilians. It was no place for conversation. The soldiers drank from cups or bottles and smoked. They stood wearily watching the train ease in, its windows framing the faces of men who had arrived only in time for defeat.

But a band began playing as we stopped, a lively Spanish bullring march, and as we stiffly got down onto the platform, it struck up 'The Red Flag'.

The volunteers from the train, grained with dirt, blank-eyed, shaggy-jawed, formed up in threes under the direction of a busy man who wore riding breeches and a crimson shirt, their bundles and bags on their shoulders and backs. Manchester and I kept together, and at the shouted order shuffled off with the dislocated column led by the blaring band.

We marched from the station into the street. There seemed to be not one complete building; just shells, single walls and windows agape. But trams were running up the cleared middle of the thoroughfare and a man was selling huge-headlined newspapers from a painted kiosk. A café was open, its front like the jagged entrance to a cave. But there were tables placed outside and people were reading newspapers and drinking coffee served by a waiter in a black waistcoat and long apron. We set off, down the centre of the street, tramping with the trams passing by us and people monotonously calling 'Salud!' The stench of smoke mingled with the smell of sunshine.

My heart had dropped as we marched. Manchester was staring solidly ahead, trudging, to the brassy lilt of the band. There was sweat on his face, running down like tears. He sensed my look and half-turned. 'Bloody 'ell,' he muttered like a prayer. 'Bloody, bloody 'ell.'

My mouth was bitter. From the side of the road a woman came and handed me a tin of water, and I drank from it and handed it to Manchester. He refused it and passed it on. 'You got to watch out with the water,' he said.

Fortunately the march was not far; no more than a mile. Now as the procession turned off from the street, I saw that we were led by the horseless man wearing riding breeches and a crimson shirt. We clattered into what at first appeared to be a large brick courtyard. Women were tending steaming urns, and there were lumps of bread and cheese laid out on tables. The women screeched and brandished sticks to keep birds away from the food. We halted and Red-Shirt told us to sit on the ground. The women, bleak-faced but trying to smile, came around with tin mugs of coffee and each of us had a hunk of bread and cheese. As I ate mine I looked up towards the open sky and saw that in fact what I had thought was a courtyard had once had a roof. Remnants of it were still hanging like black fingers from the bricks at the tops of the walls. It must have gone in an early air raid because flowers and weeds had colonised the sides; one of the women was gently spraying the flowers with a watering can. Another, younger, and beautiful in a sad way, carried a baby and with a quick and surprising smile she handed it to Manchester. Almost as surprisingly, the rough youth took it gently and rocked it in his big arms. The woman watched him and laughed. 'I'm used to babies,' he said as though he owed me an explanation. 'My sisters are always 'aving them.'

While we sat I heard my first air raid siren. It began startlingly and moaned up and down, joining the chorus of sirens in other parts of the city like an eerie part-song. Most of us got up and looked around for somewhere to shelter, fear fixed on many faces, but the women were uncaring and continued to pour the coffee and give out extra bread. The woman watering the flowers did not look away from them.

Above the siren wails, the man in riding breeches shouted 'It is nothing! *No hay nada!*'

'Don't sound like nothing to me,' grunted Manchester over a crust of bread. His cheeks bulged.

'No here,' said a woman pointing away before she formed her hand into a dive bomber.

We remained staring up at the sky, except for some of the newcomers, perhaps accustomed to war, who had stretched out on the ground to sleep. We waited an hour while the sun moved around the scarred walls and there were rumblings in the distance; and dull distinct thuds like the blows of a pile driver. Some Republican officers arrived wearing odd mixed uniforms, but each with a stick under his arm. One had a steel helmet looped around his throat and hanging over his back, another wore a hat with a jaunty feather in it, two had berets and one a pillbox cap.

The men were roused and ordered to get into line at a set-up table. An officer sat behind it on a box and others were grouped around watching each arrival as he handed in identification papers. Sometimes they asked questions but mostly it seemed to be a formality.

It was half-an-hour before the men around me were ushered towards the table. Manchester stood in front of me. 'I only got my unemployment book,' he said over his shoulder. 'I ain't got no passport.'

'Maybe they'll send you home,' I joked.

'To bloody Manchester? Not likely,' he grunted. 'Anyway, I'm 'ere now.'

As he said it there came a deep roar from the sky and across the open roof appeared five aeroplanes, low and black, in a pattern like a cross and with crosses on their wings. They came so abruptly that there was little time to move. Some men half bent their backs as if to ward off an explosion. The Spaniards turned up casual faces. '*El puerto*,' said a Spanish woman who had been doling out coffee. She pointed to the door and the street. '*Bombardean el puerto.*'

Moments later we heard the anti-aircraft guns opening fire, a numbing sound that even deadened the bangs of the bombs as they fell. Smoke began to drift densely across our oblong of sky. There were shouts from the street and an excited old man came in and began to gabble and gesticulate. The woman who had said they were going to bomb the port shrugged and said to me: '*Uno se ha estrellado,*' she made a sign of a plane crashing with her hand. 'One,' she repeated. '*Uno.*'

Manchester was handing in his unemployment card, still looking at the sky. The officer behind the desk merely copied his name onto a roll and said: 'Have you been a soldier?'

'Me? No,' said Manchester.

'What can you do? What can you do for Spain?'

'Dig,' said Manchester decisively. 'I've done a lot of digging.'

The officer nodded. 'You can dig trenches . . . or graves.' He wrote something on the sheet, handed Manchester an identity card and a ration card, and pointed him to join a group standing by the wall. Then his weary eyes took in me. I handed in my seaman's discharge book. This seemed to interest him. 'Ah, a sailor,' he said. 'That is good. We want sailors.' He wrote something on a card, gave me an identity card and a ration book, and pointed at the door. '*El puerto.* Go to there. There is the reporting office.'

'That's where they are bombing,' I said tentatively.

'Now they are finished,' he shrugged and waved me on.

I went to Manchester and shook his dumb hand. 'They're going to 'ave me digging,' he said confidently. 'What are you doing?'

'Go on one of their ships, I think. I'm a merchant seaman. I've got to report to the docks.'

'I think I'd rather dig,' he said. He smiled bravely. 'See you in old bloody Blighty.'

I went out of the door and turned down the long, straight,

ruined street. I asked directions from the officer before I left, but it was easy to see the port. Smoke stood like a dark forest over it.

The sun was hot and my spirits low. I thought of Barry Dock and Blod and Griff. The coal office seemed a good place now. I thought of going to the police or someone in authority and giving myself up. But who would want to listen here? All they could do would be to return me to France. I saw Gaston's face again as the gun went off, and the blood, and I decided to stay and wait. On each side of the street, the buildings looked like cobwebs. A tram came by, on its roof a red flag flying. It was crowded; people with dark, stony faces. They were crammed inside and standing on the platform at the back. It had a directional sign on the side which said: *Puerto*. I hesitated then climbed up onto the back step while it was slowly moving. There was just room. I made a show of feeling in my pocket. The man standing next to me, a thin scholarly shape with a sparse beard, shook his head and laughed. 'No money,' I shrugged pretending to laugh with him. 'No money.'

Shaking his head the man said: 'It is for nothing.'

'You don't need a ticket?'

'It is free,' he said. He indicated the devastated city. 'All here is free,' he said. 'All for nothing.'

Nobody left the tram, nor did it halt. Other trams were following and some lorries loaded with people. It occurred to me that they might all be travelling to some particular event, and when we reached the dock entrance I realised I was right. A growing crowd surrounded the iron gates, standing quietly but with a threatening expectation. 'What is it?' I asked the scholar.

'You saw the bombing today, this morning?' he asked.

'I heard it.'

'One of the bombers was shot down in the sea by our guns. The crew still lived. These people are waiting for the crew. They are going to welcome them.' He pulled at his stringy beard. 'Thirty-eight people are dead this morning. There have been many others. They are Germans, this crew. All the bombers are Germans. They bomb civilians, children. They do not care, mister. They are practising, you understand, for a bigger war, with your country.'

The tram was left empty at the dock gates. So was the one following, and the one after that. The lorries spilled their occupants. The people joined those waiting. The tram drivers rested on their brass handles and watched.

There was not long to wait. There was activity behind the shut gates. The scholar motioned me to join him back on the platform of the tram where, he suggested, there was a better view.

Three men in flying kit were the other side of the gates, surrounded by soldiers and police. The men's faces were stark white. The crowd fell absolutely silent, a frightening thing. Through the bars the German airmen looked out. The people looked in. Then, to a rising murmur of anticipation, the double iron gates were opened and swung inwards. The police and troops simply pushed the three young men to the crowd.

I have never heard sounds like the sounds which followed. There were three separate, then interjoining, screams from the Germans. The Spaniards burst into a massive baying, howling and bawling and waving their fists, struggling to get near them. As though they were flying the trio were hoisted into the air above the crowd. They were thrown up and smashed down again, lifted and flung, and torn by the savagery of the people. One man was still screaming with his arm completely torn off. One disappeared into the maw of the mob and was stamped underfoot. The third was lifted and impaled on the spiked railings. I got down from the tram and was sick over the tramlines at the back. The scholar looked at what I had done. 'Nobody vomits any more in Barcelona, *señor*,' he commented mildly. 'The days of vomiting are past.'

*

The place to which I had been ordered to report stood below a group of palms, stripped of their leaves, but with their trunks still standing like the bowed legs of some tall animal whose body had vanished. All around the docks, as far as the mockingly bright summer sea, was rubble, some still smoking. But there were ships unloading, each one with an anti-aircraft gun squatting beside it, prepared and pointing at the blameless sky.

Under the naked palms was a shed with 'Poste No 1' written above it, the sign slewed to one side. There were half-a-dozen men crowded inside with their backs to the door. As I entered, a sharp, high, male voice came from the front. 'Salud!' he piped. The men replied 'Salud,' in a dull way, and half lifted their clenched fists before turning and going past me and out of the door.

Their departure revealed a bug of a man wearing a steel helmet below the rim of which his red face was soaked with sweat caused by the helmet's weight. 'Salud!' he greeted me. He had sat down but he rose to his feet, hardly seeming to increase his height.

'Salud,' I replied and we both raised clenched fists, the first time I had ever done this. I handed him my discharge book, my identity card and my ration book. He pushed the ration book back. 'Keep this,' he said in English tapping the document emphatically. 'Because no eating.' He poked his finger towards his mouth.

'English,' he said screwing his eyes up over the discharge book. 'So you come to war.'

'Yes,' I replied with no certainty. 'They said I had to come here.'

'Salud!' he exclaimed, this time more mildly, although he still stood. His small fist went into the air like an uppercut from a flyweight.

'Salud,' I repeated doing an uppercut of my own.

'We have difficulty,' he said. He went to a map on the wall. 'This, Republic.' He pointed to Barcelona and described a small circle around it. Then his finger went south and curved around a much wider wedge. 'Also this Republic.' He wafted his hand across the remainder of Spain. 'This – Fascist sons of whores,' he said.

'Madrid, Valencia, Granada – we have,' he continued. 'Barcelona, we have.' His finger curved like an indicator on a dial across the sea between Barcelona and Valencia. 'This is only way between two Republics.' He ticked it up and down. Then he spread his arms. 'Republic planes fly over the Fascist bastards but cargo go in ships. Bombs. Boom, boom.'

He looked up at my face. I could feel it had gone white. 'Which ships you are in?' he asked. 'English ships?'

'I was on a liner, the *RMS Orion*,' I answered. 'Linen room steward.'

'No submarine?' he asked.

I thought I was going to choke. 'Submarine?' I heard myself repeat. 'No. No submarine.'

'Republic have good submarine,' he said proudly. He described another tick-tock movement. 'Barcelona, Valencia. Valencia, Barcelona. Fascist imbeciles always try bomb.' He spread his hands like an explosion and made another booming noise.

'Never been on a submarine,' I repeated. I pointed to myself. 'Merchant sailor. Not navy sailor.'

'All same here,' he shrugged. 'But, for you, we have. Very little, very slow. Always the Fascist bastards bomb this ships, but ships is still on the sea. Come, I show you, *Inglés*.'

He walked briskly past me to the door. '*Compañero Stalin*,' he said pointing. 'Her named for the great Soviet Stalin.'

The vessel was visibly listing to starboard even out in the harbour. She was squat and dirty and hung a ragged red flag from her stern. 'This is your ships, *señor*,' he said. He leaned against the trunk of one of the decapitated palms and scribbled something on a piece of paper. 'For you,' he said handing it to me. 'A good trip, I hope you have. *Salud*!'

'*Salud*,' I muttered taking the paper with one hand and lifting my other fist. He disappeared busily into the shed. I looked across the oily water at the *Compañero Stalin* and felt like weeping. There were several ships in the port, mostly flying Greek flags, although I thought they were probably of many nationalities, some perhaps British. Running guns and goods to Communists in Spain was a profitable capitalist enterprise. It crossed my mind that I might somehow get aboard one of these vessels and escape. Wherever it took me I could make my way home. But to what? To arrest and extradition and a French prison cell. I could still see Gaston's legs sprawled up the stairs while the blood ran from his shirt. There was no choice. My destiny lay there, listing out in the dangerous harbour.

If she appeared decrepit from a distance the *Compañero Stalin* proved worse on approach. The boatman who rowed me out to her hardly took his eyes from the summer sky. 'Stuka,' he explained unnecessarily. 'Stuka.' He looked down only to make sure we were on course. '*Del sol*,' he said pessimistically. 'Stuka – *viene del sol*.' He demonstrated how the Stukas came from the direction of the sun. As we approached the side of the *Compañero Stalin* he shook his head and made clicking noises and pointed out two large, recently and hurriedly patched plates in her hull and truncated mast.

At the stern of the vessel was a tall, almost bald man cleaning a pair of Lewis guns. As I climbed aboard he greeted me in Spanish. I walked along the dirty boards. He had scraps of blond hair around the edge of his head. 'Do you speak any English?' I asked.

'Here and there,' he said. 'I am a Dane. Per Petersen. There's a lot of Petersens in Denmark. See how the gun is burned.'

He tapped the muzzles of the twin Lewis guns. They were black like the ends of dead cigarettes. 'Plenty bang . . . bang . . . bang,' he laughed. 'What you called, son?'

'Davy Jones,' I answered. 'I don't much like the look of this wreck.'

'I don't much like,' he agreed. 'She'll go down to the bottom, that's a bet. The Stukas, they just wait for us out there.' He nodded at the glittering sea. 'But she's so far lucky. So don't worry.'

'No,' I said unconvinced. 'I won't.'

'It's good to speak English. They're all Spaniards. They know fuck-nothing.' He nodded to the hatchway which led to the crew's quarters. 'Crazy and mad. All Catalans, worse than Spanish.' He sighed. 'Communists and Spanish and Catalans, together. For Christsick. You got no gear?'

'Nothing. Lost it all,' I said.

It did not seem unusual to him and he did not ask for a story.

'You don't need much gear,' he said. 'Maybe a life jacket.'

He led me below into the filthy fo'c'sle. The fetid air seeped out to meet us. 'Stinks,' the Dane called over his shoulder. 'Stinking stinks.' Two men were sleeping in bunks on either side of a central table on which were the remnants of a meal. A bottle lay on its side. The men's feet were naked and dirty, their faces streaked with oil, their eyes shut as though in death not sleep, their mouths gaping.

'Alfonso,' said Petersen pointing to one man. '*El Greco*,' he said nodding at the other. 'Spanish Greek, for Christsick.'

As though even he did not want to be below for any longer than he had to be, the Dane went up the steps to the deck again. The sun was fierce, at its afternoon height. 'You don't speak no Spanish?' he said.

'*Salud*,' I joked grimly. 'I know *Salud*.'

'Hah,' he laughed. 'You learn *Salud*.' He put his fist before his forehead and repeated it: '*Salud*.' He walked back towards the twin Lewis guns and picked up the cloth with which he had been cleaning them. 'I sleep up here, on deck,' he said. 'With the guns. Guns don't smell.' He saw my intent look. 'See,' he said grabbing the harness. 'Like a horse.' He looped the harness about his shoulders and swung the guns in an arc and back. 'A circus horse,' he said. 'Bang . . . bang . . . bang. Got you, Fascist son of a whore.'

'It's terrible,' I said to him. 'I saw them tear three German airmen to bits this morning. By the dock gates.'

'Sure, sure,' he nodded. 'They love blood, the Spaniards. But Nazis are fuck-nothing. You wait to see them kill other Spaniards.'

'And it's all for politics,' I said looking around at the port. The ruins were like hills, foothills to the mountains outlined mistily behind the city.

'Differences,' he corrected. 'And old enemies . . . you know . . . what is the English? To fix . . . to settle . . . you understand.'

'Old scores?' I completed. He nodded. 'To fix the old scores. That's good for them. In Barcelona they dig up the dead nuns, you know. In the coffins. They show them outside the church. That was a thing, for Christsick. And the people laughing.'

'It must have been funny,' I said soberly.

'You will not know the Spaniards,' he shrugged. 'I been here years, in and away, but even I never understand them. Cave people, you know, like from thousands of years. They have something dark inside.'

He fitted a round drum of ammunition onto one of the guns, spun it fondly with his hand and took it off again. 'And the Germans and the Italians, the Fascists, they have the war because it teaches them. Like they are at school, shooting, bombing. They will know what to do when the big war starts.' He looked at me. 'How old?'

'Me? Nineteen.'

'Just the right years, age, for war,' he smiled. 'You come just in time, for Christsick.'

That calm evening the *Compañero Stalin* sailed on what was to prove the briefest sea journey of my life. Petersen handed me a steel helmet. 'Just one hour,' he said surveying the dying sky. 'Then they will not come. It is dark. We creep like the mouse.' He shrugged. 'But then tomorrow, maybe, they will catch the mouse.' He polished the barrels of the Lewis guns then crouched to look through the central sight, before pretending to fire them, making a staccato noise with his lips and swinging the guns in an arc.

'Have you ever shot one down?' I asked.

He laughed uproariously. 'With these old grandfathers! All I know is they make hell of some noise. It *feels* like they are shooting, the bullets coming out. But, who knows for sure if they are going anywhere, these bullets, because I never hit!' He rubbed his chin which sprouted needles of fair hair. 'The Spanish-Greek,' he said nodding towards the bridge. 'He got Fascists in the water, in a rubber boat. The gun was okay. He killed four. They floated around us, all dead, but then the gun did not have to shoot far. Three hundred feet maybe. But how far into the air she fires, who knows? Nobody knows until you make a hit.'

The captain, a Catalan with incoherent eyes who ran up the yellow and red striped flag of the province as soon as he got aboard, told me I was to be the loader of the gun. He had not been instructed I was joining the ship and he did not seem pleased. '*Aqui es un niño*,' he grumbled waving his hand at me. '*Un niño Inglés.*'

'He says you are a kid,' said Petersen.

'I'm old enough,' I said.

There was an age qualification for war. I had never thought of it. At eighteen you could be told to go out and die, just as at fourteen you could leave school or go into the pictures by yourself. I manoeuvred the steel helmet onto my head. It fitted; I was old enough. I did not feel like a boy. When I heard the drone I looked up from under the brim to the rippling evening sky. It was up there somewhere. I was frightened. Petersen was searcing the wide blue. 'They come,' he said. 'Somewhere they come . . . There!'

He swung the twin guns so violently he knocked me sideways. My helmet slid over my face and before I had replaced it I heard the shrieking of the aero-engines and the plane rocked over us, barely above the broken mast. Petersen was leaning back into the harness firing blindly. The guns made a stunning noise. I held my ears. His shooting was reckless. He continued firing after the plane had gone and as he swung the muzzle he chopped off the radio aerial over the bridge. The vessel heeled as the man on the wheel ducked. The captain's boiling face came out from the wheelhouse and he shook his fist at us. His words were lost as the plane came back.

'Drum, Drum,' bawled Petersen at me. I lifted a drum of ammunition and stood waiting, straight and to my surprise solidly calm, to hand it to him. He had shown me how to reload but now he did it. The swooping shadow of the aircraft appeared again, like a hand dropping on us, and the Dane swung the twin guns and blazed away madly. Bits of wood and rigging flew from the ship's upper parts. The captain was going crazy, shouting and making strangling shapes with his hands. Then, like a trick, the plane simply, almost slowly, blew up in an orange ball of fire, exploding so close to the sea that in a moment the bright fire was doused as it dropped to the surface. It sank and then came up again, still blazing. Petersen stared at it with an incredulous guilt. The captain, speechless, came out and gaped at the simmering wreck. The helmsman, the Spanish-Greek, left the wheel to look too. They were so stunned for so long that I began to wonder whether Petersen had done something amiss like destroying one of our own. But it was just shock; utter, silent, disbelieving shock. Then the Dane, abruptly released, set up a wild whoop, banged his hand on the hot guns, shouted with pain, and turned to embrace me, hitting his forehead on the rim of my helmet.

The captain and the Spanish-Greek began hooting with joy. Three more of the crew came on deck and danced. A bottle of brandy was brought to the Dane and, wiping the blood which my helmet had caused from his forehead, he gulped two huge mouthfuls. He thrust the bottle at me. I drank extravagantly and the brandy dropped inside me like molten lead. I joined in the elation. El Greco came down from the wheelhouse and got behind the guns, arguing with another man about the privilege and pushing him away fiercely, before bringing their noses down to sea level and training them on the last embers of the sinking plane. But there were no survivors for him to kill. Some of the wreckage floated disconsolately, smoking mildly, but there were no heads.

The jubilation on deck was at its pitch when another aircraft, its Nazi crosses plain even in the failing light, came from astern and neatly, almost politely, dropped two bombs, one on each side of us. The vessel dipped sharply one way then the other. There was a maddened scramble for the gun, Petersen pushing two of the Spaniards away. He held a piece of waste rag to his bleeding head. The plane did not come back. We saw it diminishing over the evening hills with the city guns putting up a spinney of white puffs about it.

Then the skipper shouted that we were sinking. The stern was going down, munching at the water, and as we watched a piece broke off and floated away as if it wanted to be first from the scene.

There was a scramble for the one lifeboat. There was no question of discipline. The captain was elbowed aside and the Spaniards, led by El Greco, hurried towards the boat which lay buried under piles of rubbish and ropes. Frantically these were flung aside. With everyone shouting against anyone else, the boat was lifted and, each with one eye on the sinking stern, the men hauled it to the side. Petersen said quietly to me: 'You okay to swim?'

As the Spaniards tipped it over the side and were fighting to follow it a regular row of fountains appeared from the boat's bottom boards. The captain, having forced the crew aside, was getting into it when he saw them, his weight causing the fountains to spring higher. With a bellow he scrambled back aboard the *Compañero Stalin*, shaking his fist at the Dane. The lifeboat was hauled from the water once more and the men desperately tried to plug the holes. I went over the side with Petersen into the cool water and we swam steadily the few hundred yards back to the harbour wall. We had reached it and slid onto the rocks there before we looked back on the sunset scene. The *Compañero Stalin* was dropping as rapidly as the sun itself, but would rise no more.

'Once,' said the Dane meditatively nodding out to sea, 'she was *Santa Catalina* but they changed it because they don't want no saints any more, you get me? For Christsick, no religion. They throw priests down holes.'

The crew had managed to plug the holes in the boat and to inflate a rubber dinghy. They were now making their way to the shore and a boat was coming from the harbour mouth to meet them. The men in the dinghy were holding something like a trophy as they neared in the dusk. They had brought the Lewis guns with them.

That night we wandered like felons about the black back-streets of Barcelona. The moon did not rise until late and the city was a place of shadows upon shadows. The sky itself looked gutted. In the streets rubble crunched below our feet. 'There is a place here, some place,' said Petersen. 'A place in the ground where we can have some drinking.'

We had eaten fish which a man had been grilling over open coals and selling down by the docks. He sold bread, black as rock, and we had that too. A shawled old woman, standing by and tearing lumps of crust apart with her hands, muttered to Petersen that the bread had been stolen. The man had to keep putting water on his fire in case it burned brightly and would be seen by the bombers. But he was bravely cheerful. He laughed with his customers as he busied himself. One man sat on a box and read a newspaper aloud, making comments which caused more laughter. When they knew our nationalities they asked us jovially when the British army and the Danish army were going to march to help them. The vision of the Danes coming to their aid much amused them and Petersen added to the mirth by pretending to march with a gun on his shoulder.

In a part of the city devoid of lights, with scarcely anything, traffic or people, moving, we found our way to a cellar off the Ramblas, the famous street of Barcelona, now a chasm of broken buildings and split trees, with bomb holes in the wide promenade, some of them unfilled. A mule pulling a cart ground along the street.

We found the cellar. We discovered it by the noise issuing from open windows along the lowest level of the street; windows oddly still containing some glass. Purple light and strummed music came from within. We went down the steps. 'This is the hole,' said Petersen.

A man in some sort of uniform stopped us inside the door. Most people had uniforms in Barcelona, some of them official. Petersen spoke to him in Spanish and the man gave a brief snort and waved us in. 'I told him we are shipwrecked sailors,' said the Dane. At the distant end, over the top of the crowded heads, was a bar, flickering like a hearth. We pushed through the people. They were standing around crowded tables, all drinking and gesticulating, talking at each other, their faces like cartoons. At the bar was another thick crowd, but Petersen was good at getting into places. He eased his way through, leaving me at the back, and returned with a bottle of wine and one glass. 'The glass is for you,' he said handing it to me. We stood in a corner. The man playing the guitar was close by but I could not see him. Hanging under the low ceiling was a blanket of acrid fumes.

'In Barcelona they have smoke all the time,' said Petersen pouring wine in my glass and taking a swig from the bottle. He swallowed it and grimaced. 'A little more smoke makes nothing.'

A wide-shouldered woman with a dark face spoke to him in Spanish and he replied. They conversed for a few moments while he took another mouthful from the bottle and, telling me with a sign to drink up, replenished my glass. The wine was thick and sour in the mouth, but I was beginning to drink anything. Petersen turned to me and pointed at the woman. 'She says that the Germans and the Italians are bombing, only taking orders from Hitler and Mussolini. Franco knows fuck-nothing. They do it as they want.'

96

'Does it matter?' I said to him. 'The bombs still come down.'

He thought this worth enough to translate it to the Spanish woman and she studied me with eyes like coal and nodded: '*Sí, sí.*' A group of men got up from a table and the woman and some men with another woman who appeared took the places. She indicated for us to occupy two of the chairs and one of the men went off and came back with an armful of wine bottles. A surprising thing occurred. The guitarist was joined by a young man wearing a clown's red nose who sang songs and told jokes which had the people holding themselves with laughter. The lady who had invited us to sit at the table had to wipe the tears of mirth from her cheeks. Petersen said: 'See they can have good fun like everybody.' But it was only for a while.

I drank on with the rest, trying to understand what they were saying, watching their rutted faces, my head becoming confused, my eyes drooping. I can remember the guitarist striking up a powerful chord and the singing starting, hard-voiced Catalan songs, with patriotic fists thrust into the air and oaths and challenges and cheers. But at one point, – so Petersen told me – adding to the laughter of the evening, I slid below the table and remained there, unconscious, before they took me out and with the drunken Dane, loaded me aboard a lorry which was taking volunteers to the front line of the fighting.

The jolting passage of the lorry over the mountain roads roused me. I was jammed into a corner, metal forced into my back, sawing away at me as we bounced. My head felt as though an anvil had dropped on it. The covering over the top of the vehicle was torn and a slice of hot sunshine cut through onto my hands, making the veins like worms.

Fearfully I looked around. There were twenty or so other figures there, all curled over in sleep or half-asleep except a scared faced youth who sat in the opposite corner to me, his eyes as blank as if he were blind.

I looked for Petersen. His half-bald head was slumped among a bundle of men in the far corner, by the tailboard. The truck began a long turning grind up an unseen hill. Standing up weakly I staggered between the prostrate men until I could touch him. 'Per, wake up,' I said. 'They're taking us somewhere.'

It took some shaking to rouse him. At last he opened his watery eyes and pushed the few strands of dismal hair from them. He focussed and then looked about him. 'For Christ-sick,' he said sitting upright. Our voices had awakened some of the young men around us. They had not been drunk, only weary. They looked like peasants, baffled eyes and unknowing faces almost black from the sun. Petersen turned to the youth nearest and asked him in Spanish. The reply was noncommittal.

'He don't know fuck-nothing,' said the Dane. 'All of them don't know.'

He said something else to the young man and he replied uncertainly. Petersen turned to me: 'He knows only we're going to fight,' he said.

Again I felt sick. 'We can't . . .' I began. 'It's not our bloody war. Why should we?'

'We have to ask,' he said. He rubbed his forehead and spat into his hand, rubbing it against his trousers. There was no room to spit anywhere else. 'That wine was piss,' he said. He smiled wryly, as though this sort of thing happened to him all the time: 'Looks like we have been Hong-Konged,' he said.

'Shang-haied,' I said.

'Shang-haied,' he nodded.

I was standing, swaying, holding one of the stanchions of the roof. The dead wine was slopping inside me. My body felt cracked, my head felt cleft, misery swamped me: 'I want to go home,' I said.

'Tell *them* that,' he advised sourly. 'When we get there you tell them. Every day the Fascist bastards bomb them, shelling them, killing them, pushing them back to the sea a few kilometers more. They are shitting. *You* tell them you want to go home.'

I stumbled back to my place at the front of the lorry and pushing away the sweating breathing bodies on either side, I slumped down onto the metal floor.

Eventually I slipped the knot on one of the ropes holding the tarpaulin top to the side and peered out. There were mountains and behind them more mountains, bare and hard, with patches of thin trees like standing soldiers on the skyline. We passed a poor white house at the side of the road. Two old people, a man and a woman shawled in black, were at the gate, waving to us without emotion. Dropping to the floor again I put my head in my hands. I squeezed my eyes as if to rid them of the reality, opening them, promising anything to God if I could only see Auntie Blod standing there with a morning smile and a cup of tea.

After another hour the truck went up a dramatically steep gradient and then clanked along a flat surface before halting. There were clear voices. The youths around me began to move and painfully sit up. Each had a cropped head, a simple face and empty eyes. They squatted like monks at prayer.

'*Prisa! Prisa!*' bawled a voice from the back. The tailboard of the lorry was struck violently with something metallic and then lowered with a clang. The back curtain of tarpaulin was pulled aside revealing a rectangle of sun and hills. My companions began to stumble and jump out. Petersen was one of the first. He was standing with a heavy black-bearded Spaniard in camouflage when I got down onto the dried red mud. 'Tell him I want to go home,' I insisted.

'Okay,' said the Dane. 'For me too. I tell him it was a big mistake.'

Regarding the man steadily, Petersen spoke three or four sentences, indicating me and then pointing to himself. At first the Spaniard seemed so astounded that he grappled for words. He repeated the Dane's words, as if trying to make sure he had heard right. He pointed to me and then at Petersen, incredulity suffusing the face above his beard. Then he let out a bellow of uncanny laughter that sent an echo bouncing around the hills. The other men stopped and turned to look. He jammed a dirty finger at both Petersen and myself and then pulled us, still laughing angrily, towards a half-walled hut twenty yards away. We allowed ourselves to be tugged. When we got to the hut the man shouted something at the top of his voice in our faces and pushed us through the open side. I had never seen anything like it.

On the ground were three bodies: an old man with his throat cut, his hair standing on end, a peaceful old woman, and a girl covered in a ragged shirt. The bearded man took the shirt away and I saw that she was naked and smeared with earth and bruises. There were wounds on her breasts and her stomach. He threw the shirt across her again. He bawled something which only Petersen understood, went outside, and returned with two spades which he thrust at us.

While we were digging their graves in the rocky red hillside, Petersen looked up at me and through his sweat said: 'I told you they would not listen.'

There were great silences in that place. At morning, high up there in the mountain trees, you could hear a stream running two miles away. A stone rolling down a chasm, a footfall, or a startled bird were crystallised in the thin, cool air. A snapped bough sounded like rifle fire and rifle fire like the crackle of lightning.

As far as the fighting fronts could be distinguished in that terrain the camp was only two miles, sometimes less, from the most forward of the Nationalist troops. We could hear them moving. Sometimes I could imagine I heard them breathing.

It was a training camp, which meant they showed you how to load, fire and clean a .303 rifle, demonstrated ambush positions, and sent you out to find and fight the enemy. Two of the dumb boys who had come with us in the truck were killed on the third day. Their weeping comrades brought their bodies up the steep road, slung on poles like slain deer.

In darkness when the sentries had been posted, the men would sit under the overhung rocks and the clumps of trees, to eat the rough food and drink a few mouthfuls of wine. There would be little talking at first but gradually they would converse. Petersen and I sat with them and Petersen would tell me what they were saying.

'They're telling their war stories,' he shrugged. 'How they did this, or killed that person.'

One squat youth, gnawing through a piece of venison and following it with a turn at the wine bottle, began talking. He was scarcely articulate. The words were slow and not easily put together.

Petersen translated: 'In his village they used to breed fighting bulls, for the *corrido* you understand, the bull ring, and when the revolution began the people there got the priest and threw him among the bulls so that he was tossed about until he was dead.' At the climax of the story the youth raised his hand as though holding something aloft, and said something which had the others laughing and clapping their lumpy hands like children. Petersen said to me: 'And when the priest was dead from the bulls, they cut off his ear as a prize, a trophy, like they do with the bull's ear on Sunday in the Plaza del Torro.'

'But the Nationalists killed those people we buried, that young girl,' I pointed out.

He regarded me coolly. 'How do you know that?' he said.

Again there occurred a surprising interlude, so alien in that awesome and sad country. One of the boys stood and began to sing, in a fine voice, a lovely sweet song. His voice went out into the hills, up into the blue darkness. It echoed and it was possible to imagine that it was another voice, an enemy voice perhaps, answering. Then, as though released, two of the young men began to dance, clapping their cupped hands like wood above heads, now bowed, now thrown up proudly like fighting cocks. There was no music but it was not needed. They circled each other edgily, each movement abrupt and poetic.

When they had finished we all applauded and shouted, 'Bravo!'

There was a sound behind us and I turned to see a bearded man, Sergeant Garrincha. There were big tears in his eyes. 'Bravo!' he repeated quietly. He saw the expression on my face and spreading one arm about the gathering he said quietly, and as though he owed us an explanation: '*Niños.*'

Neither Petersen nor I were sent out into the hills. Despite the derision of Sergeant Garrincha, when my companion explained that we were foreigners only there by mishap, some doubt had been sown and the commanding officer, a surprisingly urbane and fastidious man who polished his nails, had sent a message to Barcelona about our presence, requesting orders as to what should be done with us.

On the fourth morning Sergeant Garrincha woke us in the hut, more solicitously than usual, and said that a car would be collecting us at ten o'clock to take us back to the city. It might have been unwise to show too much joy, but I felt like shouting with relief when the car came up the road in an eruption of dust. As far as I was concerned this was the first stage of the journey back to Barry Dock. Once we got to Barcelona I was determined to find some authority which would send me home. The vision of bleeding Gaston had diminished.

The driver of the car said nothing to us but kept looking from side to side as we descended the dirt road. He wore civilian clothes, a shiny old black suit and a peaked cap as if he had been a chauffeur. He was unarmed, as we were, but from the wide top pocket of his coat projected the ears of a steel catapult.

Petersen said to him: '*Para los conejos?*'

The man remained silent but after a while replied. The Dane said to me: 'He is a rabbit shooter. Also humans.'

'He should get a gun,' I said. 'Everybody else has.'

The Dane put the suggestion to the driver who again

waited before he answered. 'He says he's afraid of guns,' said Petersen.

As if to illustrate the point we turned a sharp bend and found ourselves confronted by the muzzles of half-a-dozen rifles. The driver spat an expletive and accelerated. Only one of the men fired and the single, simple shot killed the man with the catapult. We flung ourselves on the floor at the back of the car. It swerved, fortunately away from the precipice, and bounced against the rock face on the other side. We felt ourselves whirled around and the side of the vehicle struck heavily. It stopped. The driver's head was slumped onto his chest. His cap was still on. 'I think,' said Petersen carefully, 'these are on the other side.'

'Tell them we're neutral,' I whispered.

The rear door was wrenched open and the open end of a rifle poked in. I thought he was going to fire. So did Petersen. '*Dansk*,' he called out. '*Dansk, Inglés.*'

No shot came. We looked up into the bandit-like faces framed in the opening. One of them said something and the other repeated it. They were telling us to get out. We obeyed.

They motioned us to raise our arms above our heads and like this they marched us up a track from the road. When we had disappeared into a rising gully we heard them blow up the car and a billow of oily smoke rose behind us. The sound of the explosion rolled like a drum across the mountain.

After a sharp, rough climb we came to a clearing where an army truck was waiting. They pushed us into the back and drove across the ragged terrain until they came to another, broader road along which, after two or three miles, we came to a forward post of the Spanish Nationalist Army. '*Dansk*,' smiled the Dane grimly. '*Inglés*,' he repeated pointing to me. Another five miles, during which we saw troops and some grotesque dwarf tanks moving along the road in the opposite direction, we arrived at a valley village where none of the houses had roofs. There were some goats in the street but no humans. Our vehicle turned into what had been the village square. Some segment of it had been cleared and there sitting in a ruined café, below an umbrella, and with a bottle of brandy at his elbow, was a man who was to play an important part in my life: Colonel Luigi Maroni of the Italian army.

'*Buon giorno*,' he said. 'Please sit down.'

He was tall, poised, and kind-looking; nothing like a Fascist, I thought. He ordered our guards off with a single flap of his hand. He had two extra glasses on the table for he had expected us, and he now poured two brandies. 'Danish,' he said pointing at Petersen. 'English,' the finger went to me. 'And . . .' he pointed to the middle button of his grey uniform. '. . . *Italiano*. This war is not ours. We can be friends.'

'They shot the man who was driving us,' pointed out Petersen.

'A Spaniard,' Colonel Maroni shrugged. 'They like to kill each other. It is something inside them. It is like they have been waiting years to get their knives out for another Spaniard. That man, the driver, he has shot dead two men.'

Petersen said: 'With his elastic sling?'

'With his catapult,' confirmed the Italian. He pointed to his temple. 'There. He shot ball-bearings.' He turned in a fatherly fashion to me. 'And what does the young Englishman think about it?'

'I want to go home,' I said bluntly. I wanted to include Petersen. 'So does he,' I said.

The Colonel laughed sadly and slowly. 'Me, I want to go to my home too. One of the worse things of war is not the fighting but the sickness for home. When I was in Abyssinia all I could think of in my head was my garden in Pesaro.'

'You've been in Abyssinia?' said Petersen.

Colonel Maroni forestalled him further: 'I did not like it. That is not my kind of war. Against men with spears. *This* is not my kind, this Spanish war. I am a soldier and I would like to fight a real war. Something I believed in.'

He seemed glad he could talk. The brandy bottle had been well down when we arrived. Petersen said: 'The man was driving us back to Barcelona. We came here only by mistake.

I want to go to Copenhagen and Davy Jones here, he wants to return to London.'

I had never been to London in my life but I nodded sincerely and said: 'London.'

'London,' repeated the Italian with a long sigh. 'I have been many times there. The buses and the column of Nelson and the Savoy.' He gazed at me, his eyes not seeming to focus. 'You miss the Savoy?' he asked.

I nodded that I did. He leaned forward seriously. 'Here,' he warned, 'I have only a few of my men, a few Italian soldiers, but there are many Spanish Nationalists. I do not want them to kill you.'

We both nodded firmly. 'But they will,' he added with cold certainty. 'They will try. When they cannot kill each other they are glad to kill foreigners. They are not, what is the word . . . particular. Just so that they are killing somebody. Antonio!' He called from the edge of his mouth and a slovenly soldier who had been lurking around the corner of the building appeared.

'Antonio will take you to your quarters,' said the Colonel. 'And he will guard you from the Spanish. I do not have another man to help.' He regarded the sloping soldier doubtfully. 'It must be only him.'

We stood and, still sitting, he shook hands with us, clasping both his long hands about ours. He looked as if he might weep. As we walked across the damaged village square he called and we stopped and turned. 'Tomorrow maybe, or another day, I hope we can get you away from this place. Keep yourself crossed.'

Antonio, dragging his feet in the dust, led us to one of the devastated houses. It had been haphazardly boarded and roofed with pieces of debris from other houses. The door was flimsy.

'What did he mean, keep yourself crossed?' I said to Petersen. In the room laden with dust were two chairs and two bunks and a table with trembling legs. We sat on the chairs.

'Maybe like a Catholic,' suggested Petersen crossing himself.

'Or keeping your fingers crossed,' I said.

'Maybe that too. This door will open easy.'

'We're not going to escape are we?' I said discouragingly. 'How can we get anywhere from here?'

He said: 'I was thinking of men getting in.'

I put my head in my hands. 'I want to go home,' I said.

'Stop saying you want to go home,' he retorted. 'For Christsick. *I* want to go home, and I don't even have a home. This Wop, this Italian gentleman, is our hope. We must trust him. There is fuck-nothing else.'

'I already do,' I said.

There were two heavy bolts on the door but the wood around them was hardly held in place by a few nails. Petersen examined the random planks. He went to the back of the house and I followed him apprehensively. There was a hole at the back through which a platoon could have marched. 'Not much of a prison,' said the Dane. 'Anybody could get in at us.'

There was a strong but polite knock at the front door and I withdrew the bolts to find Antonio there with a tray of food and a bottle of red wine. '*Mangiare*,' he said putting his bunched fingers to his mouth. '*Presto!*'

'Before the Spanish come back,' added Petersen.

'*Si, si*,' agreed Antonio. '*Avanti.*'

Petersen held up his fingers to the Italian and said: 'How many *Italiani? Quanti Italiani?*' Antonio selected eight of Petersen's fingers but, reconsidering briefly, put down one of them and made a throat-slitting sign.

'How many Spanish?'

The slovenly man shrugged and rolled his eyes. He extended his arms to take in the whole countryside around. '*Mucho*,' he said dolefully. '*Tanti, tanti Spagnuolo.*' He slit another throat.

He went, leaving us with the bowl of meat and rice and oranges. We ate it silently and drank some of the wine, but with caution. 'I think this is the time not to drink,' said Petersen. 'If we go to sleep maybe we don't wake up.'

We sat in the hot room all the rest of that day. Sometimes there were movements in the village and sometimes we heard gunfire from the hills, but no one came to us. As it became dark we heard the sound of men entering the square; there were a lot of shouted orders and the creaking of a cart. We sat in the darkness, scarcely breathing, and waited for something to happen. Nothing did. Several hours later, it was almost midnight, Antonio returned with two lumps of bread and a pot of honey. We dipped the bread pieces into the honey and drank the rest of the wine.

'One must watch and one sleeps,' said Petersen. 'We must guard our own prison.'

'Why don't we make a run for it?' I suggested unconvincingly. 'We could get out of here easily. We could find the road. It's not that far.'

'And give them the reason for shooting us, for Christsick,' the Dane said. 'Hunting us in the mountains like animals. That they would enjoy. I think we stay. I'll sleep, you watch, okay? Two hours.'

We survived through the night. My sleep was shallow and full of dreams of fear. At six o'clock, with the daylight seeping through the broken windows and the cracks in the door they came to take us out and shoot us.

There were six of them, slipshod soldiers, who looked as if they had been provided with one uniform between them and had each claimed a part. One had the trousers, one the tunic, one the shirt and one the hat. The other two had a single official boot each, the other foot being clad in a shoe fashioned from a motor tyre. They might have quarrelled over who should wear what. The took us across the rubble of the square. The clearness of the morning was all around; the serenity of the hills, the air petrified, a few birds sounding clear and sharp. 'Nice day,' mentioned Petersen. 'For being shot.'

They ushered us into one of the other houses. There was

some sort of commander there, a Spaniard with a lined face, but no sign of Colonel Maroni or his Italians. Petersen demanded to see the Italian officer, but the Spaniards laughed and said they had all gone away.

We were marched out of the house. Our hands were free but we now had eight Spaniards, four on each side. Most seemed no older than me; slab-faced country boys with clumsy movements and deeply socketed eyes. One, who marched on my left, had a huge angry boil on his neck. It was giving him pain. He pointed to it for my benefit and made a face to show how much it hurt him. It seemed that this might be the last ordinary contact I would have with human life. I said: 'It looks nasty, that boil.' It might have been a pathetic attempt to ingratiate myself with him, a last thin hope of getting him as a friend, an ally. He replied in Spanish and pointed to his neck again. We trooped on.

The clearing was not far, the view was magnificent, far over Spain, brown and already shimmering in the faint heat of the day. Petersen shook hands with me, and the firing squad watched and nodded approval to each other. They shook hands with each other.

'A nice view,' said my companion. 'The best one we will have.' He regarded me warmly. 'Maybe you tell them you want to go home,' he joked. Then he said: 'Don't let these bastards see you cry.'

I swallowed my tears. 'They asked me if we wanted blindfolds,' he said. 'But I said we didn't need them. We can close our own eyes okay, if we want. Okay?'

'Okay,' I said. I had already decided to close mine. There was a sheer rockface at the back of the clearing, not high but enough for their purpose. They stood us against the rock and four of the men were ordered by the commander to form the firing squad. Each of them crossed himself.

'*We're* going to die, and these bastards cross themselves. They know fuck-nothing,' grunted the Dane. 'Stand up straight,' he added. 'Die like a good boy.'

I was glad he was there. We both stood to attention.

Maybe they would miss. No, not from thirty feet. The commander had a sword which he raised and shouted an order. The rifles came up to the shoulders. I had a few words with God and closed my eyes.

Then the shots were fired.

BOOK TWO

One

There was no mistaking Dolly Powell as she came through the door of the Maison de Danse, Barry. I was weaving through a foxtrot with another girl from the old days when I saw her. She looked lovely, taller, and strewn with glittery silver. I swung my partner sharply so that Dolly would not disappear from my sight and the girl gave me a sulky glance and craned over her shoulder to see who it was.

She disengaged herself and strode away. 'Too big for your boots now,' she said bitterly. I scarcely noticed. Trying to appear tall and broad and slowly smiling, I walked towards Dolly.

'Hello,' I said as though I had been loitering there for years. 'Fancy seeing you again.'

'Look what the tide's washed in,' she answered. Her eyes were bright though. My name had been in the papers.

'Quite a little hero, Davy Jones,' she said. 'You can buy me a drink if you like. Port and lemon, please.'

'It's my pleasure,' I replied. I wanted to show her how time had changed me. 'Please, join me at the bar.' Even holding her elbow was a memory. The sharp point and the two little billows of smooth cool flesh each side. 'Any particular brand of port?' I asked as we reached the bar. My eyes were full of her eyes.

'Er . . . no,' she said. 'Any port . . . in a storm.'

We laughed at this and we came together, our bodies in contact, her soft and silver-sprinkled bosom pressing into my stiff white shirt. 'Oh Davy,' she whispered. 'Fancy you being in the *Daily Mirror*.'

'Don't let's talk about it,' I said looking towards the dance floor. 'Let's dance.'

To my annoyance the band began the Gay Gordons, an old-time jolting dance. It was not romantic. We went bounding around the floor, others looking at us below the centrally suspended and revolving globe of sparkling light. It reflected in her dress, sending kaleidescope patterns across her front. 'You've got to know a lot of women since you've been at sea, I bet,' she said bouncing close to my ear.

The rush of the dance was taking us from end to end of the floor.

'I've met a few,' I called to her modestly above the music. 'But never anybody like you, Doll. Remember out in that boat?'

'I was scared out there,' she shouted. 'But you laid down on top of me, didn't you!'

The dance stopped and I was grateful.

'How could I forget that,' I answered. The dancers began to applaud. People were sweating and laughing. The Master-of-Ceremonies announced: 'Underneath the Spreading Chestnut Tree,' so we walked off and went out of the Maison de Danse into the touchy September air. From the terrace you could look over the Bristol Channel where a few shipping lights punctuated the night. The ornamental railings were completely occupied by couples with their arms hung about each other, kissing and muttering; wiping their cheeks and mouths. We had to wait until one couple went away, arguing, so that we could take their place on the rails. I kissed her luxuriously and she slackened her lips and then screwed them onto mine with picturehouse passion. 'Oh, Davy,' she breathed. 'We've had some good times, haven't we? Remember the night Tosh fell off the lighthouse?'

My mouth moved against her neck. 'Poor Tosh,' I mumbled. We moved a little apart and she wiped her neck with her handkerchief. Then her face moved forward an inch and we kissed again deeply. 'Davy,' she murmured. 'When I saw in my dad's paper that they called you a hero . . . It said:

"British hero of Spanish firing squad". And there was your picture. My mam said I ought to get in touch with you right away.' She pulled away and looked at me convincingly: 'You've got a bright future, Davy Jones,' she said. 'My mam and dad both reckon you have.'

'There's not much future in being a hero,' I whispered. Her breasts were nuzzling me like pups. I rubbed the silvery attachments on them, at the same time looking out to sea as if I were thinking gallant thoughts. 'I wouldn't want to do it too often.'

Becoming a hero had, in truth, been both frightening and easy. There was nothing I could have done about the swift events of that morning facing that rank of rifles on the Spanish mountainside. Having closed my eyes an embarrassing feeling came over me. I was about to wet myself. It would be my final bodily act. The shots came. I screwed my chest about in an attempt to wriggle around them. Miraculously I felt no bullets, no pain. I only heard the echoes.

Cautiously opening my eyes I saw through a veil of blue smoke that the firing squad and their commander were now sprawled on the earth and did not look as if they would be getting up again. The other Spaniards were lying on the ground too.

'They have shot themselves,' muttered the unbelieving Petersen from my left.

'God answered my prayers,' I said devoutly. 'He saved us!'

We began to laugh, shake hands, embrace and dance. Again we looked towards the Spaniards. They had not moved. Flies were beginning to hover around them.

'It was not God,' said Petersen nodding towards the higher scrub around the clearing. 'It was our friend.'

Through the boulders and broken vegetation strode Colonel Maroni in his riding breeches. He had half-a-dozen men with him. They regarded the neat stack of corpses with nodding satisfaction, like artisans who are gratified by a job.

'The executioners executed,' announced Maroni, quietly but theatrically. He threw a dramatic arm wide to take in the whole scene.

We stood unmoving on the red earth. The lucky flies were really humming around the toppled Spaniards now. You almost felt at least one hand would raise itself to swot them away. The Italian officer, in his breeches and grey tunic, came towards us beaming, awaiting our thanks and congratulations which he received in plenty. 'It is not right to execute a boy,' he said profoundly. 'As a civilised soldier I could not witness it.'

Petersen, who often said awkward things, asked: 'How you going to explain?' He looked around the clearing.

'Mutiny,' shrugged the colonel. 'Mutiny and jealousy. They tried to steal from us, we prevented them, they tried to kill us. We killed them.' His eyebrows arched as if seeking approval. Petersen nodded and I said: 'Yes, sir. That sounds all right to me.'

Maroni's men were taking the dead Spaniards and putting them in a straight rank at the edge of the clearing. 'They will bury them,' shrugged the Italian. 'This is a busy war. There is no time for inquests. Only the usual questions will be asked.'

'There are many other Spaniards,' said the Dane looking around the horizon.

'Nationalist and Republican,' nodded Maroni. 'We must leave. Come, I will take you. You can go home now.'

By this time I believed that he could do anything. I felt myself trembling with it all. He held his long hand out to me and I took it, like a boy with his father, and we held hands all the way to the mountain road where a grey car was waiting. 'I will drive with you some of the journey,' he said. The Dane and I got into the back seats. The colonel climbed in beside the driver. 'Then I must leave. This driver knows where to go.'

We began to move. I lay back on the leather seat. An

116

overwhelming weariness flooded through me. Petersen nudged me awake.

From the front seat, Colonel Maroni said: 'I was born in Pesaro, the town of Rossini.' His voice softened. 'Gioacchino Antonio Rossini. His father was the town trumpeter.' He said it 'trumpeteer' and took a white handkerchief from his pocket. He gave it to the driver with some instructions.

We drove down through the rocky bends. Maroni did not seem to be on his guard. 'When you think he wrote "The Barber of Seville; a story of Spain,"' he said. 'All of life and colour. But now these Spanish people have forgotten. They do not know how to enjoy.'

He was silent for the rest of the time he was with us, only saying a few words of goodbye as he left the car. Our gratitude he waved aside and said once more, to me: 'You are only a boy.' He shook hands and said sombrely: 'This is a season of war and there will be more seasons.' He stood outside the car and gave a stiff salute which we awkwardly attempted to return. He was still at attention when we drove down the further hill and curved once more into the stony mountains.

'Thank God for Rossini,' said Petersen eventually.

'I never want to be nearer being dead than that,' I said fervently. 'I was numb. Not even properly scared.'

'You cannot be *nearer* to death,' muttered the Dane. 'Any nearer and you are already there.' He patted me affection-ately on the head and laughed gently. 'It was being a boy saved you,' he said. 'Saved *us*. Being young can be of use.'

We had reached the mountain's foot and now the driver, who had said nothing throughout the journey, raised a heavy brown finger, like a cigar, and made a hushing sound. It was bright midday but we were creeping through sunshine as though it were dead darkness. He eased the car against a wall punctured by two shell-holes. The finger beckoned around his neck and we leaned forward. '*Casa,*' he whispered.

We climbed from the car. He handed Petersen the white handkerchief which Colonel Maroni had given him, making a waving motion with it before doing so. Petersen understood and gave it another small wave. The driver nodded seriously. We began to walk down the littered road towards the house. The car turned gingerly behind us and headed back to the climbing countryside.

Petersen picked up a length of branch torn from a tree. He tied the handkerchief to it and, in an embarrassed sort of way, began staunchly marching with the truce flag above his head. 'Or the *other* bastards will shoot us,' he said.

We reached the house. It was gutted, the roof surprisingly remaining but little else. A shrub was growing through one of the window openings. The house occupied a junction in the road and looked down over a shallow valley flooded with intense sunlight. 'I hope they got some beer,' muttered Petersen licking his lips.

'Eyes,' I said. 'I hope they've got eyes.'

'We should stay here,' he decided holding the flag once more aloft. 'Let them come for us. If we go down maybe they make a mistake.'

Like people waiting for an occasional bus we stood at the junction for half-an-hour. We took it in turns to hold the white handkerchief above our heads. After that time we heard the crunching of slow wheels and a cart with a mule staggering between the shafts came steadily around the bend beyond the house. There was a woman, cased in black, her old face almost black too, leading the mule. It was my turn to hold the flag and I lowered my arm, but Petersen told me to keep it up there. The woman stopped and stared at us, unspeaking.

'*Buenos dias, señora,*' said Petersen giving a brief but gallant bow.

A man with a rifle rose from the cart, his head and shoulders appearing almost comically. He was joined by another. They did not look welcoming. The weapons were levelled at us. 'For Christsick,' muttered the Dane.

'Republican.' He pointed to me and then to himself. 'Also Republican. *Dansk* and *Inglés.*'

118

'You're sure they're not Nationalists?' I whispered.

He said he was not. But the woman turned sulkily and went to the back of the cart. She slid some bolts and let down the tail. Inside were ten crouching men and three pigs. She motioned us to climb in. We did, and silently, surrounded by odours, we began our journey; a journey that was to take me home and to Dolly Powell at the Maison de Danse, Barry Island.

The same busy and unkempt man was in his office by the blasted palm trees in Barcelona harbour. He showed no recognition until he heard me speak. Then he said: 'Ah, *el Inglés.*'

'You sent me aboard the *Compañero Stalin,*' I reminded him.

'*Sí, sí. Compañero Stalin.*' He nodded vigorously and then puffed out his cheeks. 'Boom, boom,' he said.

I said: 'I hope this next ship not boom, boom.'

He laughed silently and shook his head as though he would never understand the foibles of the young. Picking up a slip of paper from his desk he said: 'Bordeaux. Okay?'

'Mucho okay,' I agreed. 'That's what the man in Barcelona said.' The man had withdrawn my ration book, scribbled on a docket to be taken to the port, and handed it to me with a snort. 'Send some person for you,' he said. 'A man.'

The harbour official put on his cap and took me outside his office as if he were going to point the way to Bordeaux. But it was only that there was no light in the cabin, it had been cut off by the latest air raid, and he wanted to explain the document to me by daylight. 'Ship,' he said. 'Name *Gerona.* Ship no go . . .' He made a sweeping motion with his arm to the south. 'If do . . . boom, boom, boom.'

'No more boom, boom, boom,' I agreed. 'Which way does she go?'

'*Norte,*' he exclaimed like someone at the climax of a conjuring trick. '*Va al norte, al Canal Francés.*' He recited it again like a gazetteer: '*Norte, Francés. Canal. Atlantique. Bordeaux.*'

'Canal?' I said.

'*Sí. Sí.*' He narrowed his hands to make a culvert. '*Canal Francés*. No boom, boom.'

He pointed to the far side of the harbour and told me a berth number. I began to walk. Now, towards the conclusion of the war, there was scarcely a building left in the port area. Some which remained from the bombing had tarpaulin tents hanging from their tattered walls; in other places shelters had been made from planks and stones and pieces of corrugated iron. Men sat in the shadows of these working at desks. Dockers hunched in waiting groups. The red flag above the iron gates, where I had seen the Germans killed, trailed with the same weariness as the city and the people. In the tarnished water of the harbour itself the stacks and super-structure of sunken ships poked through the surface like buildings in a drowned town.

It was a long walk in the heavy sun. It was as well that I had nothing to carry. I had gone through the most fraught time in my life with no luggage. As I walked I heard a shout from behind, and I turned to see Per Petersen crazily riding a bicycle towards me. He was waving and navigating the machine around craters and piles of debris with the other hand. I had already said goodbye to him. He had been setting off for Figueras.

'I thought you had gone to the frontier,' I said. We had shaken hands and embraced because of all the things we had faced together, and now it was oddly disconcerting to see him again so soon, as though he spelled more trouble.

'So, I change my mind,' he laughed, stopping the bike. 'Maybe things will get better.' He looked around at the devastated port. 'Maybe.'

'You ought to go home,' I said with determination: 'Because I am.'

'Ah, but you got a home,' he sighed unconvincingly. 'You got Auntie Blood.'

'Blod,' I corrected. 'Blodwen.'

'So, yes, Blod. You, Davy, you got a bed to go to. Where

do I go? To Denmark. I hate bloody Denmark. It's grey, it's cold there.'

'You don't get bombed or shot,' I pointed out.

'Not yet,' he said prophetically. He was balancing the bike with his crotch. He spread out his hands. 'In Denmark there is nobody for me. Maybe I got somebody there but I don't know. I think I stay around here. The war must be over soon. I just got time to join the other side with our friend Colonel Maroni. After, there will be good chances of making money. Look here, around you.'

He indicated the dockside devastation. 'Somebody got to clean up. Somebody got to rebuild. And they won't be no Republicans. So I become Nationalist. I know how to get back there now. The same way we come to Barcelona.'

I thought he was right but I said: 'It'll be nearer now. They're advancing all the time.'

'You want to come?' he said like a challenge. 'Maybe we could make fortunes.'

My expression was enough. 'No, no,' he nodded. 'Okay, you go home. I go back.'

From his pocket he took my address which I had written out for him only a few hours before. He read the scrap of paper aloud: 'Alexandra Hill, Barry, Glamorgan, South Wales,' and shook his head. 'Sounds good,' he said. 'You go there.'

We shook hands again, this time almost tearfully. Then he turned the bicycle and rode back the way he had come. He shouted and waved and I turned and waved back. But I never saw him again. I had a letter a year later from a Spaniard who had shot Petersen dead and taken the address from his pocket. It was a couple of days after we had parted. He had died, the writer explained, by mistake, but at that time Spain was a country of mistakes.

When Petersen had gone, bicycled off into the dust and sunshine, I trudged steadfastly on along the harbour front, vowing that I would never be like him; that whatever misadventures I had, that wherever my roamings took me, I would always have some place to which I could return. What I did not know then was that returning could often be more painful than having nowhere to go.

The *Gerona* had once been called *San Joaquin* but this had been painted over by the Republicans in their distaste for religion. It was easy to see the original lettering standing in relief on the bow and on the stern, and no amount of paint would ever hide it.

Small and low and squalid though she was the *Gerona* was to take me at least part of the journey home, and if she had not been so built she would not have been able to creep through the canals of France made available to the Republicans by the French government.

She had a pair of old rifles, harnessed together as the Lewis guns had been on the *Compañero Stalin* and now aimed optimistically at the sky. A man was asleep under the weapons, his face black and swollen; I now recognised the sleep of the exhausted. Two more men were below. One opened one eye as I went down and without speaking pointed to a vacant bunk. There was an old blanket on it, stained with recent blood. Now also I knew better than to ask questions. I merely folded it up and taking it up to the rail, threw the sticky mess over the side. There was plenty of blood in that harbour.

I went below again and I stretched out in the bunk. As I was dozing off to sleep I felt something small and hard sticking into my side. It was a bullet, a spent bullet. It must have dropped from the previous occupant's body. I put it in my pocket as a souvenir, and I still have it today in my trunk.

We were to sail that evening, to my relief after darkness, and by next morning we would be crossing into French territorial waters. The captain was ashore with his wife. He returned sadly just as it was getting dark. He spoke some English. He seemed kind and tired. 'It is better it is soon over,' he said about the war. 'None of it is good. Spain against Spain, and Spain is broken. Brother and father and brother all fight against the other. The sun shines always on our country, but we have not seen it.'

By signs and a few words, I asked him where we would enter the French canals. Already I could imagine their soft green banks, the summer somnolence of the villagers, the inns and courtyards and the French girls. He replied: 'Marseille.'

'Marseille?' I said, stunned. Where I was wanted for murder.

'Marseille,' he repeated. '*Dentro de dos días*.'

At that young time of my life, it seemed that I was fated to lurch from one episode of anxiety to another. Now as we journeyed by night away from Spain, the glowering guns of the hills receding with each mile, I was only voyaging towards another peril.

All through the watches I lay in the hot fo'c'sle wondering what I should do. As a nominal passenger I was not required to take a watch, but I went on the deck at dawn and stood by the man on the dog trick, watching the shadowy mountains behind the Gulf of Lyons swell with the light.

'Marseille' said the Spaniard. '*El Santuario!*' He kissed his fingers.

'Not if you're wanted for murder,' I thought.

I decided to lie below throughout the two days we were in Marseille. Once we were within France, picking our way through the canals, I felt all but sure no one would require to check my papers or, rather, my paper, for my seaman's discharge book was still my only document of identification. Then the captain said that in Marseille the French police and customs came aboard every vessel sailing from the civil war zone of Spain.

On the second day, in the evening, with peaceful lights all over the hills, we came into the mouth of the port. The bulk of a liner bigger than the *Orion* was outlined against the city, her illuminations like a fairground, a band playing through the summer night. We slid below her hull and I looked up to her soaring decks where passengers were leaning over with drinks and sedately promenading while the music played, and for a moment I got a whiff of the life and people I had left behind; Mrs Tingley, the late Mrs Brewing, Totty, Boniface, Charlie Peace and Norris. My crew mates must have wondered where I had gone. I missed the linen room. I went below to the confined, stenchy cabin and sat wretchedly. Perhaps I would forever be a fugitive, the runaway killer of Gaston.

Prudently I remained below as we docked, feeling the blank thud of the hull against the pier and the customary shouts of warning and greeting. In no time, as if they had been impatient, official footsteps clanged overhead. The skipper called for me to report on deck. Warily I went up from the fo'c'sle.

The four other members of the crew were standing in an obedient line with their papers in their hands, the captain at the end, holding the ship's log like a priest holding a Bible. I shuffled forward to join the crew, standing at the beginning next to the man who had already had his papers examined. There were two uniformed police and a man in ominous plain clothes. He had a huge trilby hat like a cake on his head. Briskly, he motioned me to get to the end of the line which had not yet been checked. My legs were shaking in my trousers. Guilt was fixed to my face.

There was nothing for it but to stand dumbly, trying to control my quaking. I eyed the leap to the dockside. It was not far but there were other officers with a small car at the next berth.

The policeman was tediously thorough in going through the documents of the harmless Spanish sailors. He asked questions and made tiny notes in a notebook. Each sailor he stared in the face as if waiting for a flicker of suspicion. He reached me. His hand was thrust out, a short, fierce jab as if it held a gun. Tremulously, I placed my discharge book into it. He grunted when he saw it was different to the others.

'*Anglais?*' he said looking sharply up. He had a pendulous moustache, one side longer than the other. He sniffed, shifting the two parts like a see-saw. I said: 'Yes sir.' He glanced through the book and looked towards the plain-clothes man. I became solid. This was it. Putting his trilby straight, the man stepped two snappy paces towards me and gazed untrustingly into my face.

'You have been in Spain?' he said. The trilby was huge, like a roof.

'Yes sir.'

'Fighting in the war?'

'Helping.'

'Helping? You have not been fighting?'

'A bit of each, really, sir.'

'Where do you go now?'

'Home,' I said hopefully.

'How old?' he looked at the discharge book, turning it to take advantage of one of the bulkhead lights. 'You are young.'

They did not realise I had killed Gaston! The wonderful truth dawned on me. '*Voilà*,' said the trilby man. He gave the discharge book back to me and, to my gratification, patted me on the arm. '*Ça va.*'

I could not believe they were going ashore. Everything was going to be all right. I was going home to Auntie Blod.

The murderer, they say, returns to the scene of his crime, and I was walking proof as I moved suspiciously along the pavements of Marseille and arrived outside the place from which I had fled a few long weeks before, Les Trois Frères. Since then my lifetime might easily have passed.

There was stubble on my chin. It might form a half-disguise. I squeezed my eyes orientally as I walked into the dim bar.

It was early and there were only a few thin shadows sitting around. There was a record on the gramophone but the needle had caught in the groove and it moaned over and over, like someone repeating a curse or a warning. No one appeared to care or notice. Women were sitting in the dimness at the back of the place, grouped in a corner, arguing. A drunk, holding his face in his hands like a cabbage, was at the end of the bar. The barman made no sign that he recognised me. I sat at the other end to the bulky drunk and ordered a beer. The first smoke of the evening was hanging over the tables.

There was no reason, no plan in my mind. It was foolhardy to be there at all. The stairs, at the top of which I had stood and from below whose canopy I had been pushed on top of Gaston, stood as blameless as a bandstand. I walked past them, on the way to the lavatory, paused and looked minutely at the bottom step. There was no stain, no blood. When I returned somebody had moved the stuck needle of the gramophone, and three men had come in and been joined by girls who already had arms about them.

Returning to the bar stool I asked for another beer. The drunk at the far end creaked and his shoulders moved as though he were trying to straighten up.

'Gaston,' said the barman. 'Gaston.'

The name transfixed me. I squeezed my eyes even tighter and watched through the slits. The barman called towards the shadows: 'Paulette!'

It was like watching a fantasy, a hopeful dream. Paulette, who had thrust me so uncompromisingly down the staircase, came from the uncertain part of the room, anxiety pinching her face. There was no mistaking her. I put my hands up in front of me as if I had a sudden headache.

'*Chéri*,' she called when she was halfway there. 'Gaston, *chéri*.'

Gaston heaved his head from the bar. My heart bounded. There was no doubt. It was *the* Gaston! I could have kissed him. '*Merde*,' he muttered. '*Bougre*.' He was sliding from the stool onto the ground as she hurried forward emitting piteous cries, attempting to catch him. The barman grabbed the great drunken arms and held on. Gaston was like a man clinging to the edge of a cliff.

'*Monsieur!*' called the barman urgently. I realised he meant me. '*Monsieur!*'

126

He beckoned me. There was nothing for it. Contorting my features even more, I moved sideways to the other end of the counter and, trying to keep my face away from the eyes of Paulette, I helped to support the sagging heap.

Paulette said something petulantly. The barman pointed to a walking stick propped in a corner and I handed it to the grotesquely fumbling man. Two other men came from the tables and between them, Paulette and the walking stick, they managed to propel him towards the lavatory.

The barman watched them go with me. 'Gaston,' he said, shaking his head. '*C'etait un accident, avec un révolver.* He is *foutu*, how you say.'

I drank my beer and went out laughing into the night. To think I went as far as the firing squad for that bastard.

Two

The first time I married Dolly Powell was a month before the following war began. That the wedding, and indeed the entire outset of our marriage, was not the sedate success that I would have hoped was due to my reappearing mother. It had been more than a year since I had seen her, and she had made no contact even when my face was under headlines, but she made her flamboyant descent on us from London, embracing me and telling me in the same dramatic breath how she had worried herself all night about the firing squad, although by the time she saw it in the newspapers it was all history. She had been so busy at the time that she had not come to visit and had forgotten to write.

'We had reporters *here*,' Auntie Blod told her disapprovingly. I had never seen her lips so pursed. 'They got to hear about it and they were *here*, all in my front room. Men with cameras, everything.'

My mother patted me as if I had won a scholarship. 'There's clever you are, Davy,' she said fondly.

'He could have been dead,' pointed out Uncle Griff.

'But he's not,' smiled my mother. 'And now he's getting married. Is she pretty?'

We told her Dolly was pretty but she said she would reserve judgement until she saw her at the church. 'It's nice you're going to be married at St David's,' she said warily once we were alone. Auntie Blod had gone to ice the cake in the front room and Griff had left for the institute. 'That's how you came by your name. She's not Chapel, then?'

'Dolly? No. Her mam wants her to be married in the church. She doesn't trust chapel weddings,' I said.

'Hmmm, who's she, with talk like that? She's only from Barry Dock.' She became thoughtful. 'Still it's right, as it happens.'

'Because I was called after St David's?' I said. 'Why was that, anyway? I've never understood. You forgot to tell me.'

She had never told me anything, in fact, and she did not tell me then. 'Later,' she promised. 'Quite soon.'

For once she kept her word. It was during the reception, held in our house, which she had taken over, making sure she had her own personal bottle of champagne. She insisted on champagne and the bottle had cost Griff seven and sixpence. It was the only one in the room and she disposed of it.

Then she pushed poor Griff aside when he was trying, in his modest way, to be Master of Ceremonies. She began leading everybody in the latest London dances, the Hokey-Cokey and the Argentinian Tango. I can still see her swirling across the tight floor in the arms of a local builder, Gomer Pritchard. They swooped along, squeezing the guests to the walls, and disappearing out into the front hall, where they reversed and came tango-ing back again oblivious to the sobbing of Gomer's wife.

Dolly was not one to be happy at being upstaged at her own wedding, pressed as she was into a corner with the empty bottles, but I pointed out that my mother had presented us with an exotic gift, a honeymoon in London. We would have to provide our own train fares and other expenses but she would, she promised, arrange accommodation until the Monday in an apartment in the fabled West End.

It was while Dolly went upstairs to change into her going-away clothes that my mother, breathless from the Hokey-Cokey and the champagne, drew me outside and urged me through the front gate.

'I can't go anywhere *now*,' I protested. Urgently I looked at my watch. 'I'm going on my honeymoon.'

'I know, I know,' she returned. 'Who is donating the accommodation?'

'You are, I know. But we mustn't miss the train.'

Her finger, raised to her lips, was quivering. 'I will not delay you,' she promised conspiratorially. 'I just want to tell you why you were called David.' She led me by the hand, the first time I could ever recall her holding it, and tugged me up the street, to the main road and back along it to the church where I had just been married.

'There,' she said pointing to the brick wall and east window. 'That's why. St David's.'

'I know that,' I said patiently. 'But why call me after it?'

Again she caught my hand and with a plotter's high-stepping walk, like a pantomime dame, she led me once more up the church steps, upon which the confetti was still scattered like muddy stars. She pushed open the door and we went in. It was cool and, we thought, empty until the verger appeared, a man I knew because he worked on the dock. He watched us go to sit at the back. 'Too late to change your mind now, boy,' he called up the aisle. 'You've done your vows.'

'I'm not, Mr Morgan,' I called back. 'We're just here for a minute.'

'It will only take a minute,' my mother whispered to me. 'I may go under a bus tomorrow.' We sat in the back pew. She ran her hand fondly over the wood and then over my head.

'*This* is it, Davy,' she said. She was still full of champagne, emitting brief explosions of wind, but it seemed to have gone serious on her. 'Right here.'

'*What* is here?' I demanded looking at the knotted wood.

'This place,' she said. She looked at me and gave a strange, half sad giggle. 'This is where you were conceived.'

I was so shocked I could not speak. Even *being* conceived had never occupied a moment of my thoughts.

'Armistice Night,' she said, her eyes rolling reminiscently.

'Nineteen eighteen. Every time I hear the guns go off on Remembrance Sunday I think about it.'

'My father . . .' I managed to ask. 'Who was he?'

'A soldier,' she sighed. 'A simple soldier. I took him in from the night in the street. In here.' There was a break in her voice and the ringed hands caressed the wood, as if he were still occupying it.

'But . . . in church?' I whispered aghast.

'It was a cold night,' she said. 'November.'

'All right. But who *was* he?' I realised my voice was cracking. 'Who was my father?'

'A simple soldier,' she repeated. She was swaying in the pew, crying a little. 'I can never remember his name.'

Our honeymoon flat in the West End of London was a curious place. We arrived there after my mother had left us at Paddington and, as a final gesture to our day, had paid for our taxi. Dolly boasted that she had been in London before, although I had not, but however she tried to point things out, she had a poor sense of navigation. She believed that Marble Arch was Trafalgar Square. The taxi driver kept correcting her, and eventually she snapped at him to mind his own business.

We arrived at the door of the flat in a narrow street. It was opened by a young woman in a dressing gown who smiled when she saw me but looked puzzled at the presence of Dolly. Her straw hair was piled up like a clothes basket. 'Ooooh, yes, of course,' she remembered. 'Delilah said.' She regarded me sweetly. 'You look like her,' she said.

Never before had I heard my mother Dora referred to as Delilah and I concluded it must be a mistake or a nickname. Dolly was cautiously sniffing the scented air as we went into the hall which was wallpapered with cherubs and had a big gold mirror at one end.

'On our honeymoon are we then?' said the dressing-gowned blonde as we followed her. She laughed over her shoulder and pushed a limp lank of hair from her shiny forehead. 'I've had a few of them, I can tell you.'

'A few of what?' asked Dolly. I was struggling with our suitcase, stumbling along a much narrower corridor and up some tight stairs.

'*Honeymoons*, darling,' she replied blithely. 'All in 'ere!'

She opened a door at the top of the stairs and said: 'You'll be all right. We keep this private, like a sort of rest room.'

Uncertainly we thanked her. She gave me a key with a soft hand and returned down the stairs still laughing at her own joke. 'Honeymoons,' she repeated shaking her basket of hair. 'Honeymoons.'

'Funny place,' said Dolly still sniffing the scent. 'Smells like Woolworths.'

I put my arms around her waist and eased her close. 'It's not Woolworths, though, is it?' I said kissing her. 'It's ours. Our flat. In London.'

Her teeth had looked really lovely during the wedding ceremony and now they glittered again. The smile turned into another kiss, this time passionately shared. Most of the room was taken up with a bed which it was impossible to miss if you tumbled. We did, striking it with reverberating twang. Someone below banged on the ceiling and we could hear muffled mirth. Although we had made a sort of love several times before, during our ten months' engagement, it had been furtive or vertical or both. Now we were together in a room with an unmissable bed, a glorious wide, golden-knobbed, resounding bed. We forgot the knocking from below and the sunken laughter.

Gone were the battles with bloomers and buttons on the abrasive settee in my aunt's sacred front room, gone were the desperate jolts behind Thomas's Dairy, eyes squinting for intruders, or the frenzied five minutes on Dolly's single council house bed. Here we were with privacy, freedom and legality. I pulled off my coat and she took her going-away hat from its pins and laid it on the narrow space of the floor. Working from the top down I took the rest of her clothes from her. She stood upright and stock still as I undressed her, finally magnificent in suspenders and stockings, black as mourning against her glowing white skin.

For all her Welsh modesty, Dolly was the sort of woman who, once she was rid of her clothes, would not be restrained. I thought she would, in turn, undress me, but she did not give it a thought, only lay back, lovely-thighed, rolling-breasted, on the brass bed and held out her guiding arms. Urgently, I threw my clothes aside. I stood stark, prepared and joyful, bursting with bridegroom love, enthusiasm and single-mindedness. Opening my arms as if I believed I could fly, I launched myself on top of her so that the springs of the bed bent to the floorboards, and the noise sounded like the d'lang of Big Ben. We coupled at once, with no waiting or preliminaries, except fusilades of sliding kisses. It did not last long; it could not at that passionate pace. There came another, this time climactic, d'lang! We hung against each other, as we had once done in that bounding boat in the Bristol Channel. From below came a resounding cheering and a triumphant banging on the ceiling.

My Dolly blushed widely, her white body tinged pink. 'Oh Davy,' she moaned. 'Do you think anybody heard?'

If they *had* heard us upstairs there was no one to say so when we went out later that evening. Downstairs was a big eastern-looking room with three or four commodious settees with rugs and cushions on the floor. There were ponderous gold-tasselled drapes at the windows.

'Nobody's in,' I said to Dolly after carefully peering. The door had been left half-open.

'Perhaps they've gone visiting,' she said quizzically. 'All of them. Whoever they are.'

We went to a public house on the next corner, something we should never have done because some of the people from our honeymoon accommodation were there and they cheered us madly as we entered and insisted on buying us drinks. The remainder of the night is very dark. We had been drinking a lot that day, sherry and beers and ports and lemons.

Alcohol was pressed on us, even *down* us, glass upon glass. Further cheery people entered the bar. The men appeared to be well dressed and the women pretty and pert and very jolly. Not having been in London before I imagined that this was how all the inhabitants were. As the boisterous evening went on a man thumped a quaking piano and we danced 'The Lambeth Walk', laughing to exhaustion. I found myself between two women with big bouncing blouses, and Dolly and I became separated. One moment she was near me, accepting another gin and tonic while she still had one in her hand, and then she was gone. I had been given a succession of whiskies, and when I next saw her she was some distance away with a different crowd and drifting further. Eventually I could not see her at all, and although I called her, like a cry to a lost swimmer, I do not think she ever heard me over the music and the din.

I was a full three sheets to the wind by the time the people from the public house tipped out onto the street. Stumbling, I shouted for my wife, but one of the friendly women told me not to worry, that she was in good hands. I remember little after that except that I rejected the lady's offer to put me to bed, managed to unlock our bridal room and take off my clothes before approaching the bedside on all fours. After again plaintively repeating Dolly's name, I recall nothing else until I awoke for moments from the deepest of drunken sleeps to be a quarter-conscious of a warm body burrowed deep under the bedclothes.

'Dolly, Dolly,' I believe I moaned. Then down there, below the sheets, unseen, she did something I would have never dreamed Dolly would know how to do. Francine and Mrs Tingley, but *not* Dolly. She was curled below the bedclothes and she did it. I almost howled with pleasure. It was the most wonderful wedding night surprise that any bridegroom could ever have had. After it was finished I collapsed, babbling endearments.

In the morning I opened my sticky eyelids as Dolly came through the door still wearing the clothes she had worn the night before – her 'going-away' clothes – and stared at me with great and guilty eyes. I remember stupidly looking below the bedclothes but there was nobody there.

The front room of the house in Barry had always been like a small unused shrine to something, its air still, furniture and ornaments unmoved, mantelshelf photographs deadpan. Most of the people were gone now, and the pictures looked as if they had died with them. The ruby glass vases had pendant crystals which, years before, I used to touch against each other to hear them ring like temple bells. Curtains were draped so that only a narrow tent of light showed. There was a dusted plant on a table. I could never remember looking out into the street from that window. The room was reserved for important occasions, known and secret; the untimely death of Blodwen's father; the reporters who came to interview me about Spain; the first trembling lovemaking between myself and Dolly.

Now that we were married we returned to Barry Dock, to two rooms in Smith Street, the rear of an old whispering woman's house, with a window overlooking the cranes and bunkers of the port. The rooms were unpromising, but Dolly was to remain there and beautify them while I went back to sea. We had a separate entrance, through the back of the house, and this was counted highly for its privacy and increased the rent by two shillings.

Before I sailed again I went to visit Auntie Blod of course, and to my surprise found her sitting, plump legs up, on the red settee in the front room, its covering hard as carpet. She knew I would go that afternoon and she had settled herself there because she had something of importance to tell me.

'Your mother told you what happened in the church?'

I had pulled up one of the chairs which had been unshifted so long that it left dents in the rug. Blod looked at the chair as though surprised it could be moved. I thought she meant at the wedding.

'No no, boy,' she said in her Welsh way. Quietly she laid a pale podgy hand on mine. Her ruby ring, her best piece of jewellery, glittered against the plump finger overlapping the full gold wedding ring which, through the years, had buried itself in the flesh. 'Before that. Long, long before. But in the same church.' She was a chapel-goer and she said it without approval. 'That St David's.'

I had not realised she knew and, for a rare time in my life with her, I became embarrassed. 'You mean, my mother?'

Enormous tears bulged in her eyes. She nodded dumbly, precipitating them down her pink cheeks. 'She told you?'

'Yes,' I said attempting to comfort her. 'But it was all such a long time ago. After all, I'm twenty years old now.'

'Yes it was,' she agreed and added curiously. 'Since just before you could remember.' Then craftily: 'How much did she tell you?'

'Look, lovely,' I said, 'don't cry about it now. She told me that on Armistice Night she had met this soldier, and that somehow they had gone into the church and . . . well, begun me.'

'On the back pew,' she added. 'Thank God it was not in chapel, Griff always said.' She seemed to have uncovered a new sadness. 'He's a fine man, Griff,' she muttered. 'A good chap. Always has been. Except for the Institute.'

I smiled. 'That's not much to complain about. Not in a lifetime.'

'But *every* night,' she said looking up, all at once adamant. 'Every night since we were married, except Sundays. Sometimes, sitting by myself, I've thought it would be better if it had been another woman. At least it would not have been so regular.'

'He only plays snooker,' I said smiling at her and kissing her on her puffy cheek.

'It's not much of a complaint,' she conceded. 'Not after all these years. And I *have* got through a lot of knitting.'

She regarded me lovingly. 'We've been very proud of you, Davy,' she said softly. At the time I thought she was saying all this because of the natural break of my wedding that I was now belonging to someone else. 'When you think how you started, your stumbling block.' She had always called my impediment my stumbling block. 'And then becoming famous like you have, with the firing squad and everything. And only now just twenty. And married too.'

I laughed and taking her own little handkerchief from her hand dried her cheeks. They became less soft as I did so. 'I bet your mother didn't tell you everything,' she said. 'Did she say about your father?'

Slowly I shook my head. My mother had held something back. I said: 'Only that he was a soldier. She doesn't even remember his name. Well, that's all right. We can't go searching around for a man with no name after all this time even if it mattered. It's never mattered to me. I've always had you and Griff. And now I've got Dolly.'

Her wrinkles seemed to widen and she blurted out: 'Davy, he was a *German* soldier.'

I felt my mouth sag. 'A German?' I said aghast. 'But how . . .?'

'German,' she confirmed dramatically. 'And in a church too.'

'But what was a German soldier doing . . .'

'With your mother? Exactly . . .'

'No. Christ, what a thing.' I was shaking my head. 'We were fighting them. Except then, I suppose, the war was over.'

'By minutes,' she said.

'But what was he doing . . . free, walking about . . . in Barry?'

'Minutes,' she repeated with relish. 'If it had been any closer she could have been shot for treason, they said at the time. Firing squad.'

'That seems to run in the family,' I muttered. 'I just can't believe it. God, my name could be Schmitt. Or . . . Hitler.'

'I don't think it was Hitler.' The thought intrigued her. 'Although they say he was only a corporal in the first war.'

'*Don't*,' I pleaded. 'Don't make it any worse, Auntie.' I shook my head. 'I still can't understand. What was a German, a soldier, doing in Barry?'

'He was in the hospital,' she said. 'They had a camp for them, down at Dinas Powis, near there. Prisoner of war camp. Us girls used to go and see them peeping through the wire. We used to pick out the handsome ones.'

'And she met him there, peeping out of the wire?'

'No. Well, I don't think so, although anything is possible with your mother.'

I nodded. The honeymoon still puzzled me. Dolly would not mention it. We did not speak about it again for years, but I put the blame for a lot that happened long afterwards on that wedding night which my mother had arranged.

'She told me she just met him in the street,' I said. 'Outside the church more or less.'

'That's what she always said,' agreed Blod. 'He'd walked out from the hospital. Shell-shocked, they said.'

'I'm the one who feels shell-shocked,' I said. 'A *German*. And I've been all these years thinking I'm Welsh.'

It was her turn to comfort me. 'You *are* Welsh,' she said. 'Well, half Welsh.'

I regarded her morosely. 'And he vanished,' I said. 'According to her she never saw him again. She could not even remember his name.'

'Probably couldn't spell it,' sniffed Blod. 'He's supposed to have written it on a piece of paper but she lost that, like she would. Anyway he never turned up again. And here you are. There's nothing you can do about it now. But I thought you ought to know. Griff said I shouldn't tell you, but for years I've wanted to. And *there*, I've done it now.'

'You'd think she would have realised,' I said. 'Even if she'd been celebrating.'

'There's never been any stopping Dora. She told me – and she didn't tell many, naturally – that he didn't *look* any

138

different. He spoke funny but she concluded he came from North Wales.'

'He wouldn't have been in uniform,' I said seeking any excuse for my mother. I looked at her for confirmation. 'Prisoners didn't keep their uniform, did they?'

'He was in pyjamas,' she said simply. 'Pyjamas and an overcoat. Everybody was half-cut, see. All in the streets, everywhere, so nobody noticed.'

'Pyjamas,' I repeated. 'Only my mother could meet a German in pyjamas.'

She patted me again. 'Well, as your mam said to me all those years ago, it was very handy at the time.'

Her head dropped and I thought she was crying. But she raised it again and her old apple face was bursting to laugh. The white cracks were widening. She could not stem it. Her mouth began to wiggle, her head shook, then her whole body. As I looked at her, I felt a great bellow coming on. It came out unchecked. Blod was rolling, tears dripping, chest heaving. I fell forward and we put our arms around each other, howling, unable to speak.

'*Hitler*,' she managed to say at last.

I pumped my head and sobbed: 'Hitler!'

When I had returned from Spain, I had been ordered to appear before a Mercantile Marine Inquiry at Southampton where I nervously but truthfully related the reasons for deserting my ship at Marseille and my subsequent adventures. Three considering captains sat behind a green table and they sent me from the room while they pondered my future.

When I was summoned back, the middle captain, a bald man with a ruddiness which extended from his throat right over his naked head, said: 'You've managed to cram more trouble into your short life at sea than most men do in fifty years, Jones. You seem a decent sort of lad, however; you seem to have had some bad luck – and some good luck. Not many men can describe what it's like to face an execution squad. The blame seems to amount to you going to unsavoury places, such as that bar in Marseille. Keep away from that sort of door, lad. If you smell trouble, full astern in the opposite direction. We are not going to take away your discharge book. You are hereby admonished.'

Then each of the captains seriously shook hands with me. I thought their eyes were quite merry. Almost on tiptoe I went out into the salt breeze, hardly daring to make a sound in case they changed their minds. When I was well away from the building I jumped in the air and went hopscotching along the dockside pavements. Few of the passers-by took any notice for Southampton is a sailors' town and they are used to odd sights.

The Orion Navigation Company, however, declined to employ me again. Instead I made two trips on a cargo ship which carried fifteen passengers, helping with the cooking and serving at the table. I was becoming a proficient sea chef, and when I was at home between trips it was I who did the cooking.

Our two rooms in Smith Street housed a large, lumpy bed which we had purchased, and Dolly and I spent our nights of long passion under its downy covers. On the night before I sailed we emerged breathless from the quilts and she cried: 'I'll save myself for you, Davy! I'll be *really* faithful!' It seemed a strangely unnecessary vow for a new wife.

In that August of 1939 patriotism was popular. War was only days away, as firmly expected as Monday. Shops sold Union Jacks, and householders flew them from their roofs and gutters, and from the posts which supported their washing lines. Each house in Smith Street fluttered its flag and Mrs Humphries, our landlady, asked me, as a sailor, to mount a ladder to fix hers on the corner of the roof. When I went to the newsagents to buy our personal Union Jack I returned with one with pictures of King George the Fifth and Queen Mary, left over from the Silver Jubilee four years before.

Dolly took a dislike to this. George the Fifth had been dead three years. The shops had run out of ordinary Union Jacks so when I took the unsuitable flag back I replaced it with a Coronation banner with central ovals containing pictures of King George the Sixth and Queen Elizabeth. When I nailed this to the washing-line post, completing the row of red, white and blue which ran the whole length of the back gardens, Dolly objected. 'Coronations and wars don't exactly mix,' she pointed out sulkily. 'It makes me feel so silly.'

Next morning we kissed and I went tramping staunchly down the hill with my shouldered kit-bag, heading for the train and for Bristol. At the foot of the street I turned and waved my farewell. She was in a red dress, her bosom standing out in the sun, her hair awry in the wind. She fluttered her hand and then I turned, the kit-bag blocked her from view, and she was gone.

Thoughtfully I boarded the train. I loved the sea but I loved my wife too, the constant conflict of the mariner, and I felt that all had not gone as well as it might between us since our marriage. Alone now, I wished that she had put her coat on and walked to the station with me. There was another man going off with a sea-bag, getting on the train, and he leaned out from the window and kissed his woman. I had a half-hope Dolly might have realised and would be coming at a run down the station steps, but I opened the carriage window and only the porter was there. When the train set off it steamed immediately along the embankment below our two rooms. Once more I looked out hoping to see her, but the only thing that was waving was our flag.

I still have a photograph of the *SS Ocean Merchant*. She was a handsome ship, brand new, oil-burning and steaming at twenty knots. The company sent it to me as a sort of memento, and when I take it from my trunk, I again admire her grand and graceful lines, the self-assurance of her canted rig, the sturdiness of her hull that nevertheless still had a swagger about it, the two white and black banded funnels, like a pair of well-dressed twins. She was one of the best vessels ever to go to the bottom of the Atlantic.

At Bristol she had completed loading and the passengers were going aboard. War was hours away and people who came to wave them off were subdued, standing in a few worried knots. From the pantry I could look down onto the dockside and I saw that the embraces were tearful, there was much extra hugging and finally there were brave hollow shouts of 'Bon Voyage' and desolate waving of hands as we finally left the dock.

'Can you swim?' the chief steward, Mr Wilson, asked me as I cleaned the cutlery for dinner.

'Swim? Yes.'

'A long way?'

'Do you think we'll need to?' I regarded him apprehensively.

'Might well.' He was a huge-girthed man and I wondered if he would overturn in the water. 'Them Germans have got all their submarines at sea, so they say in Bristol, and they generally know.'

'But this is a merchant ship,' I pointed out.

He laughed quite jovially. 'God bless you, lad. Hitler don't care about that. Hospital ships, blind nuns, cripples, children, they're all fair game to Adolf. Then there's *mines*. Everywhere.' He sprinkled something invisible with his fingers. 'Like hundreds of thousands. Right across the mouth of the Bristol Channel.'

'How can we get through?' I dropped a fork and it resounded on the floor, making us both jump.

'Oh, I expect we'll find a way. He's a good skipper this. Maybe he's got a plan. And he has to look after the passengers, don't he?'

There was a companionway outside the pantry leading up to a triangle of deck. When Wilson had gone to supervise the laying of the table, I climbed up there and stood in the light September westerly watching the land moving by. The solid, safe land. It was early evening and I could clearly see traffic travelling along the shore, the first lights in windows, a canopy of smoke curled over a big white house, flying several Union Jacks. Longingly, I thought of our two rooms, our flag, my Dolly and our bed as big as a country. And I was out there in the lonely and dangerous sea.

Most of the night I lay awake, tense in my berth, trying to judge the time when we would be at the mouth of the Bristol Channel, imagining the menacing metal tap, the horns of a sea-mine against the hull next to my head. But nothing occurred and in the morning we were making good, sailing south-west of Ireland in grey breezy weather.

At the first lifeboat drill, summoned by a raucous bridge klaxon, all the passengers assembled at one station. There were ten men and five women. One of the women had her gas mask in a cardboard box suspended by string around her neck. When her steward came to show her how to wear her life jacket and he looked at the gas mask oddly, she shouted against the wind: 'I've come prepared for war, you know.'

Captain Brandon, a brave-looking man with platform jaw and shoulders like an aeroplane, stood legs astride on the deck and explained the emergency drill and its importance if war were declared. 'This vessel,' he announced proudly, 'is of the latest type. She is capable of twenty knots and could outdistance a German submarine. She has ample lifeboats, as you see, the crew know their stuff and the ship has a series of watertight doors. If, at any time, one section of the hull should be holed, these doors will close, thus isolating the trouble.'

'Will we still be able to float?' demanded the gas mask woman.

'For months,' replied the captain. Everyone laughed.

The next day was the first Sunday of September, a light-aired morning with no other ships in sight. At ten forty-five the passengers were told that a special message was to be broadcast over the radio at eleven. They gathered in the saloon and Mr Wilson and I served coffee and biscuits while

143

they listened to Mr Chamberlain announcing brokenly that we were now at war with Germany.

One of the men passengers choked so violently on his coffee and biscuits that, even as our prime minister's weak voice was faltering over the radio, the chief officer was pounding the passenger on the back and he eventually had to be dramatically turned upside down before his air passage could be cleared. 'Apologies everyone,' he said once his face had resumed its normal shade again. 'Bit of a shock, that's all.'

Watches were doubled. I spent a chill two hours on the bow looking for hostile aircraft, mines or submarines. Mr Wilson made a special journey forward to point out Kinsale in southern Ireland. '*Lusitania* went down just off here,' he muttered. 'One thousand one hundred and ninety-eight drowned. Nineteen fifteen.'

'It's so near land,' I said looking at the clear green headland. It looked close enough to reach and touch.

'Not a chance,' he said morosely. 'Not a chance in hell. She went straight down. Torpedo. Bodies bobbing everywhere.'

During my watch I was surprised to be joined by the lady with the gas mask. She wore its box around her neck so that it hung in front of her, as if she were collecting for charity. A fur coat was pulled shapelessly around her and on top of this bulged her life jacket. She did not speak to me but proceeded to search the sea with a dainty pair of opera glasses. 'Where are you, Hitler?' she muttered. 'Where are you?'

Night crept from behind us. There was a feeling of misgiving at dinner and the first officer told jokes. During the main course Miss Frobisher, who carried the gas mask, removed it from its box and put it over her head. The others pretended not to notice. She sat, the flat snout above her plate, and tested her breathing, her challenging eyes like black balls rolling behind the cellulloid window. After a full two minutes she took it off and replaced it in the cardboard box.

'Gas attacks are very rare at sea, Miss Frobisher,' mentioned the captain politely.

'The wind would blow the gas away,' confirmed the first officer.

Miss Frobisher doggedly stabbed at the food and replied without looking up: 'ARP stands for Air Raid Precautions, captain. And I am taking precautions.' She looked up thinly. 'Perhaps the enemy has developed a new gas that can pursue a ship.'

Everyone then had a guess as to how long the war would last. Most thought it would be over by Christmas. Miss Frobisher said: 'Three weeks,' but added sombrely: 'the Germans will win.' Everyone looked horrified. Then the captain calculated three years, and the first officer made it four, with our side as the eventual winners. Those who experienced the First World War began telling memories, some sad and terrible, but as we served the port and brandy they became happier and by late evening everyone was quite enjoying the hostilities.

After the passengers and officers had left the saloon for the night, Mr Wilson and I had to set the table for breakfast and the trays that would be taken to cabins with early tea. It was also my duty to go to the provisions store deep in the bottom of the ship to bring up supplies which would be required next day in the galley.

It was just after midnight when I went down the long steps, through and along the various decks, and unlocked the store. It was an extended narrow section shelved on each side with bulkhead lights along its middle. As I was taking tins of soup from their shelf the lights flickered, as though in warning, and then there came a massive explosion and the ship heeled drunkenly, sending me sprawling along the metal floor. My head struck the bulkhead and I lay stunned, my hands flailing. The lights went out and then, as if refusing to die, they lit again. I bawled: 'It's a mine! We've hit a mine!' There was no one to hear me down there. Clutching a metal rung I pulled myself upright only to be swung off my feet again by a second spasm of the ship. The klaxon was sounding remotely: 'It's all right, it's all right,' I repeated. 'She won't sink. She *can't* sink. It's all right.'

Then I heard the deep sliding of the watertight doors. 'There,' I confided to myself. 'That'll do it.' Then, suddenly horrified, I realised that the closing doors would imprison me, trap me in the bottom of the ship. I staggered to the entrance of the storeroom and looked along the corridor. One door, towards the stern, closed with resounding finality. Filled with fear I looked the other way. The door at the far end of the companionway was slowly moving across its gap. Shouting, as though that would stop it, I charged madly along the passage and flung myself through the narrowing hole. I fell onto the hard deck on the far side. Swiftly, I pulled myself up. At the extreme end of the next section, another metal section was easing across. Crying out, I ran and tumbled the length of the corridor and fell and finally wriggled through, inches to spare, striking my head again on the overhead metal.

Now there was one more. The ship lurched again, pitching me sideways. Somewhere above my head the klaxon was honking crazily. I thought I could hear shouts and cries. The door began to close and I went like a hurdler, forcing myself through it, tumbling into a brimming trough of icy Atlantic water. It caught me, knocking out my breath, and its power rolled me over, gasping and shouting for help.

The salt choked me, the cold paralysed my arms. I went under again, into the dark and terrifying depths before gasping to the surface, my strength knocked out, my chest swamped, my heart banging. The overhead lights had gone out. My hand struck and then grasped a metal ring set into the bulkhead. I hung on with every ounce of strength. Hung on and then, using two hands, pulled myself half clear of the churning water. It rolled me like a float. Again I struck my head against metal and I almost let go and fell again. I heaved myself up, shouting and cursing. It was terrible. I was so frightened, convinced that now I really would die.

With my final effort, and using the impetus of the water which again swept around me, I got to my feet, onto a ledge and, waiting for the next surge, tugged at the ring and pulled myself clear. I was on a wide ledge, crouching and whimpering, with the water below me rising.

Trembling with shock and cold, I crouched on the ledge, holding on desperately while the sea gushed around below me. I had to get out of there. I reached above me into the void and at first touch my hand contacted a hatch handle. It turned. Frantically I pushed against it and felt it shift upwards. I raised myself on the ledge and thrust both hands flat on the hatch. It moved upwards letting in a slender light.

'Good, good,' I encouraged myself. 'G . . . g . . . good b . . . boy. C . . . c . . . c . . . come on.' I do not know whether the stammer had returned because of the fear or the cold. It made me stop talking to myself, however, and I gave all my will and strength to forcing the hatch. Gradually, as the light fanned out, it opened. Sounds came in, like noises from hell; screams and shouts and the eerie creaking and cracking of the ship; the useless continuing klaxon.

I was almost there. One gasp-heave and the hatch clanged back. Trying to get my breath, I thanked God silently, but then I cursed aloud as I tried to lever myself from the hatch only to tip back again. I was not giving up now. I was almost there. Gathering everything I had I got my weight through the round, narrow hatch and with another heave I slithered out into the passage above. Lights were flickering. Water was swilling up and down the deck but only inches deep. On my hands and knees I began to move.

Doors were wildly swinging and furniture and glass were scattered in the exposed cabins. Crawling, trying to regain my strength and keep my balance, I progressed along the heaving corridor. When I had almost reached the junction at the distant end around the corner came another figure on all fours. For a moment I thought I was hallucinating. It looked like a pig or a dog. It was Miss Frobisher wearing her fur coat and her gas mask. The klaxon had stopped and I could hear she was grunting.

'Miss Frobisher,' I croaked. 'Miss Frobisher.'

The black snout turned. 'Are you all right?' she asked in a muzzled voice. She lifted the rubber from around her chin and repeated the question through the aperture.

'Yes, yes,' I breathed. 'Thank you. Follow me. We can get out.'

'Splendid. You crawl, I'll follow,' she nodded.

We crawled along the remainder of the passage, the only way to make progress because the enclosed space was constantly pitching. It was like being thrown about in a tin can. I went first and she was close behind, the snout of her gas mask nudging my backside. She was still grunting. There was an iron door at the end and I pulled myself upright with its handles and then helped her to her feet. The fur coat was saturated. She clung to me like a walrus.

'Steady,' I encouraged, holding on to her. 'Steady, Miss Frobisher. We'll get in a boat, don't worry.'

The black rubber face nodded in return encouragement. I pushed the levers and the door swung open, helped by another lurch of the hull. We climbed out onto the open deck.

The scene was amazing: our ship was heeled over to port. They were trying to launch a lifeboat. And standing off only a few cable lengths distant was the black outline of a German U-Boat. The searchlight from her conning tower was flooding over the scene. I thought they were going to machine-gun us. I crouched and pulled Miss Frobisher down with me.

To my astonishment the thin lady managed to get upright. She waved her fist slowly but defiantly and shouted something within the confines of her gas mask. Then I saw that the Germans were, in fact, illuminating the lifeboat. I still believed they were going to open fire. But from the conning tower came a voice through a loudhailer. It was calling instructions, encouragement. For a moment I thought perhaps we had been doomed by mistake, that this was one of our own submarines.

Then came the hollow echo of *'Achtung! Achtung!'* There had been no mistake. Miss Frobisher had taken off her gas mask and now, quivering-faced, she turned to the sea and the submarine. 'A nasty, uncouth language,' she said quietly. 'From a nasty, uncouth nation.' She made to replace the rubber mask over her face.

'Miss Frobisher,' I pleaded. 'Leave the mask off now. We'll have to go into the boats. You won't need it, I promise.'

'I don't trust them,' she muttered with finality. 'I have a bad chest. Gassing would do it no good.'

Stoically she replaced the mask. The visor was fogged. I took her wet, thin hand and tried to lead her down the sloping surface to where the boat was being launched. We had almost reached the rail when the ship gave a deathly sigh and heeled violently. We were projected across the deck. Nothing could stop us. The angle was steep and the ship was bowing to the ocean. I fell and slithered to the side. Miss Frobisher somehow, like an ice skater, kept her feet, which was fatal, because she was thrown against the rail and in a second had gone over the side into the waves. I remember screaming out for someone to help her. 'Man Overboard!' I shouted. Then idiotically: 'Woman Overboard!'

A grinding of wood and metal came from the guts of the ship. Then a series of short, thick, explosions. Fire had broken out forward and waving flames were coming from the hatches and companionways. Pulling myself up by the angled rail, I looked down into the dark water. The U-boat's searchlight, curved around the scene. One of the lifeboats was upside down in the sea. There were heads like fishing floats around it. They were still trying to launch the other boat. There were yellow rafts below. 'Miss Frobisher!' I called blindly over the side. The ship gave another convulsion, another warning. 'Miss Frobisher, are you there?' I had no life jacket but I knew I would have to go soon. There seemed no point in joining the *mêlée* around the hanging lifeboat.

Crawling up the rail I bellowed upwards, giving notice of

my intention: 'God help me!' and pitched over. I hit the sea
and went right under into the freezing, awful blackness. But
I was fighting now. I had got off the ship and I was going to
survive. As I surfaced, one of the empty yellow life-rafts was
floating nearby and I swam to it and heaved myself up onto
it. I lay shivering and shocked. The searchlight came around
once more then it was extinguished. Voices came over the
water. She was going. A last shout came through the loudhailer. 'Good luck!'

It was getting light. The U-Boat slid under the waves
leaving a sea covered with oil and debris. One lifeboat was
upright in the water several hundred yards away. It was
crowded with heads. Other heads were clinging to floating
objects and there were still those hanging onto the upturned
lifeboat. The ship was lying on her side, like an elephant
resting, the dawn reflecting on her light flanks. From the
direction of the new day came first an aeroplane which circled
the scene and dropped two life-rafts and half-an-hour later a
British destroyer.

We were picked up quickly and taken from the water. A
sailor put a blanket around me and gave me a mug of coffee
laced with brandy. 'First sinking of the war,' he said with a
sort of admiration.

I sat dumbly on the deck, too exhausted to move or thank
them. They were bringing others over the side. Our captain,
pathetically angry, said: 'Brand new ship. She was brand
new. Look at her. Look what they've done.' As if she heard,
the SS Ocean Merchant groaned for the last time, like a suicide
who can take no more, and with blunted fountains spouting
around her, sank below the Atlantic. A medical orderly came
to take me below. I was only a minor casualty. As I was
going I saw them bring Miss Frobisher's body over the side.
Her fur coat was caked with oil. She was still wearing her gas
mask.

By the early and empty evening we were back in Bristol; a
western September sky, gulls and trams, and people going

home, all as if nothing had ever occurred. It was so strange to be brought from the chill prospect of a death in the Atlantic to a place that was so placid, so unaware. In the few days, hours almost, since we had sailed so much had happened to me but nothing had happened to Bristol. I wanted to warn it, to point seawards, to shout: 'The Germans are out there!'

It had rained in the daytime and along the docks were dull-eyed puddles; outside the gates I could see some children swinging around a lamp-post and men propped up outside a public house. I wanted to run to the gates; tell them what had happened to me, about the lives we had lost, and how the ship had gone down in fountains and flames.

'You must tell *no one* of this,' said the naval officer in the warehouse at the dockside. He had set up a table and chair among bales of goods, some of which, I noticed, came from Germany. A lightbulb dangled low from the tall ceiling like a spider on a thread. A sailor sat alongside the officer with a list of names, making notes. The civilian survivors had been taken off to a hotel. Two of the men had been weeping but the women were dry-eyed. The officer questioned me on my personal story and I told him what had happened with the watertight doors, and then about Miss Frobisher and her fur coat and gas mask. It was the first sinking of the war and my interrogator had a brand new ledger in which to record the fact. He had written in capitals at the top of the page *SS Ocean Merchant*. He wrote in longhand steadily as I spoke and with no change of his expression. I had been paid off and a new discharge book issued. My book, which had followed me on so many adventures, had now finished its journeys and was lying on the ocean bed. A troupe of eager ladies had come to the docks and given us replacement clothes, random trousers, heavy jerseys and several woolly hats apiece.

'*No one, nobody, not a soul*,' warned the officer putting his finger to his lips in case I had not understood. 'It never happened.'

'Yes sir. I mean, no sir.'

'As far as the world at large is concerned,' he said. He was not much older than me, but light-haired with a round, pompous face. 'As far as it is concerned, you have just been out for a pleasure cruise. And now you're back.'

'What . . . what can I tell my wife?' I asked.

'Nothing!' he replied, so sharply it was almost a squeak. 'Women have mouths. She'll tell the neighbours, the neighbours will tell their relatives, and in no time Hitler will hear.'

'But I've only just sailed, sir. I'm supposed to be away a month or more.'

He looked annoyed. 'Wait,' he said pinkly. 'Orders are required here.' He stood and briskly ran his hands down his uniform before picking up his new cap, putting it on and marching away. I was one of the last survivors to be questioned. Only a handful were outside the walls of bales awaiting their turn. The officer disappeared through a temporary corridor. The sailor who had been taking the notes looked up at me.

'What was it like, mate?' he asked.

'What?' I thought it might be a trap.

'Bein' sunk, torpedoed.'

'Wet,' I said stubbornly.

'You don't have to 'ide it from me,' he said. 'I've been sittin' 'ere listenin'.' He nodded towards the gap in the bales. 'Straight out of trainin' that one is. They don't know. Just ask the questions they've been trained to ask. This is that snotty's first job. You're the first sinkin'.'

I nodded. 'It was horrible,' I said.

'Scared, I bet.'

'Bloody terrified,' I said.

A piping voice, like a school prefect's, came from the echoing end of the warehouse. 'Tell him not to be so damned stupid, Ronnie,' it called.

'I'll do that,' called Ronnie in return.

'Ronnie,' muttered the sailor. 'Ronnie.'

The pink officer came back. 'Don't be so damned stupid, Jones,' he said. He sat down. 'You mustn't tell a soul. Tell the little woman that you got the 'flu or something, never sailed in the first place.'

'Yes sir. All right,' I said, in no doubt about how much Dolly would be convinced by that.

'Anyway, sign your statement here.' He took a single sheet from the sailor who had been writing it down at the same time. I signed and he looked at the signature as though surprised it was not marked with a cross. 'Very neat,' he approved.

'Right, then. Off you go home. Better luck next time!'

I was unsure whether I was required to salute him. He saved the situation by thrusting out a determined but flabby hand and shook mine. 'Good show,' he said.

I went out of the dock gates and turned towards the station. Good show. That's what it was, a good show. Like a variety performance. I could still feel the terror and the cold, still see the crawling, furred, and snouted Miss Frobisher. Still hear the screams and the klaxon. My arms and legs ached. I had a bruise the size of a dinner plate where I had hit the water. A good show.

In the train other passengers sat around me and talked animatedly about the war. Everyone was jolly and seemed to be glad that the years of uncertainty were gone. One man, with tufts of white hair like feathers on his head and eyebrows, said to me: 'You'll be the right age then.'

'Yes, I suppose I will.'

They began examining me, as if my caution had alerted them. There was another man, dressed in a prim grey suit, a woman in a huge coloured pullover and another thin woman wedged into a corner by the first woman's bulk.

'*You'll* have to fight,' squeaked the thin woman from the corner. 'Everybody will.'

I almost said wearily: 'I have.' Instead I nodded and said: 'I know.'

'Don't be a conchie,' warned the man in the grey. 'Nobody can stand conscientious objectors.'

'Give them white feathers and shoot them, I say,' said the

153

big woollen woman. Her fat eyes narrowed as though sighting a gun.

'Shooting's too good,' responded the man. He patted my knee. 'You get out there and have a go,' he advised. 'As soon as you can.'

I very nearly let it out then. I had seen something they had not, a nightmare. But I stopped myself and pretended to doze. The men both got off in Newport and I changed at Cardiff for Barry. It was gone midnight. There was a train at one o'clock. On the platform was a drunk who offered to share a bottle of rum with me and I drank it with him until the train came in.

When we reached Barry an unwholesome weariness came over me. I tramped up the slope from the station, as if I were somehow left unclean by my experience. The rum was making me roll as I walked. I sang a little on the empty hill and tried to concentrate on my Dolly deep in our bed.

The house was dumb and dark. Going around our back door I let myself in with my key. Calling up the stairs so that I would not frighten her, I ran unsteadily up to fall into her arms and weep and tell her my terrible sorrows, and to hell with the secrets.

I put the light on. On my side of the bed, sitting up, blinking, was a soldier. He was wearing his rough khaki shirt and his battledress top and trousers were on the floor. Dolly was hiding below under the bedclothes.

'Dolly . . . *Christ*! Dolly . . .' I choked. The room was reeling. 'What's this?'

Her flushed face edged out. 'Oh Davy,' she cried. 'You're back early!'

She sat up, pulling the sheet up in front of her to hide her nakedness. From *me*, her husband. 'I've got some bad news,' she said.

'It looks like it,' I croaked.

She said: 'Your Auntie Blod died this afternoon. Three o'clock.'

With them still upright in the bed I sat on the corner of it

154

and began to cry. I cried and cried and cried. Dolly began to cry to and then the shirted soldier joined in, lustily wailing the name 'Aggie! Aggie!'

'It's the war,' sobbed Dolly. 'It's the bloody war.'

'The war's only just started,' I pointed out, still sobbing. '*Sunday.*'

It was so. But, new though it was, it had already begun to take its toll.

Three

Blodwen looked as comfortable in her coffin as she had been in her back room. She seemed snug and almost smug, as if anticipating a cup of tea, a pink smile below her resting eyes, her podgy hands across her chest.

'He's made a tidy job of her,' summed up Uncle Griff, referring to Evans Above, the undertaker who lived on Barry Hill. After the funeral, at which he sang louder than anyone except my mother, who also sobbed loudest, Griff went home for the drinks and biscuits. 'Good pals, we were,' was all he said, and that evening walked to the Institute where he played his customary silent game of snooker. He continued to work for the iron foundry, live in the house and go to the Institute until after the war. The front room was shut and he rarely spoke of Blod again. Sometimes, the neighbours said, they could hear him at night singing alone in their bed.

My wife told me that the soldier had been a mistake; that she had no idea how he came to be in bed with her, indeed she had been as surprised as I was, although I doubt that. 'He was at the forces' canteen,' she said sprinkling my chest with her penitent tears. 'And he seemed so lonely so I asked him back for a cup of tea. We had the tea but he kept putting rum into it when I wasn't looking and I must have passed out. I found the empty bottle.' The tears ran thicker. 'And then you came in. Oh Davy, I thought it was a ghost.'

'It very nearly was,' I told her.

'And then your auntie going and dying and everything. It's a terrible war. That Hitler's a bastard. *There*, I've said it now, a *bastard*.'

'A bastard,' I agreed. I embraced her and kissed her ears. I did not want to lose her.

We went the next day down to the beach. The fairground was shut because of the war and the autumn, but we walked around it, pretending to have rides and to shy at invisible coconuts. The wind rattled through the shuttered sideshows and the rigid roundabouts as it might through a deserted village. There was hardly a ripple in the sky or the water. We walked away from the dead fair and down onto the sands. We held hands like new lovers and surveyed the loneliness of the Bristol Channel. Soon I would have to go back to sea.

'Why did you go to the forces' canteen, Dolly?' I asked. I could still see that shirted soldier.

She paused and turned on the flat, washed sand regarding me sincerely, as if she were glad I had asked. 'It's my war effort,' she said simply. The breeze disturbed the curls on her forehead. 'Everybody's got to have a war effort.'

She was my wife and I deeply loved her and wanted to keep her. Soon I would be going away again and I needed to know that she was thinking of me when I was out there on the wide sea and she was in our bed.

From where we stood we could see the cap of the old lighthouse from which Tosh had tipped that childish night. Neither of us had been there since. Now, without either suggesting it, we began to stroll in that direction. She dragged her feet through the cold sand as if she were still reluctant, but she allowed me to help her over the rocks and then we went up onto the grass and eventually climbed the green slope to the base of the tower.

The cottage where the retired coastguard had lived was derelict and shuttered. 'He's gone,' she said. 'Dead I expect. Lots of people are.'

We reached the lighthouse door and sat on the step together, as if we were still in childhood. 'I'm lonely when you go away,' she muttered.

'I have to go to sea. I was only gone three days last time.'

'If you could be a soldier,' she suggested 'you wouldn't be

away all the time. Some of them go home to their own beds every night.'

'Some of them,' I said carefully.

'Or be in the air force.' She giggled now and pointed up to the blank afternoon sky. 'Up there, wiggling your wings at me down here.'

I laughed with her. We walked around the foot of the lighthouse and tried the door but it was firmly locked. Around the far side we looked up at the gallery from which Tosh had plunged. The iron rail had never been replaced. 'Whooooo,' said Dolly softly. 'That's how he went. 'Whoooo . . .' she made a plummeting movement with her hand. 'Down and down.'

An edgy wind came like a small warning across the grass from the sea. 'Why don't we go home,' I said. 'And have a cup of tea in bed.'

She put her soft arm around my waist and we began to stroll down the brief hill. At the bottom she looked back and up and I did also.

'He'd have been good in the air force, Tosh,' I said.

'A dare devil,' she nodded. 'Flying through the air.'

I was grateful to get her home and into our bed. I made the tea and took it to her on a tray. We had some buns and butter too because there was still butter to be had then. She smirked and put her finger in the butter and mischievously smeared it on me. We were naked and I put some on her, on her nipples, and we fooled about like that until a lot of butter was used up and not much of it on the buns. It made a mess of our only pair of sheets and that night we had to sleep on the underblanket. Making love with her was luxury but more frequent, and I was sad when three days later I had to leave again, for Liverpool, to join another ship bound for Portland, Maine. I would have been even sadder if I had known then that I would not have her again for many years.

When I returned from the next voyage it was just before Christmas and she had gone. Our bed had gone too, our big, billowing bed, wide and accommodating as the sea, the symbol of our marriage. Our room looked like a bomb crater without it. I was still panting from my run from the station; running uphill with my sea-bag on my shoulder, so eager was I to see Dolly after two long months. People who saw me laughed or pointed me out to others. I did not care; all I wanted were her surrounding arms, and the comfort of her breasts.

Our back door was locked but I still had my key. It was about four on a Sunday afternoon, winter and almost dark. I dropped my sea-bag and clattered up the stairs, calling her name. Never again, not after the last time, would I want to shock her; or myself.

The door of our living room, which was a kitchen as well, was open but the light was not on. I put my head around the door. It was tidy and empty, not Dolly's style. I told myself not to be a fool. 'Dolly,' I called quite mildly. 'Doll, where are you?'

I took the single pace to our bedroom and opened the door. The last shreds of December daylight were coming through the window. They were sufficient to illuminate the terrible fact: our bed was not there. Our bed, the one thing we had bought together; it had almost been our home, our bliss, our marriage. Gone.

'Dolly!' I cried out again. Then 'Dolly!' angrily. And finally a low, 'Doll,' as I sat on the empty floor. Oh God, where had she gone? Or been taken? Taken by someone who took our bed too? I crumpled back against the wall by the frame of black material that we had used as a black-out for the window and afixed there so happily and finally on many a night. I fingered it as if it were a nightdress. Then I heard the door open below. I sat up.

Who's that up there? On a Sunday. What you doing?'

'It's me, Mrs Humphries,' I called back. 'I've come home.'

'Home!' She was a coarse woman and it came out like a curse. She began to thump up the stairs. 'This ain't your bloody home! Not till you pay up!'

She appeared at the door frame, like an evening witch. My

position on the floor seemed to enrage her more. She stamped into the room and kicked me twice with her tattered shoes. 'Get up!' she bawled. 'Don't you sit on my floor.'

I stood up. She was half my size and she burst into tears. 'Sods!' she wept. 'Sodding sods, you are.'

'Where is my wife?' I asked her calmly.

Her wet eyes glistened at me in the dimness. 'Where?' she repeated. 'That's what *I* say: "where is she?" If you don't know, I don't. She buggered off, that's all I know. The sod.'

'She took the bed?' I had a faint hope that Dolly might have gone to start a home for us elsewhere.

The old woman looked defiant. 'I sold the bed,' she said. 'For my money. Rent owing and the money she took when she went.

'I don't believe it,' I said firmly. 'I want to know where she has gone.'

A sort of sympathy came over her. 'I don't know,' she replied more evenly. 'Better ask her mother. She won't tell me. She says it's none of my business. So I've sold the bed to get my money.' She regarded me in the deepening shadow. 'I don't know what a boy like you was doing with her.'

'She's my wife,' I told her. 'There's no "was" about it. She still is.'

'You're a fool,' she said. She turned and went to the door. 'I want my key back,' she added holding out her hand.

'You can have it,' I replied putting it into the thin palm held out, pale as paper. 'I don't want it now.'

Picking up my bag I went through the door and down the stairs. She came down with me and curiously opening the back door, said: 'You never came across my brother George Hopkins, did you, while you been at sea?'

The kit-bag was on my shoulder. Her voice had subdued. 'No,' I answered. 'Never did. There's a lot of people at sea.'

'He's under it now,' she said. 'Lost in October,'

'I'm sorry,' I said genuinely. 'I've got to be going.' I began to walk away.

'All right,' she said. She hesitated. 'And good luck.'

I went around the side of the house and up the hill again. It was cold but I was sweating. Inside I felt as empty as our bedroom. The houses were terraced, their doors opening onto the streets. From one of the doorways, out of the dark, a man who must have known me shouted: 'Home again?'

It was strange walking through the black-out town. In September when the war had started the evenings still had a few hours of light but now everywhere was like pitch. Bicycles and what few cars there were had blue shaded lights and the bus that went down to the station moved almost by instinct, its headlights reduced to slits, its windows blanked out like a double-decker.

Dolly's mother's house had sandbags against its windows. They had always thought of themselves as superior to other people in the street. Her father, who was timekeeper on the dock, came to the door and when he saw me said: 'Oh, it's you.'

'Where's my Dolly gone, Mr Powell?' I asked.

He did not invite me over the threshold. Instead he turned and called into the house. 'It's David Jones. Wants to know where our Dolly's gone.'

An inner door was opened and shut so no light issued from the small hallway. Her mother was a wide woman and her shape took up most of the doorway. 'It's Dolly you want?' she said.

'He'd better come in,' said her husband unsurely.

'All right,' she said. 'Just for a minute.'

She regarded my sea-bag doubtfully, then disdainfully. Leave that outside,' she said. 'They get filthy.'

I put it down outside and went in. There was an elaborate opening and shutting of doors so that the lights did not escape. 'There's a war on you know,' said Dolly's father. 'You might not realise it, being away, but there is.'

'He's an ARP warden,' said Mrs Powell nodding her head towards her husband as we got into the room. The settee and the chairs were uncut moquette and there was a china lady in a blue dress sprawled across the clock, under the mirror on its chain, above the mantelpiece. On the shelf were Christmas cards and in a corner there was an artificial Christmas tree. There was proper coal on the fire, not dust as other people used. Mr Powell always brought proper coal home from the docks.

'Showing lights,' said Dolly's mother. 'There's people here, in Barry, signalling to the Germans.' She looked as if she would have liked to leave me standing but she put a white fastidious cloth on one of the chairs, covering the back and the seat, and indicated I could sit.

'Germans themselves,' sniffed Dolly's father. 'Jews, but they're still bloody Germans. Signalling the bombers with torches and by not having a proper black-out.'

'There's been bombing?' I said aghast. 'In Barry?'

'Not yet,' put in Mrs Powell, seeing her husband hesitate. 'But there will be. And those are the people who'd signal them. I'd shoot them all.'

'All of them,' said her husband.

There was a pause. I looked from one mealy face to the other. 'Where's my wife?' I said.

'Dolly?' she answered, as though the two were not one and the same. 'She got fed up, waiting.'

'So she joined the air force,' said Dolly's father promptly and proudly.

His wife regarded him as though he had stolen her line. 'She's in the WAAF,' she corrected. 'Women's Auxiliary Air Force.'

'Where is she?' I repeated.

'Don't take that attitude with us, David Jones,' said her mother. Her pompous eyes became aggrieved. 'She's a young woman. She can't wait about while you're gallivanting all over the place, America and the like.'

'Where they don't have a war,' Mr Powell put in knowledgeably. 'Where they don't have any black-out. Plenty of everything.'

'She was lonely and she wanted some life. You were never there. She's only young.'

162

'I'm a sailor,' I said. 'I can't walk home.'

'That's the trouble. She should never have married you. She needs somebody to look after her, not somebody who turns up when it suits him. Other men don't go off for months. Not as soon as they're married.'

'Where is she in the WAAF?'

'Somewhere in Scotland,' replied the man primly.

'Where?'

Pink blotches came to his crafty face. 'You may not know it,' he intoned. 'But no one is allowed to give away service addresses. It's secret. The enemy might find out.'

I stood up. 'I think you can take it I'm on our side,' I said. Reaching for the mantelpiece I took the hateful clock with the woman spread across its top and held it above my head. They both went white.

'Don't you dare!' Mrs Powell said hoarsely. 'I'll get the police.

'That's our anniversary present,' he whispered.

'Our twenty-fifth,' she said.

'Where is she?' I repeated.

'Arbroath,' he said, taking the responsibility.

'In Scotland,' she said. 'But she won't want to see you.

I put the clock back on the mantelpiece. 'I want to see her,' I said. 'I love her.'

'Arbroath? It's a long, long way, boy,' said Griff. 'The trains the way they are . . . could take days.'

It was strange Blod not being there. Griff had shrunk a little. I found him at the Institute, chalking his cue, working out strategy. The place felt warm and beery. When he had finished his frame we sat down by the bar. 'You joining up?' asked one of the older men.

'He's in the Merchant Navy,' said my uncle.

'You want to get into uniform,' said the man. 'Get into the war proper.'

'Maybe we ought to have a uniform,' I said afterward.

'Aye,' he agreed. The man had angered him. 'They'd know

then. A peaked cap and an anchor embroidered on a jersey.'
I smiled. 'Any more for the Skylark?'

'All you've got is that daft silver badge,' he answered.
'Who can see that?'

He leaned forward and peered closely at the badge in my
lapel. 'MN,' he grunted. 'Who knows what that means? They
might around here but they won't in half the country. They'll
think you're a bloody miner or something.' He studied me
seriously. 'How has it been?' he said.

'Oh America was fine. Lit up. No rationing. People buy
you drinks and tell you to kill Hitler for them. But the
Atlantic isn't much fun. We had two ships sunk in the
convoy. One right to starboard. Yards away. The men were
on fire in the water.'

'And you come home to find your wife vanished,' he
sighed.

'She wanted to do something to help the war,' I told him
lamely.

'Always was a keen sort of girl,' he said. He shook his
head: 'There's a lot like that. The war's made them all the
keener.'

We went back to the old house. 'Not like it was,' said Griff,
although it seemed the same, just a bit colder. 'Just somewhere to sleep and have a swill now. She always kept your
room for you, the bed made, just in case,' he added. 'It might
need airing though.'

'It doesn't matter,' I said patting him on the shoulder.

'When you've been in the sea, torpedoed and wet, I don't
suppose a bit of damp worries you,' he half-laughed.

That night I slept in my old room, remembering it as it
was when I was a boy. I opened the curtains and let some
moonlight in. I was full of a weary sorrow. The next morning
I went to the station to get the train to Cardiff and then up
to Scotland. I had a week before I was due to join the ship
again. On the way to the station I passed a second-hand
shop, Jenner's, that had been there for years. In the hard
times it had financed half the town. Now, like a prize exhibit,

I saw that the middle of the window was occupied by a bed; *our* bed.

Entranced, I walked towards the window. On the brass headrail was a label. It said: 'War-damaged bargain.'

I went inside. The man did not know me. 'It's five pounds,' he said. 'Lovely bit of bed, that is. But you have to take it away yourself.'

'Thanks,' I said. 'But I can't take it now. Maybe I'll come back for it.'

It took thirty hours to reach Arbroath. Every train was crowded and I had to stand much of the way. Men in uniform were given priority for seats because they could be *seen* to be fighting the war.

Hung with fatigue I went out of the station at Arbroath into a Scottish evening drizzle and went straight to a lodging house across the street. It was nine o'clock. The man who kept the house said: 'I hope you'll be a good sleeper. There's a dance tonight and they'll be fighting in the street about twelve.'

'Where's the dance?' I asked him.

'The Corn Exchange,' he said looking at me carefully. 'But you'll be in no fit state, I'm thinking, to be doing yon Hokey-Cokey. Anyway it's Services only.'

'I'm Merchant Navy,' I said.

'Aye, that would count. I'll be putting the kettle on so you can have a cup of tea and a wash.'

I shaved and changed my shirt. Then I walked down the grey street to an old square. The blunt noise of a dance band issuing from the Corn Exchange increased as two soldiers and two girls opened the door and came out. They went along the pavement with their arms about each other, singing.

'Armed Services only,' grunted the man at the door when I wanted to buy a shilling ticket. He was portly and wearing a stained dinner jacket and a sweaty shirt.

'I'm in the Merchant Navy,' I said. I pointed to my badge. 'Are you Armed Services?'

'If you're looking for trouble,' he said in a nervous way, 'you can't come in. We don't want any trouble.' He handed me a ticket and I gave him a shilling. 'Not many people do,' I said.

Pushing aside the thick curtain within the entrance I walked in. It was so full and so smoky the band was invisible. There must have been five hundred people in the resounding room, crammed onto the dance floor and standing four deep around its edges and at the busy bar. At once I heard Dolly laughing – there was no mistaking it. The rich gurgle floated over the music and the chatter of the dancers.

Edging my way through the crowd I reached the fringe of the floor. There she was, all curls, dancing with a big airman, who had his back to me, laughing at something he had told her. She was in uniform, her arms looped around his neck and before my horrified eyes she leaned towards him and kissed him fruitily on the lips. It was a long kiss and by the time they disengaged their faces she had moved to the music so that when she opened her eyes the first thing she saw was me.

I took three paces onto the floor, shouldering aside the intervening couples, and tapped the big airman on the arm. Dolly was trying to say something, to him or to me, but the words had frozen. Her face was like a crust.

'Excuse me,' I said to her partner.

'This ain't an "excuse me" dance,' he said over his shoulder.

Catching his arm again I said: 'It is when you're cutching with my wife.'

He half turned. He did not believe me. 'Fuck off,' he said. Dolly stood back from him. She looked beautiful in uniform, her hair full over her shoulders, her breasts pushing out the buttons on the pale blue tunic. 'Davy,' she croaked.

Her partner turned fully now. He was a thick-looking man with sticky hair. 'Fuck off,' he repeated.

166

I hit him directly on the chin and I continued hitting him across the floor. He staggered back through the dancers mowing them down as he went. There were protests and screams. I got him against the low dais on which the band was suddenly wavering and with a final punch sent him sprawling over the drums and their drummer who burst into tears.

Then I turned to look for Dolly but only in time to see half-a-dozen eager military police coming at me. I tried to explain that I had only come to find my wife and that everything would be all right now. They crashed into me like a scrum, throwing me into the weeping timpanist. One hit me on the head with his baton. Then they lifted me bodily and carried me from the Corn Exchange to the police station.

'As a rule the fighting does'na start till towards the end,' said the police sergeant as he opened the cell where I sat. 'It was the earliest outbreak I can recall, laddie. Still, it's Christmas.' Then, as an afterthought, he said: 'There's one of the WAAFs wants to see you. Says she knows you.'

Dolly came into the cell and sat on the bench opposite. I stared at her delicious legs in the grey-blue stockings. 'Christ,' she said. 'You look a sight.'

'Doll,' I said. 'I just came to find you.' My arms went out to her and she leaned forward into an embrace, but only briefly. 'Fancy leaving,' I said. 'Just going off like that. Mrs Humphries has sold our bed.'

'She would, the old cow,' she said without concern. 'You broke Sonny's jaw, you know. He was only dancing with me.'

Miserably I regarded her. 'Sonny was kissing you,' I explained simply. 'You're my wife.'

'It was nothing,' she shrugged. 'Only a bit of fun. There's a war on, Davy.'

'So everybody keeps telling me. I wouldn't know, of course, I've only been bloody-well torpedoed. I'll bet none of those fat bastards there last night know what it's like.'

She sniffed. 'Your language,' she complained. 'You never

used to swear. Everybody has a bit of fun in wartime. It's called Living for the Day.'

'Fun? Other people seem to be having my share,' I said bitterly. I leaned towards her. 'Listen, Dolly, I love you. You're my wife. I want you back with me.'

'In those two rotten rooms,' she sulked. 'With you miles away all the time. America and places. I was going mad.'

'I wrote to you,' I protested. 'Three times a week at least. I didn't get one letter back.'

'They wouldn't have caught up with you,' she said still sullen. 'I wrote to you but how can you expect to get letters when you don't know where you'll be next? It's not even like the army or the air force where you more or less know where somebody is.'

I put my face in my hands. It still ached from the Military Police. 'Look,' I said. 'I'll come out of the Merchant Navy. I'll join the army.'

'It won't make any difference now,' she pouted. 'I'm here. I'm helping to fight Hitler in case you hadn't realised. I'm on searchlights.' she regarded me firmly. 'I might as well tell you, David, *I've never had such a good time in all my life*. I don't want to be married any more.'

It was almost Christmas. Someone had put a fir tree on the platform but there were no lights on it, only straggling pieces of silver paper. Beside it a ragged man played carols on a violin. I was glad to leave Arbroath. Sonny the airman's jaw had not, despite Dolly's fears, been shattered, although my dreams had. It emerged that he was not supposed to have been at the dance at all. He should have been minding the searchlight or something, but he had crept away to be with my wife. In the dubious circumstances no charges were made against me and I was released from the cells. At the lodging house the man refused to take a night's payment for a bed in which no one had slept. He came to his door and wished me luck and a Merry Christmas as I walked across the station. I thought he was the only decent person there.

The journey back was just as grey and broken as it had been going to Scotland. The train was suffocating with servicemen going on leave for the first Christmas of the war. With their greatcoats and their kit-bags, they seemed to be double the size of ordinary people. Some of them had bottles of booze and they drank through these and sang, quarrelled, or went to sleep. After four changes of train I came to a village station, Packwick, on the borders of England and middle Wales, in Herefordshire. Here, with a bang and a resigned gush of steam, the engine broke down. The heating had already done so. We were crushed in the carriages. Some passengers got out and stood about on the platform. It was a small, wet place with no refreshment buffet. On each side were winter fields under a sky low and dank. The trees looked ready to break. The air smeared on the face coldly. From somewhere unseen came the lowing of a lone cow; a rook croaked, people coughed.

'What a fucking hole,' said a soldier standing next to me. 'Makes you wonder what we're fighting for don't it?'

I liked it. I liked its nothingness, its anonymity; its impartiality too, for in that place they would all be strangers. It was like the sea.

'I'm going for a walk,' I said to the soldier.

'I would, mucker,' he said. He had a Birmingham accent. 'Walk 'ome if I was you. This bleeding train's not going anywhere for hours and hours.'

A short stone tunnel led out of the station. It was as though I was shaking them all off, the Birmingham soldier, all the others on the train, Sonny the airman, and Dolly as well. With every step I felt I was pushing them aside. Let her kiss her greasy-haired searchlight minder. When I emerged onto the soaking country road, with full ditches, dripping hedges and low sky, I felt a gratitude, because I had become alone.

I could have taken either direction. There was a signpost, like a wooden man, arms stiff. Wrackly was one mile, and Packwick one mile the other way. It did not matter then. If I had chosen Wrackly my life might have been quite different. I stepped out for Packwick.

After only a quarter of the distance I heard behind me a clopping horse and the hard grind of wheels and a baker's van came into view, bouncing cheerfully along the shiny road. The man reined the horse in with a single soft word and examined me from his lofted seat. He had a narrow but ruddy face and wore a black bowler hat and black jacket that did not fit him.

'You a serviceman, lad?' he inquired.

'Merchant Navy,' I said.

'Grand,' he responded. 'Want a ride?'

'Thanks.' I climbed up beside him. There was a smell of fresh bread from the van behind and I had a momentary memory of Francine, and her room above the bakery, far and long ago.

'Where you going?' he said.

'I don't know,' I answered honestly. 'I just got off the train.'

'Don't know?' he repeated doubtfully. 'Don't know? You surely know where you're going. You're not a spy are you?'

I laughed. 'No. It's just that I had to get off that train. I'm going as far as the nearest pub.'

'That'll be the Stag's Head in Packwick,' he said. He had flicked the reins and we were again skimming along the road. 'Could do worse.' He had a broken loaf by his side and he handed a piece of it to me saying: 'Fresh this morning.' Then he said: 'Why would you do that? Just get off the train.'

'It was crowded,' I said at first then, almost to myself: 'I'm crowded.'

He nodded. 'I know what you mean. It's a good pub, the Stag's. Not short of beer which is more than you can say for a lot of places.' He shook his head. 'This war's a terrible thing.'

A few low, reflecting rooftops appeared. 'Packwick,' he said. 'You could miss it if nobody told you. Here's the Stag's. I'll come with you.'

The horse seemed to know it was meant to halt in the yard. Its driver loosely hitched the reins over a post. The Stag's Head was old but unpicturesque. In summer there may have been roses and wisteria but now the cracked white walls were all but bare, a rain butt was overflowing, the yard was muddy. My companion opened the low door, however, and we entered a warm room with a wood fire in the grate. The ceiling was low and smoked, its beams bent. A big, slow man was wiping glasses behind the bar. A wireless set was playing dance music.

'Jeff,' said the van driver. 'I found a wandering sailor.' He turned to me. 'I don't know your name, son. Mine's Billy Houghton. And this fine-looking bloke is Jeff Blewis, landlord of this pub.'

'I'm David Jones,' I said shaking hands with them both. I thanked Billy for the ride.

'Long way from the sea, aren't you?' said Jeff. 'Couldn't be much further from it in this country.'

I told them I had been to Scotland to see my wife and I was going south to join a ship the day after Boxing Day. Unasked, the landlord put a tankard of beer on the counter. 'Half, Billy?' he asked although he knew.

'Half, Jeff,' agreed Billy.

'Years at sea myself,' said the landlord pushing the pint towards me. I thanked him. 'Five continents. Every ocean,' he said. 'Wouldn't like to be on it now though.'

'It's not comfortable,' I said. 'It's all right when you get there, America or somewhere, the Caribbean, because you're away from the war then, half the people don't know it's happening, but getting there and back is different.

'Half the people in this country don't know it's on,' said Jeff. 'Don't you reckon, Billy?'

'Half them round here don't,' agreed Billy. 'Just think it's a good excuse for a night out. Still it won't be quiet as this for long, I don't reckon. Hitler's not going to sit back and let life go on like usual. He's got something up his sleeve.'

'Any disasters?' the landlord asked me.

I could have told him I had known plenty recently. I said: 'Torpedoed once.'

'Horrible,' he said. 'Where was that?'

I was past keeping secrets. 'Atlantic,' I said. 'Two days out. Only hours after war was declared.'

'That was unlucky.'

'It was. I was all right. I was picked up. But we lost some crew and one passenger.'

'How long will you be here,' he asked. 'What about Christmas?'

I laughed. 'I'd just forgotten Christmas,' I said. 'I've got to join a ship at Avonmouth on the day after Boxing Day. God knows what I'll do until then. My wife's in the WAAF in Scotland.'

'Stay here if you like,' said Jeff almost eagerly. 'We've got rooms. People haven't come away this year.' He looked at me. 'It's quite reasonable.'

Almost with relief I said: 'Well, yes, all right. I was going nowhere in particular. It was just I couldn't stand being on that train any more.'

'That's good,' beamed Billy. He looked pleased to have been the harbinger. 'Can you sing?'

'A bit,' I said.

'Good,' he said. 'We have a good sing-up in here at Christmas, don't we. Jeff?'

Before the light diminished that afternoon I pulled on my duffle coat and went out and walked over the still fields at the back of the hamlet. There was a line of ragged trees at the boundary of the first meadow and a winter-thick stream coursing through a muddy channel. Cows were in the pasture beyond, their sluggish shiftings the only movements in the dimming landscape.

The room they had given me at the Stag's Head had an old wooden bed, firm and big, a window with flowered curtains lined for the black-out, and a rustling wicker chair. There was a decorated basin and jug on a washstand and a chamberpot sitting coyly below the bed. Down the passage was a bathroom. A towel had been left while I was out walking. I went down to the bathroom and let the gas geyser gush enough hot water for an indulgent bath, and I lay for half-an-hour, feeling my weariness drifting away from me.

It was still only five-thirty. I returned along the twisted corridor to the room, folded the quilt over me and dropped into a heavy sleep.

A knocking at the bedroom door roused me from a dream that I was back in the Arbroath prison cell. I stared around the formless room thinking it was true. Not until I had called, the door had opened and the light had been switched on did I recall where I was.

'Jeff said to call you to see if you'd like something to eat.' I blinked in the light, half asleep and not able to see her. 'Yes, yes,' I said. 'Thanks. I just dropped off.'

'You've been travelling,' she said.

She was pleasant, serious but soft, her face a little long and her eyes deep. Her hair was dark and short, she wore a woollen sweater and a pleated skirt. She smiled gently.

'I'm Paula. I'm Jeff's daughter. And I know you're David Jones.'

She went out and closed the door. I lay stretching in the bed, a kind of relief running through my mind, as if I had arrived somewhere at last. Rain and the branch of a tree began to tap-tap on the curtained window. I got up, shaved and dressed and went downstairs.

The door which led to the bar had a step immediately on the inside and I opened it and stumbled forward. Someone shouted: 'Drunk already!' There were a couple of dozen people there, middle-aged, coated and scarved, cheerful. From behind the bar Jeff said: 'Sorry, son, should have warned you about the drop.' He placed a tankard of beer on the bar. 'Happy Christmas,' he said.

They chorused: 'Happy Christmas' and, embarrassed, but made glad by their friendship, I raised the tankard. The door opened and a party of three cheerfully disorganised women and one man came in, shaking off the rain. 'It's Henry's Harem,' called the man who had shouted 'Drunk already'.

'Come on through the back,' said Jeff. 'There'll be plenty of time for drinking afterwards. Paula's made some chicken pie and she makes it lovely. Have it in the kitchen.'

I followed him through a door at the back of the bar. Paula was laying a place at a red-clothed table, a lamp hanging low over it. She smiled: 'Hungry?'

'I am,' I said. 'I hope this is not making a lot of trouble for you.'

'It's a pleasure to have somebody to eat it,' she replied. 'Dad's a real baby these days, doesn't want this, can't eat that. My mother died last year and he hasn't had a proper meal since.'

She cut through the pie crust and we both watched the steam rise from it. 'One thing you can be sure about is chicken,' she said. 'You can always get a chicken. Mind you, around here rationing is not so bad. It makes up for having to live in the country.'

'Don't you like it, the country?' I asked. She was putting the food on a plain plate.

'Would you?' she asked. 'Wet and grey, you get sick of it. A bus once a day and that gives you an hour in Hereford before it comes back. If you miss it, you walk.'

The food smelled good. She went to the bar and brought back another pint of beer. 'I suppose if you live here, it's different,' I said. 'But it seems a good place to me. A peaceful nothingness.'

She nodded and sat at the table, her hands clasped across the cloth in front of her. Her skin was light, her hands rounded. 'I don't think I ever will get used to it,' she said. 'But what with the war and my father being here by himself there was not much choice. I lived in the south, Winchester, with my husband. He was a Territorial so he was one of the first to be called up. He's in France now.'

'No Christmas leave?'

'He's not coming home,' she muttered unhappily. 'I was

hoping, but he's not. I wouldn't mind, but *nothing's* happening is it? No real war is going on. Not in France. There are no battles. He's there, the Germans are there, I'm here.'

'All quiet on the Western Front,' I said.

She nodded. 'When I hear that on the wireless I grind my teeth. We'll probably hear about them playing football with the Germans because it's Christmas or singing carols across no-man's-land. I just wish he'd come home for a few days.'

'Sometimes you can't,' I shrugged. 'My wife gets fed up. She says the same to me. And I'm in the middle of the Atlantic.'

'Dad was saying you were at sea.'

'Dolly joined up, the WAAF,' I sighed. 'I've just been to see her in Scotland.'

She gave me a slanted look: 'You left her just before Christmas?'

'She's busy,' I said. 'She's on searchlights.'

'I know how it is,' she said, rising from the table. 'You'll have some more pie, won't you?'

I accepted and thanked her. She put it on the plate. 'We've got a turkey for Christmas Day,' she said. She moved towards the bar door. 'Come through when you're ready,' she said. 'They have a sing-song and play some silly games.'

That Christmas Eve, with strangers in an unknown place, was the happiest and kindest I was to know for a long time. There was good nature, singing, and faces pink with pleasure. Two soldiers and an airman with a girl came in. The three random ladies who were called Henry's Harem insisted that I sat with them in their corner. One was Henry's wife and the others her sisters from London. They sang with great verve, out of tune, and threw big Cockney arms around me. A man with ruby cheeks played the piano. I kept my singing low, but at the end of one song one of the sisters called out: 'This boy's got a ruddy lovely voice: 'e's been singing beautiful, right in my ear.'

Billy, the baker who had brought me to the Stag's Head, stood up: 'Come on, sing something for us, Davy?'

'Come on, Davy,' urged the soldiers and everyone chorused: 'Come on, Davy!'

'What shall I sing?' I asked them, still sitting between the two broad women. Jeff from behind the bar called: 'Give us a sea-shanty, son.'

I said: 'Yes, all right.' The ruby man on the piano said: 'You start, sir, and I'll follow. I'll soon catch you up.'

So I sang to them, one of the old shanties, and soon they were chorusing:

> 'Marr-i-ed,
> To a mer-ma-id,
> At the bottom of the deep blue sea.'

I half turned in the song and saw Paula looking at me, her lips moving a little to the words.

As Jeff had said, we were about as distant from the sea as it is possible to be in England but even now, years after, I like to think of the old sea song rolling from the closed-up darkness of the inn and spreading over the country night.

'I reckon we want a Christmas carol now,' said Billy. 'Give us a carol, lad.'

With a single note from the piano I sang: 'In the Bleak Mid-Winter'. When I had finished, there was a gap for a moment and they all began to clap. The two big London sisters were in tears, one lending the other a handkerchief. I looked around to Paula, but she turned quickly and went out of the room, returning with mince pies and sandwiches. Glasses clinked across the bar and we played games, including one where the victim, hands behind back, had to pick up an apple with their teeth from a bowl of flour. Everyone had seen it before and they knew what would happen. When Billy's turn came and he was kneeling, low over the bowl, one of the London sisters stepped smartly forward and pressed his head into the flour. He straightened up, his face caked, blowing white lumps from his mouth.

176

When they had all gone jovially home and the door was barred, I helped Jeff and Paula to clear the bar and wash up in the kitchen. 'Good job I kept apace with the glasses, washing up, or we'd be here all night,' sighed Jeff. 'It was a good evening, though. One of the best.'

It took more than half an hour to wash the plates and cutlery. Jeff had gone to finish clearing the bar.

'They cried when you sang,' said Paula studying the forks she was drying. 'Did you see them? I felt like it too.'

'Why?'

'I don't know,' she said not looking up. 'It was just the way you sang.'

I began to tell her about my first voyage and how I had cooked and sung for the captain and crew of the *Myrtle Montgomery*. She called her father and he came into the kitchen. 'You must listen to this,' she said and asked me to start again. Jeff sat on a chair. As I recounted the story his grey head nodded and the creases at the side of his mouth turned upwards into a grin.

Afterwards he said he was going to bed. Paula made a pot of tea. I was still drying dishes when she said: 'Sing the carol again, will you. In the Bleak Mid-Winter.'

'You sing it with me then,' I suggested.

'I'll try.' We sang together, both softly:

'In the bleak mid-winter,
Frosty wind made moan,
Earth stood hard as iron,
Water like a stone.'

When we had finished we both laughed in embarrassment. We drank the tea, put out the lights and went up the narrow wooden stairs. She led the way and waited for me on the landing. When I got there she gently put her arms about me and mine went about her. Her body felt small against me. She kissed me on my cheek and I kissed her on hers. We said goodnight to each other and went to our rooms. Never mistake domesticity for love.

*

At ten on Christmas morning Billy called in his van to take me to church. Paula stayed with her father to prepare Christmas dinner. We drove in the van, the horse clopping brightly over the empty echoing road. In the damp church I was wedged between the London sisters who sang dreadfully, but loudly, determined to match me and each other.

'It's really, really nice singing with somebody who can sing,' the one who had been flat said as we walked through the village.

'Best *I've* ever sung,' said the one who had been out-of-tune throughout.

They each clung to one of my arms, their bracelets sounding on their plump wrists, and insisted that Billy and I should go to Henry's house for sherry. We drank it in front of a coal fire in a small grate, with an eighteen-inch imitation Christmas tree on the table. The sisters had, unknowingly, each knitted a hat and a scarf for the other as presents, and the mirth was uproarious when they put them on. They were identical patterns. Then Henry poured another glass of sherry all around and said: 'Happy Christmas. Let's hope by the next one this war will be all over.'

We drank solemnly to that and Billy took me back to the Stag's Head. It was busy with customers. I went behind the bar with Jeff and Paula and washed glasses as they served. At two-thirty everyone left to hear the King's broadcast in their own homes and we sat in front of the wireless set, utterly silent, as though any word would disturb his halting delivery.

'He gets his words out a bit better now,' said Jeff when he had finished. 'Never wanted to be King anyway.'

It was five in the afternoon before we were able to sit at the dinner table. The last turkey I was to taste for several years sat glistening in the middle of the table and Jeff carved it with care and ceremony. The pub was deserted that night. Billy had stayed and we ate fully and drank moderately, lingering at the table until far into the evening. When he had arrived Billy had put his horse into a stable at the back of the yard. When he left I went with Paula to see him off. The horse did not want to go out into the dark, drizzling night, into the shafts. 'He likes it in there,' said Billy. 'Dry and warm. But he's got to go home and that's that.' We laughed. He had enjoyed the wine. 'He knows the way.'

We went back and listened to the radio, the three of us sitting in the worn kitchen armchairs. Jeff dozed and eventually woke and announced he was going to bed. Paula and I sat for another hour laughing at a special Christmas edition of *Music Hall*. Then we walked up the stairs and embraced on the landing again. Her head dropped down on my chest, wearily it seemed, and her hair was under my chin and in my nose. 'Goodnight,' she said kissing me again on the cheek. 'We're both shipwrecked, aren't we?'

'Goodnight Paula,' I said, returning the kiss. 'I think we are.'

On the afternoon of Boxing Day a special bus rattled around the countryside to pick up villagers who wanted to go to Hereford to the opening of the pantomime or to the picture palace. It stopped outside the Stag's Head at one-thirty, and Paula and I boarded it. Its passengers were wrapped against the wind and the drizzle and from the mass of damp coats and wound scarves came calls and greetings. Children, like bundles, sat four to a double seat, their faces bright, their voices piping. Sitting in the bus with her, shoulder touching shoulder and leg against leg, we said little to each other. She pointed out a spired church or a hill half-lost in the misty day and said how nice it was in the summertime. It continued to drizzle dismally. She removed the scarf from around her head and shook her thick hair. She did not look at me. I was thinking of going the next day to Avonmouth and the Atlantic.

In the cinema we sat in the middle of hundreds of steaming people, wet raincoats folded on laps, excited children jumping and laughing, a mass grinding of bull's-eyes and Christmas chocolates. In the row in front a woman cracked nuts with a nutcracker. The film was a comedy, Mickey Rooney as Andy Hardy. In the darkness we held hands.

The bus did not leave for half-an-hour after we left the cinema. There was a café open at the bus station, and we sat at a marbled table there, facing each other drinking cups of tea.

'Why is it like this?' she asked soberly. 'Is it because we've both been disappointed in other people?'

'I don't know. It's just very strange.'

She said: 'I shall miss you. Until tomorrow I won't know how much but I only know I'll miss you.'

Our fingers contacted briefly across the damp pale green table. The bus driver came into the café and called out the names of half-a-dozen villages. We went out and boarded the bus, sitting unspeaking against each other while everyone around was laughing at what they had enjoyed at the pantomime or the pictures.

It was quieter in the bar that evening. Paula served me a dinner of cold turkey in the kitchen, and afterwards I sat on a stool and talked to Jeff behind the bar about his days at sea. He closed up at ten-thirty, and Paula suggested he went to bed while we cleared up. There was not much to do and after half-an-hour we had finished. She suddenly went to the door and pulling the long black-out curtain around her like a cloak looked out. 'There's a moon,' she called back to me. 'The rain's gone.'

I went to the door, putting my arm around the curtain draped about her shoulders. The moon was crouching among some trees as though wondering whether it was wise to venture further. 'Shall we go for a walk?' she suggested. Without waiting for an answer she turned and took her coat from the peg behind the door leading to the bar. I helped it around her slight shoulders then I pulled on my duffle.

We went out into the yard, pulling the door quietly closed. She looked up at her father's bedroom, the curtains drawn and in darkness.

'We'll go a-roving by the light of the moon,' I whispered.

'But not very far,' she whispered in return. 'Give me your hand.'

We went around the corner of the inn across the cobbles of the stable yard. Faintly, a dog sounded. Everywhere else was as silent as the moon.

Her profile was pale and composed, her hair had turned black. We walked cautiously over the cobbles and to the door of the stable where Billy had kept his horse. It was secured by a peg of wood. She released my fingers, took out the peg and with a touch of her hand pushed the door easily inwards.

Inside the darkness was split by wedges of light shining through the many cracks in the old wooden walls. 'It's always warm in here,' she whispered.

We pushed the door behind us, turned face to face and, with a great and happy relief, fell towards each other, arms about bodies, lips to lips. She was throbbing against me. 'We're not going to worry about this,' she said as though to assure both of us. 'After tonight we may never see each other again.'

We kissed again, her legs against mine, her small breasts pressed to my chest. She led me to the back of the stable where there were bales of straw. 'We keep it here for Billy,' she said as though an explanation was needed. 'He doesn't have enough storage space in his little barn, because he has . . . to . . . use it . . .' Her hands went to my thighs and she rubbed me softly '. . . as a stable . . . for Dobbo.'

'Dobbo?' I asked stupidly.

'Billy's horse,' she said. She first took her coat and laid it across the straw. 'Keep yours on,' she instructed almost absently. 'It will keep us both warm.' We clutched each other. 'My God, I'm going to enjoy you,' she said. We dropped onto the straw and made love there, my duffle coat still on my back but spreading over us like a blanket. She held onto me fiercely, beginning to cry.

The straw was warm about us, the moon striping our moving bodies. For strangers we knew each other very well and we were grateful for each other and for our understanding of each other. A sudden lightness came upon her, as though a burden had gone. Our smiles beamed through the half-light. 'I could not come to your bed,' she whispered. 'I wanted to, but I couldn't.'

'Jeff?' I said.

'I wouldn't let myself,' she said.

Her smile became impish. 'Let me have your duffle,' she suggested. I took it off and gave it to her. She rolled away from me, her exposed skin glowing white in the shadow, and put the coat hugely on her back. Then she pushed me easily back into the straw and sat over me, astride, moving her legs up my thighs, the coat like a thick, engulfing tent around us. Her taut breasts looked down like staring eyes as she leaned over me and easily brought me into her again.

I left at six-thirty the next morning. Billy called to take me to Hereford where he had to deliver some bread. I said goodbye to Jeff and paid my bill of three pounds, seventeen shillings and threepence. Paula wrapped in her coat came to the door in the dark and we kissed while Billy was attending to the horse.

'I do hope we will see each other again,' she said. Her eyes came fully into mine.

'Of course we will. We will write to each other. You will write to me?'

'Yes. Let me know where. Goodbye.'

'Goodbye Paula.'

Billy came back from fussing with the horse. 'Dobbo don't like getting up these mornings. He likes his warm straw.'

We smiled at each other when he said that, then I kissed her on her pale cheek and she kissed me on the ear. Again we said our farewells and I climbed up on the baker's van. Billy snapped the reins and the horse trotted away along the straight bleak road towards Hereford, towards the train, towards Avonmouth, towards the sea, towards the war.

Four

One thing has never left me in all my years of travelling the sea, and that is the experience of going south in winter. Off Cape Finisterre, in Spain, the seasons alter; the dark of the north, with its snow, rain and stormy days, softens within a few hours, and the ship is pushing on through deep blue, almost black, sea; fat, lazy waves are embroidered with white hems that now and again glisten like splintered glass in the touch of the sun. The sky often remains grey but the breeze is warm. White unhurried birds follow the mast as it moves towards the summer of the southern ocean.

Even the anxieties of a war passage could not damage this feeling; indeed it was almost as if the transition were a frontier, not only between climes but between danger and safety. The sun came out and someone played a gramophone on the foredeck.

That was the first time I was ever aware of the change, on the voyage which began after Christmas from Avonmouth. My temporary happiness over the things that had occurred, Paula, and the warmth of that drab, damp village, ebbed away as the train wound its tedious way west and arrived at Bristol; Bristol, always a crossroads for me. I waited in the rain for a bus to Avonmouth. It was half-an-hour late.

'Been waiting long, mate?' inquired the conductor dolefully.

'Since Christmas Eve,' I said putting my sea-bag under the stairs.

'You had a better time than I did then,' he grunted

punching a ticket. He handed it to me and nodded at the sea-bag. 'Getting out of all this then,' he said. 'The bloody rain and the bloody war.'

'The war's out there as well,' I told him.

'I wouldn't know,' he shrugged. 'My legs are unfit for service.'

He ran up the stairs to the top deck. A woman with a scarf tied around her fat face, as if she had toothache, leaned over from the seat across the aisle. 'He's a scream, he is,' she confided. 'You need people like him to cheer you up these days.'

At Avonmouth I trudged a mile to the ship. She was taking on cargo; she displaced ten thousand tons, American-built, an anti-aircraft gun at her stern, depth charges along her rail, and a pair of rapid-firing pom-poms forward of the bridge. She was called the *Jasper Johnson* and we sailed just after midnight. By New Year's Day, the opening of that fateful year of nineteen-forty, we were in the southern ocean destined for Cape Town.

That entire year I occupied voyaging far from the dangers of home. From Cape Town to Mombasa, to India, Madras and Bombay, to the East and to Australia and the Pacific. From each place I sent letters to Dolly and to Paula. No response came from Dolly but in Sydney I received three letters from Paula. They had followed the ship. The third told me she was pregnant.

'Tim, my husband, eventually got some leave in early January and we were together for a week, here at Packwick and in London. I find I am expecting a baby. I will write to you some time and tell you whether it is a boy or a girl.'

Sitting on deck in the peace and the autumn sunshine of Sydney, with the harbour and the hills of the city around, I felt the gulf of the world, of life, and circumstances between us. The last sentence was as firm a goodbye as I had ever known. I kept the three letters. In the light of what happened they were read again years later and even now I still have them. They are in my trunk.

It was strange knowing of no danger while the German armies were invading France, far away. The ship was moored in the middle of the harbour, just prior to sailing for Auckland. On the final night I was returning with three of the crew from shore leave at midnight. We were all sober, for that captain would take no drunks, and we were about to sail; but the man in charge of the boat, a little journeyman who took his business anywhere in the harbour, was wildly drunk.

He was singing and turning the boat to port, to starboard, to port, across the night harbour, in time with his song. We did not take much notice since those sort of men are frequently like that; it is to do with the frustration of being penned within a harbour. It was very dark. We were halfway across to the ship when I saw the red and green bow lights of a vessel on a cross course to us. It was close and closing. 'Ship to starboard!' I shouted.

'Where?' he bawled back.

'Starboard!' It could have been my last word. He threw the tiller the wrong way and we struck the oncoming bow head on. She was only a coaster but she was big enough to lift us from the water and throw us aside like driftwood. I actually felt the steel of her hull as I was flung aside from the boat, pushing at it hopelessly with my hands. Something struck me on the head and I woke up floating among debris in the harbour. In those few moments of consciousness my only thought was sharks.

'Plenty of munchies in the harbour,' said the man in the next bed. 'They must have gone to doss or they'd have had you, mate.'

I was there for three weeks with a broken leg, concussion and bruises. One of my shipmates and the boatman were drowned. The ship had sailed without me and I was left in Sydney, first at the hospital, then at a seamen's convalescent home, and finally at a dockside hostel.

A padre came to see me, a pale and mirthful man from the

Missions to Seamen. 'Ever hear the story of the bloke called Jones, like you, who went to heaven?' he said. He sat on his hands, like a boy. 'After a bit his widow, she died too, and she went up there and told St Peter she wanted to contact her husband. Now there's a lot of Joneses in heaven, and he asked her if her old man had a nickname. "No", she says. "All I know is that when he was dying he said if I went with another bloke he'd turn in his grave." 'Oh, right, mate,' says St Peter. 'I know him. We call him Revolving Jones.'

The union sent an official to the hostel, where I was anxious to ship out. 'Got one berth. Sailing for Panama,' he said. 'Suit you?'

Eagerly I said it would and that night I went down to Port Jackson and stood, astonished, on the wharf. There she was, the *Spirit of Lupus*, a four-masted barque, covered with ropes and rubbish, waiting to sail for the South Seas.

She was a romantic mess; caked hull, tangled rigging, unwashed deck, rusty ironwork; a slovenly ship, an unkempt native crew, a suicidal captain and his wife who believed she could sing opera. But when the prow was bowing to the long blue waves of the Pacific and her grubby sails were full of the trade winds she was a beauty. We sailed up into the islands, in those days tatty places with lagoons for harbours and villages made from coconut palms. We traded in copra and in things the natives wanted like sewing machines and cigarettes.

On the first morning of the voyage we had just cleared Sydney Heads and I was working on the foredeck. The sea was brilliant in the first sun, the wind like velvet. An echoing shriek came from the bridge, and there was Darwina Tumble, the captain's wife, singing. I was her only audience and she resounded above me. Gulls shied affronted from the ship.

It was grand opera, I think; the breeze adding to the scene by flying her mass of ringletted, black hair straight out behind her. Her face was wide and handsome, her mouth huge. She was wearing yellow pyjamas and they swelled as she struggled to the apex of the aria. She never reached it.

She faltered to a stop, breathed profoundly again then, eyes on the sky, flung aside the bulging silk pyjama jacket. A pair of breasts like tureens were exposed. They seemed to expand before my astonished eyes as she pitched again towards the climax of her performance. I crouched behind the forward lifeboat.

There were four Kanakas, natives of the Pacific islands, as crew and one of them appeared that morning and cautiously looking about him, said: 'Missus done sing-song.' I came out from behind the lifeboat.

The captain was morose and often threatened to take his own life. He regularly told the crew that he was going to set the *Lupus* ablaze when they were distant from land and help, or that he was going to run her across a reef in some waters infamous for sharks.

Five days out we made an evening landfall on a small island in the Austral group south of Tahiti, where the barque was greeted by the chief and his wives and special natives. They were in need of fresh cigarettes and they had to get their copra out, but their real anticipation was for the arrival of the great singing white woman.

We sat in the centre of the village and ate pigs, chickens, a turtle and a goat, in the company of the elders of the island, with the children and most of the women standing outside the main circle. Bottled beer and native potions were drunk and the prime moment of the night was heralded by a single thud on a tribal drum followed by a flurry on the ukelele by the chief, a mountainous man, his stomachs folding like aprons over his grass skirt.

Darwina Tumble, in a necklace of shark's teeth and a skirt as big as a native hut, pounded to the centre of the gathering, the cooking fire at her back, throwing her form into massive silhouette. The islanders seemed dumb with excitement. You could hear the distant breaking of waves against the reef. The chief gave a single plonk on his ukelele and she flung herself into an aria. She bellowed, she trilled, she howled, she warbled and wavered, she performed little childish jumps when she got to a coquettish part, and her fine large face was wet with tears and perspiration as she trampled on the last of the song. The natives were ecstatic. Captain Tumble, a leg of pig in one hand and a pot of drink poised before his mouth, nodded.

Darwina, encouraged, took a bite of goat, wiped her mouth with the back of her hand, and launched into a loud lullaby. The islanders were hopping, the chief planging ecstatically on his ukelele. The applause at the end shook the palm trees.

'Right!' bawled Darwina triumphantly. 'Right you are then, mates. Community singing. How about "You Are My Sunshine"?' The rapture which greeted this announcement would be impossible to describe. They howled, they pounded their feet until the ground trembled, they waved their arms, and then at the flick of her fat finger they dropped to silence. She began and they followed, not far behind.

> 'You are my sunshine, my only sunshine,
> You make me happy, when skies are grey.'

The words proved too complex for many of the singers, and the tune for all of them. It was a mad cacophony, two hundred wild natives all singing different songs, the chief banging his furious ukelele and Mrs Tumble howling above all. It was riotous, the most hideous noise, everyone bellowing at the pitch of their tuneless voices. Eventually the whole nightmare collapsed, fell to bits, and an exhausted silence dropped over the place. The chief lifted his ukelele and cried out triumphantly and everyone cried out too, none more loudly than Darwina Tumble.

The weather turned fitful. Captain Tumble stood beside the helmsman at intervals during the rougher passages, utterly silent, staring straight towards some destiny that we could not know.

He had spoken no more than a dozen words to me since I joined the *Lupus*. I quartered with the natives in the stern where the barque bucked most in the bigger seas. The

Kanakas tended the sails, graceful and strong as the sails themselves. My duties were on deck, stowing, cleaning and painting. We scarcely saw another ship and those we saw were far away. It was as though we had sailed into an oblivious world.

Another island drew itself up from the horizon as the sea eased and Darwina appeared on the upper deck and performed deep breathing exercises. By evening we had slipped through the reef and into the lucid pond of the lagoon. On shore was waiting another eager committee of natives.

The cigarettes and the sewing machines were unloaded. Every hut had a sewing machine although the natives had need of few clothes. They were used for other purposes. Some of the island boats used them as anchors.

'This is not a singing island,' Darwina Tumble confided to me on the jetty. I was surprised that she spoke. 'It's a dancing tribe.'

That evening after the feast Darwina sang to them and the tone-deaf natives joined in 'You Are My Sunshine'. There was a tremendous moon and the villagers danced. At first it was sedate, the music provided by boys playing pipes and tapping drums, but later it became lively. The moon looked like a window behind the palms. There were ukeleles. The young girls of this island had sweet breasts and eyes and it was not unknown for them to offer themselves to visiting sailors.

One of the men told me that the chief wanted to speak with me. He was sitting, beer bottle in hand, behind a wooden table and beside him, in an upholstered armchair, was an old lady with a finely gnarled face framed by a few feathers.

Captain Tumble appeared. 'The chief,' he explained, 'wants you to dance with his mother. She likes you because you're young. It's her birthday.'

The chief added something which I did not understand. I

gave a short bow and held my hand out to the old lady. There was a stirring among the islanders.

It took two natives to get the chief's mother to her feet. Her eyes were deep holes but far down they shone sharply at me. Her arms were clanging with bangles, and she took some of these off before she was helped to the dancing area. I followed.

It was the strangest dance. We remained on the same spot, me holding her upright, not easy because she was a wide woman, while she turned in a slow but rhythmic circle. We swayed in time with the flutes, the drums and the ukelele. Everyone else had cleared the floor and was standing, smiling but intent, at the edge, while we performed our long and graceful pirouette at the centre. She was a grand old lady; her sunken eyes were bright and she smiled at me like a tortoise. The dance did not last long. She said one word, and not loudly, but the music ceased and the same two natives came to transport her back to her armchair, this time carrying her, for she was tired. I gave a short appropriate bow again, and the chief's mother sat down amid silence, although once she was seated there was a great outburst of clapping and shouting. I could feel myself blushing. Genially the captain beckoned me over. Darwina Tumble began to sing: 'For He's a Jolly Good Fellow', a song parts of which the natives knew for they joined in lustily.

The chief rose from behind his table and reaching over put a wheel from a sewing machine, on a long bootlace, around my neck. 'That's a great honour,' Captain Tumble pointed out. The chief said something profoundly and the captain translated: 'His mother thanks you too. She enjoyed the dance.'

When they came to carry the old lady back to her hut at the end of the evening, they found she was dead. The natives began wailing and I began to feel insecure. The chief kissed his mother's leathery hands and they bore her away still in the armchair. He turned to me and my heart quaked. With difficulty he assembled a sentence: 'My mamma was a hundred years old this day,' he said.

When once more we were in the open ocean Mrs Tumble resumed her brazen-breasted arias from the front of the wheelhouse. The sea was benign and at night there were extravagant stars, below which she sang.

The captain, however, scarcely appeared at all, leaving the steering and navigation to the helmsman. The crew knew the signs and frowned. He was visited by bad ghosts and seaborn moods. He imagined drowned sailors rising from the depths and voices calling on the trades. He drank prodigiously and when the vessel veered the bottles could be heard rolling. The natives repaired a breach in the lifeboat.

We were heading north-west towards the Solomons and I suspected that as soon as we reached Honiara we would lose the crew. The weather worsened, there was a chop on the sea, winds came flat and low, there were towers of copper clouds. Then it rained as it can only rain in those latitudes. We were off the reefs of the Dongas Strait at gone midnight, the helmsman staring into the streaming blackness, watching the blink of the lighthouse on Suna Island, easing the nervous vessel away from the shoals. All the sails were stowed and we were moving under the poor power of the auxiliary engine, making scarcely two knots. Sometimes it appears that we were going backwards. I have never been afraid of bad weather but the *Lupus* was creaking and straining more plaintively than any vessel I had ever heard before. She dipped and rolled and a wracked breathing came from her lungs. The wind wanged through the rigging like a harp. It was sullen and dangerous, no night to be at sea.

It was also no night for the captain to go mad. But he did. As mad as any captain has ever gone. We were off the Suna Island light, edging closer, with the Kanaka helmsman putting all his skill and muscle into keeping us off the reef, when Captain Tumble appeared in the wheelhouse. I had just brought the helmsman a cup of Oxo which the skipper knocked from my hands with a shivering cry. The blow thrust me back against the bulwark. The helmsman shouted a warning. The captain, bellowing oaths, crimson-eyed and stark-faced, caught hold of him and threw him against me. The door was next to my arm and, wanting to get out, I opened it letting in the wind and the drenching rain. With a howl Captain Tumble turned and flung us both out. We fell down the ladder on to the pitching deck. He slammed and barred the door and turned the *Lupus* hard to starboard.

'Reef,' said the soaked helmsman pitifully. 'Skipper steer for reef.'

His compatriots, alarmed by the sharp alteration of course, fell out onto the deck. Tumble was bellowing from the wheelhouse, his shouts above the beating rain and shrieking wind.

'The lighthouse,' I muttered. I shouted: 'He's heading for the lighthouse!'

The Kanakas began to throw rubbish from the lifeboat. 'Get missus!' I shouted. 'Get missus quick!'

She was already there. She staggered onto the deck, for once truly like a figure from grand opera. 'What's the fucking bastard up to?' she howled.

'He's going to ram the light! We'll go on the reef!' I shouted back. 'Can't you do something with him?'

'*You* do something!' she demanded. 'Break the bloody door down!'

We rushed up the ladder, getting in each other's way, desperately trying to force the door. It would not give. The bars were made to withstand a mutiny.

It was an incredible scene: the black night, the battering rain and the wind, the waves coming over the side like grasping hands, the sea picking us up and careering us relentlessly towards the reef. The lighthouse seemed to flash more rapidly, as though in panic. The Kanakas could not shift the lifeboat. Frantically they tried to sort out life vests. Darwina Tumble was stretched flat against the pitching bulkhead, each hand clutching a stanchion, legs thrust apart, chest thrust out. She began to sing.

The howl of her voice above the wind stopped the Kanakas in their search for life vests. I turned and saw her, great soaked arms and bosom, rigid thighs, splattered hair and streaming face, mouth open against the storm. She sang what I now know is the Easter Hymn from 'Cavalleria rusticana' by Mascagni:

> 'O rejoice, for the Lord has arisen,
> O rejoice, he has burst from the prison.'

At the pitch of all this, the storm and the hymn, and the impending doom, Captain Tumble flung open the door to the wheelhouse and stood crazily waving his arms at us and the heavens. 'Stand by to ram the lighthouse!' he bellowed.

We rammed it ten seconds later. We struck the reef and the vessel was thrown up like a racehorse at a jump. The bow slithered over the coral and struck the short lighthouse true amidships. The impact was tremendous. The bow went into it like a knife, splitting the wood and coral from which it was made. The light was actually thrown from its mounting and crashed onto the forepeak. There was instant blackness. I was thrown back against the bulkhead with Mrs Tumble. We hung together while the drama crashed around us. The hull cracked and the masts snapped like knitting needles. The noise was too great to hear any cries. Then the impact abruptly ceased and the *Lupus* slithered sideways over the reef. All the breath was knocked from me by the collision with Mrs Tumble. I was clutching onto the great wet woman; the next moment she was on top of me, then we had been swept over the rail and into the enclosed waters of the lagoon. We were saved.

The sun, rising mockingly after the bad night, roused me. I was imprinted in the black, volcanic, sand. Mrs Tumble was lying on her back a few yards away, her large form projecting from the beach like an island itself. She was snoring. Aching, I eased myself into a sitting posture and looked out at the lagoon, flat and innocent, and beyond it the feathered reef. The stump of the lighthouse stood like a broken tooth. There was no sign of the ship.

'It's gone,' said Darwina firmly from my right. She was sitting up in her own impression in the sand. We had made two perfect moulds. 'It's gone and so is Tumble. Good riddance, both of them.'

'We ought to go and see,' I suggested. 'He might be out there on the reef.'

'I don't *want* to find him,' she replied belligerently.

'What about the boys?' I said looking around. The beach curved, black as a tarmac road, to each side of us, but the view behind was blocked by crowded palms.

'They'll turn up,' she said confidently. 'Those Kanakas always save their own skins, don't worry. I wonder, is there anything to drink?'

Her big, dried head turned one way, then the other, as if she expected to see a conveniently open bar. 'And eat,' she added. 'I wouldn't mind a pork pie.'

Incredibly some figures appeared on the reef near the stunted lighthouse, and we quickly saw that it was our crew and they were carrying burdens. They came over the coral, splashed through the shallows of the lagoon, and approached along the sand. 'Skipper gone,' said the headman smiling. 'Sharks got him okay.' He nodded to the boxes they bore. 'We get tucker before ship gone.' They produced a large and unsoaked carton of Australian meat pies. Darwina selected two of these as if she had known they would arrive. She bit deeply into one, still sitting in her outline in the black sand, and then took a bite at the other, presumably to prevent anyone else claiming it. 'I've got to tell you something,' she said to me, the pie rammed and rolling in her mouth. 'My real name is not Darwina.'

We each had a pork pie and there were some bottles of beer. The boys sat diffidently a little distance off, talking deeply among themselves. 'What's your real name then?' I asked.

She swallowed heavily and washed it down with a swig of beer. 'Beryl,' she replied. 'Darwina was my stage name. I'm from Darwin, see, like Melba called herself after Melbourne. But she had the luck.'

'What are you going to do now?' I asked.

'Have another pork pie,' she said taking one from the carton. The boys stopped conversing and looked around at her as though the pies had been counted. 'I mean, what will you do from now on?' I said.

'Get rescued and start again,' she replied easily. 'Tumble was no bloody good anyway. Drunken old thing.' A little admiration came into her face and her voice. 'Still, he rammed a lighthouse. Not many men have done that.'

I agreed and we sat staring at the sea. 'I'm going home,' I said. 'As soon as I can.'

'There's a war on,' she pointed out. 'You'd be better off staying out of that lot. Stay out here where it's safe. Come back to Aussie with me. You can be my manager.' She paused and added: 'We could go to Broome.'

The boys had spied something out to sea, and were chattering and pointing. A boat appeared, moving quite swiftly, heading for the gap in the reef. 'We're going to be rescued, sod it,' grumbled Darwina. 'I wouldn't have minded staying here a month or two.'

As though seeking consolation she picked up the final pork pie and gnashed at it. The headman looked at her but she returned the stare steadily and he turned his attention back to the arriving boat. It was chugging into the shallows now. It stopped and a white man, his pot-belly slung above a pair of massive shorts, dropped into the lagoon and waded ponderously towards us. 'You knocked the fucking lighthouse down!' he complained in an Australian voice and when he was still in the water. 'How d'you come to do that, for Christ's sake?'

'It got in the way of the fucking boat,' Darwina belliger-ently howled back.

He appeared to know when he was outcursed and as he reached the beach he came up quite decently and asked us if we were all right. 'Noticed the light had gone at three this morning,' he said. 'But I wasn't coming out then. I'm on Manacuna.' He nodded towards the blank horizon. 'Over there. We'd better get you of here.'

Obediently we stood. He took note of our outlines in the black sand. 'Like coal dust this stuff,' he said.

'I was brought up with coal dust,' I said. We were wading out to his boat.

'You're a Pommie,' he said.

'Welsh,' I said.

'Still a Pom,' he shrugged. He helped Darwina over the gunwhale of the boat, with the aid of the crew, a major lifting job. 'Well, the war's over,' he said to me.

'Over!' I felt the joy run through me. 'They surrendered!'

'Who's "They"?' he said.

'The Germans, Hitler,' I answered slowly.

'Not on your life,' he said staring at me. 'That bugger went through France and everywhere like a dose of dysentry. France, the lot. France packed it in. Then England packed it in.'

'We gave up?'

'So I heard they reckoned over the radio. The King's in prison. Churchill was shot. It's all over, mate. You'd be better off staying on that beach.'

That the news was less than the truth I did not know until I reached Honiara in the Solomons a week later. The time between was miserable, fearing what the Nazi storm troopers might do to Dolly, thinking of poor garrulous Uncle Griff being executed for abuse, wondering if Hitler would spare Paula and the Stag's Head.

There was an American freighter lying off Honiara and one of the crew told me that the war was not over, that the

King was not behind bars, and that Churchill remained unshot. Wireless reception in the smaller islands was notoriously uncertain. He took me over to the vessel and we listened to a news broadcast from Manila which confirmed the truth.

'I've got to get home,' I said to the radio officer. 'Somehow I've got to.'

He took me to the captain who at once signed me on as an extra deckman. 'It's against the book,' he said shaking my hand. 'But who cares? One more guy to fight those bastards. That's good enough for me. Welcome aboard.'

We sailed to Honolulu and then to San Francisco. There I was issued with twenty dollars and new papers by the British Consul and given a railway warrant which took me across the United States to New York. I had to change trains in Chicago and at the station were four young men who were going to join in the war too. 'I've just got to get to London,' said one in his adopted American voice. They all agreed. 'And quick,' said another.

We had to board the train. The whistles blew over my reply and the engine hooted. Some people had come to see them off, the men straight-faced, the women weeping. Not wanting to disturb their farewells, I moved along to another window. As the engine steamed and hooted and we began to move away, I saw arms projecting from the carriage ahead of me and the people on the platform drawn up, their palms raised flatly in the Nazi salute. I got off at the first station and waited all night and all day for the next train.

After only one night in the seamen's hostel on 23rd Street, New York City, I was handed another rail warrant and another five dollars and told to go south to Wilmington, Delaware, to join a British ship leaving for Liverpool. I had been away and out of touch for so long it was difficult to think what the war was like; armies over-running entire strong countries, refugees, tanks rolling on roads, air battles. Every day the American newspapers were full of photographs of the bunkered British watching through binoculars, of criss-crossed skies and dive bombers over the Channel coast.

On the train, the moment I spoke, the whole compartment became alert and interested. One woman pressed fruit on me. 'You're British,' she said. 'You must be hungry.'

It was no use explaining that I had been in the South Seas. They would have none of it. I was British so I must have been in danger. Under their insistence I admitted that I had, in fact, been torpedoed a year before. The woman who had donated the fruit – I was by now eating a huge peach – began crying, her cheeks as wet as my chin. A man in a gingery coat demanded to know my address in Wilmington, and I had to tell him it was the Seamen's Mission Hostel but that I was expecting to sail for England within a day. At this another woman began to weep, and an old man, stuffed with emotion, stood up and cried: 'We got to wipe out those Nazi bums!'

They chorused: 'Kill 'em. Kill the Nazi bums!' People from other parts of the train began to gather and join in. 'Let's get the doughboys over there!' One man shouted and some began to sing: 'Over there! Over there! The Yanks are coming, over there!' There was an embarrassing attempt to sing 'God Save the King' with everyone emotionally standing, swaying with the train, which I had to lead because I was the only one who knew all the words. It did not subside until we reached Wilmington by which time I was dotted with lipstick and damp from women's weeping. My hand had been pumped and my shoulders pounded. Five dollars and a packet of chewing gum had been slipped into my pocket.

The man who had wanted my address had not merely taken it in the moment's emotion. I had been at the hostel for only three hours and was eating a steak in the canteen when I saw the superintendent pointing me out to a man wearing a grey suit and an alert expression who marched briskly to the table and said in a British accent: 'You're Jones, I believe.' His left eye had a flicker in it.

'Yes,' I said. 'Sir.'

'Good chap, Jones,' he said. He bent over the table, confidingly. His eye increased its twitching and it was difficult not to look at it. Others were eating at the long board but they were out of earshot. He said: 'Must have words with you, Jones. Matter of national importance. But finish your chow, old chap.'

In the superintendent's office amid piles of books, magazines and used clothes, and a German helmet with a hole in it bearing the date '1917', he introduced himself. 'Walmsley,' he said. 'Lieutenant Commander actually. But since we're here, Stateside as it were, you can call me Mr Walmsley.'

'Thank you, Mr Walmsley,' I said.

'I'm based in Washington,' he continued. 'My job being to keep the Yanks on our side, chivvy them along. Propaganda, the Boche would call it. We call it Information. We just like them to know that we're a bonny lot of chaps fighting a war for them until such time as they see fit to join in.' He nodded to the holed helmet. 'It was nineteen seventeen last time,' he said. 'We can't wait as long as that again.'

'It looks like we're losing, doesn't it, Mr Walmsley?' I said.

'We're most certainly not winning,' he said glancing around. 'We're hanging on by our toenails.' His eyelid fluttered.

'When I was in the Pacific I heard that we were finished,' I told him. 'Churchill was dead and the King was behind bars.'

'You know how rumours spread,' he sighed. 'We should have better propaganda.' He became briefly thoughtful. 'Perhaps we should open an office out there. Honolulu, somewhere like that.'

'Why did you want me?' I asked. 'I'm sailing tomorrow morning.'

'You're not,' he said briskly as though glad to be sure of something. 'You're off that trip. I've arranged that. You're here for at least a week. You'll be helping to get America into the war on our side.'

'Me?'

'That chappie you spoke to on the train, the one who knew where to find you . . .'

'I gave him this address. He kept on. I thought it would be all right.'

'Certainly, certainly. There's a limit to all this secrecy stuff. He passed it to Mrs Eleanor Colling, who's a big-wig here in Wilmington, chairman of the Aid to Britain Committee. On Saturday they are having a parade to demonstrate their support for our war effort. They want you to carry the flag at the front.'

I was flabbergasted. 'The flag?'

'*Our* flag. The Union Jack,' he said a little testily. 'You're British, you've seen action, you're big and strong enough to carry quite a decent-sized flag. You're our man, Jones.'

I was trying to gather my thoughts. 'But when will I get a ship?' I said.

'Eventually.' His eye dropped like a wink. 'If this comes off we could have you carrying the jolly flag all over the place. Every state.' The idea had just come to him and he liked it. 'My word, that would be a thing!'

'I'd rather not, Mr Walmsley,' I said firmly. 'I want to go home.'

He looked astonished. 'Back there?' he said. A flush of delayed patriotism flew over his face. Twitching like a signal, he patted my shoulder. 'Stout man,' he said.

'My wife . . .' I began.

'Ah yes. Well, I've got a wife over there too. Worried to death about her. God bless our brave wives, I say.' He looked at me as powerfully as his twitch would allow. 'But war is war,' he intoned. 'Like jolly old Sister Anna, you must carry the banner.'

'Yes, I see,' I said.

'Good. We must get you a uniform.' He turned side on and sized me up with his stable eye. 'You don't have a uniform do you?'

'Uniform? No. I'm Merchant Navy, Mr Walmsley. I

haven't even got my badge now. I lost the lot in the Pacific. They were going to fit me out with some gear here.'

'No uniform' he mused, 'No badge.' He grimaced. 'Not that a badge would do much good. Nobody would spot that in a parade. You'll have to wear something.'

'What's the matter with my sea-going gear,' I suggested. 'I can get fitted out today.'

He remained thoughtful. 'That's no good,' he decided. 'A sou'wester might help. A nice yellow one.' He sighed. 'No, you'll have to have a uniform. The Yanks won't understand if you march in your everyday togs, sea-going or not. If you're in a war you've got to have a uniform. That's the American philosophy. Jesus, there are people here already decking themselves out with tunics and hats and even medals and they're not even in it yet.'

'What sort of uniform?' I asked guardedly.

'We might have to temporarily transfer you to the Royal Navy,' he said. 'Or the Marines. If we can get hold of Merchant Navy officer's rig then so much the better, but it's got to fit you. They won't like it if it doesn't fit. Bad propaganda.' He patted me on the shoulder. 'Don't worry, Jones. We'll solve it somehow. If I can't get the genuine article, I did see a shop in Wilmington that does carnival novelties and fancy dress and that sort of thing. Perhaps they'll have something.'

'I could go as Nelson,' I said unhappily.

The uniform was genuine, that of a second officer in the Merchant Navy. It even had a medal ribbon on the breast. When I put it on and looked at myself in the mirror at the Seamen's Mission I realised what might have been. I marched at the head of the parade in Wilmington that day, immediately in front of another British sailor decked out in a combination of oddment clothing.

'It's sort of half boy scout, half fire brigade,' he decided. He smiled mischievously. 'With a dash of Women's Land Army.'

He was neat and bright-faced. 'My name's Malcolme,' he said. The smile spread again: 'With a final "e".' Before the parade he checked his strange outfit; khaki shirt, blue trousers and pointed hat. 'These lollipops won't know,' he said. 'I'll tell them I'm in the Royal Fuckabouts. Yanks will believe anything.'

We marched with modesty and style. The Union Jack was a heavy one and my arms ached by the end of the three miles through the decked streets of the town. Thousands turned out to cheer and the bands played bravely. At the end of it Lieutenant Commander Walmsley arrived at the dispersal point while we were drinking lemonade and congratulated us. 'That should bring them into the war in no time,' he enthused. He took me aside. 'Mrs Colling has asked that you go to the party at her house tonight,' he said. He glanced at Malcolme. 'Foskins they haven't invited because they can't quite make him out. What was he supposed to be today, by the way?'

He asked Foskins. 'I don't know,' replied the lively man. 'I just put on whatever fitted. I thought I looked rather fetching.' He placed the pointed hat on his head at an angle. 'I may wear this when I go out tonight,' he smirked. 'Maybe I'll put a feather in it.'

I asked Walmsley if I should wear the second officer's uniform to Mrs Colling's house. 'You *must*,' he insisted. 'That's a certainty. They want to see you in your uniform.'

'But I'm not entitled to it.'

'I've cleared it with the British Embassy,' he said. 'It's counted as part of the war effort.'

'It would be a help if I knew what the medal was,' I said.

He peered at it closely but inconclusively. 'We could look it up, I suppose,' he suggested. 'On the other hand, just be vague – they'll like that.'

At the party I told them it was for learning to tie knots. 'You British,' chided Mrs Colling as we danced. It was a white, wide house with a colonnade and long windows opening out onto a terrace and the warm garden. 'You're so modest. I won't ask you how you *really* got it. I know it will embarrass you.' She was a handsome woman with red hair and glistening eyes. Her outstanding chest was under my chin as we danced. 'Tell me about when you were in action,' she whispered.

I did my best to smile disarmingly. 'Commander,' she called to Walmsley who was seated casually in a wicker chair surrounded by other guests.

'Madam?' he replied.

'This young man flatly refuses to tell me about his medal. And he won't say a word about being in action.'

'Oh, he's been in action,' Walmsley loudly confirmed. 'He's been torpedoed.'

All around the table they gasped. Mrs Colling led me solicitously from the floor and a man stood up insisting that I took his seat as if I had just been dragged dying from the water. A drink was pressed into my hand. 'Tell us, *please*,' begged Mrs Colling breathlessly. 'We all want to hear.'

Their eyes were expectant. Some of the women were beautiful in the way that rich American women are. For a moment I had a memory of Mrs Tingley sitting in bed on the *Orion*. One woman reminded me strongly of her. She leaned over the table, her bosom below her silk dress sliding and coming to rest on it. Her eyes were intense.

Consoling myself that I was merely telling the truth, I began: 'It was a strange business. Because war had only been declared a couple of days before. We had hardly cleared Kinsale in Ireland . . .'

They listened avidly, glasses suspended halfway to lips. When I had finished Mrs Colling began clapping. Everyone joined it. 'Now you must dance with me,' said the woman with silken bosom and intense eyes. 'I insist.'

She led me to the floor and arranged her bloused chest against me. After we had danced she kissed me on the cheek. 'You poor boy,' she murmured. 'And by golly, how brave.'

I had several more drinks and then went up the main staircase and along the gallery at the top to the bathroom. It was luxurious, entirely white; porcelain, walls, towels and carpet. As I pulled the catch to leave I felt the door pushed inwards and there was the lady with whom I had danced.

'Oh, sorry,' I said. 'I didn't realise . . .'

She pushed her way in very firmly. I took a step back. She faced me, pinned me with her startling eyes and, with her hands behind her back, clicked the bolt closed again. 'My name is Deborah Michael,' she said. 'I think you ought to know that for a start.' Then she slid her marvellous arms about my neck. I felt myself stiffen all over. Her lips came to mine. Her eyes remained open, examining my astonished face. 'You're very nice-looking,' she said. I thought they would hear my heart beating over the sound of the band downstairs. We kissed with great enjoyment. 'My husband won't miss me,' she mumbled.

'Your . . . your husband?' I repeated easing myself from her.

'He's downstairs,' she said. She came up against me again, kissing me and unbuttoning my trousers. 'Full of gin.'

'But . . . we can't . . .' I stumbled. 'Not here. Like this.'

'We can and right here like this,' she replied, her voice loaded. 'It's my contribution to Britain's war effort. My admiration.'

She fell to her knees and, as though she was used to dealing with sons, pulled my trousers and underpants to my ankles. She clutched my legs. 'What fine British thighs you have,' she muttered. 'And, just look at that! My God, it looks brand new. I must kiss it!'

I stumbled back and sat on the quilted cover of the lavatory lid. I felt my eyes bulge. At any moment I expected her husband to be rattling at the door. My hands went to her breasts. 'Take them out,' she demanded disengaging only briefly. 'I want you to have them.'

They were exquisite, pale cream and like large fruits. We swivelled and she fell onto the white floor. 'It's all right,' she assured me strangely. 'I go to ballet class.' She put her hand around me and like someone using a pulley tugged me down onto my knees. 'Don't go away,' she whispered. 'I'll get out of my pants.'

I offered to help but she insisted on doing it herself, curiously folding them quite neatly and putting them on the side of the bath. She eased up her skirt saying, 'It's crease-proof.' Her stockings were held by slim suspenders which formed a frame for her bun of light hair. Her thighs parted and we did it frantically there on the bathroom floor. Someone tried the door. 'I'll be just a minute!' she called out brazenly. We lay panting on the carpet.

'We can't walk out of here together,' I whispered. 'I hope they're not waiting outside.'

'They can go to hell,' she panted, lying back. 'My God, *I* nearly died in action then.'

It was with no small regret that I handed back the uniform and its medal to Walmsley. He shrugged, regretting it himself.

'It's your decision, Jones,' he sighed. 'You could keep the rig and have a great time. And all official.' He beamed slyly. His eye batted. 'You *liked* being an officer, didn't you?' he said.

'It has its advantages,' I admitted.

'And it could keep having them,' he insisted. 'You're made for this part, son. It's right up your street. Good-looking, big, clean-cut British lad like you. You could be parading around half the States, a genuine hero, flesh and blood, not someone out of the newspapers or the movies. Women . . .'

Avoiding his face I said: 'I have to go home, sir.'

'To wife and war, eh?'

'I'm not so sure about the wife,' I admitted. 'She's engaged in anti-aircraft operations, searchlights. But the war's there all right.'

He had a last try. 'Listen you'll be doing more for the war effort by touring the United States, telling them about it, than being just another man jack standing up to face Hitler.'

He made a final stab. 'America and Britain both need you,' he said.

I thanked him and repeated in almost a whisper: 'I've got to go home.' Resignedly he folded the uniform across his arm and gave the medal ribbon a slight brush. 'All right, okay, it's your decision. I suppose I could order you to stay. The Washington Embassy would endorse that. You're a bigger hero in Wilmington than Winston Churchill. But if you must go, then you must go.' He held out his hand and we shook firmly; then he tapped me across the shoulder. 'You're a good chap. Makes me feel I want to get back there myself.' His eyes dropped for once together. 'But I have duties . . .'

He marched out stiffly and I felt glad when he had gone. Parts of me were still sore from Mrs Michael. She had cried when I finally left the party in the early hours and so had several of the others. They came to the door of the house as I was leaving with Walmsley in the navy car. They were weeping and waving and one of the men started to sing shakily: 'There'll Always Be an England'. People were standing to attention, and when they had run out of words they hummed it. Walmsley and I stood straight and embarrassed at the door of the car. I was trying not to look at Mrs Michael. Each time my eyes wandered to her she was piercing me with maternal fierceness. My organ ached.

One of the men called for three bulldog cheers. When they had given them we were able to get into the car. Mrs Michael's loaded husband shouted: 'Give Hitler hell, son!' and added: 'Give the bastard hell!'

It was taken up like a war cry: 'Give the bastard hell!' Mrs Michael collapsed emotionally against her husband's unsteady flank where she lay sprawled like a mermaid clinging to a rock.

Now I was faced with the ocean, full of danger and lonely fear. I knew it was right. Somewhere in my mind was a romantic hope that because of the war and the way people felt, the new sharpness of life, Dolly and I would find each other again. I dreamed that she would be waiting for me on the dock and I would walk down the gangplank and fall into her lovely arms. I even imagined us standing at the search-light together, our own personal searchlight, seeking out the bombers and blinding them with our light.

I knew it would not be at all like that. I would go back to no one except lonely Uncle Griff. There would be no home, no giving arms, no deep bed. The uncertain sea was the only certainty in my life. Even then I felt that my unsatisfactory destiny was to revolve; around and around the world, always coming back to the same place, the same places, because there would be no starting point and no finish, just another circle. Revolving Jones.

BOOK THREE

One

The ship I was to join was lying at Baltimore. When I got there she had already sailed. At once I suspected a plot on the part of Walmsley to keep me helping Britain in America. But at the dock office a man with a great stomach and a cigar told me that it was a normal security measure to confuse the Germans.

'There's spies,' he said. He was sprawled almost horizontally in his swivel chair, moving a little to the right and then to the left, the puffs of the cigar like the arc of fire from a field gun. The smoke drifted over his shirted stomach as the haze of battle might over a hillside. 'Everywhere there's spies. So we don't tell 'em the time of departures. Sometimes even the crew don't know. They got to make an intelligent guess.' He reached for a message tape from the desk. It was ticking through a glass-domed printer behind him, a machine like an enclosed old clock. 'But you struck lucky,' he said. 'You sail midnight. And she's a US ship. Safe and with good American chow. She ain't going to be sunk by no U-Boat, just believe me. Those Krauts are scared of Uncle Sam. They don't want him in the war.'

'That's good,' I said genuinely. 'I don't like being torpedoed.'

'Can't be nice,' he agreed. 'There's another Limey guy going with you. Malcolm . . . they can't even spell Malcolm . . . they got an "e" on the tail of it. Foskins.'

The ship had just come out of dry-dock and she was lying, large and spruce, not far from the harbour office. The man eased himself from the chair and took me to the door, pointing her out with stabs of his cigar. 'See the second US flag after the coaster,' he said. 'You'll be safe on her. Have a good trip.'

Foskins was already on board. We were to share a cabin. 'What about this, cherry pie?' he said with his bright grin. 'First we're stars of the parade and now it's a luxury cruise.' He looked down at his blue shirt and dungarees. 'I was sorry to get rid of the rig though. It caused quite a sensation that night, I can tell you. It's amazing what you can get away with in uniform.'

'I know,' I agreed. 'Amazing.' I sat on the opposite bunk. 'Well, they won't sink this one,' I said.

'Ooooh, I'll say they won't. It'll be a real skive, too, believe me. They have it so cushy these Yanks. And they won't give us much to do. We're extra crew but they'll just ask us to wash up the forks or something gentle. And we'll be paid.'

She was fifteen thousand tons, roomy and confident, the Stars and Stripes at her stern. She sailed at midnight and at eight o'clock the following morning, in fog, she was called to heave-to in the Atlantic. I heard the American captain shouting through the loudhailer. 'This is an American ship. This is a *neutral American* ship. Do you hear me? This is an American ship.'

Foskins came into the cabin with lather on his chin. 'I only shave once a week,' he complained. 'And this has to happen.'

'What is it?' I said. We had a porthole but the ocean on that side was hung with mist.

'Somebody who wants to know who we are,' he said cautiously. 'Like a German.'

'This is a neutral ship,' I pointed out fiercely.

'Don't tell me,' he said mildly. 'Tell them.' He looked at me, his eyes glinting. '*We're* not neutral, cherry pie.'

Muffled shouts sounded. There was a long interval while the ship lolled in the foggy sea. Then the Captain's voice came through the speaker in the gangway outside the cabin. 'Hear this now. All crew on deck. All crew on deck.'

'Does that mean us?' I said.

'Not if I can help it,' he said. 'I'm going to hide.'

The bosun came to the door. 'Okay you guys, this means you too.' He looked at us carefully. 'Try and look like Americans,' he advised. 'They're coming aboard.'

We followed him up to the deck. My heart felt stiff, my legs felt uncertain. 'Don't worry, dear,' said Foskins. 'We'll bluff it out. Talk like Mickey Mouse.'

We looked over the indistinct water. A large shape lurked in the fog. 'It's no U-Boat,' said Foskins. 'That's a bloody cruiser.'

Most of the American crew were already assembled. They stood in slightly shamefaced ranks as though they had been insulted but could not answer back. There were three lines and we joined the rearmost. Above us the captain was leaning over the wingbridge. Coming through the foggy water was a launch. We could hear but not see it. Cold and concerned I stood waiting. Foskins was like a wax model staring straight ahead. 'Just our luck,' he muttered.

The sound of the boat engine eased and there were shouts from below. A rope ladder had already been let over the side. The American captain, a tall studious man, came down to the deck. A cap with a gold arrangement came over the hull. The man who followed it was in German naval uniform. He had a businesslike pistol in a holster at his side. He was followed by four sailors, all carrying tommy guns.

The German officer saluted. The American captain seemed to think about it, but then returned the salute. 'This is an American ship,' he repeated to the German. 'You have no right to stop a neutral ship. You have no right to bring armed men aboard my vessel.'

'Too bad,' said the German officer with a distinct American accent. 'You must report us. There will be an apology.'

'I already have,' replied the captain. 'A US warship is on its way.'

The German was unconcerned. 'We cannot have an incident,' he said. 'We will not detain you long, captain. I just want to see the cargo manifest.' It was ready for him. The captain took it from the second officer, hovering nervously behind him, and handed it to the German. 'Non-strategic materials,' said the captain. 'Bound for Lisbon.'

'Nice place, Lisbon,' replied the German almost insolently. 'One of the few peaceful places left in the world.'

'The United States,' the captain pointed out calmly, 'is at peace. At present.'

'Sure, sure,' nodded the German. He looked around at the lined-up crew.

'I'm going to wet myself,' whispered Foskins. I tried to keep my elbows stuck into my sides, tried to keep my legs and my face straight and my eyes expressionless.

'Your crew is entirely American?' asked the German.

'Two Argentines and a man from Panama,' said the captain.

'And two Limeys!'

The accusation was squeaked from a trembling man at the end of the front line. He turned and pointed his shaking finger at us. 'These two. They're Limeys.'

'Green!' snapped the captain. 'You're on report.'

'I should care,' chattered Green. 'We shouldn't have these guys on board. I feel vulnerable when they're on board. I got kids.'

The German officer walked to us and regarded us quietly. Two of the armed seamen were behind him. Another two remained in position on the deck. 'Limeys,' said the German. 'Please step out of the rank.'

'Those two,' mumbled Green. He pointed again and began to sob.

There was nothing for it but to step out. 'You are English?' said the German. 'I am,' huffed Foskins. 'And proud of it.'

'Good,' said the German gravely. 'Good for you.' He turned his attention to me. 'You also? English?'

'No,' I replied. 'I'm Welsh.'

He shrugged. 'It's the same as English,' he said. 'But smaller.' Turning briskly he confronted the captain. 'We must take these men with us,' he said. 'They will be treated

214

as prisoners of war. No harm will come of them. You have my word. Your ship will be allowed to proceed.'

There was nothing the American could do. We saved him the trouble by stepping forward and we moved towards the ladder with two of the armed guards in front and two following. The captain called: 'Wait! Wait one moment.'

He took three paces towards us. The Germans raised their tommy guns but a snapped word from their commander made them lower the muzzles again. The American captain shook both of us by the hand. 'Good luck,' he said. 'I'm sorry. There is nothing I can do.' He glanced at the Germans, taking them all in. 'At the moment.'

He turned to the German officer. 'Give my regards to Adolf Hitler,' he said.

'I will personally,' returned the German just as easily. 'When he gives me my Iron Cross.' He laughed and held out his hand. The American did not move. 'Okay,' said the German. He saluted stiffly and ushered us towards the ladder.

'I'll give Green's regards to Hitler!' shouted Foskins defiantly over his shoulder. He was about to descend the ladder. He turned and looked at the man who had betrayed us. 'Fucking lollipop,' he said.

We went heavily down the steps. Looking up I saw that all the American officers and crew had crowded to the rail, startled-faced, to watch us go. I began to wish I knew more about the Geneva Convention. Foskins and I were told to sit amidships on the small cutter. 'They have all sorts of amateur theatricals in prisoner of war camps,' mentioned Foskins looking at the Atlantic. He turned and grinned ruefully at me. 'You have to look on the bright side, don't you,' he said.

The ocean was grey and greasy. As the shape of the American ship subsided into the fog so the bulk of the German warship grew in firmness. When we were very near, almost below her bow, I saw the name, *Kiel*.

Foskins looked disgusted. 'How come they're out here prancing about anyway?' he demanded. 'Where's our navy?'

The German officer answered. There was a touch of a smirk at the side of his mouth. 'The British navy is in port,' he said. 'Waiting for the invasion of England. Or on convoy escort, trying to guard English ships from our U-Boats. A full smile now occupied his strong face. 'We have the Atlantic for a playground,' he said.

We came alongside the cruiser. Her grey side loomed over us like a metal hill. Whistles shrilled and sailors appeared at the head of the ladder hung over her hull. We were ushered up the side. A young officer looked astonished to see us. The man who had brought us across said something to him in German and he saluted. 'Please,' he said to Foskins and me. 'To come with me.'

'What a lovely big ship,' said Foskins eyeing the young officer in his mocking way. 'I bet she goes fast.'

'Thirty-five knots,' replied the youth seriously. 'No ship can catch us.'

'Oooh,' said Foskins. 'Really fast.'

The officer opened a door. 'Here, please,' he said. With stiff politeness he showed us into the large cabin. 'I must lock you,' he said apologetically producing a key.

'Aren't you supposed to search us for weapons?' suggested Foskins looking at him shyly. He appeared to have quickly recovered his spirits. The man shook his head and went out, making a performance of locking the door. Foskins sat on one bunk and I sat on the other. 'Well, here we are, cherry pie,' he said his gaze going around. 'Not a bad nick. I've been in worse.'

'They'll treat us all right,' I said. 'They have to. The only thing is, God knows how long it will be for.'

'Bye bye the war,' he said. 'Pity really. But we can attempt to escape and that sort of thing.' He looked about us and his boy's grin returned. 'We could try tunnelling out.'

We laughed and were still laughing when the same officer and a rating came in with a pot of coffee, two mugs and a plate of bread and sausages. They appeared puzzled. 'Why so laughing?' asked the young officer. 'You are prisoners.'

'We thought we might try to escape,' I said glancing at Foskins.

'By digging out,' added Foskins making a shovelling motion. The German shook his head. 'Not possible,' he said uncertainly. 'This is a ship. We are at sea.'

They went out shaking their heads. Again we laughed and drank the coffee and ate the spiced sausages. We felt the ship get under way and begin to move powerfully and smoothly. 'She's new,' observed Foskins. 'She don't rattle like our ships.'

After an hour the officer returned with the rating who collected the mugs and plates. Both seemed gratified that we had eaten the sausages. 'German food,' said the officer. 'Good?'

'Scrumptious,' said Foskins rubbing his belly.

The young man could not make him out. His eyes narrowed a little and he became less friendly. 'The captain will talk with you now,' he said. 'You must come with me.'

We followed him out onto the open deck. The ship was moving purposefully through the ocean now clear of fog. The sky was grey as the sea but shreds of sunshine were beginning to touch the ridges of the waves. We were heading east, towards Europe. Two armed sailors stepped out each side of us as we went aft. The German sailors on deck, scrubbing, cleaning and polishing like charwomen, as sailors do on every ship on every sea in the world, watched us keenly.

We were told to sit in an outer cabin. Foskins was called into the captain's presence first and after ten minutes he emerged and I was told to replace him. 'He's a nice man,' he whispered. 'For a Hun, ever so nice.'

The German commander was sitting at his desk looking puzzled. He asked me to repeat my name and then said: 'It will be necessary to get all your personal details on this form. You are now a prisoner of war.'

'So I understand,' I said. 'Although I didn't know you could be taken prisoner from a neutral ship.'

'This happened,' he shrugged. 'Stranger things will happen

before the war is ended.' He looked as though he wanted to ask me something. 'This other man,' he said leaning forward on his elbows. 'Malcolm-with-an-"e" Foskins. He is a strange one.'

'You think so, sir?'

'Very much I think so.' He appeared embarrassed. 'Is he what they call a cissie?' he said. 'A man who likes only men.'

'What makes you think that, sir?'

He looked at me guardedly. 'What,' he asked. 'Is a cherry pie?'

They moved us to quarters on the upper deck, a double cabin with a small open exercise area. The sun came out and we sat stripped to the waist watching the German seamen polish the guns. 'I hope we don't run into the navy,' I said. 'I'd hate to be on the wrong side when the shooting starts.'

'They do keep their guns nice and clean,' he said like a domestic. 'Just look at the brasswork. Lovely, simply lovely. I wonder what they're like when it comes to shooting?'

The question was not left long unanswered. At seven o'clock the following morning klaxons began to screech and boots pounded along the deck. 'Action stations,' said Foskins sitting up in his bunk. 'The navy's here.'

The door to the small open exercise area was left unlocked and we crouched out there. It was a bright morning and in the long visibility we could see a solitary shape moving on the horizon. Below us the men were busy around the guns. They began to swing in the direction of the shape.

'It's a merchantman,' breathed Foskins. 'Left behind by the convoy, I bet. They're going to sink her.'

The captain was calling sharp orders from the bridge. Below us the crew of a gun were curled into their firing positions. We were closing rapidly, the cruiser cutting through the water like an athlete. We were soon so close we could see the red ensign. Desperately she was trying to make smoke. It was pouring from her two funnels. But too late. The gun below us fired with a deafening bark and a halo of fumes. The shell hit the water short of the target like a suddenly sprouting tree. The aft guns opened fire. They were bracketing the ship, getting the range. It did not take long. We watched the second salvo and then the third, which struck the vessel true at her midships. There was a huge ball of flame and smoke. You could see the old ship lurch under the force of the blows.

'Lollipops!' screamed Foskins. 'Fucking lollipops!'

There was a fire hydrant and a hose coiled on the bulkhead next to us. He was only a small man but he was hard and valiant. I stood speechlessly as he uncoiled the hose. I half tried to stop him. 'Get out of my way, son,' he shouted. Strongly he pushed me to the deck and I was still struggling to my feet when he whirled the wheel of the hydrant and a vicious jet of water shot out from the hose nozzle. He held it like a weapon, staggering to the rail and directing it at the German gun crew below. It bowled them all over the deck. They rolled and slithered. One man slid right to the ship's rail and lay there unconscious. He later died, one of the few men to die in the war from a fire hose. Foskins was laughing like a madman, taunting them. He turned the nozzle onto a party of marines coming at us along the deck mowing them over with the shock stream of white water. They flew comically in all directions, like bowled over ice skaters, and trying to get to their feet, only to be knocked sideways and back by the next jet.

I could not see who shot him, but somebody did. A spray of bullets came from below, chipping lumps out of the metal around us. I was crouching and Foskins called out a small, almost polite curse and dropped on top of me.

He died in the ship's hospital two hours later. I was holding his hand. He said to me: 'My mum always wanted me to be an officer. She said it had more dignity.'

'But not so much fun,' I said.

The surgeon, who had done his best, was there when Foskins last opened his eyes and said: 'Fucking lollipops.'

'What is this he said?' asked the German doctor holding his pulse.

'It was just a saying he used,' I said. 'Fucking lollipops.'

He shrugged. 'Not big famous last words.'

'He wasn't a famous man,' I said.

Later, when they were making out the official report and asking me questions, I looked at the date on my statement. It was the fourth of July. I had been twenty-one years old that day.

For three more melancholy days we sailed east. The summer clouds were low and thick, the sea fretful, and I was full of sadness for Foskins. The Germans buried him decently at sea with a coffin draped in a Union Jack, presumably kept for just such an occasion. It was the afternoon after they had buried their own sailor, killed by the fire hose. I went to both burials. They fired rifle shots over both men before they jettisoned them over the side.

The German cruiser had picked up survivors from the merchantman, hanging pathetically onto an almost submerged lifeboat. They were all Indians and they seemed colder and more frightened because of it. From the deck you could see their eyes shining up. The officers had been British but they had not lived. The Indians regarded the Germans with terror, their faces shivering their skins purple. They had not calmed very much when I was sent below to explain to them that we were being treated as prisoners of war and would be landed in France and taken to a camp in Germany. They thought I was a German and they prostrated themselves on the deck before me.

They had only a dim idea of where France and Germany were. The cruiser's cook, however, made them a huge dish of meat curry and they ate this with great hunger. It cheered them a little and five of them went to sleep while the sixth stayed awake and sang an Indian chant, like a lullaby over them.

At daybreak on the fourth day we came in sight of the

coast. I had been allowed to remain in the upper cabin and to go out onto the narrow open part where Foskins had been shot. His blood had been wiped from the bulkhead but it had stained the wooden boards underfoot. The bloodstain had turned to the colour of ink.

There I stood on the fourth morning, looking towards the smudge of land, when a German junior officer on the deck below looked up and pointed. 'France,' he called to me. 'Brest.'

How strange that I should be back there; and on the same sort of weeping morning as that on which I had first arrived with Captain Bracklesham on the *SS Myrtle Montgomery*. Brest, where Francine had lived. Francine . . . perhaps she was still there.

The mouth of the harbour began to open like a revelation. Now I remembered the displacement of the land and the various channels and the long line of buoys in the grey water leading into the port. If I had expected to detect an air of defeat and occupation over the place, then it was not apparent. The outer harbour was still moving with ships and boats. A pilot cutter appeared, more punctually than on the previous occasion, and the civilian pilot (I could almost swear it was the same pilot, although he appeared more spruce and obliging) came aboard. He smiled and saluted everyone in sight. The German sailors lined the decks as we slid with quiet grandeur into the harbour.

There were French warships lining the quays as they had been on the previous visit. Now the ranks of pom-pom hatted sailors cheered as we swept by. Sirens were sounded. We were the first German ship to enter the port since the French surrender.

On the dockside were anxious-faced stevedores ready to take the ropes and hawsers. Nowhere had I seen dockers so eager and so efficent. They were six to a mooring rope. Ashore I could see buses moving briskly in the streets. A band began to play and a civil deputation of Frenchmen lined up. Everyone appeared to be anxious to be seen doing their best. The Germans allowed me to remain alone on the small open area and men on the dockside waved to me, some raising their hands in a sort of half-Nazi salute. At first I tried to waft my hands dismissively, indicating that I was not a German, but it made no difference and all I could do in the end was to wave back shamefacedly.

Then they took us ashore, the six Indians and myself; they put us in a wire cage next to a slaughterhouse. At first the Indians were convinced that the squeals of the animals were human beings being executed. When I told them that they were cows and pigs they were even more distraught and began to wail and weep. They could not understand what was happening. They had little idea about the war; they knew they were in France but believed that the French were on our side, opposed to the Germans.

The French, at least the French in Brest, were not on our side. Some of them came strolling by the cage in which we were confined and looked at us as if we were animals. They put their faces close to the wire and put out their tongues. Some brought children and pointed us out derisively.

We had only been there a day and a night when about fifty British soldiers arrived, traipsing tiredly through the town, watched stone-faced by the population. They only had a couple of German soldiers to guard them but they were too defeated to run away.

'They 'ate us, the French,' one of the soldiers said to me. We had to sleep in the sheds meant for cows. There was dung still drying on the floor. This had upset the Indians even more and they wailed until the Germans took them off and put them into more suitable quarters. Even then they believed they were going to be shot because they made a terrible scene as they were being taken, and I had to be summoned to tell them that nobody was going to kill them.

'Poor heathen buggers,' said the soldier. 'They don't know what anything's about. I bet they wished they'd never joined the bloody British Empire.'

He said that the soldiers had been in another camp and

222

before that had been wandering lost for days. None of the French would help them. 'Not even a measly drink of water. They reckon we ran away and left them.' He sat against the cowshed wall. Food and cigarettes had been distributed and the British sat wearily smoking. Some had already toppled over to sleep. The man who spoke to me had taken off his boots and showed me his feet. 'You couldn't get anything more like raw meat in that ruddy slaughterhouse,' he grunted. 'Never mind. I'll have plenty of time to give them a spell. Years.' He said they had arrived in France just in time to be captured. 'As they was takin' the rest of the army off from Dunkirk, they were landing us this side. Didn't make sense,' he said bitterly. 'But not much does. That Churchill is a bastard for a start. He don't care about the working class. He shot the miners. A right bastard. Always was.'

On the following morning a German officer came to the enclosure and said that we were being taken by train to Germany. 'First class?' asked one of the soldiers wryly.

'Of course, first class,' said the German unsurely. 'It is all first class from now.'

They gave us soup and bread and a packet of five French cigarettes each and loaded us into trucks. I gave my cigarettes to the soldier. He looked amazed as he accepted them. 'Never give bugger-all away, mate,' he advised putting them in his battledress pocket. 'Not when you're in the shit. Keep everything that might come in useful. You wait till we're behind the wire. You'll see how it works then.'

As the trucks trundled down the hill from the compound into the town I tried to spot some place I might recognise. I thought I might even catch a glimpse of Francine although I knew that this was foolish. But, hardly had I dismissed the fantasy, when the truck turned down a street and I realised that it was the cobbled road on which stood the baker's shop. There it was! The bakers came out to stare at us with hostile eyes. I was at the side of the truck and trying to look around the corner to see Francine's door. It was painted the same bright red and there was a hanging pot of flowers outside.

The truck in front paused at a junction and our vehicle jolted to a halt. At that moment I saw her, Francine! She was in the window over the baker's shop. It had been five years but I knew it was her. My heart leapt.

'Francine! Francine!' I bellowed over the side of the truck. 'Francine, it's me!'

The employees, who had come from the baker's shop, looked upwards at the window. Then Francine opened it, pushing it up and leaning out, her face fuller and her breasts hanging over the sill. 'Francine!' I howled again. 'It's me, Davy Jones!'

For a moment she stared in disbelief. Then she spat the biggest gob I have ever seen. It struck one of the bakers staring up from the pavement and he howled in disgust. Then she slammed the window so violently it shuddered. Our lorry began to shrug forward.

The British prisoners had watched the scene with awakening interest. Now bitter-faced, I turned to look at them. The soldier who had spoken to me looked embarrassed for me. 'Did you know 'er then?' he asked.

'I used to,' I said. 'Way back.'

There were other dejected British soldiers at the station. About a hundred and fifty were waiting on the platform, watched at a distance by the unmoving French and supervised by the Germans as they boarded the train. One of the prisoners, a sergeant, said to me: 'We seem to have lost, home and away.'

The compartment had wooden seats. Every soldier sat blankly, hot and dead-eyed, until as the train pulled out from the station, one thick-backed youth near the window got up and thrust his upturned thumbs out in the traditional British sign. His hair was cropped like a hedgehog close to his neck. The sergeant who had spoken to me came angrily through the door and shouted: 'Take your bloody thumbs in, lad! Take 'em in!'

Half looking around, the boy obeyed slowly. His face had

become red. 'Just showing them that we're not downhearted,' he said, adding 'Sergeant.'

'Well don't,' said the NCO. His eyes bulged. 'No more thumbs up. It's finished, all right!' he darted around the tired, shocked faces. 'I'll strangle the next bastard who does it.'

He looked hard at each face of the men on the wooden seats. He sighed and grunted: 'Marvellous' and went out.

'That's Sergeant Holloway,' one of the soldiers told me tonelessly. 'He gets worked up about things.'

The train clattered east, over the flat country. Quiescent Frenchmen were taking in the harvest, knee deep in yellow fields below a hard blue sky. 'Like one of those paintings,' said the man opposite me. He was older, his face brown and deeply lined.

'Do you think we'll pack it in?' I said.

'If we've got any sense,' he said looking up with grey expressionless eyes. He regarded me across the small aisle. 'How come you're in civvies?' he said. 'Secret Service or something?'

One or two laughed like brief dog barks. 'Merchant Navy,' I said. He was not being antagonistic.

'Get shipwrecked?' asked a round, grocer-faced man. They laughed again.

'Sort of,' I answered. I did not tell them any more. They did not want to know. Each had his own misfortune. They were down and weary and being taken to a captivity where no end would be in sight. We all leaned back on the wooden seats in the burning, enclosed air, almost stifling despite the open window. There were only two German guards to each of the carriages. Sometimes the train, which was old, eased to a metallic crawl. We passed fields and streams. It would have been easy to simply open the door and jump out, down onto the embankment and away. But to where? Nobody tried it.

We were beginning to realise that our conquerors were organisers. There were seats for all the prisoners. One of the guards came around with a bucket of clean drinking water and an enamel mug, handing it around. We stopped after three hours at a country station where the Germans had set up a field kitchen. They handed out bread and bowls of vegetable soup and gave each man an apple and a pear. 'Like Christmas,' said the man with the grey eyes. I remembered the train into Spain, the men sitting on the floor and the donkey.

We skirted the northerly suburbs of Paris. The men crowded to the right-hand windows in the corridor to catch a distant glimpse of the Eiffel Tower like a cobweb against the greying sky. There were a few jokes about making a run for it now and getting some *oo-là-là*. None of them had ever been to Paris. We were still in the country and the hot corn-bright fields were still all around us, men and women in headscarves working in them, heads down, as if in indifference or shame. Some of the soldiers tried shouting but not one of the workers looked up, although they were near the railway.

We were still going east, never leaving the fields, and the evening was coming on, when a noisy shadow, like a swiftly flapping hand, flew across the train. Men at the windows looked up shielding their eyes. The plane turned and came back the other way, its guns distinctly firing. We looked at each other as though we had been cheated; someone had changed the rules.

'Down! Down!' bawled Sergeant Holloway from the corridor. 'Get on the floor.'

We flung ourselves on top of each other. Men were trying to burrow underneath others, fighting them; they cursed and rolled, punching each other in fear. The plane howled over us, its guns stuttering. The roof overhead was splintered as though pierced by invisible nails. There were screams and smoke. A soldier, blood bursting from his chest, stood up pointing to it speechlessly and fell across the rest. The plane flew the whole length of the train, strafing as it went.

The train was stopping. 'Doors! Open the bloody doors!' I heard Holloway shout. 'Get out under the trees.'

The doors were flung wide almost before he had finished. I disentangled myself from the pile on the compartment floor. Above me was a man, a dead weight, and I had to roll him aside. The youth who had put his thumbs up out of the window, was sitting in the corner, crying like a baby. He was cradling his stomach and blood was creeping through his fingers. 'Shooting prisoners,' he wept. 'Innocent prisoners!'

The plane was coming back. I stumbled to the door and jumped out. All along the train men were falling out of the carriages and tumbling onto the embankment. There was a small stone yard and a copse of short trees. Everyone flung themselves under cover as the plane came back, their hands hugging the backs of their heads, pressing faces to the grass. The machine guns raked the train again.

'It's one of ours,' said Holloway quietly. He was a few yards away. He pushed himself up onto his elbows and watched the aircraft. 'Stupid fucker.'

A paper-faced man appeared in the open doorway above us and pitched forward onto the embankment like an actor in a melodrama.

'What can we do?' I gasped to Holloway.

'Ask him to stop, if you like,' he said calmly. 'Here he comes again. Sometimes I don't understand this pissing war.'

It was a Spitfire, the roundels on the wings easily seen. It came back, its guns firing exuberantly. The train had caught fire and mercifully its smoke was screening us. 'He's having a lovely bloody time,' the sergeant spat. As he said it there was a dull, almost slow-motion explosion from far down the line. An orange light lit the early evening and a ball of smoke flew up. 'He's down,' said Holloway.

'He hit the railway bridge,' said another man standing up.

'Serve him right,' said Holloway.

Two hours later German military trucks arrived to take us from the burned train. The British prisoners had helped to put the fire out, making a human chain of water carriers from a farmyard in the nearby lane. Most of one carriage and part of another were destroyed. Twelve prisoners, a guard and the fireman of the engine had been killed by the guns of the plane.

We sat wretchedly in the copse until they came to fetch us. 'That,' said Holloway. 'Was insult to bloody injury.'

When the trucks arrived in the lane they were driven by German soldiers but in the back of each one were two Frenchmen wearing unpleasant expressions and green arm bands. They had no guns but carried thick sticks. The lane followed the direction of the railway track and little more than a mile away it bent over a bridge. The remains of the Spitfire were flung along the banks beside the railway. It had struck the ground before reaching the bridge.

'Not looking where he was going,' muttered one of the soldiers. 'Looking over his shoulder.'

'*Les Anglais*,' said one of the Frenchmen. He spat in a thoughtful way over the tail of the lorry. No one said anything.

They took us to the town hall at a small place and we squatted on the floor for hours. Some local women, silent and abashed, served us soup, bread and coffee. They seemed glad to leave and we were not sorry when they had gone. Not one looked at us, met our eyes. Candles had been brought in when the food came, for the daylight was going, but the last of the Frenchwomen to leave, a thick-angled old lady in a peasant dress, snuffed the candles and took them with her, leaving us in the darkness.

'Don't think much of us, the Frogs,' said someone as we settled down to sleep on the floor.

'Don't think much of them either,' said another man in the dark.

There were few other words. Grunts and sighs and snores. There was a window open and against it a bench. We had taken it in turns to stand on the bench and urinate out of the window into a yard at the side. Some children congregated to watch but none of the men took any heed. There were two bucket lavatories beyond the inner door.

At eight the following morning the French women returned with bread and watered milk. Some held their noses when they came into the room. Then we marched through the brief town, ragged, dirty, unshaven, to the railway station where another train was waiting for us. We passed the school on the way and two teachers lined the infants up at the railings to watch us trudge by. Some of the men looked up at the children and the man next to me mumbled sadly. Most looked straight ahead.

It was the first time we had marched together and I realised that, although they were grim and unkempt, the other men all wore some semblance of khaki battledress and kept doggedly in step. I was still in the blue shirt, short collared jacket, thick blue trousers, and rubber-soled shoes I had worn when I left Baltimore. As I marched I remembered rolling with Mrs Michael on the white floor of that faraway bathroom.

Not only the children stared. People appeared from their homes as we tramped by, some mouthing short comments, little snarls, as though their disgrace was mirrored in our captivity. We were glad to reach the station.

Half-an-hour later we were going eastwards once more towards Germany. The seats were wooden, the air was torrid and the smoke from the engine drifted in through the windows. Someone at the front of the carriage began to sing. He sang harshly but with determination, and others joined in, a sort of mumbling which straggled from compartment to compartment. More sang, stronger now, although there was no change in the men's expressions, just their mouths opening and shutting, the words wooden. Two guards came along to watch us and everyone chorused: 'We're going to hang out the washing on the Siegfried Line!' which sounded foolish and hollow. The guards did not understand it, except for the words 'Siegfried Line' and they merely grinned because they did not care what we sang. They were the conquerors and there was no spirit in our song.

As the train edged east so the countryside changed, unlike

the golden fields of the west. We were now travelling through farmland churned by war; craters and tank tracks sculpted in dried mud, buildings holed and roofless, towns and villages with rubble still piled in the streets. A funeral was going through one village, the mourners walking and the coffin borne on a horse-drawn hearse. The short procession stopped dumbly at a crossing to let the train rumble by. We ceased our singing and stood silently watching it from our windows. Then we went through a town where hardly a wall seemed to remain. The inhabitants picked their way through the debris, pushing carts, carrying loads. Boys played on a pile of rubble as if it were a sandcastle.

Holloway, the sergeant, said to me: 'Ever see anything like it?'

'A bit,' I said. 'I was in Spain in the civil war.'

For the first time he looked surprised. 'Bit young for Spain, weren't you?' he said.

'I didn't intend to be there,' I told him. 'It was by accident.'

All he said was: 'There's no age limit anyway.'

By afternoon we had passed through the devastated country and crossed into untouched Germany. It was astonishing to progress suddenly into bright-roofed hamlets, the sun polishing their cobbles, into summer fields and swollen woods, over streams and rivers; towns where people looked curiously at our train and then often began to smile and wave. It was as though we had travelled from an enemy country into a friendly one. Some of the men in the windows waved back quietly.

'They're not bad, the Jerries,' said Holloway. 'For Germans.'

At nightfall we pulled into a large station and without fuss were ushered from the train and assembled on the platform. There were still only a handful of German guards with us. These were relieved now by a platoon of nervous-looking young soldiers under a short, squeaky officer.

'*Guten Tag*,' he said in a short bark. Someone brought a

230

box and he unselfconsciously stood on it so that everyone could see and hear him: 'This night you will be here, on this place, this station, and the next day you will go to the camp. *Heil Hitler!*'

It was the first time in real life I had ever seen anyone do that. *Heil Hitler.* The Nazi salutes in Chicago, also on a station, had been mimed. But this man raised a stiff thin hand and squeaked it. The German soldiers snapped to attention but we stood in our rough bunch and said nothing. A party was detailed to unload a pile of mattresses from a lorry outside the station and these were distributed. The waiting rooms had been left open and some men claimed spaces in there. Others put their mattresses on the platform or on the benches.

Others had been detailed to unload a smaller vehicle carrying food and urns. The squeaky officer summoned Holloway and asked in his high voice: 'Is any man that can cook? We have no cooking soldiers.'

'I'll ask,' responded the sergeant politely. He turned: 'Any man here with cooking experience?'

I stepped out. 'I've done some,' I told him. 'On board ship.'

'Good, just the job,' he said. 'Anybody else?'

Two other men came forward. One had worked in a café on the Great North Road and the other in a hospital.

'All right, Jones, you take charge,' said Holloway. He turned to the German officer. 'It's okay. These men can manage.'

The man seemed relieved. 'Good,' he said sharply and copied Holloway: 'These men can manage.' He addressed me. 'Also for my men. You cookers can manage for my men also?'

'We can manage,' I said.

'Manage, manage,' he repeated to himself in a privately pleased way. He ordered men to carry the boxes and tins of food into the station buffet, which was large, with restaurant tables and chairs. There was gas and electricity. We opened the containers. The food was mostly in tins; beef, potatoes and other vegetables. In an hour all the prisoners were sitting on the chairs eating and beginning to talk. The German soldiers sat at their own table with their officer sitting away from them, oddly, behind the buffet counter by the big brass money till.

'Bloody good, son,' said Holloway to me. 'You'll be all right in a prison camp. If you're the cook then *you eat*. Never forget that.'

Those were the first days of my captivity, which continued for almost three years. It was difficult to know what to expect. The stories of the Huns and their ill-usage of prisoners had been handed down from the war before this war. Our treatment on the trains travelling east had been fair; at times the youthful soldiers on guard appeared more nervous of us than we were of them. It came as a great surprise, however, on reaching the prison camp at Baden Baden in the south of Germany, to find many of the prisoners going around on roller skates.

'The Red Cross sent them,' said the camp leader, a bronzed captain in the Royal Artillery. 'They come up with some odd-bod things at times, and since they send them we feel it is only right they should be used. They also sent us a trampoline. When the chaps are not skating they are bouncing up and down on that.'

He had his own office, which incorporated his living quarters, the bunk fixed to the wall behind his desk. There were photographs of a number of women on the wall and a variety of children, the pictures segregated into little islands some distance apart from each other. 'They all write to me,' he said. 'But, God, it gets so busy in here that it's difficult to find time to answer all the letters. I have to have a real blitz on letter writing once a week or they'll stop sending the parcels.'

He looked almost fondly from the window. He was a thin, hard-wrought but genial man, with an explosive moustache.

Twenty or more prisoners were roller skating around the exercise yard. 'Used to be a Jerry school, this,' he said. So there's a decent playground for the skates.' He briefly examined me. 'I suppose you don't skate,' he said. 'Being Merchant Navy?'

He had already asked me for news of the war but he knew as much as I knew. 'The Jerries tell us,' he said lugubriously. 'And why should they lie?' His thin shoulders shrugged. 'They're going to beat us by an innings.' He straightened one of the women's pictures and then aligned another with it.

'Nearly all army here,' he continued. 'Brown jobs. But it's only a reception camp so almost everybody gets moved off in one direction or another. There's a couple of Merchant Navy chaps at the moment, but they're Polish. They try to make out they're Welsh because they're afraid the Jerries will victimise them. Since you're Welsh you'd better help them pretend.'

'I can cook,' I said firmly. I wanted to get the claim in early. 'I used to cook at sea.'

He looked surprised. 'You won't have to here,' he said. 'The Jerries do it. They bring in women to cook. Ugly women but they're not bad. A bit over-fond of the greasy sausage. We also have cookery lessons for any of the chaps who feel inclined, a chef from the Grand at Eastbourne and he's very spot on. You ought to join in. You won't be here long enough for taking any of the courses they've started at the main camps; civil engineering, forestry, accountancy, that sort of thing, but cooking you can leave off and start again somewhere else.'

'How long will I be here, sir?' I asked.

'Six weeks, ten weeks, who knows?' He shrugged his bony shoulders again. 'Not much longer. They have special camps for navy and Merchant Navy. What do they call them . . . *Milags*, that's it . . . for the Merchant Navy. Nobody hangs around *here* for long.' He smiled in a satisfied way. 'Except for me. And I'm here until we win the bloody war.'

It was late afternoon and the shadows of the roller skaters

were long on the tarmac playground. It was tempting to wonder what had happened to the children. Men were waiting at the side to take over from those who had finished coursing around. Some of the prisoners were very good, whirling and twirling at speed with one leg held out stiffly in front of them. They were clad in a variety of khaki uniforms, they were healthy-looking and seemed happy in a schoolish sort of way. Beyond rose a formidable barbed wire fence with a watchtower which, as far as I could see, was unmanned. Outside the fence were summer trees and a long field in which grazed rounded German cows. In the blue distance were forested hills.

All the men who had arrived on the train were put into long huts divided into rooms, each with four bunks. Sergeant Holloway, smoking a Woodbine, was standing in the evening sunshine that day, wedged up against the door of the billet, observing the prisoners on their skates.

'Great place to spend a war,' he said to me. 'If you're a circus performer.'

I watched the rollers with him. 'There's a trampoline as well,' I said.

'I know. I was wondering if you could train yourself enough to bounce over the wire.'

I looked at his wry face. 'Do you think it's worth escaping?' I said.

He patted my shoulder. 'No, not really, son,' he said. 'Where is there to escape to? By the time you got home you'd probably find the Jerries had just beaten you to it. I think we might as well hang around until this lot's over. And the way it's going we won't have too long to wait.'

'They'll let us go then,' I said hopefully. 'Home?'

'They did the French.' He puffed a wrinkle of smoke and then regarded the cigarette as if he could not make up his mind about it. 'As soon as the Frogs waved the white flag their prisoners were freed. Imagine that! "Here comes Daddy! He's coming down the street, Mummy!" Clever old Hitler knows about weaknesses. As soon as we pack it in he'll send us home.' He finished the cigarette, threw the butt on the ground and stamped on it. 'But you're not left with a lot of pride.'

He turned back into the hut and I followed him. There was a central table in the day room of the building. It was piled with clothing, German magazines and ripe plums. 'You're the first,' he said. 'They've just brought this stuff over. The others are being deloused.' He glanced at me. 'Have you been deloused yet?'

I shook my head. 'I didn't know you had to be,' I said.

'You have to be,' he answered. 'Well, you've got the pick of the free gifts. Take an armful and a few plums, they're nice, and get deloused. The others won't like it if you're scratching.'

I took a pair of army trousers and a blue jersey from the pile and then two shirts and two pairs of socks. Below the table was a rank of army boots and I picked up a pair of these. I began to eat one of the plums. A large form filled the sunlit doorway. The man, perspiring and fat, almost rolling as he walked, came into the hut. He was in a huge khaki shirt, trousers held up with braces and an officer's stiff cap. He greeted us like a lost uncle. 'Hello there! I'm the padre. John Willy, they call me. Either of you believe in God?'

Holloway said he did not. I nodded. 'It's all the same,' beamed the padre. 'Even *I* only see Him as a possibility.' He sat on the edge of the table. He had a large envelope and he buried his podgy hand in it. 'Letter forms,' he announced. 'You'll be wanting to write to loved ones, so you do it on these flimsies. They're rationed, so use up all the space you have.' He handed the forms to Holloway and then to me. 'We have one poor chap who can only write in block capitals,' he mused. 'So his letters tend to be short. I keep meaning to get one of the practising Christians to write for him if I can. Trouble is, everybody gets so dashed busy.'

'Roller skating,' said Holloway.

'That and other things. There's the concert party. The trouble is people don't stay long enough to get involved in

235

any long-term activity. Off they go somewhere else. So we can't rehearse anything properly. It has to be a variety bill with different acts: comedy, recitations, ballet and so on. Still, it's pretty good. Either of you do anything?'

'Jones can sing,' said Holloway, nodding at me. 'I heard him on the train.'

'Good,' said the padre. 'You're in then. Since you're a believer you can come to church too, I hope. Sing in the choir. It's only hymns. As I say, nobody is around long enough to manage "Elijah" or anything.' He beamed again, this time in a challenging manner at Holloway. 'Quite a few of the lads come to church,' he said. 'Never been near the place before, most of them. We're thinking of having a football match against the Unbelievers.'

He said he had to go because he had more social calls to make. We watched him bounce over the playground, waving and greeting men on the way. Holloway sat on a chair near the door and lit another Woodbine. He put his head into his hands, the cigarette projecting like a little chimney from his cupped fingers. 'And I thought they would all be tunnelling like fury,' he said.

Two

The long sameness of those days, weeks, months and eventually years, has caused them to fuse into one clouded memory. Some things are clear, fixed in place, but not many. In the middle of a war I was at peace, fed, clothed, given a roof and a bed, and required to do only a little beyond remaining in one place, to perform the same light duties that I performed the day before and the day before that, and would do again tomorrow and the day after. There was, however, for a long time, no seeing an end to it.

I must have been one of the few prisoners of war to receive divorce papers while I was behind the wire. From Baden Baden I had written to Dolly, to Uncle Griff and to the landlord Jeff at Packwick. I did not write to Paula but merely asked after her. Griff replied first, telling me about the snooker championship and that Barry Dock had been bombed. Jeff sent me news that Paula was having a baby and, despite the air raids, was living near London to be close to her husband. Dolly, or rather, her solicitor at Arbroath where she appeared to have settled for the duration, as they used to call it, sent the divorce papers.

The grounds were cruelty and desertion. In the circumstances I could certainly have defended myself on both counts, particularly on the second, but I merely acknowledged the papers and agreed to what she required. Dolly also forwarded a claim from the Inland Revenue.

Life in the prison camp suited some of the men. The two Poles in my billet played hushed chess all day and chatted interminably in their own language at night. They insisted on pretending it was Welsh.

There was another man, a small, hard, fellow from Cornwall, called Curnow; a fisherman who had been drunk and missed his sailing from St Malo and been captured by the advancing German who did not know what to do with him.

'Best bit of oversleeping I ever did,' he said sitting smiling in his bunk. 'Look at me here. No worries, no troubles. No work, no wife, no mother-in-law. Being looked after.' He beamed. 'And there's more room here than on a Falmouth trawler, I can tell you. I could stay here forever.'

He did not; in fact none of us did. Every man was transferred to another camp once they had been documented and processed through the German system. More prisoners arrived, although the flow was diminished because, for the first time in the war, armies were not in direct confrontation. The Germans were on one side of the Channel and the British on the other, held up until the next move. The men that did arrive came to the camp with grim expressions, expecting a poor life, only to become optimistic the moment they saw the prisoners on roller skates. There was talk that the Red Cross would be able to send ice skates in time for the German winter.

After seven weeks, during which time I became proficient at several figures on skates, including the difficult number eight and the even more difficult five, my name appeared on the dreaded transfer list. I was going to a camp at Alessandria.

'Egypt,' guessed Curnow the fisherman confidently.

We searched the map of Germany borrowed from the camp commandant's office, but could not find it. None of the Germans seemed to know where it was. At six on a fine autumn morning I reported with my kit; the forest was turning orange, the sky clear with an edge to the air; there were twenty of us, including the pair of Poles and Curnow, assembled by the main gate. A truck came to pick us up. It was the custom for a group of the other prisoners, close

238

friends and billet-mates, to see the departures away, and Sergeant Holloway was among them. We shook hands. 'You're an unusual bloke, Jones,' he said.

'So are you, sarge,' I replied.

'I can't wait to get out of this cushy hole,' he muttered. 'Get to a real camp with searchlights and watchtowers and escape committees.' He grinned. 'I'll be back in Blighty in a year,' he said. 'Fighting these bastards.'

He probably was too. I never saw him again, the man who wanted to fight a war like a war. He waved and turned his big back as the truck took us away. We asked the solitary guard where we were bound but he did not know either. We were going to Munich and there we would be transferred to a train.

'The salt mines,' forecast Curnow flatly. He pointed downwards. 'That's where they're sending us.'

At Munich we were coralled into a corner of the station, confined by an ornamental rope barrier that had obviously been used in the past for ceremonies. No one was left to guard us. The Germans did not treat the possibility of escape seriously. We stood in a self-conscious group, appropriately by the lost property office, and watched the crowds and the activity on the wide concourse.

They were playing martial tunes through a huge horn loudspeaker. The Germans were so jubilant, so victorious at that time, that they all appeared to be marching to the music, civilians as well. They strutted to and from their trains, some projecting snappy Hitler salutes to each other as they passed. A platoon of troops arrived and halted loudly; girls in frilly regional costumes formed groups to watch them and give them flowers. The young men did not know what to do with the flowers so they stuck them in their forage caps and asked the girls to kiss them, which they did and more, embracing and giggling. A sergeant stood by benignly accepting a crush from one of the girls, her big bosom swollen under her pure, pretty white blouse. I felt a pang of envy.

The troops were called to attention and the girls stepped

back obediently at the same snap of the order. Their chatter ceased and their faces became as serious as the drilled faces of the soldiers. They did not move again except to perform polite waves as the platoon marched onto a platform where a train was waiting.

More soldiers arrived, to be kissed, hugged and bedecked by the costumed girls. The vignette, it appeared, had been thoroughly rehearsed. As the order was called to bring the troops to attention, so the girls fell back and made their modest waves as the young men strode off.

'Makes you wish you was on the winning side, don't it,' muttered Curnow. He looked thoughtful. 'I wonder 'ow long it will take our maids to start kissing Germans?' he said. 'Not too long, some of them where I come from.'

The German soldiers were all boarding the same train. Eventually a man in army uniform, but clerkish and wearing thick glasses, approached us unsurely and read our names from a list. When we had each acknowledged we were there, a further clerkish man arrived, this one with a heavy back as if he were carrying a knapsack below his tunic. '*Jahwol*,' he nodded to the first clerk and peered through his glasses at the list attached to its board. He turned and regarded us: 'Nobody has escaped?' he said in heavy English. He had enjoyed the joke before. Some of us, including me, smiled shamefully. 'This way, march,' he ordered as the slighter man swept away the ornamental rope with a bureaucratic flourish.

We shambled out onto the concourse, making our niggardly protest by not being in step. The two bespectacled Germans were in front, the bigger one calling out: 'Left, right, left, right.' He marched with his back humped and his head pushed forward and down so that his eyes were on the ground, just ahead of his feet. The other clerk, still strutting, was wiping his glasses and flexing his poor eyes. He collided with a luggage barrow.

The civilians watched us shuffle towards the platform. We had to pass in front of the girls in their costumes. They looked

240

as embarrassed as we felt, their eyes turning away. "Ow about a kiss for us?' called Curnow to one of them. Her face went pink and she said something under her breath.

'Can't remember when I last 'ad a kiss from a nice girl,' he said to me sideways.

'It'll be a long time yet I expect,' I said.

'Well,' he philosophised. 'It'll only be like being at sea.'

The half-blind German leading the group halted angrily and several of the captives stumbled into him. 'No speaking!' he shouted at us. 'No speaking by prisoners!'

The smaller clerk joined in, prancing up and down the line snapping: 'No speaking! No speaking by prisoners!' From the assembled girls, still standing only yards away, came a flurry of applause.

Thankfully we shambled on, through the metal gates to the platform. The train was steaming, ready to go. The platform was clear of soldiers; their heads were projecting from every carriage window. We were halted at the rear of the train and ordered into a series of vacant compartments. I sat down near the window, next to Curnow.

'Another cook's tour,' I said. The air was already humid. The Poles had taken out their chess board. One of them set it on his kness. 'I never thought I'd see the world from a train.'

'After this I don't reckon there'll be much chance of travelling,' said the Cornishman. 'Unless it's from one end of the salt mine to another.'

'What makes you think it's going to be the salt mines?' I asked.

'I'm Cornish, you're Welsh. Those two are Poles. All mining races,' he said. 'They've picked us out.'

'Let's watch the sun,' I suggested. 'If we turn left, then it could be Silesia, and the salt mines. If it turns right we could be heading anywhere in Germany.'

The sun kept steadfastly to the front of the train. We travelled south, through elegant mountains, until we crossed the border into Austria. The train stopped at Innsbruk and then continued. In the early evening, when the sun was well down in the west, the train eased to a halt but we could not see far enough ahead to know where we were. Eventually some railway officials came along the corridor. They looked in at us curiously and one said. '*Buona sera, signore.*'

We were in a region of cloudy mountains. This was an inland place and, as a sailor, I could not imagine where it was. Sailors are notably parochial. Curnow said: 'I'm all at sea.'

After a few miles of puffing painfully around the scalloped track the train pulled into a siding. We were ordered down onto the embankment and marched alongside the train until we climbed onto the wooden platform of a small station. The German soldiers came to the windows to join others who were looking out with curiosity. The faces watched us in silence which we returned until Curnow, who enjoyed the last word, turned to the final German face in the final window and said: ''Ow be you goin' along then, Fritz?''

The station building had two new-looking flag masts supporting two flags, each half the size of the building itself. They curled lifelessly in the small wind like useless sails. One was the striped flag of Italy and the other the Fascist banner with its axe. We were formed up on the platform and the train began to draw away. Curnow waved coyly at the German soldiers.

One at a time the prisoners were called into the station waiting room where a busy and confused Italian was entering items in a large book like a Bible. There were only routine questions and an examination of identity papers, but he made the maximum difficulty. He painstakingly heard my name spelled and entered my Uncle Griff's name and address as next-of-kin. I wondered how Griff would have felt had he known that his details were going into enemy records.

Two old buses pulled up outside the station. There was no town nor village near. It reminded me of the station between Packwick and Wrackly. I wondered if Paula would ever write to me.

The Italians got us aboard the buses with a great amount of chattering, disagreements and waving of arms. Eventually, as if they had accomplished a major manoeuvre, they slammed the doors and stood back, panting and sweating, while the drivers started the engines. 'Wave,' called Curnow down the bus. 'Everybody wave at the Wops.'

Our bus was alongside the other vehicle and, as it pulled away first, every prisoner waved cheerily to the group of Italians outside the station. The men in the other bus saw what was happening and gladly waved too. One or two of the Italians, unable to comprehend the taunt, began to wave back but the fussy officer shouted angrily at them and they stopped. We laughed and then began to sing: 'There'll always be an England!' The men in the other bus saw that we were singing and they also began. The drivers looked over their shoulders and the vehicles started to wobble. There were only two young Italian soldiers, boys, at the front. They stood looking frightened while the singing became louder. They held their rifles as if they had no notion how to use them, then stood, perplexed and staring. The driver stopped at a village and the other bus stopped behind. Our driver got out, ran along the street and returned with a policeman and a priest.

The policeman had a sullen moustache and long eyes, the priest was in his cassock and cloak and appeared in an ill mood. There was a brown blotch of food on the side of his mouth.

We had ceased singing and now silently watched. The policeman had a revolver but it looked dull and unused. Neither he nor the priest said anything. Inhabitants from the village began to gather, staring up without hostility at our faces framed by the bus windows. Some smiled uncertainly and the children looked shy, and hid behind their mothers' dresses. But no one spoke. The scene was frozen. Eventually the priest muttered bad-temperedly to the policeman who relayed the words with similar expression to the bus driver

243

who told the two young soldiers. The priest and the policeman left and the villagers summoned a brief cheer for them.
The bus driver returned to his seat and the guards now sat
on a seat alongside as if they could not bear to look at us. We
re-started our journey and the accompanying bus did the
same. Once more we all began to sing.

We sang heartily and patriotically for the next half-an-
hour, until we arrived at the shape of a large dark house. The
youthful soldiers stood up and, as the driver switched on an
interior light, we saw that our guards had both been crying.
They clattered from the bus and were replaced by four
soldiers of more seniority of age but with expressions of even
greater uncertainty. Lights went on in the house and we
could hear a woman shouting unhappily. A donkey began to
honk. One of the Italian soldiers was deputed to go on some
errand and returned thirty minutes later with a serene old
officer. He wore medals and epaulettes as if he had just left
the stage of some musical comedy. His moustache was waxed.
As he spoke its ends went up and down.

'There is a mistake,' he announced loudly. 'It was not for
three days that they expected you would come here. There is
no camp for you. Tonight you must sleep in this, the bus.
Tomorrow you will begin building your prison.'

Italy had entered the war two months earlier. Italian border
troops had moved into the French Riviera, but had been
halted and turned back by the token contingent of French
forces at Menton. The Italians retreated to their side of the
frontier and waited for the French to surrender to the
Germans, which quickly occurred.

'Everybody here should realise that because the Italian
authorities appear incapable of organising anything it does
not follow that life is going to be easy.' We were assembled
in the one big tent that had so far been erected, a hundred of
us inside and two hundred sitting on the ground outside. The
prisoners had arrived in unexpected convoys over the course
of the second day. A truck had to be sent to tour the area to

buy food. Standing on a farmhouse chair at one end of the tent was a Merchant Navy officer, Captain Frank Franklyn, a bald man wearing a heavy seagoing jersey despite the warmth of the afternoon. 'Those of you who've been in German camps will know that the Jerries are fair enough and have the camps well organised. But it is going to be different here in Piedmonte.'

'The Italians are not accustomed to taking prisoners of war and so nothing has been properly organised. Food, accommodation, even things like letters from home, are going to be matters of unhappy concern for everybody here. The *second* thing we have to do is to build our own prison camp, huts, latrines, wire enclosure, everything. The *first* is to get some tents erected today so that we have somewhere at least to sleep while we're doing the main job. It is important that we get some huts erected fairly soon because Piedmonte means the foothills, and we're right under the mountains here. It soon gets cold, very cold.'

He looked, almost glowered around. 'I am the camp leader. The Italians are anxious to leave the internal organisation to me. We will not be ill-treated here, just at the mercy of general inefficiency, which means that a lot of things can go wrong, everything from not having enough to eat, to inadequate sanitation and an outbreak of cholera.' He regarded our upturned faces seriously from his perch on the chair. 'I have received only one direct instruction, from Major Sabantini, the Italian commandant,' he said in a measured way. 'Civilian shoes. No prisoner is permitted to wear shoes – boots are allowed only. Those who don't have any will be given a pair. They say they *can* organise boots. This is a precaution against escapes. Escapees wearing boots will be recognised more easily. So no shoes.'

He raised his voice: 'And no escapes either. If any of you have any bright ideas of going over the wire – when we've eventually put it up that is – then forget it, because we need every man here to help in the construction of this camp.

245

Otherwise we're going to freeze.' He looked towards the men outside. They could all hear him.

'In October,' he continued, 'that's in one month, in case any of you have lost count, it starts to rain in these parts. And it's not a gentle Liverpool drizzle. It's thick as soup, but colder, and it goes on day after day. We'll need some roofs over our heads by then, and I mean proper roofs not canvas. Then it stops raining and it snows.'

He looked about him doggedly, chin thrust out this way and that, at all the attentive faces in the tent and those peering from outside. 'The first thing we are going to do,' he said, 'is establish the skills of each man. Where's Mr Perkins . . .' He half raised himself and searched among the faces. A stub of a man in the centre of the tent stood and said: 'Here, captain.'

'Right you are.' Captain Franklyn addressed the men again. 'Mr Perkins is a purser. His skill is writing things down. And there was a clerk somewhere . . .'

A young man with a trimmed beard stood. 'Here, sir. Havertree.'

'Don't go around saying your name's Havertree, son,' called the captain. 'You'll end up in charge of the latrines.'

It was the best joke most of us had heard for weeks and the laughter was uproarious. 'All right,' said the captain, a touch of apology in his tone. 'You can help Mr Perkins. Come on out.'

They set up a table and two chairs, and a hard-covered exercise book was produced. 'We don't want shipwrights wasted on digging ditches,' announced the captain. 'So line up here and Mr Perkins will record what you can do. But first . . . any cooks?'

Half-a-dozen men moved out of the crowd. 'Right, come on first,' called Perkins the purser. 'We've *got* to have a cup of tea.'

I joined the line and found myself in charge of stores. Perkins said: 'The captor nation – the Eyetyes – will provide the stores. You have to order what you need, or what you hope you'll get, and make arrangements for the stuff to be under cover, and under guard, in the camp.'

The men left the big tent and before another hour the camp was beginning to take shape. The mountains piled up behind us, like a barrier holding back the deep blue sky, then the town of Alessandria and the bronzed country falling away to the coast at Genoa. By nightfall all the tents, our temporary living quarters, had been erected and cement brought in for forming the foundations of the permanent huts. An area was set aside for the latrines and bathhouses, at this time only holes in the earth and buckets of water. The region was crossed with canals, however, and an arm of one of these passed half a mile below the camp. After work for the day the prisoners went in sections down there, fifty men to one guard, and poured buckets of water over each other.

Sick men were to be treated at a civilian hospital at Alessandria or, in minor cases, at an Italian army camp before the town. An area was marked out for the cookhouse.

'Downwind,' said the practical Perkins. 'No smells drifting over the camp. There may come a time when there's not enough to go around.' A tent was erected for the stores and I watched it rise up with some sort of pride. The Italians brought in cases of food by lorry and I organised the sorting of this under canvas. They said they would bring in milk and other perishables each day. The cooks lit two old fashioned boilers with smoky chimneys and constructed a range from stones and bricks with a long metal top. Firewood was collected and piled. 'Like being in the boy scouts again,' said Curnow who had attached himself to my stores crew claiming that he knew about the storage of fish. At the end of the first day, with a sunset spilling over the land bordering the distant Mediterranean, three hundred seamen sat down wearily to an evening meal of lamb stew and fruit and bread. The cooks made gallons of tea and the prisoners sat around talking and eventually went tiredly to their tents. There were no complaints.

The huts were built before the rains arrived in October.

The captives constructed the barbed fence that was to imprison them and hammered in the stapled wire. Some of them were whistling.

A desultory group of Italian soldiers occupied a hut between the expanding compound and the canal and once every two hours one of them, often smoking a cigarette and usually willing to exchange two of his for one of the Red Cross Woodbines of the prisoners, would wander over to see we were still there.

Part of my duties were going to Alessandria with the stores truck. I wore clothes indistinguishable from any other man in the town, the only clue that I was a captive being in my bulky boots. It was a pleasant place, set on the Tanaro River, and there was little sign of war, although there were more women than men, and many of the men were old. But it seemed as if its life, amid its flaking buildings and turning streets, was unaltered. People gathered to talk under the trees, there were shabby, comfortable restaurants, cafés in courtyards and shops with their goods spread across the pavements. I was always in the company of a shambling Italian soldier and two slow men, Luigi and Gianni, who worked for the food distributors. At first they seemed to be more apprehensive of me than I was of them but, as the regular journeys to the town went on, they became easier. There was always a moment, during the visit, to go into one of the courtyards and sit in the shade drinking coffee or wine.

'I *like* it here,' said Curnow solidly one day. He was working, moving sand, and he said it without looking up. He spoke the thoughts of others. They were all sailors, accustomed to being away from their wives and families, and some frankly welcomed not having to face the duty of going home. 'No responsibilities,' summed up the Cornishman. He continued to shovel. 'If we could go out to a dance once a week, meet a nice woman or two, then you couldn't better it, could you?'

'You're not drowning in the sea,' said another man watching Curnow work. 'Like some.'

There was no news. The Italians shrugged when you asked them and said the war was as good as over. Mussolini and Hitler ruled the world between them. Letters from home were censored and there was no chance of listening to a wireless. Only the men who sporadically arrived at the camp, merchant seamen picked up by submarines, knew what was happening. 'Bombing's been bad,' said a man from London. 'Terrible. London's on fire. When we was sailing from Tilbury the docks was burning. I was glad to get out to sea.'

We had a guilt about being safe in our captivity but there was little we could do about it. The ban on escapes still stood. A football field had been laid out and matches organised. The Italians would come and watch and there was talk of them playing football against the prisoners. Men were taking correspondence courses organised through the Red Cross. I began studying for my third officer's examination. Captain Franklyn, the camp leader, set test papers in navigation and gave lectures in seamanship. Other men with special skills or experiences gave talks; a concert party was formed.

While the compound was being built the Italian commandant arrived rarely. He would have a glass of wine with Captain Franklyn and leave his inspection tour to a subordinate officer. He lived somewhere in the town and on some mornings was seen out riding with a woman.

When the huts were completed and the barbed wire surrounding them and us had been fixed to the last strand, we heard that the commandant had been replaced and that the new commanding officer would be attending the official opening ceremony.

No one seemed to see anything strange in a ceremony to mark the completion of the prison by the prisoners themselves; it was a matter of attainment for we had started with nothing and now we had a home. We even flew a homemade Union Jack over the gate on the ceremonial day but, after some debate with the Italians, this was replaced with some mixed red, white and blue bunting. A red ensign, brought out to decorate the messroom, was allowed to remain.

It was a special occasion and there had not been anything to celebrate for a long time. Each man was issued with a bottle of beer and a large tea party was organised with extra rations from the Red Cross parcels pool. The Italians brought a piano into the mess. We turned out smartly for the arrival of the new commandant. Our wire fence glistened in the late autumn sunshine, our huts were shipshape inside and out.

A small elderly Italian band played at the gate when the new officer arrived in an open car. He was greeted by Captain Franklyn and shown around the camp we had built. He remained at some distance from me until almost the moment of his departure. Some of us had formed up at the gate to sing 'Run Rabbit Run', a neutral and innocuous song, and were just about to start, the new commandant approaching, when I saw his face.

'God,' I breathed. 'It's . . .'

'You look like you know him,' said Curnow.

'Know him?' I muttered. 'He saved me from a firing squad.'

At the end of the ceremonial day Captain Franklyn called all the men together in the new long mess hut. Everyone was given another bottle of beer. We sat at the big tables the shipwrights and carpenters had made. The mood was jovial. When the captain came in with Perkins the purser some men started cheering and soon we were all joining in. Then the men sang: 'For He's a Jolly Good Fellow'. It was so loud and uproarious that two of the indolent Italian guards were stirred enough to come to the door and peer cautiously in. Their heads were greeted with renewed cheers and they withdrew swiftly and bashfully.

'Good, good,' said Captain Franklyn putting up his hands. Silence dropped over the mess. 'Congratulations,' he said bluntly. 'To everybody. It's been a very workmanlike job.

We've now got a good ship, weatherproof and comfortable. The only trouble is she is not sailing anywhere.'

A serious silence at once fell. His voice became quieter: 'As prisoners we have no choice but to remain here. At the same time we have to realise that our country is at war and that it is our duty to do anything we can to help our country.' His head poked inquiringly around the room, like that of an eagle on a perch. The guards had closed the door politely behind them but, at a nod from Franklyn, Perkins pushed back his chair and tiptoed towards it, opening it, looking out, closing it and turning the key exactly in the lock.

'Coast clear, Mr Perkins?' asked the captain without looking sideways.

'Coast clear, sir.'

'We have constructed a very good stockade here,' Franklyn continued. 'Not a loose nail anywhere. We've played fair. Now it's our duty *to get over it*. We will be forming an escape committee.'

A groan went up from some of the men. The captain looked shocked. His eyes searched the audience. 'It is our *duty*,' he repeated. 'As prisoners of war, we must attempt an escape.' He stared along the faces. 'Any questions?'

For a few moments there was no movement. Then a massive man, a New Zealander who had delighted in showing his muscles and feats of strength during the construction, both to his fellows and particularly to the guards, stood ponderously.

'Sir?'

'Yes, Bannerman.'

'If we escape, sir . . .'

'Yes.'

'Where will we be going? Where will we be escaping to?'

'England,' said Franklyn briskly. He was not going to add to that. He got up from his seat and followed by a fretful-looking Perkins strode out of the building, leaving behind silence and Bannerman still standing. His shoulders, like bulwarks, strained his shirt. 'Well, mates, Bill Bannerman ain't escaping,' he announced. 'Bill Bannerman's staying right here for the rest of this bloody war.' He strode out and we all began to trail after him, each man dropping his beer bottle in a bin outside the door. Curnow had not finished his beer. He stood by the bin and lifted it to his lips but then threw it in, still half full. 'Mucked up a nice evening,' he said.

We shuffled to our new huts. Curnow followed me in and gave the wood walls a disgruntled punch. 'Built to last,' he said. 'All tight and cosy.'

'It'll blow over,' I told him. 'Talking about escaping is one thing, escaping is another.'

'The big bloke was right, though, when he said where was there to go. There's not a sausage. Look at the map. At least we've got the Eyetyes here. Everywhere else is Jerries.'

'There's Malta,' said one of the other men, an elderly seaman called Freemantle. Few welcomed the suggestion. Some moved away.

'*If* we've still got Malta,' said another man.

'We had it last week,' asserted Freemantle. 'I saw one of the Eyetye newspapers. There was a map showing who had got what. Malta was still ours.'

'Always wanted to go to Malta,' muttered Curnow.

Outside it began to rain noisily, battering the new windows, but the hut was firm. The lights were put out at ten. Like boys at school we got into our beds, four to a room.

After a few minutes Freemantle's voice murmured: 'You could almost swim to Malta.' No one spoke.

The rain set in hard and we had to dig extra ditches to carry the water away but in general the new camp stood up well to the weather. When Captain Franklyn was making his rounds one day he came to the stores and asked me some questions about supplies. It was the first time I had been able to speak to him. 'The new commandant, Colonel Maroni, sir,' I said diffidently. 'I know him. I've met him from Spain.'

'And how did that come about?' he asked.

'The civil war, sir. He saved me from a firing squad.'

'Jesus, did he now!'

I described quickly what had happened in the mountains of Catalunya. The captain sat down on a box and listened thoughtfully. He whistled and grinned at the end. 'Saved your bacon there, son,' he agreed. He rose. 'When he comes on his rounds I'll bring him across. See if he remembers you.'

Two days later I returned from Alessandria and was helping to unload stores when I saw Captain Franklyn and the Italian commandant approaching. It was difficult to believe that the two were enemies. They were laughing. There were two Italian soldiers behind them and a young officer, who talked flamboyantly to Perkins.

'Jones,' called Franklyn.

'Sir?'

'Colonel Maroni, this is Jones. You have met before.'

'We have?' The commandant eyed me with curiosity. 'And what did I say to you?' he asked.

'That you came from the home town of Rossini,' I told him.

'Pesara,' he nodded. 'That is correct.'

'And Rossini's father was the town trumpeter,' I added.

Pleasure warmed his face. 'Where was our meeting?' he asked.

'Spain, sir.' The other men had stopped unloading the truck and were listening.

'Ah.' He was regarding me more closely. 'In Catalunya?'

'Yes. You saved me from the firing squad.'

'Jones!' he abruptly exploded. He shook with amazed laughter. 'Goodness God!' he said turning to Franklyn. 'Every time I see this boy he is a prisoner!'

Three

As the months went on it grew cold. Winds fell from the mountains, whistling around the huts at night, and eventually, two weeks before Christmas, it snowed deeply. Clearing paths and roads gave us some occupation. There had been plans for the prisoners to go out in working parties, to the railway and in the forest, but no move was made to organise these and most of the men had to occupy themselves learning languages or engineering or land management, or taking part in discussions on the world they would like to see after the war. There was nothing else to do.

I was in genuine employment, for the stores kept me busy five hours a day. Other men volunteered to go out in wood-gathering parties, and these were very popular because apart from twenty prisoners each week being permitted under escort to go to the cinema in Alessandria, where they sat like grateful children in the back two rows of the stalls, there was scant chance to get beyond our wire. Some woodworking tools had been brought in, and the carpenters and ship-wrights were making furniture and other things. Three of the inmates had lost legs in action and the carpenters made each of them wooden legs plus spares.

We had Christmas dinner with extras from the Red Cross parcel pool and the private parcels which the prisoners received from their relatives, and pork brought to the camp gates by a group of shy Italian civilians. On Boxing night we had a concert party and on New Year's Eve a dance.

The dance, naturally, was very odd. We had a gramophone and a pile of records. There were formation dances: the barn dance, the Gay Gordons and the Dashing White Sergeant, which had been taught in the camp classes. Some of the men jitterbugged together.

At the end of the evening, as the year turned, we all sang 'Auld Lang Syne'. We made a big circle outside in the snow because there was no room in the mess hut where the dance had been held. It must have looked rare, three hundred men holding hands in a great ring, singing about people who were far away. Some Italians came to the gates and stood watching with the guards. They were silent and they went away silently.

After it was finished we all shook hands and wished each other a Happy New Year, 1941, and then went, hands in pockets, back to our huts. We left a circle trampled in the snow as big as a circus ring. I looked out of the hut window and saw it illuminated by its own whiteness. Beyond it were the dim lights over the wire and outside the heavy mountains clothed in misty cold.

Curnow, who slept in the bunk above me, climbed like a boy, into his bed.

'Jonesey,' he muttered from the bunk above.

'Yes?'

'I'm homesick.'

There were groans and curses from the other men in the room. 'Shut up, Curnow,' grunted one man. 'You're making it worse.'

'The blokes with one leg will be back in Blighty soon,' persisted the other man. 'Lucky bastards.' We all knew they were about to be repatriated. They had been plodding happily around the camp on their wooden stumps.

'It might be worth cutting your leg off,' grunted Curnow.

The days dragged and drifted on. The seasons changed but little else. We heard rumours that the war was changing. The Americans were now fighting. The Italians began to mutter among themselves. Our guards said they had always hated the Germans.

One morning in the hot May of 1943 a message was passed

to me to attend a special navigation lecture by Captain Franklyn. We used maps and charts as part of these lectures and by now I was well advanced in my studies for my third officer's certificate, strange since I had not been in sight of the sea for almost three years. At this session there were three men who were not studying for examinations. Curnow, who had never shown ambition to increase his sea-going status and was summoned from his vegetable garden, was among them, looking apprehensive. Captain Franklyn produced a map from the bottom of a pile of navigation charts. 'This,' he said, 'is a map of the Piedmonte area, right down to the sea.' He looked up at us with his sharp eyes. 'It will show you, I hope, the way to get home.'

A thrill, half-fright, half-joy, went through me. 'If anyone wants to back out now, then do it,' Franklyn said quietly.

No one moved.

'Grand. It has been carefully planned. We have friends inside and outside the camp.' He glanced up as if he would not welcome questions. 'We're talking about tomorrow,' he said. 'You four will form the stores crew. Jones in charge as usual. You will go to Alessandria and contact will be made there. After that you have to follow your noses and your luck. This map shows the route to Genoa. You may not need it. The Italians will help you. At Genoa or some place on that part of the coast, you will be taken on as part of the crew of a vessel sailing for one of the ports in unoccupied France. Wherever you land up there you will be looked after and eventually – and it may take time – smuggled out into Switzerland or Spain. I hope you have all been paying attention in your Italian lessons. You're going to need them.'

That same afternoon the New Zealander, Bannerman, was shot dead by one of the Italian guards. He lay like a big mound of earth in the sunlight by the gate. It was like a petrified scene, all still, not a sound after the crack of the shot. Then there was a commotion. An ambulance arrived but it was no use to Bannerman. They transported a dead man away. The Italians said the shooting had been an accident.

The incident caused the postponement of our escape attempt. Life went on its unchanging and unchallenging pattern; the summer spread around us, cricket was organised and a volleyball net set up. The visits to the cinema were increased to two a week.

After two months Captain Franklyn and Perkins the purser came on their morning rounds and Perkins winked at me and said, 'Tomorrow.' When I got back to the billet Curnow looked over the rim of his bunk and nodded. I nodded back.

This time there was no interruption. Four were to make the break. The two other men were called Rand and Billingham. We took the stores lorry into Alessandria and began to load sacks and boxes at the warehouse which I had visited nearly every day for three years. Nothing happened until the back of the vehicle was almost full. Then Gianni, foreman at the warehouse, came to me and said: 'Let us go.'

My stomach tightened. I followed him. He was a big man with a flowing moustache. He walked, almost strolled, through the warehouse, conversing with me in Italian. I kept nodding and smiling. We went between the piles of sacks and crates out into the white sunlight of the yard at the rear. Another truck was parked there, piled with greengrocery and bags of flour. There was a crevice between the goods and at the back of this, like men hiding in a defile, were Curnow, Rand and Billingham. I could see their eyes. Gianni was calm. I could feel myself shaking. I climbed up among the sacks. Gianni's big teeth were vivid below his thick moustache. He pushed up the tailboard and shouted '*Si, si!*' The driver started the engine.

We crouched in the dark. We felt the lorry swing through the tight streets and saw the flowered windows of the town turn past over the top of the tailboard.

The truck left the town and we could smell the canal before being held up as we crossed one of the bridges. The driver braked and we heard him shouting. My teeth were clamped together. I shut my eyes. We restarted and overtook a donkey cart which we could see plodding along behind us, the driver waving the whip at the back of our vehicle.

It was difficult to know how many Germans were in this region of Italy. We had seen them marching in small units and sometimes they set up a random road block and inspected vehicles.

The heat became dense as we drove. The driver kept doggedly going, we could hear him loudly singing. After thirty or forty miles he stopped to fill up with fuel. There was a lot of banter in Italian with the man pumping the petrol. Before we set off again two bottles of water were thrown casually over the tailboard to us.

The day outside became more shaded. By early evening we had reached a small town and we could hear people walking in the streets. Some men were talking loudly and laughing, probably in a bar. There was the smell of dust and horse dung.

Beyond the town we again stopped. Curnow clutched my arm and rolled his eyes. There were strong German voices outside. The driver became voluble and got out of his cab. They trudged around the side of the vehicle and we solidified, pressing ourselves as far out of sight as we could. We never saw the Germans for they remained below the tailboard and they didn't look into the back. Eventually the driver clambered back into his seat and we set off. After a couple of miles he began to sing again.

We halted again and this time, we knew, we were at the gates of a port for there was the remembered smell of the sea. Official voices were again raised but now they were Italian. The driver shouted a farewell and drove on. In our cramped, dim place we nudged each other. It was going to work.

The truck pulled up again and this time remained stationary for more than an hour. The driver appeared to have gone away. Then we heard voices returning. These stopped too but after ten minutes we sensed someone softly approaching the tailboard. Tensely we waited. It was quietly dropped and a floating hand beckoned us to get down from the truck. So cramped were our legs that we almost fell out. We stood stamping our feet silently to bring back the feeling. We were on a cobbled dockside with a ship tied up. The man who had pulled down the tailboard did not appear afraid. He pointed to a gangway going up to the dark deck of the ship.

We climbed to the deck. I was knotted with excitement. No one else was there. The little man went like a monkey across the ropes and tackle and slid through a hatch and we followed: Rand first, then Billingham, then Curnow, then me. As we went down the companionway so the sickly heat below decks came to us. There was another hatch which led into a store-room, where machinery, parts and tools were lying around. There was a high porthole. The man motioned us to stay. He shut the door and locked it. We sank to the floor. We had not exchanged more than glances for six hours and we remained silent now.

After more than two hours we heard feet on the deck above and the unmistakable sounds of a ship preparing to sail. Voices drifted down to us, cables rattled, and then we felt the ship move, jerkily at first but with increasing power and smoothness, out from the harbour and into the sea. We were on our way to freedom.

We were at sea for two days and two nights. We only saw one man, the small Italian who had guided us aboard the ship. On each of the two days he brought us a bowl of pasta and some water.

It was necessary for us to urinate through the high porthole and this was only achieved by standing on Billingham's shoulders. He was the biggest man and he suffered this duty without protest even when Curnow and then Rand said that they additionally wanted to crap. When Billingham had his turn he had to plant his feet, one on my shoulder and the other on Rand's, and push his backside through the porthole. It was not easy.

On the evening of the second day we felt that we were

approaching the shore because we could hear the sounds of other ships and feel their wash against the hull. We sensed that the vessel was slowing. She reduced to dead slow and there was a firm bump and a grating on the hull as she came to a jetty. We crouched and waited, apprehensive but eager as dogs in a kennel. It was three hours before someone approached and we heard the catch on the outside of the door slipped. It opened. The man had a torch. He directed it into our eyes so we could not see him although he was bigger than the Italian. '*Suivez moi*,' he grunted. We rose wearily and followed him.

It was a warm night, bulky with clouds. From the deck we could see that the harbour around us was small. The Frenchman loped ahead on rubbersoled shoes. Down onto the dockside we followed him and into a dark storage shed. He briskly locked the door behind us.

'God help me,' grumbled Curnow as we felt our way around the dark space. 'We've been more locked up since we escaped than we was before.'

We could only sit on the floor and endure another wait. Lack of room meant we went to sleep propped against each other. I woke to hear Rand snoring and roused him. It was humid in there and it stank. Wan daylight hung below the door and we heard signs of activity outside. Early boats were entering the harbour. We could smell fish.

Carts, their rimmed wheels grinding on the dockside stones, and some grunting lorries arrived. We could smell the fish being unloaded. Then, sharply and silently, the door of the store was opened and we crouched as the daylight streaked in. Only a brown and heavy-haired hand appeared. A dirty finger beckoned us. We went out blindly into the low, early sunlight where three men were standing. The third word spoken to us since our arrival in France was, '*Ici*.' The man indicated one of the horse-drawn carts. Crates of fish were being loaded onto the back but a space had been left in the middle and into this we crawled. The stench of the fish was powerful. The workers filled in the open space around us with more crates until eventually the cart was loaded and began to grind away. Water and scales cascaded from the fish. We squatted, sodden and overwhelmed by the odour, for almost an hour until the cart came to a halt. Once more we waited. As the crates around us were lifted, another beckoning finger summoned us and we climbed out.

We were in a streaming gutter beside a fish market. No one looked at us, until a man in a flapping rubber apron approached. Casually, as though we were day labourers arriving for work, he directed us to unload the cart which had been our refuge. Other carts arrived and several lorries. Old men and young women gutted the fish at long slab tables. They shouted and gesticulated at each other and laughed crudely. They paid no attention to us. Buyers, men wearing hats, were at the centre of the market picking out their fish. There were no Germans and no police.

A large, clean car drew up on the far side of the street, away from the market debris. A driver got out and opened the rear door for a man wearing a light grey suit, a tie with a white shirt and a straw hat. He was in his forties, brown-faced but smooth, as though the tan had been carefully acquired.

He strode across the cobbled street, being directed around puddles and squashed fish, by the man in the rubber apron, until he reached the buyers' side of the market. He had a metallic watch and rings which reflected the sun. The workers dropped their voices and their eyes. Other buyers fell back respectfully as he viewed the fish and pointed to them. Then he glanced up and for a moment I was certain that he looked directly towards us. Quickly I turned away and went towards the final truck being unloaded. The man followed by the aproned overseer, with a list clipped to a board, went back to his car where he signed the list as it was held out. The driver opened the rear door and the man got in. The driver handed him a cigar from a box and lit it for him before getting back behind the wheel and driving away.

The workers had become subdued now. The shift was

nearly done. Women were washing their raw hands under taps. Men were lining up at a scarred desk to be paid, and the women joined in the line behind them. Curnow, Rand, Billingham and I had spaced ourselves out along the fish slabs so that we would not be conspicuous in a group. The man in the apron, with no change of expression, called us over and paid us a few francs. As he did so a small shuddering van appeared and pulled up. The overseer wiped his hands on his apron, said to me: '*Monsieur*,' and motioned with his eyes towards the van. Then he did the same to Curnow. We looked at the others but no sign was made to them. The man put up the palms of his hands in a sign that they should stay.

Curnow and I climbed into the back of the van. It had a ragged canvas cover. The driver wore a jersey and a greasy trilby. He drove away as soon as we were in the back. It was not far. After a mile along a road hanging above the sea, the vehicle turned down a slope of profuse bougainvillea. It steered into a yard and we looked out onto the back of a substantial white building. The driver motioned us to get from the van and we did so, to find ourselves standing high above the aching blue of the Mediterranean. It was midday, tranquil and warm, with the smell of flowers overcoming even the scent of the fish which clung to us.

Stooping as he loped, the driver made for a low door, overhung with creepers, and we followed. It was a cool, long, stone passage, leading into a courtyard with half-a-dozen small doors facing the yard. The Frenchman went directly to one of these, opened it and unsmilingly said: '*Ici.*'

We went into a plain clean room, two beds, a washstand and a screen. 'All they say is "*Ici*",' said Curnow looking around. 'Where d'you reckon this is?'

'Safety,' I said. The man returned and handed two towels to us, indicating that we should follow him. We went out into the enclosed sun of the courtyard once more and into a stone room where a single tap poked from the wall. '*Lavez vous*,' he pointed. We stripped off our foul clothes and poured water on ourselves. It was four days and a lot of fish since we had washed. The man came back and gave us each a pair of rough linen underpants, a thick pair of socks, two shirts and two dark blue smocks and two pairs of blue trousers. He looked down at our feet and went out again, returning with two well-worn pairs of wooden clogs.

We returned to the room to find a pile of bread and cheese on a board on the table, with two bottles of beer beside it. We ate hungrily and as we did so the man again came back, this time with some grapes.

He left us to eat. Then we both stretched on the beds and immediately slept. It was dark when I awoke and stared around the room. Curnow was snoring quietly. It was the opening of the door which had roused me. I pushed Curnow's shoulder and he awoke too, his eyes trying to remember where he was. A woman wearing a white overall was standing in the dim opening of the door. 'You must come this way,' she said.

Into the courtyard we went. The night was close and full of the smell of flowers. Stars crowded the space between the white walls. From somewhere came the enticing odour of cooking. We walked behind her broad swaying bottom into the house. She mounted some wooden stairs and opened a door which let onto a finely furnished landing, carpeted and hung with old pictures, a leather chair in one corner. 'You must come this way,' she repeated half turning. We followed her into another corridor, darkly panelled, at the end of which she knocked on a door and opened it. '*Monsieur*,' she said to someone inside, '*Voilà les Anglais*.'

Curnow and I went into the room. The curtains were drawn and it was soberly lit. There was some deep furniture, pictures, and a big desk, sitting behind which was a man who looked up as we entered. It was the man in the grey suit who had come to the fish market. The woman went out.

He came around the desk and shook us each by the hand. 'Gentlemen,' he said quietly. 'I am Alfred Laurent. This is the Hôtel de la Rive. Welcome. You will be safe here. For a time.'

*

I was there for ten weeks. The war was blazing all around us, and there we were in that sunny, becalmed place. Apart from the German officers who came regularly to dinner at the hotel from their leave centre a few miles along the coast, there was no great danger of our discovery. We watched the officers at their tables by standing sideways and peering through the crack of the kitchen door.

The Hotel de la Rive stood above massive scenery; rocks rounded as elephants, an endless blue sea and a sky more endlessly blue than that. Cypress and olive trees hung from the rocks. There were extravagant flowers; bougainvillea, fuchsia, and other tumbling plants. A hard path went from the hotel down to a yellow beach which tapered away to a miniature harbour.

Guests at the hotel were people from Nice or Monte Carlo or as far as Toulon. Sometimes French naval officers from the Vichy government base there would come for several days, defeated men trying to put a brave face on it. If the Germans came to dine the French would transfer to some other restaurant or would sit in the most distant corner of the dining room. They saluted each other in passing and smiled, the French smiles rooted to their faces.

Civilians who came for weekends were subdued, with little spirit, and although they often drank sufficiently to cheer themselves, the jokes were old. An official from Nice had too much wine one night and began to address loud and acid remarks to a group of Germans on the far side of the room. His wife and friends, and Monsieur Laurent, got him briskly out. His wife came back to apologise to the Germans who laughed and seemed to enjoy it.

Curnow and I had started by emptying the bins, cleaning the floors, doing the washing up and general porterage. Our fellow workers never acknowledged that we were odd men. They spoke to us in French, which we scarcely understood. One morning a simple culinary task had to be done and the chef was annoyed because two of the staff were ill. I picked up a knife and from that moment Curnow and I were

264

promoted. They believed that Curnow was also a cook, I was able to manoeuvre him to perform uncomplicated tasks, and they brought in two local men to empty the bins.

Four German officers and four Frenchwomen had enjoyed dinner one evening and decided to compliment the chef and his assistants. We were called to parade at their table. One of the Frenchwomen took a fancy to little Curnow and began asking him questions. He smiled stupidly and did not answer. He rolled his eyes towards me and this made the officers and their women laugh even more. Monsieur Laurent saved us. He appeared at the door, having been summoned sharply by a waiter, and in two strides was with us, patting us on the backs and bowing to the Germans. He pointed to Curnow and then indicated his own ears. '*Il est sourd,*' he said. Curnow, never lost for initiative, opened his mouth like a hole and pointed into that as well, making a piggish noise as he did. The officers and the ladies laughed even louder. The German officers gave us each a tip. We then backed out, comically, because they laughed and applauded our little dumb show. Once in the kitchen Curnow shook with anger. The chef suggested that we went back to our room in case they came to look for us. We pocketed our francs. '*Boche,*' said the chef grimly. Before putting his tip in his pocket he spat on it which was something he also did with dishes to be served to German officers, mixing it well into the food. It was a small revenge.

As we became accustomed to the place so we moved more freely. Language was the barrier because however much we came to understand neither Curnow nor I could ever chance speaking French in public. Curnow was anxious to make the acquaintance of an obliging local woman, and he had made overtures to one or two who came to the hotel to work as maids or waitresses. Monsieur Laurent, who missed very little, said to me: 'Your friend Mr Curnow. Please tell him there will be time for women after the war.'

We went down the steep shale path to the shore on many

afternoons. Below the hotel the beach was difficult to reach and used by few people. The neighbouring harbour section had been encompassed with barbed wire by the French. There was also a gun emplacement which was rarely manned and quite often locked up. Below it people sometimes sat under coloured umbrellas. Preparations for an Allied invasion were not serious.

The French knew the war news and talked about it openly. In October the British army in North Africa had rolled back the Germans and Italians at El Alamein, an offensive that was to take them the width of Africa to join up with the Americans who had landed on the other coast. United States planes bombed Le Havre, in Northern France; the people in the south sadly shrugged and said it was a pity. The German invasion of Russia was still stemmed at Stalingrad. In the Pacific the Japanese were still advancing and dying but their time was running out. Five hundred Italian prisoners of war drowned when a U-Boat sank a British ship.

I used to go swimming on afternoons from the quiet beach. Life was unreal. The autumn sun was like a golden gong, people sat under awnings and drank pastis. It was as if this place had been removed, not only from the war but from the world.

Alone one afternoon I swam out to sea, turning on my back and looking at the land; big grey rocks, deep mountains behind, rising dark and green to the intense sky. There were pale houses among the cypresses, boats nodding offshore, the movements of a slow horse and cart along the Corniche road.

Swimming back I became aware of a woman walking on the beach. She had a dog, busily running on the sand. I could see that she was calling it. She wore an orange dress and a straw hat. I paddled offshore for a while waiting for her to go.

She showed no inclination to do so, however, and the autumn water was becoming chill. Also it was time I was back in the kitchen. I swam a few hundred yards in the direction of the harbour and began moving towards the sand from there. She strolled with her dog in that direction also. I turned and trawled my way back to my original course. She turned and went that way too, as if she were patrolling, or even waiting for me. There was nothing for it but to go towards the shore.

She remained, her hat shading her eyes, the dog barking. I trudged from the sea. It was impossible to avoid her. '*Bonjour, madame*,' I said, assuming the mumble that I always hoped would disguise my accent.

'How are you, *monsieur*,' she responded. 'And how is your small friend who cannot speak and cannot hear?'

Antoinette Durer lived in a apartment overlooking the sea at Nice. She was the mistress of, among others, a German colonel stationed in the north who visited her twice a month. 'He is very kind,' she explained revolving a drink in a long glass. 'But he remains my enemy.'

The window looked onto the Promenade des Anglais. 'Now the English have gone away,' she said. 'How long will it be before they come back?' I went to the window. Below, the palms were sifted by an early winter wind. Blunt grey waves came up to the beach. People walked wearing long coats.

'I am sorry,' she said, 'that you have to leave your small friend behind – Monsieur Curnow. He will be safe. This time there is only room for one.'

She was going to get me out. This delicate woman who had waited on the beach, this woman with the cloudy eyes and long light hands was going to get me out, and home. 'It was so amusing that night,' she laughed. 'When we congratulated you on the dinner. Our German friends thought you were simpletons.' She shrugged. 'It is easy to tell lies to them.'

'It would be hard not to believe anything you said,' I replied. '*I* would believe you.'

'They think they have won, it is finished. So, they ask, why should we lie to them?' Her eyes clouded. 'Another drink?' she asked. I gave the glass to her. The black dog was tucked up like a snail under a potted palm in the corner of the wide room. She handed me the Martini. 'How long have you been away from your home?' she asked. I sank into the chair.

'Three years altogether,' I told her.

'You have a wife?'

'She divorced me.'

'Why was that?'

'One reason was desertion.'

Antoinette put her fingers to her surprised mouth. Her lipstick was pale. 'I am sorry to laugh,' she said. 'But that does not seem very . . . sporting.'

'Those are my feelings. But that was that.'

'So there is no one?'

'I have an uncle. And somewhere I have a mother.'

She eyed me over her glass. 'It is not a close family?'

'You could say that. There is not a lot at home for me. I just want to get there.'

'You must fight the war,' she nodded seriously. 'As all of us.'

'This is very dangerous,' I said. 'For you.'

She shrugged. 'I have friends in good places. Also here in Vichy France there is not the surveillance from the German military. We are, after all, French, whatever has happened to us. We do not like the *Boche*.'

She went into the kitchen, put on an apron and prepared a meal for us. The small table was set in the circle of a lamp. She changed her dress and was serving soup. 'It's difficult to believe this is happening,' I said to her.

'It is all true,' she smiled and shrugged. 'There is a bottle of wine. Will you please open it.'

I fumbled with the bottle and with the corkscrew. 'I have champagne,' she said. 'But Heinrich gave it to me and he counts the bottles.'

'It must be nice to have a friend like Heinrich,' I suggested. I sat down opposite her at the table.

She did not want to discuss it. 'It is useful in many ways,' she said. 'Tell me your adventures. How did they catch you?'

As we ate the meal I related some of the things that had happened to me. Sometimes she laughed but always her eyes became intent again. She said at last: 'I cannot believe that so many things could take place to one man.' She raised her glass. 'But now you are here,' she said. I raised mine. 'I am here,' I said.

After she had made coffee she went to the window and brushing aside the curtain looked out onto the dark Promenade des Anglais. 'Once,' she murmured, 'all this was so fine, you know. Rich people and sunshine. Now we are just holding on, as you say. Hoping for the best to happen.' She took a final glance from the window and moved away. Then she stopped and darted back, quickly tugging the curtain and bending her knees to see below the heads of the palms in the avenue. 'Oh,' she said hurriedly. She put her coffee cup down on the table. She went back and peered out again. 'Oh, *mon Dieu!*' She turned, her face full of alarm. 'Quickly,' she gasped. 'Heinrich is here! It is his car.'

Panic caught me. 'What shall I do . . .?' She grasped me by the arm.

'Come. The next apartment. Quickly.'

She picked up my blue jacket and bodily pushed me out of the door into the corridor. 'The table,' I said pointing back into the room. 'He'll see . . .'

'It is okay,' she said. She pushed me again. 'Come now.'

The adjoining flat was only a few paces down the corridor. She rang the bell and knocked urgently. It was at once opened by an old woman.

'Madame Tranchard,' said Antoinette briskly. '*Pour vous.*' She thrust me bodily into the doorway, so forcefully that I landed in the shaky arms of Madame Tranchard. Antoinette's feet sounded, hurrying down the corridor. I heard her door slam.

Not at all flurried the elderly woman invited me to sit down while she sedately poured me a tumbler of brandy. She paused to listen at the door, her face creased with joy and cunning. There were voices in the corridor. '*Les Allemands,*' she said and spat lightly on the floor. She rubbed it into the carpet with her foot.

The rest of the night was like a purgatory. I slept in a single bed wedged against the wall of a tight room immediately next to the one occupied by Antoinette and Heinrich. I was barely six inches from them. He grunted and moaned and set the bed springs singing. I could hear her talking to him. After a while it stopped but then it began again. The bed sounded, I heard water being poured. They conversed again but then were quiet. At three in the morning they awoke, just as I was inching off to sleep. I lay there, squirming and bereft in the dark, while she spoke softly to her enemy and lover.

The train steamed into Marseille again. I was at the same platform from which I had left for Spain five years before. Antoinette spoke occasionally, low-voiced, in English as we walked from the station. In Unoccupied France at that time no one took any heed of anything. They went on with their work and their families, steadily, hardly raising their heads to take in what was going on with life in their country or in the world. People in the streets and shops and in restaurants, always speaking in undertones, not, it seemed, listening to anything or anyone beyond their own conversation.

Outside the station was a horse-taxi, a motor car with shafts, the driver and the animal with their heads sagging at the same weary angle. The horse snorted as Antoinette spoke but the man remained soundless. There were few vehicles in the streets; some cars with enormous gas bags, as big as the cars themselves, carried on their roofs. We went to an address about a mile from the station. In the back of the slow vehicle Antoinette handed me some francs. 'You must pay,' she said. I took the money. At the destination the driver accepted it wordlessly and with a long sigh flipped the reins and started his horse back towards the station. It began to rain.

Antoinette pulled my sleeve and we stood back below a

shop awning, until the taxi had gone. The horse crapped like a comment on the bonnet of the car as it drew away.

We began to walk along the street. After turning two corners we went into a crouching door, a cobbler's shop lit by only a fanlight onto the street, where a gnomish, hairless man in a filthy apron was sewing stiches in a ragged pair of boots. Antoinette spoke to him and, with half a glance, he pointed to a curtain leading to the back of the shop. '*Montez l'escalier,*' he called after us.

We went up the stairs, spiralling sharply. It was dim and dust grated below our feet. 'These places are not first class,' she muttered.

There was a door at the top and she knocked and immediately opened it. The room was unoccupied but it had two armchairs and a couch, two weathered lamps, and old photographs askew on the walls. There was a table and on it a pot of coffee and two cups. As if she expected it to be there, Antoinette poured the coffee into the cups. She added powdered milk and brown sugar.

'Am I allowed to ask where this is?' I inquired.

'A house to hide in,' she answered. She nodded at her coffee. 'They charge extra for coffee. Some make good money from the war.'

A woman with a twitchy face appeared, her hands held in front of her as if to ward off a blow. Only Antoinette spoke. The woman already understood and her eyes rolled in the direction of another door. '*Monsieur,*' invited Antoinette. We went from the room into a bedroom with two single beds pushed against each wall. There was a towel on a rack and a basin on a stand. The woman went out again silently.

'We must both be here,' said Antoinette. She examined the room. 'It is not the Ritz. But it is safe. I hope it is safe.'

She said she was going out and would bring back some food. After she had gone I looked out of the window onto wet roofs and lay back on one of the dark beds watching spiders on the ceiling. Rain guttered from the roof over the window.

When she returned I was asleep. Her entry made me sit

upright in alarm but she touched my forehead with one finger and smiled down at me through the gloom. It was five o'clock and it was already almost dark. She had brought food in a brown carrier bag and we went into the other room and spread it on the table. There was bread and pâté and a square of doleful cheese. She had also brought a bottle of wine.

'It is not the best repast,' she smiled. Her knees were close together just below the hem of her skirt. 'In Marseille,' she continued, 'they are taking it more badly than in Nice. They believe that the Germans will march into the Unoccupied Zone at any day and what freedom they have will be gone.' She blew out her cheeks sadly. 'They see no end of this in sight.'

'Not many people do,' I said.

'It is better than being occupied in the north,' she went on. 'Or in Holland or Belgium. Perhaps even in Germany. Things have gone on too long in Germany, so my German friends say to me.' She looked up. 'The best place to be is in England.'

'When will I be there?'

She said she did not know. 'We must contact a group here. They make the arrangements.'

The wine was thin and sharp. 'Does Heinrich think that things are looking bad for them?' I said.

She knew what I meant. Her eyes came up and she smiled sombrely. 'Heinrich was on some special mission, so he came to see me. I did not know. Madame Tranchard entertained you well?'

'She was very kind,' I said.

'You slept?'

'After a while.'

Her hand went suddenly to her mouth. Her eyes enlarged. 'Oh . . . you were in the *petite . . . chambre*.'

'Yes.'

'Oh, that is too bad.'

She put down her glass and leaned towards me. Her face

272

was close. Her slender eyes searched my face. I scarcely knew what to do. My fingers went below her pale chin. Her eyes closed but I kept looking at her. As we kissed the old twitching woman padded into the room and, as though we were not there, began to remove the plates and the cutlery and the glasses from the low table between us. Her hands went below our stilled embrace to collect the empty wine bottle. We moved apart and she gathered everything onto a tray, scraping pieces of food together and then plodding from the room again.

'The service is good,' I said.

Antoinette's hand was against her mouth. 'Here they do not see, they do not hear, they do not know.' She laughed shortly and soundlessly. Then her eyes came back to me and mine to her. She stood and held out her hands in invitation and I took them.

We went to the bedroom and, after a backward look into the other room, she turned the key in the lock. I stood stupidly. She became very deliberate, as if she had entered a small trance. Her eyes were cloudy, her face grave, her body still. A helplessness came upon me. Eventually she murmured, as if tired: 'Please will you take my clothes.'

I touched her blouse and began to undo the buttons. As I did it she eased herself out of the rest of her garments, tossing each thing aside. Her skin glowed in the dimness. Her arms were slim. My hands went to her sharp breasts and I touched a woman intimately for the first time in three years.

Her face averted, she unbuttoned my shirt, peeled it over my shoulders, and bent forward to kiss my chest. She rubbed the tops of my arms.

'These,' she mumbled. 'These.' Vaguely she waved her hands at the narrow beds. 'We must make them like one.'

We performed a movement like a dance, a turn and a sidestep, to get from the space between. Then I bent and pushed the beds together. They blocked the door.

At that moment someone tried to open the locked door. They would not desist. It was rattled irritably. Antoinette nodded and I pulled the beds apart again and turned the key. I only allowed the door to open by nine inches but in the crevice I could see the shaking chops of the old woman. One eye shone in at me. A bright, terrible eye.

She was trying to thrust a tray and the coffee pot and cups through the aperture. She would not be deterred. 'No coffee, thank you,' I said. '*Pas de café, merci* . . .' She continued to force her burden through the crack. I had to accept it. '*Merci, madame. Merci. Bonsoir. Bonsoir.*'

I closed the door on the trembling face and the pointed eye and brought the tray into the room, pushing the door and locking it. I sat on the bed with the tray on my knees. Antoinette, her upper body still naked, was regarding me with simmering mirth. 'They charge extra for the coffee,' she said.

Taking the tray from me she walked to the washstand and placed it there. 'So many things can go wrong in two minutes,' she said. I watched the shadows and shapes change on her body as she walked back, the slight tremor of her breasts, the inward arch of her stomach, her mobile hips still concealed by her skirt. She examined my face very seriously and touched her finger to her lips. I manoeuvred the small beds back together once more. She patted them as they abutted. 'This is how we will be soon,' she promised. 'Joined.'

By this time I could hardly wait another moment for her. I tugged my trousers down like a navvy in a ditch. Gracefully she turned away and took off her skirt, her pants and her stockings. She remained wearing a half-slip. She pushed my shoulder with one finger to ease me back. We were shadows. The only light came from the uncurtained window, the pale drift from the night sky. There was now no sound of rain. Her body arched above me, curved and lean. I felt the luxury of the single silken garment moving up my thigh as she bent towards me. My hands went to the cool, full, skin of her bosom.

'What is the difference?' she inquired in her oddly serious manner. 'Between big and large?' She propped herself on her

274

elbows to ask, her face moving up to look at mine in the dusty light.

'There is no difference,' I said. I could not wait any longer; I shifted my body below her, she slid lightly as a snake over the top of me, the lace and silk of her slip caressing me. I was going to kiss her but her hand diverted my mouth. 'More of that later,' she whispered. 'We must get to this.' From above me she eased herself onto me and me into her.

The luxury of her body drenched me. Three years is a long time. She was the most beautifully sexual woman. Her cool skin took on a sheen of perfumed sweat as we moved together. I made myself keep my eyes open for I did not want to miss a moment of her. Her face was intense, wound up; her eyes tight. Damp glistened on her breasts, her mouth was agape. Her demand, her urgency, took me by surprise. Crying out she stifled herself by thrusting her hand across her own mouth. I was consumed with the marvelous fury of her. She stiffened and fell forward onto me and lay gasping for a few moments, her hair flowing over my wet face. Almost mischievously she eased herself into a kneeling position, her legs still athwart me, her backbone straight, her chin canted, her stomach stretched. We were hot, almost steaming. She pushed her damp hair away from her face, to the back of her neck and inhaled deeply, her pinpoint nipples rising and falling, her ribs visible under her shining skin. '*Bien*,' she said, so quietly it was almost a thought. 'Now, *chéri* . . . She looked down at my flat face. 'Now, we will make more love . . . but slowly.'

Afterwards I was sitting propped against the wall, her head in my naked lap.

'I was jealous of Heinrich,' I told her. 'I was in the bed against the wall like this.'

'Ah!' It was a small bark. Her face remained against my ribs. I could feel her laughing. 'You did hear.'

'All night. I wasn't eavesdropping but . . .'

'Eavesdropping?' She repeated it carefully. 'Eavesdropping.'

'Listening when you should not be.'

'Ah, so you were a spy.' She laughed the same laugh. 'Heinrich, he only pretends. He cannot. He is sixty years old and he was damaged in Russia.' I could feel her looking up at me.

'Oh,' I said. 'Poor Heinrich.'

'Yes,' she said genuinely. 'He is useful in many ways, you understand. He is sad for his wife in Germany.' She moved her head and smiled in the dim light and put her finger on my lips. 'Do you want to sleep now?'

'If you like,' I said.

'I would like,' she said. We pulled the meagre blankets around us and she slept in my arms for the only time that would ever happen.

At first light she left. While I was still waking and asking her where she was going she kissed me on the cheek and then on my mouth. I reached up and touched her gentle face, scarcely a touch because she turned and briskly pulled back one of the beds. She put her finger to her lips and squeezed out of the door. I never saw her again.

The broken-faced old woman brought me food twice during the day. It was evening when she returned for the third time. She was with a young man, small and darting like a monkey. '*Monsieur*,' he said. 'Come now.'

'Where is Mademoiselle Durer?' I asked.

He made a face, briefly spread his arms and repeated: 'Come now.' As we went from the building I was aware of the hag's eyes in the downstairs shadows. The street was swirling with thin rain. We padded along together through a skin of side streets and to the corner of a main thoroughfare. It was bleak as a drain. I followed him, trotting alongside a crumbling wall with the fronds of unkempt trees hanging across it. There was a stone plinth and a set of smashed steps. The young man opened the door ahead and, to my shock, I found myself for the third time in my life in Les Trois Frères.

My astonishment stopped me. When the youth looked around I halted in the doorway. We had come in a back entrance, almost below the stairs where that night Gaston had tumbled and the gun had gone off. Like a returning ghost I went forward.

The big gloomy room was almost vacant. Part of it had been closed off and there were tables and chairs piled behind a screen. A few men were sitting at a table and three more at the overcast bar. A woman knitted.

We walked around the dusty tables towards the men. One turned as we approached. It was Gaston. I thought I would faint. He stared at me in the dimness. '*Anglais*,' he grunted. He pulled a chair from the table and indicated it.

The other men shifted around, showing little interest in me. It was as casual as making room for another player in a card game. A waiter appeared behind me and put a glass of pastis on the table. They began to converse, low and earnestly, questions and cross questions going over the table. It was as though I were not there. One man produced a sheet of crumpled paper, consulted it and put it in his sock, lifting his solid leg to the table to do so. Gaston got to his feet with difficulty and rolled away. He was still not walking well. He stumbled towards a telephone on the distant wall. The man sitting next to me, observing my interest in Gaston, said: '*Blessé* . . .' He glanced at me to see if I comprehended. 'Bang,' he said pointing his finger like a gun and clutching his testicles.

'Oh,' I said. 'Really?'

Gaston tottered back. He spoke gruffly to the others. The matter seemed to be serious. One man was delegated to speak to me. 'Would you have a woman?' he asked. He made a money motion with his fingers and thumb.

'No thanks,' I said. 'No francs.'

It seemed to settle something. The man said: 'Tonight – you go.' I was aware of someone behind my chair and I turned to see Paulette, the girl of that night years before, Gaston's girl, who had unknowingly despatched me on so many adventures. In her hand was a half-knitted sock and she looked much older. Gaston told her that I had no money. She shrugged and made to go away but Gaston took the sock and showed it to the others.

Two men came and sat at the next table. Gaston asked them questions. Expressionless, Gaston rose and shook hands with me. The other men hardly looked up. The recently arrived pair took me out into the street where a horse-taxi was waiting. They sat without speaking facing me in the taxi, both smoking thick-smelling cigarettes. Once more I arrived at Marseille station. One of the men walked to the end of the train already at the platform and the other indicated that I should remain with him. We boarded the train, into a compartment containing only a priest reading a letter by the light of a torch, his lips working over the words. My companion touched his forehead and muttered but the priest ignored us. My guide and I sat down facing each other next to the windows. The train shifted.

Blinds were pulled down in the compartmnent in which a solitary small bulb burned. Once I inched the blind away to look out on the void moving past the train. The Frenchman seemed to be dozing but when I moved the blind his eyes opened and he motioned me to replace it. We stopped several times and many people got on and off but no one came into our compartment. Once an elderly pair fussing with bags and bundles tried to enter, but the priest grunted at them and they shuffled away. He must have been part of the arrangement for he stayed with us all the way to Lyon and then departed still muttering over the letter, the end of which he never reached.

I dozed and when I awoke the other man who had come with me had replaced my first escort. He was likewise blank-faced and wordless. The train rolled through the French winter night.

It was daybreak at Lyon. The station was full of people, moving in mass rushes to and from the platforms. There were *gendarmes*, but they were swamped by the crowds. The police where checking people's papers, however, and as we left they stopped the first of my travelling companions. He produced an identity card and some other documents. His companion joined him and, producing his papers, dropped them on the platform. They scattered and there was a small commotion while the man retrieved them and displayed them to the policeman. In the meantime I had walked past.

Casually I kept walking towards the *Sortie* sign. Before I reached it both my guides were with me, one in front and the other a few paces to my right.

That day I spent in a room at the rear of an undertaker's premises, redolent with the french polish smell emitted from a coffin with lit candles at each corner. At midnight I was taken in a rattling village bus, with four other men lounging about the tattered interior, to somewhere outside the city. It appeared to be a casual journey, the driver conversing over his shoulder with the other passengers.

We pulled into a yard smelling of dung. Everyone got down from the bus including the driver. They hung around waiting, sitting in the shadow of one of the stone walls, but smoking and talking quietly. They knew what they were doing. At two in the morning I heard the sound of a plane flying low and my companions stood and stubbed out their cigarettes. The aircraft came in low and there was a flash of lights from the field. The plane made one pass and then turned and landed.

'*Vite vite*,' said one of the men touching my arm firmly. I ran with them.

The plane took off within ten minutes. I had never flown before and throughout I never saw the faces of the crew. They sat in their flying helmets like two coconuts against the lights from the instrument panel. We flew for two hours.

The *Lysander* began to lose height. Nothing could be seen of the ground but in a moment a line of lights, like stitches, appeared ahead and without a second look the pilot brought the aircraft in. We landed on a bumpy field. None of us

279

moved. The plane was approached by running men; four were pulling a cart and they pumped fuel aboard with a handpump. It took only ten minutes, then they backed away and disappeared. The pilot started the engine, the sturdy plane jumped eagerly from the ground and we rose into the still-dark winter sky.

Half-an-hour after daybreak we were over the English coast. Through the lightening clouds I saw the dog's ear of the Isle of Wight. At once we began to lose height. I saw dim trees rushing by and felt the wheels touch. My joy was stunned by a cry from the pilot and then we hit something. It lifted the plane which slewed to one side, slid along the landing ground and careered into a lake.

I found myself struggling in freezing water and thought how strange it was, after a life at sea, that I should drown surrounded by dry land.

BOOK FOUR

One

At Christmas, so they told me, they put a paper hat on my head and tried to make me laugh with a blower toy, the sort that unwinds and makes a whizzing sound. Apparently I did not laugh.

In March I was told that an army officer was coming to the hospital to see me. My legs were free of plaster but there was still another operation to come. The officer was a sleepy sort of man, his uniform as shapeless as pyjamas. He asked me if I was feeling any better but did not wait for an answer.

'You turned out to be a bit of a disappointment to us, Jones,' he told me seriously. The bedside chair was too small for his backside. 'Us in Intelligence, that is.'

'I did?'

'No fault attached to you, of course. It's the way things happen these days.' He smiled encouragingly. 'But it was lucky for you in a way. *You* were kept especially alive.'

'Especially?'

'Absolutely. Especially. There's no harm in telling you now because the whole thing's finished. But we thought you were someone else, a French chap. Can't tell you his name but let's call him Paddy. We were expecting him over that morning on the *Lysander* and you turned up instead.'

'Paddy,' I said carefully, 'would have been welcome to my seat on the plane. We hit a bloody deer on the runway.'

'A small herd,' he nodded. 'Penetrated the wire. Full blown stag got stuck on the aircraft's nose, they tell me. Strange sight.'

'I nearly drowned in a pond.'

'We're sorry,' he said. 'But we had no idea. Paddy came over a week later.'

'I'm glad.'

'Well, I'm sure he was jolly useful. *You* were just the practice, you see, the dry run. We knew he was coming out but the French are woeful at letting anyone know. They decided to put a dummy, that's you, in to see if the thing worked before risking . . . er . . .'

'Paddy,' I said.

'Exactly.'

I regarded him steadily and said: 'I thought it was all very elaborate just to get a common prisoner of war out.'

'Oh, they *wouldn't*,' he confirmed. He sighed and looked at the wan spring day coming through the window. It inspired him to get up and walk over to gaze. 'Decent view,' he said. 'Across the forest.'

'I haven't seen it,' I told him.

'Oh, it's quite decent. There's a herd of deer over there.'

'They're probably waiting for me.'

He laughed, sat down again, and sniffed. 'Don't be too browned off, old boy. From what the medics say you're lucky to be alive, even though you got top treatment. Thinking as everybody did that you were someone else. No identification. God, what was the score . . .?'

'Two broken legs, arm, ribs, fractured skull, swallowing pond water, and other bits I still don't understand,' I said. 'Oh . . . and shock.'

He detached his bottom from the chair. 'Well, we're pretty busy, as you might gather, with the invasion coming up and one thing and another, but I thought I'd take some time to come and see you. It looks like you'll miss the rest of the war.'

'That's a shame,' I said.

He looked uncomfortable. 'Must be off,' he said. 'Cheerio. Glad you're on the mend.'

The nurse, a nice hairy girl with big hands, came in

afterwards. 'He was a funny one, wasn't he?' she mentioned tucking in the bedclothes around me.

'Intelligence,' I said.

'Oh, I see. Yes, of course. They were all here when you were first brought in. You got graded A1. Made a big stir, I can tell you. Grade A1.'

'Pity I missed it all,' I said.

'Oh, it *was*,' she said busying herself around the bed. 'That's why you got a special room on your own. They had men coming and speaking to you in French and everything. It went around the hospital like wildfire.'

'Well, I'm sorry I let everybody down,' I said.

'Oh, I wouldn't worry about that,' she went on still fretting about the room. 'Not everybody can be somebody. It's quite nice when they *think* you are, when you consider it. You get the very best treatment anyway. Grade A1.'

Now the Intelligence officer had come and gone I was moved into a general ward, although, as though in deference to my former status, I was put at the end, in a bed next to the window where I could see the spring. Once I was able to get out of bed regularly I sat by the window and looked over the spreading green of the countryside and a glimmer of river.

When my identity was established, I had been asked for details of my next-of-kin. I gave Griff's address in Barry but a short sombre note came back informing me that he could no longer be considered my next-of-kin because he had died in the previous year. They tried to contact my mother but failed. People moved in wartime. With a wild hope that perhaps she might take pity on me, I thought of suggesting Dolly but I knew it would be hopeless. I had no one for a next-of-kin.

When they let me go out, in early summer, I used to limp down by the reedy river and sit against a tree on the bank. I was there the morning in June when patterns of planes fanned over the sky, heading for the invasion of Normandy; bombers and fighters and gliders being towed like donkeys.

I was not sorry to be sitting by the gurgling river while they all went to war. I was becoming angry. Angry with myself. Of all the blundering, benighted bastards. Marriage, wars, it was all the same. Each wobble of fate had led and landed me in danger, disgrace, disillusion. I brooded on it. Treatment Grade A1 – because I had been mistaken for *someone else*. The story of my life. Who had tumbled down the stairs on top of Gaston? Who had been swimming in the Atlantic within hours of the declaration of war? Who had carried the banner at Wilmington? Who had been cuckolded, creased, cocked-up, ill-conceived, and enthusiastically fucked about for the entire twenty-five years of his life? Answer, David Jones. Revolving Jones, the wandering good guy. I sat on the river bank and vowed that next time I got Treatment Grade A1. It would be for *me*, the genuine article. Something seized me. I looked up at the planes in the sky, opened my arms, and shouted: 'David Jones! I'm David Jones! Here I am, David Jones!' against their noise. They, of course, ignored me. Why I did it, I don't know. It was all the experiences, I suppose, and the hospital, and someone else's special treatment. I was weeping and shouting at the same time. I disturbed no one with my cries, nothing but a couple of river birds who flew off but soon settled on the water again. I made little impression on them either. I stood up and walked disconsolately back to the hospital while above my head thousands of strangers were going to free the world.

The river stretched itself before entering the Solent and the English Channel; there were small inlets in the estuary where they had been building landing craft to be used in the invasion.

These places, where the plump trees lolled over the tidal mud and water, were now strewn with silent debris. The barges had gone and behind was left scattered wood and metal. In the sudden quiet seabirds were rummaging among the abandoned materials and in the newly-turned mud from which the last completed craft had been launched.

There was a yard on the shore, above the tide. The roof of a boat-building shed showed over the trees. The solitary rebound of a hammer echoed within the shed. I went towards it, walking around the empty estuary like a castaway seeking companionship.

There was a concrete ramp, white in the bright forenoon sun. A half-finished landing craft was on a cradle. Two men were unhurriedly working on her, one hammering. Sitting on a bench watching them was an older man in a red shirt. We muttered good mornings. 'The last one?' I asked nodding at the craft.

'Not this one,' he replied shaking his head. 'Last one's gone. She's over there now, this minute.' A nod indicated the direction of the English Channel. 'Might be on the bottom by now,' called one of the men from the boat.

'She won't,' replied the older man. 'Too well made for that. Germans won't sink *her* in a hurry.'

They had a jug of coffee and the seated man poured me some in a mug without asking if I wanted it. 'We got some sugar somewhere,' he said searching about him. 'Off the ration.'

He made room on the bench and I sat down. A new roar of aero-engines filled the sky. He stood and went unhurriedly to the front of the shed. The man in the landing craft continued hammering but the planes drowned the noise. I followed the older man to the open end of the shed. The wings and bodies of the planes made crosses. 'Like looking at a cemetery,' he said. 'In the air.'

The formations moved off, the sound diminishing; the sky cleared. He turned to go back into the shed. 'My name's Will,' he said. 'Spendlove.' He walked to the bench and sat down. 'Didn't think we had that many planes. Mostly Yanks, I s'pose.'

I told him my name. 'That's Shaggy Pearce, making all the noise,' he said indicating the unfinished hull. 'The other bloke is Sammy. He's going next week. Called up for the army. Ought to be in just in time for the end.'

''Ow do you know?' demanded Sammy from the deck. 'It might go on years yet.'

'No it won't,' said Will dismissively. 'Beginning of the end, it is. Like Winston said.' I was wearing hospital blue trousers. 'How long you been in hospital?' he asked.

'Few months,' I said. I added: 'They thought I was someone else.'

'Oh I see,' he nodded as if this happened all the time. 'Well, you look better now.' He nodded towards France again. 'You won't have to go back again then?'

I smiled at him but indicated Sammy. 'Like he says, it might be years.'

Will picked up a saw and appeared to be counting the teeth. 'I don't reckon it will,' he said again. He touched the hull of the landing craft and then studiously closed his fist and tapped it. 'Won't be any need for this,' he said. 'We turned out half as much *again* as what we were supposed to. Working all night and all day. But this one was too late.' He looked out onto the tranquil estuary. 'You wouldn't have known this place a month ago. It was like the Armada. Everything. Now. It's all gone and we're left.'

'Like me,' I said. 'I can't say I'm sorry.'

'Been through blood and shit have you?' asked the man called Shaggy Pearce who had been doing the hammering. His head and shoulders were above the hull. Will looked up disapprovingly. 'Shaggy,' he said.

'All right, blood and fire,' said Shaggy.

'A bit,' I said tapping the hull. 'What will happen to this?'

'God hisself knows,' said Will. 'We'll finish her. There must be a few not quite done, in and out along the coast. They might need them. Replacements and suchlike. But you don't generally use these things more than once. They either get the blokes ashore or they don't.'

'Probably end up as a cockler. Something like that,' said Sammy. 'After the war they'll be two-a-penny.'

'Cockles?' asked Shaggy over his shoulder.

'Landing craft,' answered Sammy.

Shaggy began hammering again and Sammy's head disappeared below the deck. Will bent the saw in a purposeful way. I went back along the bank by the reed beds, towards the hospital lunch.

I went down to the boatyard every day. With Will and Shaggy I discussed how the invasion was going, looking at the maps in the newspapers, sitting in that calm sunlit place, with scarcely a sound but the honk and piping of estuary birds. It seemed only a natural progression that I should take Sammy's place. I had never done any real carpentry but Will said that it did not need any. 'If you can saw along a straight line and turn a screwdriver the right way.'

It was a curious occupation, building a boat for a war that was not going to need it. 'They said to go on with the contract,' shrugged Will. 'It might be wanted.'

My hospital treatment was almost finished, my bones healed, my limp gone, and my strength repaired. I began to love that place and its silent days, so far from the war. We listened to the wireless and read the newspapers and watched the planes, but that was the nearest it came to us or us to it. They were bringing wounded men into Southampton and they were clearing the hospital for more. I was discharged in July and I went to live with Will's family in Millcreek village.

Strangely I discovered an aptitude for woodworking and throughout that summer I remained there. Will's wife, Mary, mothered me. I had a brass bed thick with white eiderdowns. The window, directly below the eaves, where there were martins' nests, looked out on the village street. Each day I was awakened by the bottles of the milkman. The horse always favoured the cottage to discharge its first pile of the day and Mary was always scolding it, although she claimed the droppings for her rhubarb patch. At night we would listen to the radio, read the *Daily Mirror* or go to the inn to play darts. The last bus left the village for Lyndhurst at eight-thirty and there were few other vehicles.

Will paid me three pounds a week and I gave a pound to Mary for my keep. I kept a pound for spending and went to the thatched Millcreek post office and paid the third pound into a savings bank.

We finished the barge and Will took on another contract to refurbish a small harbour craft damaged during the assembly of the invasion boats. Throughout all this, this new peace, this new activity, this new life, I was aware that no one knew I was there. There was no one who needed to know. Where my mother was, what she was doing, I had no idea, and I found it difficult to care. Who, in any case, was there to ask? Then, one morning in November, I received a letter from a solicitor in Barry; a letter forwarded from the hospital, complaining of the difficulties they had experienced in tracing me and asking me to contact them.

The following day I wrote and they replied that Griff had left me his house and his few belongings. The house was worth three hundred and fifty pounds. I was rich.

It was another four months before I left the estuary and travelled to Wales. That was the final, long winter of the war; the countryside was gloomy, the towns bombed, the people fatigued. I reached Barry after dark feeling like a stranger. The solicitors, Ephriam Morris and Bevan, had left the key to Griff's house under the soggy doormat. The people next door had moved. One of the Blodwen's front room curtains had sagged, hanging like a dead sail. The door key was cold. I turned it in the lock, opened the door, and stood hesitating on the mat, like a stranger waiting to be invited in. A whiff of old air came out. The light in the hall went on when I pushed down the switch; Griff must have left some money in the meter before he died.

Walking into the stale place was walking into my past. Hardly a thing had been moved. Griff's familiar coat was hanging on the hallstand. I wondered who had taken charge of him when he died, who had buried him, who had mourned him.

Someone had been in the house, the solicitor I imagined, because letters were piled against the wall behind the door, like a swept-aside snow drift. They had not bothered to pick them up but pushed them into a pile when the door was opened.

Walking through the corridor, along the landing, and into the rooms I felt like a returning survivor. Everything was much as it had always been except that the clock, of course, had stopped. It was only an eight-day clock and Griff wound it every week. Things were in their places but it was damp. I could trace the run of my thumb across the table in the front room.

The lights went out after about ten minutes. I had a shilling and I put it in the slot. In the kitchen there was mould, even inside Blod's prize teapot. A dead mouse, a look of resignation on its face, was sprawled in the food cupboard. A tin of condensed milk had exploded and, in gorging itself, the mouse had become stuck in the ooze.

It was nine o'clock. I went out of the house once more, seeing the curtain next door flick as I slammed the front door. Down the once familiar hill I walked. Although the black-out was over there seemed to be a reluctance to light up. All the way down there was scarcely a glow showing out onto the wet pavements. People had become used to being without light. But the fish and chip shop glowed like a beacon in a sea fog.

They had no fish. There had been none for a week, the man said. It was a different man, but a woman who had always worked there, carrying the buckets of chips to and fro, was still making her greasy journey. She did not recognise me and I said nothing to her. They had sausages and chips so I had that. There was a table, rough as an old crate, with saggy chairs, one each side of it, a tin pot of salt and an empty vinegar bottle at the centre of its oilcloth top. I made to sit down.

'That's the caffee,' said the man. 'You have to have tea and bread and butter if you sit there. We got no butter. So it's bread.' He hesitated then added: 'A penny for the plate and knife and fork.'

'Posh eh?' I answered, sitting down. 'All right, mate, tea and bread and butter with no butter. And the plate and cutlery. Have you got any vinegar for this bottle?' I picked it up and shook it.

'There's a war on,' he said.

'I heard about it,' I said. He brought the plate. The sausages looked poorly sitting among the chips.

'There's a crack in the plate,' I said.

'We do our best. There's a war on,' he repeated.

He brought the tea and the bread with no butter and put down a bottle with a trace of vinegar in the bottom. 'Found that,' he said. He added it up on a pad. 'That's an extra three-pence farthing,' he said.

I gave him fourpence and told him to keep the change. He went to the back of the shop complaining: 'When this is all over some people will have to watch out.'

As I was eating a man came into the steamy shop wearing an army greatcoat over his ordinary clothes. The khaki of the coat was glistening for it was raining again. 'Nice night,' he said. He went to the counter and ordered chips. He dragged his left leg.

'Pallister,' I said. 'You're . . . Pallister.'

He shuffled around and peered at me. 'Jonesey,' he said eventually. He laughed harshly. 'You knew me by the leg.'

'I knew it was you,' I said. We shook hands.

The fish shop man folded Pallister's packet of chips. Pallister sat down on the other chair facing me and opened the newspaper wrapping. 'That's the caffee,' said the man. I glanced up at him and he went to the rear of the shop without saying anything further.

'You haven't been around, have you?' asked Pallister. 'I would have seen you.'

'First time back tonight,' I said. 'My uncle and auntie died.'

'Have you got their house?'

292

'Yes,' I said, surprised.

'Good for you. That gives you a start when the war's over. Everybody's going to need a start and those that have the best start will end up the richest.' He picked up the chips with his fingers and the proprietor sulkily brought him a fork and a knife with a chewed bone handle. 'Where have you been?' Pallister asked me.

'At sea,' I said. 'Prisoner of war. Hospital.'

'Some story,' he said, but asked me nothing more. I remembered that he had been a clever boy. 'What about you?' I asked.

'Haven't shifted,' he said. 'Couldn't, with this bit of a leg. Been a fire-watcher right through.'

'Plenty of fires?' I asked.

'Enough. Have you seen down the docks.'

'No. I've only just arrived. An hour ago.'

'The station too. That funny old chap who was the porter, he copped it.'

'I couldn't see much,' I said. 'It was dark when I got in.'

'Round the goods yards mostly.' He looked reflective. 'Then we had the Yanks. More trouble than the Germans.'

'Haven't seen anything of Dolly, I suppose?' I asked. His face clouded. 'Dolly?' he said.

'Dolly Powell.'

'Oh, at school. The girl with the . . .' He made a cupping motion with his hands.

'That's her,' I said carefully. 'We got married.'

He took a chip from his mouth. 'I didn't know,' he said.

'We're divorced now. She joined up. Went into searchlights.'

'Bloody mad, all of it,' he said. 'The lot. Here's me, I couldn't get a wife or a woman, not even when all the able-bodied blokes had been called up. I thought I'd have the field more or less to myself around Barry, the leg wouldn't matter, and then the Yanks turned up.'

'I'm living down in Hampshire now,' I said.

'That's good, I bet.'

'It is. When I came out of hospital there didn't seem much reason to go anywhere else. I'd had my war.'

'Done enough,' he nodded. 'Are you working?'

'I've been in a boatyard,' I said. 'What about you?'

'Figures,' he answered. 'Francis the accountant. Remember Dewi Francis? I've spent the war adding up.'

He leaned over the yellow remnants of our chips. 'You've got to be *ready*, Jonesy,' he said. 'Prepared. Once it's over, the war, you've got to be *first* in the race. It's going to take a bit of time for everybody to get sorted out, those that come back. Back in civvy street, back in jobs. If you get a head start, and you're clever, you can make it. There's going to be a different sort of rich man around then. We ought to keep in touch.'

Trudging back up the hill I thought again how dark the town was. There were gritty lights at the corners of the streets and behind a few curtained upper windows, like coloured postage stamps, but little else.

As I let myself into the house the smell of disuse again came out to meet me. I put the hall light on and it glowed damply. The accumulated letters were still piled behind the door where my initial opening had swept them. Now I picked them up, two handfuls like fans, and put them on the table in the living room. On the mantelshelf was a photograph of Blodwyn and Griffith on their wedding day. I could never remember seeing that before. Perhaps Griff had found it somewhere and put it up there to remind him what they were like when young. I picked it up. They were smiling. I smiled back at them.

Several of the letters were addressed to Griff hoping that he would be better soon. There was one from the institute giving notice of the annual general meeting, another exhorting him to buy National Savings. There was also a letter addressed to me, dated more than a year before:

'Dear David,
It is a long time since we met on the liner *Orion* when

294

you so kindly read to me. This is just a little letter to tell
you that I have thought about you in this terrible war.
My son is a soldier. I do hope you keep safe. I enclose a
photograph of myself taken on vacation in Florida this
year.

    With good wishes,
    Helena Tingley.'

I found myself grinning and surprised. I had written in her
address book and she had sent me several Christmas cards.
The indistinct photograph showed a handsome woman on a
small donkey. 'Florida 1943' was written across the bottom.
Some day I must write to her.

I went up to my old narrow bedroom. It was bone-clean
and cold. In the bathroom on the landing I found Griff's
razor still on the shelf. I went along the short space to their
bedroom. Tidy and chill again. Everything in place. Someone
must have been in and cleared up after Griff died. Their
room, where they used to sing on those former midnights.

My sleep was disturbed; I woke to stare at the shapes of
the once familiar place, now strange. I had left the curtains
open. I lay on the mattress with a blanket spread over it and
another on top of me. At last I slept and woke to the slate sky
of a winter's morning.

Almost as soon as I went downstairs there came a timid
knocking at the kitchen door. It was the woman from the
house adjoining. They were new people. She was holding a
cup of tea, like an offering, and looked shy and confused.
'Thought you wouldn't have anything in the house,' she said.

She carried the cup and saucer in. 'I can get you some
toast or something if you like.'

I thanked her but refused. 'He went very sudden, your
uncle,' she said. 'Me and Mr Evans, we'd only just moved
in. Are you going to live here?'

'I might,' I said. 'I don't know yet what I'll be doing.'

'They tried to contact you but they couldn't,' she said. She
regarded me tentatively. 'The rumour went around that you
was in prison.'

'Prison *camp*,' I told her. God, they thought I was in jail. 'It's different to prison. I was a prisoner of war. I escaped.'

She looked a little frightened. 'I didn't say it,' she protested nervously. 'It was just going around.' A small light came to her face. 'But anyway you're here now, whatever sort of prison it was.'

'I've been in hospital since,' I persisted.

'Fancy,' she said. 'So you don't know?'

'What?'

'Whether you'll be living here.'

'I won't for a while anyway,' I answered. 'I'm working away. I have to sort matters out as far as I can. I'm going to the solicitor this morning.' I had a thought to ask her to forward any letters to me but then I thought again. She took the cup and saucer and I thanked her and she returned to her own kitchen door.

My intention had been to walk down into the town, see the solicitor, and get immediately on a train; I wanted to get away. But the route down the hill passed within a minute of where Dolly's parents lived. I strode steadfastly past the junction, but on the other pavement my feet turned right and took me to her remembered porch. The brass on the front door shone like new gold; they still lived there. I knocked. Her mother, her chest thrust out, answered.

'Oh it's you again, is it,' she said. She began to polish the knocker.

'Turned up like a bad penny,' I said.

To my surprise her truculence faded. 'You'd better come in,' she said. 'Wipe your feet.'

I rubbed my shoes heavily on the doormat. Once more I entered the meticulous house, every flounce of curtain in place, every cushion balanced on its proper edge, every ornament beaming. The clock with the drooling girl was missing. In its place stood a photograph of Dolly. She was in a tropical uniform and a bright sun was shining on her lovely face.

296

'Dolly,' sniffed Mrs Powell as if I had not recognised the picture.

'She's moved from Arbroath,' I guessed.

'Ages. She's in India.'

'India!'

Mrs Powell picked up the picture and rubbed her sleeve on the glass. 'Lovely, isn't she.'

'Yes,' I said honestly. 'She always was.'

'India for the duration,' she said. 'As far as I know.'

'I didn't realise they had searchlights in India,' I said.

'Oh it's not searchlights. She's into something much higher than searchlights,' said Mrs Powell.

'That's very high,' I said.

Her lips tightened. 'I suppose you're going to ask after Mr Powell.'

'Oh yes. How is Mr Powell?'

'Gone.'

'Oh dear, oh dear. Dead?'

'Wish the swine was,' she said with all the spite she could muster. 'Went to Daventry. War work. But he soon found work that wasn't to do with the war. A Belgian tart. You might as well know. Everybody else does.'

'I'm sorry about that,' I said feeling a gladness within me. 'Belgian eh?'

'Tart,' she repeated. 'They come over here, running away from the Germans, cowardly lot, and then these goings-on. They *steal* our husbands. He says he wants to marry her, the fool. At his age. You wait till she has to do his washing.' Her anger was giving way to tears. 'Wait till the war's over,' she said inconsequentially.

'It happens in wartime,' I said looking at Dolly.

She sniffed back her sorrow. 'Not that I cared. He was like a bloody haddock.' She smiled bravely. 'It was just when the Americans arrived so I didn't care. When Dolly was on leave we used to go out together. Like sisters. People used the think we *were* sisters.' She sucked her cheeks in and rammed out her bosom. 'Made me feel young again, those Americans – I

297

won't call them Yanks – I can tell you. Real gentlemen too. Your uncle died I hear.'

'Yes he did. Griff.'

'Left everything to you, I expect?'

'The house. I'm just going to see the solicitor about it.'

'Well, it's an ill wind, don't they say.'

'They certainly do.'

It was time for me to go. 'What happened to the clock? Your anniversary clock?' I asked as I reached the door.

She fell for it. 'Took it with him,' she muttered. 'Stole it, more like.'

I moved off down the garden path. 'Fancy that,' I said. She saw I was smiling. It was the best smile I had smiled for years.

The office of Ephraim Morris and Bevan, Solicitors, was in an alley off the docks, the coal dust of ages wedged in its wrinkled brickwork, coating its doorstep and sills. They were on the first floor, up an open flight of echoing stairs. 'It's only a loft really,' said the young Mr Morris, the founder's grandson, from the top of the stairs. 'Apologies for that.'

'No trouble,' I answered. 'I've been at sea.'

'Aye, it's a bit like that,' he agreed testing the stair-rail with his foot. He was slight, pink and youthful, almost juvenile in his appearance. 'Couldn't get in the army,' he said as though to forestall a question. 'Lowest grade, C3. They said in my condition I would only be of use to the enemy.' We went into a low office, with a grimed window overlooking a yard. He sat behind the desk like a schoolboy. 'So I had to stay in Barry and face the bombs,' he said leaning across with a tight beam. 'Our Mr Bevan was killed, you know? Please sit down.'

'No, I didn't. I'm sorry.' I sat down.

'Blown to atoms, smithereens,' he added with a gratified dolefulness. 'Hardly a scrap of him left. Formally identified by his turnip.' He took a worn gold watch from his waistcoat, swinging it mildly on its chain. 'And we had to move offices, of course. Nothing left. All the files went too. A few people in Barry breathed a sigh of relief about that, I can tell you. That's why we're here in this crib. You've come about what?'

I regarded him with surprise. 'You wrote to me,' I pointed out. I handed him the letter. He looked as though he was having difficulty in recognising it. But he said: 'Ah, yes. Your uncle. Different name, of course, Carmichael and Jones. We need the file. Recent files are all right.' He rang a little handbell on the desk, the only shining thing in the room. A timid woman sidled around the door. 'Mrs Morris,' said the youth. 'File on Carmichael please. Mr . . . er . . .'

'Griffith Carmichael,' I told him.

The woman went out. 'My mother,' the young man whispered nodding after her. 'Like everybody else, she has to do her bit. The bomb on the office upset her.' He smiled seriously. 'You ought to have seen the dust,' he said. 'Rose two hundred feet they say.'

'No one else hurt?' I asked.

'Only poor Bevan. It was seven in the evening and he'd stayed behind to do some work. Just shows it doesn't pay. No, I was at the pictures. Heard it go off, of course, but it was a horror film, *The Door with the Seven Locks*, and it's not a film where you can go out in the middle. Ah, here's the file.'

Morris took the file from his mother. There were only a few documents. 'Pretty simple,' he said. 'Your uncle dies, wife already dead, leaves house to you. No other surviving relatives.'

'I thought I might have a mother somewhere,' I suggested.

'Nothing about a mother,' he said rummaging through the papers. Then he found something. 'Ah, wait. Here we are. Dora Jones. Is that her? Or *was* that her?'

'*Was?*'

'It's a death certificate,' he said simply. He held it out and I took it in fingers that had become cold. I read the name again. 'That's her,' I said. I looked up at him. 'Was,' I added. 'I've been out of touch.'

'You really were,' he said. 'You'd better keep it. It must

have been tucked in here for some reason. Probably as proof that a previous will is no longer applicable.'

The certificate said under *Cause of Death* – 'Motor Accident, Multiple Injuries'. I could look at it no longer; I felt I wanted to cry. 'If you want to go outside or anything,' he suggested watching me. 'Bit of a shock, obviously. Come back some other time.'

'It's all right,' I said. 'I can't come back. Not in the near future. I'm living in Hampshire.' I could not imagine that she was dead.

He said: 'Oh, well, the will is straightforward enough. Griffith Carmichael left his house and contents to you. There was a bit of money but it went in funeral expenses and somebody cleaned the house up afterwards. Usual sort of thing when there's nobody else around, no family. Where were you, by the way?'

'In a prisoner of war camp,' I said.

'Oh, they let you out early?'

'I got out.'

'Good for you. Well, that's as good a reason as anybody could give for enforced absence.' He looked at the will again. 'There's a few small bequests. His billiard cues and balls to Mr Lewiston and Mr Bryn David, at the Barry Institute. If you give me your present address I will send the necessary papers to you, for the transfer of the property. Then it is all yours. What will you do? Sell it? I'd hang on to it if I were you; prices are bound to go up after the war.'

As I was leaving, going out of the alley, he came running after me. 'One more,' he called boyishly. 'Tucked into the file. Nearly missed it.'

He handed me a letter so covered with marks, crossings-out and inscriptions that it was difficult to isolate my name. 'Someone must have popped it in there,' he said. 'These things have a funny way of turning up.' He looked at the envelope in my hand. 'Looks a nice jigsaw, that does.' He was reluctant to go back.

To my surprise he took the letter back from me. 'See there!'

he almost squeaked. 'Addressed to you in the prisoner of war camp. *Two*.' He held the envelope close to his eyes. 'One in Germany, one in Italy. And . . . see, you look here . . . It says "Not known" and "Gone Away". Funny in the circumstances.'

'Life is,' I said. He handed me the envelope. It was scattered with various other addresses including the Orion Shipping Company. Morris said: 'Aren't you going to open it?'

'Yes . . . well . . .'

'Go on. Open it. I've got interested now.'

I opened it. 'What is it?' he asked. 'Good news this time?'

'It is. It's my examination result,' I said. 'I'm now a third officer in the Merchant Navy.'

After I had returned to Will and Mary at Millcreek I wrote to the coroner of West London requesting details of my mother's death. The reply enclosed a summary of the evidence given at the inquest in April of the previous year. She had been killed while a pillion passenger on a motorcycle driven by Sergeant Rayburn Scanlon of the United States Army. There had been a collision with a bus in Harrow Road, Paddington; both the riders on the motorcycle were killed. That was that. She had often talked about being hit by a bus.

Will said to me: 'What are you going to do? Go home?'

'Eventually,' I answered. 'I'll have to go back there to finally sort things out. Sell the house and that.'

'We've got a new contract coming up. Big assault craft. Damaged in the landings. They're bringing them back gradually.'

'Who's going to be needing them now?'

He shook his head. 'War'll be over by the summer. No, a man called Perring's bought it. He wants it fitted out like a small car ferry. He's an army major.' He shook his head in admiration. 'There's those who are thinking ahead,' he said. 'They'll be the one's to make their fortune.'

The craft arrived in the estuary ten days later and we worked on her through the rest of the winter and into the spring. We painted out her number and painted in the name *Fanny Bailey*. Will had three other men working with us. One day one of them found a crucifix, silver on a chain, wedged among the deckboards.

When the vessel was almost finished the man who had commissioned the job came to the yard. He was still in uniform; his sleeve hung like an empty bag. Will handed him the crucifix. He sniffed as he held it in his one hand. 'Question is, was it lost or did he throw it away in disgust?' he mused.

His name was Harry Perring and he was to be part of my life. He climbed all over the vessel. 'She was my command, this one,' he said softly rubbing the hull. 'Bloody thing. That's where I lost this lump.' He waved his empty sleeve. 'Up the front there.' He grinned engagingly. 'You didn't find it did you? Never saw the damn thing go. Looked around for it afterwards; after all, your arm is your arm, but couldn't spot it. There were a few other arms and legs missing. And heads.' He summed me up. 'You been in the services?' he asked.

'Yes sir. Merchant Navy,' I answered.

'He's been torpedoed, wrecked, taken prisoner on the high seas, escaped from a prison camp, got mixed up with the French Resistance, and was in a plane crash,' summarised Will proudly.

Perring laughed. 'Quiet war, eh?' He moved around the hull, pushing and prodding it. 'Some people missed all the excitement.' He grinned wryly. 'Poor devils.'

It was calm and comfortable down there by the estuary. The war was in its dying weeks. I could have stayed there forever, building boats, perhaps getting married, and maybe I should have done.

We finished the contract in April and I told Will I was leaving and going back to sea. 'Why would you want to do that?' he asked. 'You've been like one of the family.'

'You've been *my* family,' I told him. 'When I needed one.'

*

I sailed the night the war ended. All Southampton was dancing, the streets crowded with bobbing heads, people riding on buses through the bombed and patched town, waving flags. At the time I thought it must have been like the night my mother said she met the German soldier.

It was difficult to reach Southampton Docks because of the happy people. Girls were kissing indescriminately; sailors, soldiers, airmen, air raid wardens, firemen and men who had done little. There was dancing in front of the Guildhall. Bottles and banners were raised on every street and corner. Struggling not to be separated from my suitcase by the press of the crowd, I was kissed and enfolded as if I were just returned instead of just departing. My new uniform was tugged and hugged by girls, women and drunks. At last I reached the dock gates, down the slight descent from the town, and gratefully went through them away from the celebrations. The gatekeeper was sitting lugubriously watching the lights spread around the buildings, shaking his head at the travelling sounds.

''Ow long before the next one, that's what I want to know?' he said as he looked at my pass. 'Second berth down, sir.' He pointed but I could already see her, the hull curving up, her deck lit, her funnels against the illuminated sky. An old excitement came to me. The uniform felt almost as stiff as the cap. There was no one on the dockside and it was almost eerie walking along there, between the cables and the railway tracks, below the necks of the cranes, the long dock lit by yellow lamps while the tumult of the end of the war still sounded over the roofs of the warehouses.

There was only a watchman and a sleepy steward on the ship. The steward took me below to my cabin. 'They can shout and laugh,' he said as we went along the deck and the sounds reached us again. 'Lost two sons, myself. One at sea, one in the air force. I've got nothing to celebrate.'

He showed me the cabin and went off to make a pot of tea. When the door was closed I sat down on the chair in a corner and gazed about me. My own quarters; the wall space occupied by a porthole, a picture of the ship, with the words: *SS Lawful*, 8,000 tons, written below. Someone had crossed out the first letter L. There was a bunk, a washbasin wedged into a corner and a lavatory which also combined as a shower.

'Not much room in there, sir,' said the steward returning with the tea. 'You can sit on it and have a shower at the same time. You *have* to in fact. No leeway to do anything else.'

He put the tray down on the table which unfolded from the bulkhead. It was eleven-thirty. We were due to sail at three in the morning. I sat in my chair and drank the tea. Then I arranged my sea books on a shelf above the berth. Also I had the wedding day photograph of Griff and Blodwen which I had taken from the house, and another of my wedding to Dolly. She was still with me, wherever she was.

The Captain, George Hart, came aboard at midnight. He looked through the documents and said: 'First voyage with a ticket then, Jones.' He was a lined-faced man with steely hair. The creases in his cheeks filled out as he whistled. 'Good God, got your ticket in a prison camp, eh?' He looked up and grinned, sending the creases in a different direction. 'Had some sort of confidence in the future, did you?'

'Yes sir. It also occupied the time.'

'Where was it, this camp?'

'Northern Italy, sir.'

'Oh, the hokey-pokey merchants had you.'

'They helped me escape,' I told him.

'You got out! Good. You sound a resourceful sort of chap. That's excellent. Mainwaring the second officer's all right but he has hallucinations. Thought I'd got shot of him last voyage, but somehow he's back. If he tells you he can see icebergs or the moon's dropped out of the sky, don't take it too seriously.'

When we sailed I was on the bridge. At three o'clock two tugs, both bedecked with victory flags, and the crews noisy, pulled us out into the Solent. We came about and sailed through the limp, dark water, away from the celebrations still undiminished in the city. All along the coast was glowing. Off Bournemouth we saw fireworks.

Mainwaring, the second officer, came to the bridge and viewed the passing land. 'Not sorry to be sailing,' he said. He put his hand to the side of his mouth. 'They say that Russian troops have landed in Portsmouth,' he confided.

Once we were clear of the Isle of Wight and into the Channel I went below. The steward had made me a cup of cocoa. I drank it and got into my bunk because I was on watch at six. Stretching out, I pulled the blanket over me and lay back full of happy sensations. The heartbeat of the engines was drumming through me and the ship was beginning to bow in the open tideway of the English Channel. I was a sailor again. Outward bound.

Two

The sea felt different now. We sailed down through the Bay of Biscay, the green rollers like moving hills, white-topped, the sky windy, the wind joyful. Now the danger had gone; there was no breathless wait for the submarine, no watch for aircraft. There was still a look-out for lost and lurking mines, but our course took us far out, first on a line to Madeira, and then down into the South Atlantic to Dakar in West Africa.

We docked at Madeira, the port and town of Funchal painted by the sun. Around the harbour were American troops manning guns that had never been fired. It was as though nobody had told them about the end of the war. The Portuguese islanders walked past the guns and soldiers as though they were not there.

I went ashore with Richard Mainwaring, the second officer. 'I only do the hallucination act to amuse the skipper,' he said. 'The Russians are coming!' he called to some Americans polishing an anti-aircraft gun on the dockside.

Walking the steep cobbles of the town in tropical whites I felt like a stage character. The sun flashed on our buttons. Girls looked out from a window and waved to us. Mainwaring returned the wave regally. 'We'll have some tea at Reid's, I thought,' he said. He had a strident stride and I had trouble matching it. We stepped out like two white storks. 'Famous hotel, you know, Reid's. Tea with Madeira cake.'

We arrived at the tall hotel, built above the rolling ocean. There was a tea dance in the palm court, elderly people slowly spinning to a well-dressed waltz. Their dancing raised particles of dust which hovered in the sunshine from the long windows. We stood at the top of the wide steps leading to the floor, its tables spreading out onto a flowered terrace, plants and palms like islands; spotless waiters spun with tea and cakes from silver trays. The dancers and the people drinking tea observed us carefully. Faltering men looked with amused hostility. Their fat and frail partners were in summery dresses and boa feathers. The head tea waiter bowed. 'For two, if you please,' said Mainwaring loudly.

'Oh, they're *British*!' squeaked a woman sagged in the arms of a hairless and disdainful-looking man. 'British.' 'British,' 'British.' The recognition buzzed about the palm court. The orchestra came to a sulky stop. The musicians, dressed in pantaloons and blouses, observed us with black-circled eyes. The leader, jerked into a puppet-like movement. His baton flew wildly and the bored players struck up 'Rule Britannia'. Everyone around the floor stood and applauded.

'Better take a bow,' suggested Mainwaring. We both stood, smiling our embarrassed thanks. My uniform creaked with stiffness.

The tune finished and the band returned to playing something softer. A tall trembling man in a faded blazer approached, followed at a wife's distance by a lady in a cream dress. We stood.

'Jolly good,' said the man. 'Rupert Curry-Banks.' He thrust out his hand.

'Formerly Camel Corps,' called his wife from his back.

He glared over his shoulder. 'Wrong war,' he barked. His hand flapped in a rearward motion, regretful and dismissive, like a half-hearted flipper. 'My wife,' he grunted. 'I have the honour to be Chairman of the British Committee.'

'Residents of Madeira,' muttered Mrs Curry-Banks.

Mainwaring shook hands heartily and introduced us. 'Yours is the first civil ship in here since the end of the war,' said Captain Curry-Banks.

'It *is* ended, isn't it?' said his wife with a pinch of anxiety.

'I *told* you,' he said stiffly over his shoulder.

'There have been so many rumours.' Her smile was like a

rent in a cobweb. 'You can never believe the wireless here. We always thought the Germans had a finger in it, didn't we?'

He stood impatiently while she finished. 'Would you dance?' she suddenly asked me. 'I've run out of conversation.'

Her husband glanced at me. 'Dance with her, will you, old chap?' he asked as if asking me to take his dog for a walk.

'Delighted,' I said. Her arms were like old sugar. A frail smile appeared again. Her waist was padded as if she were wearing a life jacket. We danced with our arms stuck out like the bowsprit of a sailing vessel. 'It is so lovely to have a relatively young partner for a change,' she hummed. 'I've been dancing with these old codgers throughout hostilities. If the war is *really* over then things can only change for the better.'

'It's over in Europe,' I confirmed. 'Not with Japan.'

'I knew there would be a catch,' she sighed. She wriggled with her corset. 'I always thought they were quite nice, the Japanese. So servile.'

'Have you been in Madeira the whole of the war?' I said.

'Nowhere else to go,' she confirmed. 'Couldn't go home. What would we do there? We'd have only been in the way. Rupert talked about joining the Home Guard, in fact he tried to start a branch here but the Portuguese wouldn't allow it, being silly neutrals.'

We revolved tentatively around the palm court. Several skittish ladies made remarks. 'It will mean an end to the knitting, I suppose,' she remarked sadly. 'The Knitting Committee *and* the National Savings Committee and the Books for Bombed East Enders.'

'You sent books to east enders?'

'Yes, those being bombed. We wondered what they would do, you understand, to occupy their time in the shelters and the underground stations and suchlike during the raids. They couldn't sing cheerful cockney songs all the time, could they? So we collected books for them. Unfortunately not many were sent. Shortage of shipping space or some excuse.'

308

The band gathered itself into a foxtrot. 'Then there are the air raid shelters,' she remembered. 'They've taken ages to dig. The locals would not do the work because of not being in the war, so our chaps had to do the spadework themselves. Mr Bamforth and Colonel Meeney both had heart attacks. Dropped dead while digging. War casualties, in a way. We had a nice service for them. Even the Germans sent wreaths.'

'The Germans?'

'Those in Madeira of course,' she said. '*Not* from Nazi Germany. These people have been here for years. Almost as long as the British. We've kept a proper distance, naturally, during hostilities, which is only right, but I imagine now it's all over they will start coming to the tea dances again.'

When the foxtrot trailed off she held out her weak, fleshy hand and I led her back to the table. A waiter was pouring tea and there was a silver stand lined with slices of Madeira cake.

'You're back,' exclaimed Captain Curry-Banks as though greeting a patrol never expected to return. He stood and put his wife's chair below her. I sat and accepted a piece of cake and a cup of tea from Mrs Curry-Banks.

Her husband turned briskly to me and asked: 'Have a good war, did you?'

'Excellent,' I said.

'Good for you. Enjoyed it, did you?'

They had two daughters in their twenties, Beryl and Joan, who would be pleased to show us around the island. 'They've had very little opportunity of meeting the right type of young man,' said Mrs Curry-Banks sadly. 'There have only been the Americans.'

They sent a horse-drawn carriage for us at ten the next morning. It drew up on the quay alongside the ship. The deck crew peered over the side as we left, the horse clopping on the cobbles, the bells on its reins sounding.

The house was about two miles from the town and far above it, so you could see our ship in the port clearly from the terrace. From there the hills dropped away like a folded skirt, down to the hem of the sea. The house was white with half-moon arches; there was a gnome fountain and the walls were engulfed with roses and wisteria.

'Grow absolutely *anything* here,' said Captain Curry-Banks as we drank morning coffee on the terrace. His wife was getting ready for the day. 'Not that she's *doing* anything today,' he added with a sour laugh. 'She rarely does. But she has to get *ready* for it nevertheless.' He pointed up beyond the ochre-tiled roof to the hills, leaning against the Atlantic sky. A few strewn clouds stood out like pennants on the peaks. 'Up there you can grow cabbages,' he announced. 'Potatoes, carrots, everything. And down below bananas. First class place for vegetating.'

Confident steps and chatter sounded behind us. We turned and rose as two young and strong-looking women came down the outside staircase. Both had browned faces and big bodies, the spring of tennis girls in their descent. Each had fair short hair and clear eyes. They had already shared us out.

'You and I are going up the mountain,' said Beryl. She wore corduroy trousers. 'There is a village in the crater. Some of the people never come out.' She regarded me with tense eyes. 'They all marry each other,' she said. Their father had wandered away and was trying to arrange a climber more to his satisfaction. 'They,' she continued, nodding to her sister and Mainwaring, 'go elsewhere.'

'You don't ride then?' she called over her shoulder, her bottom astride the donkey in front. My donkey hit my backside and my crotch like a fist at every step.

'At sea you don't get a lot of chance,' I called out. Her broad back shrugged under the white shirt.

'Nor tennis, I suppose?'

'Limited opportunities,' I answered.

We plodded without conversation after that, always ascending, the road becoming tighter and wending through banks of bright flowers. At every pace I gritted my teeth. Feeling was going from below my waist. Once we were confronted by a village funeral party, the coffin carried by six men, a procession of people in black behind them, children clutching flowers. A woman supported another who was weeping. They halted to allow us to go past. The crying woman regarded us with metallic eyes. 'Going up has priority,' Beryl called to me.

'Even for a funeral?'

'Even for a funeral,' she shouted back. 'If we'd stopped they'd have become confused and the whole thing would have gone to pot. They'd have probably dropped the coffin.'

I called to her: 'I'll have to stop, Beryl. I'll have to get off. I feel as though I'm paralysed.'

She revolved. 'If you get off now, you'll never get back on,' she warned in an annoyed way. 'And it's a bloody long walk.'

We juddered on for another hour. The sun was hot but the air fine and clear. At each elbow in the mountain road we could still see Funchal and the misty sea. The ship was still in view, diminished to a splinter. Eventually, Beryl thrust out her hand like a cyclist, indicating that we were leaving the road and taking a rocky track. Every bump of the donkey's back bruised my legs, my backside and my crotch. A mile up the track we came to a plateau overlooking an astounding drop. The donkeys knew it was time to stop. Beryl slid off her mount easily and waved her hand into the chasm. 'Take a look.'

Dismounting the donkey was agony. It shifted, sensing my discomfort. Beryl laughed: 'Oh God, you do look a scream with your leg stuck out like that.'

'It doesn't feel all that funny,' I said. 'Could you help me, d'you think?'

She strode over and helped me. Her hands were confident. The donkeys snorted and wandered away with its companion. I stood like a swaying drunk.

She put her arms out to support my body, steadying me, her big chest leaning against mine. 'You *are* in a bad way,' she said more seriously although her eyes were still mocking. 'You've gone white in the face. Don't fall down the crater.'

Like some stricken combatant helped from a battle, I leaned on her while we took the few paces away from the edge of the crater. There were some patches of grass among the stones and she lowered me to the ground; my legs were bent like a spider. She went towards her donkey and I inched my legs forward, extending my feet. She returned looking concerned like a first-aid helper, and spread a tartan rug on the grass and stones. Then she moved behind me and put her strong arms below my armpits. With support from my own hands on the ground and my legs giving painful leverage, I managed to move crab-like onto the rug.

'This is embarrassing,' I told her. 'Thanks. Aboard ship you get the wrong sort of exercise.

Her expression had altered. 'You could do with a drink,' she said, her face near to mine.

'Where's the bar?' I said. 'I can't walk anywhere.' She laughed pleasantly now, and strode purposefully away again. 'I have the bar with me,' she called back. The donkeys had roamed and were both drinking at a stream which issued into a pool before tumbling silently over the lip of the crater. Beryl brought back a leather bag and from this produced a bottle of red wine. 'This will help,' she said.

'Embrocation might be more to the point,' I smiled ruefully. 'You must think I'm a fool.'

'Not at all,' she said looking through the wall of the bottle at the contents. She expertly uncorked it and handed it to me to drink from the neck. 'Forgot the glasses,' she apologised. 'How long since you've been on a donkey?'

'When I was seven,' I told her. 'On the beach.'

'Far too long,' she sighed sagely. The wine was rough but welcome. 'Do you want to see down into the crater? That's why we came.'

'Can I crawl?' I asked seriously.

'Sooner or later you're going to have to get to your feet again,' she said. 'Otherwise you won't be able to get on the donkey.'

'Oh Christ. All that way down.'

'All the way,' she confirmed. She handed the bottle back to me. 'Have a drink and then I'll show you the village.' I drank deeply. The wine was making me feel better. Slowly I turned myself onto my hands and knees and began to crawl towards the rim of the precipice. She laughed into her hand. 'Stop now,' she said. 'Don't go slipping over. It's difficult to get out. Just ask the people down there.'

Elongated on my stomach I peered down into the wide, dead crater. Far below I could see the houses of the village, patterned and white like a snowflake. The sound of a barking dog came up to us.

'They live and die like that,' she whispered. 'Trapped. It takes the men a day to climb the tracks to get to the next village to collect supplies. Most of the women spend their lives down there, looking up at a circle of sky.'

She turned away from the edge and I revolved on all fours and began to crawl back too. Away from the crater her mood changed again. Like a child sensing a game she laughed sharply, and to my amazement swung her leg over my back, sitting lightly on me and holding my ears. 'Gee up, burro!' she hooted. Her laughter echoed from the rocks. We were at the rug. She tumbled from me and rolled me gently over, sitting astride my stomach. 'Do you want me to rub your poor legs?' she inquired, her concerned face again coming close to mine.

I looked into her intent expression. 'It might just help,' I said studiedly.

Sitting on my midriff, but taking her weight on her knees and shins and leaning backwards, she trailed her hands behind her and began rubbing my trousers. She rubbed from the knee up to the arch. My hands reached up to hold her breasts, one on each flank. I began to move gently so we were massaging each other. Then I removed one hand and undid the buttons of her shirt to the waist. My fingers touched the lace of her brassière. She stopped rubbing my legs, and reached up her own back, under the shirt, and released the hook. Her full soap-coloured breasts, their centres like flowers, rolled out into my hands. 'They're beautiful,' I said thickly. 'Beautiful, like you.'

'I'm very proud of them,' she replied doggedly. 'They're better than my sister's. So I'm told.'

I had never seen a woman unbutton her own trousers before. She did it now, deftly flicking the corduroy open at the front into a triangle. Once more she put her hands behind her and undid my buttons as well. Her hands went in and after leaning back, the movement causing the snouts of her heavy breasts to rise as though savouring the mountain air, she fumbled and found what she sought. I could feel the sunshine on its nakedness.

She glanced over her shoulder. 'I think I have a use for that,' she said like a customer in a second-hand shop.

'Use it then,' I muttered.

Afterwards we became very friendly. We lay on the rug in the hilly warmth and she questioned me about the sea and what had happened to me in the war. I told her and she lay listening until she sat upright and exlaimed: 'All that time, in that camp, you had no . . . women friends?'

'None,' I answered simply and truthfully. 'There were no facilities.'

'*I* have the facilities,' she whispered.

Once more we made love, the rug below us, the sky above. Two hawks like voyeurs cruised overhead. We rested again, lying on our backs looking up. There was another bottle of wine and we were drinking that. 'It's disgusting stuff this,' Beryl said. 'But good.'

She handed me the bottle. 'We haven't been back to England in six years,' she said. 'They wouldn't let us. Joan and I both wanted to go and join something, if only the girl bloody guides, but they wouldn't have it. They skulked here, with Germans skulking the other side of the town, and we had to skulk with them. There's been a lot of skulking. Thank God for the Americans.'

'They've been quite a distraction,' I said. 'At home too.'

'We would have gone mad without them. Can you imagine being stuck here for years while the rest of the world was having a party? I can't tell you how many times I've been deeply in love.'

It seemed to be time to go. We were quite drunk from the wine but the donkeys knew the way and I was sufficiently spent to gain the back of mine without great pain. We wobbled down the mountainside.

The rocking of the donkey and my own instability made it a difficult journey. The ring of countryside seemed to be revolving around us. Once I fell off and two men, sitting by the roadside, decently helped me to remount while Beryl looked on sulkily. I was dozing like a lover around the animal's neck by the time we reached her house. I fell asleep in a chair. Mainwaring arrived an hour later, woefully holding his ribs, and we got a taxi back to the ship, waving goodbye forever from the window.

Mainwaring said: 'We went on a toboggan.'

'I've been on a donkey,' I told him. 'I'll never be able to walk straight again.'

'They shove you down about a mile of a bumpy stone hill on this toboggan thing and it bangs the insides out of you. I thought I'd broken my back.' He grinned and looked at me. 'Apart from the donkey, was it all right?'

'It was,' I nodded. 'What about you? Apart from the toboggan?'

'It was,' he smiled. 'Worth every bruise.'

As soon as we sailed, the weather blew up badly and we had a foul passage down the Atlantic to Dakar in West Africa. Bow-legged I staggered arthritically about the ship. Mainwaring collided with bulkheads.

'Too much donkey-riding is no good for a sailor,' observed the skipper after he had asked what was crippling me. 'Altogether different movements.'

The storm abated as we rounded Cape Verde and made for the African port. We came in on a hot morning with the desert rising in the distance like a yellow sea of high waves. Dakar could be sniffed two miles out, the rancid reek of an equatorial harbour. There had been some mystery about the cargo we were to load. The Captain was given no manifest until the night before we docked when it was transmitted over the radio. I was on deck watching a blazing sunset extinguished by the sea and walked around the deck to sniff Dakar and hear the noises of Africa and the city.

Captain Hart came along the deck with the manifest. He followed my gaze over the shore, the diffuse lights and thump of music. 'War surplus,' he muttered. 'We've got a cargo of what is described as War Surplus. And the damned war is only just over. In fact it's not over.' He studied the manifest. 'Vehicles, guns, stores. Somebody is onto a fat profit.'

The following morning we were alongside the dock and I saw what he meant. Pyramids of sand coloured materials lined the wharf; crates, tents, ranks of jeeps, cars and trucks marked with the white American star. Tall Senegalese men were working ashore taking orders from fussing Frenchmen, and soon the cranes were swinging.

It took three days to stow the cargo. Then we sailed and plodded back to Liverpool where men in large cars and coats turned up to inspect the goods as they were unloaded, waving sheaves of paper and cheque books in each other's faces. We then turned the ship around and went back for more, this time to Casablanca.

In the market place in the city every sort of radio set could be bought, army watches, electric razors, the novel ball-point pens, tins of food and meat, bottles of Scotch, and millions of pairs of nylons. All the crew went ashore and bought as much as they could, especially the nylons. I bought half-a-dozen pairs although there was no one immediately to whom I could give them. I would have to start rebuilding my life.

The ship had to go into dry dock when we returned to Liverpool but it was only for a week, during which Japan surrendered and the war was really ended. I went down to South Wales. They were selling ice cream by the beach again

316

and some of the fairground was working. After the long war people were out blinking at the sun.

The house was as I had left it, cocooned, petrified, still. The rooms were lighter with the August days but it was no more welcoming. There was another drift of letters behind the door, one addressed to my Uncle Griff marked 'Please Forward' and another still wishing him a swift recovery. People did not stay in touch.

Mrs Evans brought her husband round from next door. 'Hang on, boy,' he advised. He had a moustache stained tobacco-yellow and greasy spectacles, the frames repaired with insulating tape. 'Just wait a bit longer and you'll find you've been sitting on a fortune. Worth hundreds they'll be, these houses.'

'We're banking on it,' confided Mrs Evans. 'Hundreds.'

I went to see Morris the solicitor. He appeared more junior than ever. 'Status quo,' he said. 'As we say. Nothing moving on your front. I could find a buyer for the house for you if you like. People are beginning to get back now. They've got gratuities to spend. Funny word "gratuities", isn't it? Sounds like something for nothing.'

I told him that I did not want to sell the house. I might yet return and live in it. Even if I were at sea for the rest of my life I would need somewhere to which I could return at the end of a voyage. 'I got somebody to go up and open a few little windows,' he said. 'Let some air in but not intruders. If you're not back by the onset of winter I'll send them up to close them again.'

He directed me to Dewi Francis, Accountants. He appeared to be on the point of inquiring what my business was there. It was noon on a dull warm day. A rattling charabanc, the fat arms of women and the faces of pallid children pressed like suckers against its windows, rolled down towards the beach. In the brief park in front of the town hall people were opening sandwiches. The girl at the lobby desk of Francis, Accountants, twirled a handle to call Pallister on the telephone. 'He's just coming down,' she said. 'You'll hear him.' She picked up her red plastic handbag and left, as though giving up a bad job.

Pallister stumped down the wooden stairs. He held out his hand before he had reached the bottom step. Then he put a cautionary finger to his lips. 'Let's go and have a pint,' he said with a smile which slid down one side of his face.

The Shipwright's Arms was on the street next to the docks. As a boy I had loitered in passing of a morning and sniffed the previous night's beer. I once saw a man kicking the closed door and weeping. It was a hard-worn place, untouched by paint and polish for years. The publican pulled the beer pump handles and said sombrely: 'They all think it will be the same as before the war. But it won't.'

'Everyone's a prophet,' said Pallister. We sat on a tough seat in a corner, stained with drink like an ancient map. 'Everybody thinks they know what's going to happen now it's over,' he repeated. 'But I bet I guess better than most. They've elected a Labour government, because the Tories were in power when the war started. Sentimental, not practical. Bevin is a foreign secretary who has trouble speaking English. The prime minister squeaks. God, Attlee makes Chamberlain a bloody Colossus.

'A lot will emigrate to Australia, and that ought to clear the decks a bit. Me, I'd go to South Africa. Labour's cheap, the country's hardly touched by the war, and they've got gold.'

'What everybody wants.'

'Don't you, Jonesey?' It was a careful inquiry. He paused in lifting his glass so that he could study my reaction.

'I suppose so.'

'How long have you been in the Mercantile Marine?' he asked succinctly. 'Ten years?'

'More or less.'

'And what have you got to show for it? A junior officer's ticket. You've got a house, but that was your uncle's, and what else?'

'It hasn't been a good time for prospering,' I pointed out.

He caught me by the shoulder and said: 'Look out here a minute. Let me show you what's in front of your eyes.'

We walked through the scarred door and into the dockside sun. We could look out beyond the harbour to the Barry Roads where, as I remembered since my childhood, ships were waiting for berths. 'There's holes in half of that lot,' said Pallister limping along in front of me. He walked further towards the sea, as if to bring the scene into focus. 'Bomb holes, torpedo holes, mine holes, shell holes, mouse holes. Some of these ships are like cheese. They've been patched up and patched up right through the war. Now they need a bit more than patching. Somebody's got to do it.'

'But there've been firms in Cardiff, Newport, Bristol, for years,' I said. 'Specialists. Ship repairs, boiler scaling, the whole lot.'

'Listen to me,' he said firmly. We walked back into the public house and sat in a corner again. 'I've got an idea. What the shipowners need is running repairs, and when I say *running*, I mean *sailing, en route*, on the hoof, if that's not getting it arse-up. They want to keep their ships at sea for a few more years, until new ones are built. Trade is going to go on, trade's going to increase. Business has *got* to improve, boy, even under a Socialist government. We've gone five years producing *nothing* except war materials. That doesn't bring in money. We'll go bankrupt; this country will go under, it'll end up as just another American colony. And the Yanks, the only people in the world with any money, they're going to be sending stuff to Europe under this Marshall Plan. Having knocked three buckets of shit out of the place they now want to rebuild it for nothing.' He grinned wryly. 'Like you used to make a sandcastle on the beach, knock it down, and then build it up again.'

I said: 'This business of yours, where's the money coming from? We've got to have tools, materials, pay men, have an office.'

'I've got four hundred and thirty-seven pounds,' he said quietly. 'Saved. You've got a house you can sell, or mortgage.

We go in fifty-fifty. I've even got a name for us: Pallister Jones. That didn't take much thinking out.'

'But everything is going to be in short supply.'

'We'll get materials,' he said grimly. 'You've seen all this war surplus stuff that's being flogged about.'

'We brought two cargoes back from Africa,' I agreed.

'There you are – and there's more. Wood and metal and tools. Millions of tools are lying about. And don't tell me there aren't those who've been hoarding. There *are* stocks of materials around. They just need to be found. There'll be skilled men coming back, wanting work.'

'When you said "on the hoof", how would it work?'

'Ah, that's the beauty. We have offices all along the Bristol Channel, and in Liverpool, Southampton, London Docks, all over eventually. We can start a repair job in Cardiff, say, and continue it in Milford Haven and then finish it in Liverpool. The ship doesn't have to be laid up. As long as she can float and she can get up steam. Our trump card. Others have all their facilities fixed in one place, where they've been since the days of sailing ships, but we'll be mobile. They won't have to stop moving, picking up cargoes, for us.'

He declined another beer. 'I've had years to think it out,' he said as we shook hands before parting. 'Fire-watching. You're too intelligent to sail the world.' His hands described a globe. 'It's only round.'

'I'm only a boy from Barry School,' I said.

'So am I,' he replied, the grin slipping sideways down his face.

On the following voyage we sailed again to Casablanca for another cargo of war surplus. Captain Hart surveyed it from the bridge. It stretched far back from the harbour, a serpentine tank of yellow vehicles, crates, enough tents to house the inhabitants of a city, spare parts, motor tyres, machine tools, and a complete field hospital, minus the instruments and drugs which had all been stolen. Animated Arabs and Frenchmen circled the pile, pointing, checking, scribbling, gesticulating, chattering. 'Somebody,' said the skipper thoughtfully. 'is going to make a fortune out of that booty.' He glanced at me. 'But it's not you nor me, Jones.'

Mainwaring came to the bridge. 'There's a plague of locusts coming this way, sir,' he reported casually. Captain Hart rolled his eyes and said: 'Not another.'

'And severe sandstorms,' said the second officer firmly. He glanced at the captain and then at me. 'Enough to bury this ship.'

'As long as it doesn't bury the cargo. The ship isn't important,' said the captain. He turned and went down from the bridge. Two cranes were rolling into position amid the dirt of the dockside. Hatches were open and the Arab stevedores prepared to load the cargo, already shouting to each other in their sharp voices, sentences as long and impassioned as a prayer.

It took two and a half days to load and the job was slipshod because off Cape St Vincent, the south-western extremity of Portugal, one of the savage storms that can run up that seaway at any season overcame us and two trucks and an anti-aircraft gun broke loose in the hold. It was three in the morning when the alarm sounded. I rolled out of my berth, and was flung back against the bulkhead by the violent pitch of the sea. I struggled into my deck gear and pulled myself up to the bridge. The captain was next to the helmsman. The storm was tremendous; as though we were rolling in the midst of black, moving mountains. One of the bridge-side portholes had smashed and the rain and wind tore in.

'Mr Jones!' shouted the captain above the noise of the night. 'Number two hold. Cargo's loose. I've sent some men down there. Go and take charge. Get it stowed.'

Swinging from rail to rail I ran and half-fell down the ladders. The big lights were on in the hold, blazing over a frightening scene. The trucks and the gun on its trailer were running amok. All were poised at one end, thrown there by the pitch of the bow; the transfixed crew, Indian lascars, were bunched to my right on a raised platform. The chief man, Adolf, was shouting something in their language. Then, as the ship dipped at the stern, the two trucks, followed by the gun, trundled like toys and rushed towards us. The first vehicle collided with the bulkhead, already pounded to scrap, and the second lorry smashed into its back with a grinding of metal and a shattering of glass. The gun, like a giraffe, was trying to mount the back of the second vehicle.

Adolf came across to me, hanging on rails and handles as he did. He was a good seaman, with sharp black eyes and a postage-stamp moustache from which he derived his nickname. 'Orders sir!' he demanded.

I was speechless. He knew I did not know. 'First, we try stop gun,' he provided for me. 'Get a hawser round it. Otherwise we fucked.'

'Okay do that,' I said with what authority I could pull together. 'Well done, Adolf.'

He swung back to his men. They were resourceful seamen. They clambered around the perimeter of the hold, over the heaving cargo. I followed them. We were on an island of crates in one corner. The lascars began spreading a wire hawser. It was a matter of timing. We reckoned there were five seconds while the descent of the bow kept the gun jammed against the forward bulkhead, before she started rising, the hold tilted, and the trucks and the gun began their thunderous career again. As the gun came back and crashed against the forward bulkhead, the second vehicle colliding with it and then, with a further shudder, the first truck rolling backwards into that, Adolf began to count, shouting the numbers as he totted them up on his fingers. He got to seven, two more seconds than we had thought. But the length of time depended on the size of the wave rocking the ship like a see-saw.

We all watched while the hideous convoy began its run again, rolling and smashing forward. It hung poised amidships until we felt the hull rocking down and the vehicles rolled back. This was the moment. Adolf bawled an order and the lascars moved like beetles. The hawser was thrown over the front of the gun and the men on the other side grasped and secured it. It worked.

When the bow rose again the gun held. Only the two trucks went on their rampage. The lascars laughed, their white teeth visible from across the hold, and Adolf looked around at me with a brilliant grin. I shouted encouragement.

The trucks returned, backing down the hold. The cabs were like mangled faces, the tailboards twisted wreckage. The second truck hit the gun and hung against it, almost hugging it. Seven seconds again. Then it rolled clear. Another shout from the chief lascar and another cable was thrown across. Now the gun was secure. 'One down, two to go!' I shouted. Adolf grinned and waved.

It was the last I saw of him because, as the truck next came back and struck against the gun, there was an explosion and a great gush of red fire. Smoke and flames billowed.

'Out!' I bellowed. 'Everybody out of here!' The lights were still on, but the gushing smoke filled up the hold, the flames were roaring like animals. On my stomach I crawled along crates and over the bonnets of vehicles. I could smell the cool air coming from the hatch and I rolled, fell and staggered towards it. The metal step was in my hands. I pulled and levered myself up.

The lascars, jabbering with fear, tumbled out after me. I broke the glass on the fire alarm and pulled the lever. The siren sounded eerily through the pitching ship. I picked up the communication tube and blew down it. 'Where's the fire, Mr Jones?' demanded the cracked voice from the bridge.

'For'ard hold, sir. A fuel tank went up. They should have been drained.'

'Fight the fire, Mr Jones.'

I looked about for Adolf. The lascars were crowded around me. 'Fire hoses!' I shouted.

They began to reel the hoses out. 'Where's Adolf?' I was shouting.

One of the lascars, the second man, said: 'Adolf-Hassim in the hold. Dead man.'

It was a nightmare. The fire clamouring in the cavernous hold, the ship tossing crazily, the brave, thin, dark men trying to get the water to the blaze. I could feel myself shaking. I went back into the hold. The fire was fiercest at the distant end but the smoke was choking and filling the whole space. I put a piece of rag to my mouth and crawled back along the crates and sacks and vehicles of the cargo, praying the loaders had drained the other fuel tanks. The men were bringing in the hoses from both sides, lying flat and playing the water on the flames. It was impossible to get any nearer. 'Adolf!' I bawled. 'Adolf!' But he was not answering.

I crawled back over the cargo. Captain Hart and Mainwaring came down from the bridge. 'Where's the chief lascar?' asked the captain.

'He's in there, sir,' I said. I was choking and oily-faced. The captain sent me to the upper deck, into the stormy night. Hanging onto the rail, I gulped the clean salty air. The ship was still throwing about, but some stars were showing. Our fire sirens howled across the water.

I went to the bridge and took over the watch from the bosun. The radio officer was sending out distress signals but no ship would be able to get near us until the weather abated.

At daybreak the fire was reported extinguished. The sea had eased. A Portuguese ship was standing off us but we told her we did not now need assistance. In the hold there was a sculpture of burned and twisted wreckage. Beneath it somewhere was the body of Adolf. It would need a crane to find him.

On the bridge the skipper said: 'We're going into Lisbon.' There was something intense in his expression, as though he were near to tears. 'They've sold the ship,' he said to me. 'The owners.'

I could not credit it. 'What, just like that? While we're at sea?'

'They did it, as it turned out, while we were on fire at sea,' he growled. 'The new owners will have to claim the insurance. We're just merchandise, Jones, just merchandise.'

324

'Including poor Adolf.'

'Him as well.'

The telephone box was on the dockside under the shadow of the ships, so it had seen and heard more than its share of dreams and dramas; a cubicle of last farewells and the notice of arrivals; for final splitting quarrels and tearful reconciliations; for revelations that someone was back from the dead, or sailing away forever.

'Hello, is that Graham Pallister?'

'Yes. Who's that?'

'David Jones. Are we still going into business?'

I heard his deep breath from Barry to Southampton Dock. 'You've made up your mind,' he said.

'It was made up for me. The ship caught fire, a man was killed. Then we heard they'd sold the ship.'

'Sounds like a true story. Where are you?'

'Southampton. I've just come by train across Europe. I'll be there tomorrow.'

'Eight o'clock tomorrow night,' he said decisively. 'I'll be in the Shipwright's.'

Across the road from the telephone box was a public house called the Sailor's Return. I sat in a corner with a double Scotch. Seamen who travelled to the lands and towns of the earth were exchanging complaints about suspect ships, drunken masters and slave conditions; stinking weather and cargoes, money that was short or a long time coming. There was no talk of adventure, little delight in the sea or foreign parts or different skies. The conversation was of disappointments, treachery and ineptitude.

I walked up the rise to the station and at the top turned and looked at the masts and funnels lining the great Southampton Docks, one ship against another. A siren sounded, smoke curled from a red funnel, and above the dock buildings I could see the slow-moving masts of another ship coming in to her berth. The salt air had a changed smell and taste on land. I could see gulls wafted like leaves of paper in the middle distance wind and hear their half-starved cries. Resolutely I turned my back on it and walked into the station. I bought a ticket to Lymington Harbour and caught a bus from there to Millcreek.

Mary was in the garden of the cottage, sweeping the path, which she did three times a day when the bus was due. Nobody ever got off that bus without Mary knowing. She cried out when she saw me, half happiness, half tears, and called in her broad voice for Will. He came to the door, his glasses slipping from his nose, his *Hampshire Chronicle* askew in his hand.

I sat in their familiar room, safe and homely, and told them of some of my adventures. Afterwards I walked down to the inn with Will while Mary cooked supper. I told him what I planned to do.

He nodded: 'There's scope,' he agreed. 'There's even scope down here, not to mention the big places. Boats needing repairs. As long as you've got the money to start you off.'

We would have more than a thousand pounds, I told him. The house would be mortgaged, both Pallister and I had saved some. 'What about men?' he asked.

'Are you available?' I smiled at him.

'Too old now. Too old to leave here anyway. Fifty years I've been working here.' He grinned. 'Like they say these days – up the creek.'

'In the future we may want to work out of Southampton,' I said.

He thought there might be some local men who would be interested. 'Shaggy, you know, and little Sammy, when he comes back from the army.' He laughed with a little grunt. 'Only got as far as Aldershot,' he said. 'He's always home with his mum, trying to make out he's a soldier back from the battles.

'Maybe the war's changed things so that folks will move about a bit more. In Millcreek, as you well know, there's them that thinks Southampton's the other end of the earth. And . . . well, London might as well be Moscow or the moon.'

I went to the bar and bought an Old and Mild, which Will always drank, and a Scotch for myself. 'Johnny Walker,' Ted the landlord asked, 'or Bell's?' For years there had been no choice. 'Bell's please, Ted,' I said.

'Things have got to get better, haven't they,' he ruminated as he poured the whisky. 'Now we've won. No point in winning otherwise, I say.'

I returned to the wooden table. It had been there longer than anyone knew, scarred with the dents of dominoes, tattooed with the patterns of years of drinking glasses. They said it was once used for clog dancing. 'It's the materials – that's going to be a big problem,' I said to Will. 'There'll be men and there'll be work.'

'Ask Ted to sell you this,' grinned Will patting the table. 'Good bit of wood.' He became thoughtful. 'But there *is* stuff around,' he said. 'All stockpiled in the war. Wood, metal, fittings, all sorts of things.'

'If you hear of any, let me know,' I said.

'I will. I'll find out.'

The following day I went back to South Wales and met Pallister in the Shipwright's Arms at eight.

He noted the ports on his fingers: Haverfordwest, Milford Haven, Pembroke, Swansea, Barry, Penarth, Cardiff, Newport, Gloucester, Bristol, Avonmouth, Ilfracombe. 'That's a start,' he said.

'*How* do we start?' I asked.

'We start,' he said, 'by forming a partnership, Pallister Jones, or Jones Pallister.' He arched an eyebrow. 'I'll toss you for it,' he said. We tossed. He won. 'Pallister Jones,' he repeated. 'Capital fifteen hundred pounds. Equal shares. I'll organise the office work, accounts, everything like that. You look after the jobs, seeing the work gets done. I'll also make sure we get paid.'

'Do we get paid?' I said seriously. 'From the start, I mean.'

'Three pounds a week,' he said. 'Each.'

'What about the office? Where will that be?'

'Your house,' he said as if it had been obvious. 'For the

time being. We don't want to have to start paying rent before we have to. It's near enough to the dock.'

'What about the council?' I said.

'When they find out we'll apologise and move. By that time maybe we can.' He glanced at me. 'We don't want anybody making waves. Business, you realise, is made up of lots of small dishonesties.'

'All right.' He always impressed me with his confidence and how he never failed to have matters clearly categorised in his head. 'We've got an office, we've got partners, three quid a week each,' I said. 'What do we do next?'

'Work,' he said simply. 'Tomorrow, Jonesey, we get on a bus, on a succession of buses, and we go to every one of the places I've named. Right around the Bristol Channel. One by one, and spy out what's going on. We'll start here and go eastwards, to Gloucester and then around the other side down to Ilfracombe. We can go in the other direction from here next week. You've got a suit, haven't you?'

I had bought a suit for a wedding at Millcreek. 'Good,' he said. 'I think mine's a bit frayed at the elbows and cuffs and the left turnup – that always goes because of the leg. I'll get a new suit.' He looked up swiftly. 'At my expense. I've got some clothing coupons. Have you got a briefcase?'

'I think Griff may have had one. I'll look.'

'I thought he worked in an iron foundry.'

'In the office.'

'Excellent. See if you can dig it out. We'll meet at the bus station at seven o'clock.

He got up. 'Let's go and have some fish and chips,' he said. 'At that miserable place. We'll sit at the table – the caffee. To hell with the expense. Then I'm going home to write up the minutes of our first meeting.'

He held out his hand, his grin sideways and, as full of anticipation as he was, I took it.

Three

Despite his limp Pallister was always in a hurry. We rushed from town to town, me running ahead to delay a bus while he loped behind shouting encouragement. It seemed odd that he should be doing the urging. At every port he scurried about, dragging his leg, bursting into the offices of harbour masters, engineers, boiler scalers, and chandlers, shuffling along the docks, swinging with his thin hands down the gangways of ships.

He always seemed to find what he was looking for, putting his pointed nose in the air like a dog. In Gloucester, which we reached on the first evening not having eaten all day, he stood on a wet, seven o'clock pavement and, swinging his bad leg like a pendulum, which he did to ease it when it was tired, he half lifted his face, turning a trifle and peering along a strange street. 'This way, Jonesey,' he instructed abruptly. 'I know where it is now. I remember.'

What he remembered was a bed-and-breakfast house at the end of a dismal row, but charging only three-and-sixpence a night for a room and an evening meal of potatoes and gravy, topped by a spoonful of mincemeat.

We slept in one lumpy double bed. 'Wait until we stay in the Savoy, in London,' he promised. 'And we'll laugh about this.' He took his support off his wasted leg. 'My ball and chain,' he grumbled.

'I can't believe how you get about so quickly,' I told him. 'Rush, rush, rush. How many buses have we caught today as they were driving off?'

'All of them,' he laughed. In the chill room we got into the tawdry bed in our shirts and underwear. 'When I stayed here before it was two-and-sixpence,' he reminisced. 'Now it's another shilling. Shows how things are going through the roof.'

The landlady, a great-necked, tall, haughty-looking woman, like an old swan, had warned us to put out the light as soon as we got to bed. Now she reinforced the warning by banging her flat hand against the door. We extinguished the single bulb.

'I've never been to so many ports in one day,' I said lying back on a rigid pillow. 'Not on a bus, anyway. What did we get out of it, d'you think?'

'Contacts. Phone numbers. All sorts. I've ordered some business cards and some headed paper from that daft old printer in Penarth. Llew Llewellyn. He's slow and the machinery is left over from Caxton. But he's cheap.'

'You seem to think of everything,' I said.

'Not everything. When it comes to the actual jobs,' that's going to be up to you. I hope you can bawl at people.'

'I can learn,' I said.

'When we get to the Savoy,' he said quietly, 'we'll have a bloody suite, overlooking the Thames, and have women in. When you've got money, Jonesey, everything works for you. With women especially.'

When I woke at eight Pallister was already up and dressed and had gone to Gloucester Docks. He returned for a breakfast of porridge and fried bread. 'Gloucester's small stuff,' he said. 'Mostly canal barges, but I've made a few friends.' He ate his breakfast greedily and then slipped out into the small kitchen and returned with two more slices of fried bread. 'Start eating it quick,' he said. 'And don't let on. This has got to last us all day.'

We had stuffed the bread in our mouths and our cheeks were bulging when the landlady appeared. 'Did you have two extra slices?' she asked, her tall chin going up.

'No. Just what you gave us, missus,' said Pallister, his mouth full.

330

He looked at me for confirmation and, still chewing, I spread my hands. She went from the room and returned with our bill, stretching her long neck as she presented it. Pallister asked for a receipt which she wrote out tortuously. 'I *know* I fried two more,' she muttered.

We caught the bus to Bristol. 'Shilling each,' said Pallister. He folded the tickets neatly and put them in his wallet.

We spent another day trailing from office to office, walking the docks at Bristol and Avonmouth, arriving in Ilfracombe in the evening. 'Nice sort of place,' said Pallister looking from the town hill down onto the crooked finger of the harbour. 'I might come on my honeymoon here.' Something caught his eye far below. A motor boat was towing a small fishing vessel to a mooring alongside the quay. 'Wonder what's the matter with her?' he said.

'She's having trouble steering,' I said watching the manoeuvrings of the two craft.

'Let's go and see,' he decided. He began to lope down the steep path to the harbour. I followed. He went down the hill in jerky bounces like a lopsided kangaroo. I marvelled at him again. We reached the road below the hill and went along to the quay. It was all I could do to keep up with him. The fishing boat had tied up and the other craft was chugging away, leaving a rotund and morose man sitting on the deck. She was called *Girl Friday*.

''Evening,' said Pallister. He had slowed at the end of the quay and we had approached casually. 'Trouble?'

'Steering's gone,' said the man grumpily.

'Serious?' asked Pallister.

The man glanced up as if wondering what interest it might be to us. 'God knows,' he said. 'I thought I'd fixed it temporarily but it went again when I was out there.' He nodded towards the Bristol Channel. 'Cost me a quid that tow did.' He sighed dejectedly. 'I was going to France next week,' he said. 'The wife's going to be disappointed. First trip since before the war.'

Pallister assumed the attitude of a man who harbours

favours. He rubbed his chin and opened his briefcase. He consulted deeply what I knew to be a bus timetable and then said to the boat-owner. 'We might be in a position to help.'

'How's that?' said the man looking first at me and then at Pallister.

'We're with Montgomery Pallister Jones,' said Pallister. 'Marine repairs. We operate mainly along the South Wales ports but we're considering opening branches on this side. That's why we're here, seeing what the prospects might be.' He opened his hand and swung it towards me. 'This is Mr Jones, I am Mr Pallister.'

'Do you deal with steering?' the boat-owner asked.

'Specialists,' replied Pallister blandly. 'Let's take a look at it.'

He stumbled down the gangway onto the deck. 'War wound,' he muttered to the boat-owner. 'North Africa.' I followed dumbly, merely nodding to the man. Enough had been said.

He took us below and to the aft end of the small boat. Within the saloon the furnishings were worn and torn and the veneered wood warped. The man said his name was Phelps. 'Anything that is reasonable,' he was saying. 'But I'm not spending a fortune.'

'Exactly,' nodded Pallister. He regarded the steering wheel.

He turned to me: 'Want to take a look,' he suggested, 'David?'

'Yes . . . of course, Graham,' I mumbled. I took hold of the wheel and spun it. That, at least, was something I could do with a convincing touch. Both men watched me keenly. 'Wheel doesn't belong to the boat,' I said.

'No. Quite right,' said Mr Phelps, impressed. Pallister's smile began to drift down his face. 'It's a wheel from a boat I had before.'

I opened the hatch and clambered down below. The engine was oil-covered. The steering mechanism was tangled and broken. I pushed my head up through the hatch. 'It's a mess,' I said. 'But it's repairable.'

'Good,' said Mr Pehlps. 'How long? How much will it cost?'

'You can have our estimate by tomorrow morning,' Pallister assured him. 'Eight o'clock.

'Eight. That's good. So I'll . . . we'll be able to go to France next week?'

Pallister said: 'Let's not make too many promises we can't keep. As we said we're here on an exploration job. We don't have any tools or equipment in Ilfracombe. But we'll get some. We might have to bring a couple of chaps from Cardiff.' His eyes flicked up to me. 'Or maybe Mr Jones can do something about it himself.'

'It will take two,' I said honestly.

'We'll get somebody, don't worry, Mr Phelps,' he reassured the owner. The man repeated: 'Just as long as it's not a fortune.'

'It *won't* be a fortune,' said Pallister glancing around the saloon. 'This could do with a paint job,' he observed. He touched the torn and faded seats. 'And some new upholstery.'

'Give me a quote for that too,' said Mr Phelps helplessly. 'I'd like to take her to France. My wife, I mean. And the boat of course. Things have been difficult since I came out of the RAF and I'd like to make it up to her. This might be the last chance.' He looked sorrowfully at each of us. 'She's not a patient woman.'

Nodding sympathetically we went up the gangplank to the dock again. We walked away and, under Pallister's whispered instructions, we mumbled to each other as though discussing details. There was a public house on the edge of the harbour. We sat down with two half-pints of beer. 'Job number one,' said Pallister holding up his glass. 'Saving a man's marriage. Good job you noticed the wheel was wrong. That impressed him.'

'Who,' I asked him, 'is Montgomery?'

He regarded me slyly. 'Field Marshal Montgomery,' he answered. 'Eighth Army, Battle of El Alamein, all that,'

'You said our company was called Montgomery Pallister Jones,' I pointed out. 'Who is Montgomery?'

'Field Marshal Montgomery,' he insisted. He leaned forward. 'Psychology. If I'd have said to our Mr Phelps that we were Pallister Jones, and that I was Pallister and you were Jones, *there we were*, presented to him – the entire ownership. He would think, "Well, they must be tin-pot if *both* of them are here." So I moved Montgomery in as managing director. He's not with us today, he's doing big business elsewhere, back in our palatial offices in Cardiff. See?'

'You think of everything,' I said again.

'You let me do the talking,' he said. 'You be the strong, silent, reliable one. Mr Phelps didn't realise it but he reacted to the name Montgomery. It's a good name at the moment. A hero's name. A British hero's name. Brown or Smith would not have sounded half as impressive. Our Montgomery may be nothing to do with the gallant soldier but he *sounds* as though he might have a connection. It's called instilling confidence.'

'You've read it in a book,' I said.

He smiled and said: 'You spent a lot of time waiting around when you're fire-watching.'

'I think I can fathom out that steering,' I said. 'It's more or less the same principle as they used on the landing barges, wheelhouse aft and cables. His cables are tangled like knitting wool. But they'll untangle.'

'Good,' nodded Pallister. 'But you'll need help. What about materials? For the saloon I'm thinking. Wood and upholstery for the seats. And tools of course. Don't look so pessimistic, Jonesey, we'll get them. We'll start right now.'

I have still never seen anyone work like Pallister. He limped around the pub asking questions, talking to people, telling short jokes, buying the occasional half a pint, as if he had been a familiar for years. After an hour we went out to a café and had sausage and chips and tea. The woman there said she had a room, that was a touch damp, but we could have it for the night at a cost of two shillings in advance. Pallister wrote it down in his notebook. We then went out to another public house and a third. Each time we sat with two small beers and Pallister moved around making friends.

Eventually he jolted through the crowd in the bar and said: 'I think I know where we can get some upholstery stuff. I'll deal with it. We've finished in here anyway. There's another pub up the street. Wander up there and see if you can find your man, to help on the boat. You'd better find some wood too and some tools. I'll leave that to you. If I'm back after you I'll knock on the window.'

I walked up the climbing street to the other inn. It was less crowded. I asked the landlord if he knew a man who could work on the repair of some steering gear. 'Tom Rollings,' he said immediately. 'He's retired now but he might not be against doing a bit of work. He's got greyhounds.'

Rollings lived half a mile away. I trudged there wishing I had the same effrontery as Pallister. There was a light in the upstairs window of the cottage. I knocked tentatively. The window above me opened. 'Who's there, this time o' night?' demanded a round face. 'Who be it, Tom?' I heard a woman's voice call from the room.

'Mr Rollings,' I said craning up. 'I'm sorry it's so late. The landlord at the Dragon gave me your name. I need someone to repair some steering and it has to be tomorrow. I'll pay you immediately.'

That made him thoughtful. 'I'll be down,' he grunted. The window closed and I saw candlelight travelling down the stairs. It glowed in the fan over the cottage door. Several keys were turned and bolts pulled. The door creaked open and Rollings stood there in a long nightshirt. He had a shotgun under his arm. 'Come you on in,' he said amiably. He put the shotgun in a corner. 'Sorry about that. Force of habit, you might say,' he explained. 'Had all sorts around here during the war. Yanks and all sorts. You had to be careful answering the door by night.'

He led me into a low room and, unembarrassed, sat in his nightshirt and cracked slippers while I told him what I

335

wanted. A second candle began to tremble down the curved staircase. Another nightshirt appeared, this time occupied by Mrs Rollings, her hair in curlers made from pieces of newspaper. 'What's he wanting, Tom?' she asked her husband.

'Bit o' work on a boat. For tomorrow.'

She continued to ignore me. 'How much?' she said.

'How much?' Tom transmitted to me. 'I got greyhounds.'

'I've looked at the job and it shouldn't take more than a day,' I said. 'Thirty shillings.'

'Thirty shillings,' Tom's wife said to Tom.

'What time?' he asked.

'Ten o'clock,' I said. 'I have to get some wood and some tools from somewhere. There's some work to be done on the cabin as well.'

'Ten o'clock,' said Tom's wife. 'And there's work on the cabin too.'

'Want any help with that?' asked Tom. 'I've got tools. All mine when I was working regular. Is the wood for panelling and that?'

I said it was. 'Well,' he said slowly, 'if it's not a big job I might have enough wood too. Better than it lying about. Good stuff. Pine. Had it since before the war. I was keeping it . . .'

'It's his greyhounds,' explained the woman.

'Three pounds for me and the use of the tools and three for the wood and I'll do it all,' he said.

'Three pounds for him and three for the wood,' echoed his wife.

'Done,' I said shaking hands with them both. 'We'd better start earlier then, now I don't need to go looking for wood. She's called *Girl Friday*.'

'Seven,' he said. 'On the wharf is she?'

'Seven,' said his wife. 'After he's run the greyhounds.'

I returned to our room at the back of the café.

Pallister was not in the room. At three in the morning I was awakened by a tapping on the window light. There was

336

a cold corridor outside the room and a rough wooden door. I opened it and let him in. It was raining.

'Soaked,' Pallister complained. He had a bundle below his arm. 'But I managed to keep that dry.'

'What is it?'

It was wrapped in a square of tarpaulin. He unrolled it quickly. 'Red damask,' he said. 'Feel the thickness.'

'Incredible,' I breathed. Then I looked quickly at him. 'Where did you get it?'

'It's an old army camp cinema,' he said. 'Roof burned off last year and the camp's empty now. I met a chap who knew that some of the seats were upholstered, just like ordinary seats in the pictures. Reserved for officers and women. When the roof fell in they just left them. They had a bit of cover on them, stuff like this.' He touched the tarpaulin. 'But they were all going mildew.'

'But this is a whole roll,' I said.

'Luck,' he said. He blinked with innocence. 'There was this tucked away in a cupboard. They must have been going to re-cover some of the seats. But the fire happened and hostilities ceased and that was that. Tucked away and forgotten.'

He saw me looking straight at him. 'It was a long way on that bloke's motorbike,' he said taking off his coat.

'It's pinched then?'

Pallister looked shocked. 'War surplus,' he corrected.

At seven o'clock Tom Rollings came along the stone quay, with his tool-bag thrown over his shoulder. It was a sharp, low morning with spots of rain in the western wind. We had already been aboard the *Girl Friday* for an hour. Phelps had greeted us pessimistically. 'It's not just the boat, you understand,' he mumbled. 'It's the wife.' Pallister told him the price: twenty-five pounds, to be paid five pounds then, and twenty at his satisfaction on the completion of the job.

When Rollings appeared on the quay, Pallister said heartily: 'Ah, here comes our Mr Rollings,' as if he had employed the old man for years. He continued this familiarity once Tom was aboard, and while Phelps was in earshot. The old man was puzzled. 'Do I know this gentleman?' he whispered to me.

'Mr Pallister,' I whispered back. 'He's the big boss.'

Rollings surveyed the twisted steering cables and groaned. 'Looks like somebody been knitting with 'em,' he said. Down in the unkempt saloon he sniffed the mildew and ran his hand over the woodwork like a doctor touching a patient. 'Nothing been done for years,' he said. 'But there's a lot like that.'

There was no sign of the wood he had promised. Pallister had brought the roll of damask material and was pulling and arranging it over the bulkhead seats in the cabin like a haberdasher's assistant in a shop. Mr Phelps went ashore saying he would not be back until the afternoon and in the manner of a man who would rather not know the worst. He walked off without looking back. It was as well he did, for no sooner had I asked Tom when the wood would be arriving than he cocked his ear and said: 'She be 'ere now, gov'nor.'

The grind of metal-rimmed wheels sounded in the vacant morning. I went out into the damp air. Pallister was standing by the rail watching a trembling handcart being pulled over the cobbles of the quay by an old woman bent at an angle by rheumatism and the effort of towing the cart. 'There 'un is, God help her,' said Tom Rollings, his head emerging from the hatch. 'My dear wife, Mrs Rollings.'

I hurried ashore to assist the old lady but she cackled and said: 'Too late, I be already here.'

We unloaded the wood onto the deck. It looked excellent, strong and deeply seasoned. Tom was already measuring the lengths with a carpenter's rule. 'Just do nice,' he said.

Without a further word, as though everything had been long-planned and settled, the old lady began tearing out the tattered upholstery in the cabin. 'Is Mrs Rollings working too?' asked Pallister.

'Let 'un get on with it, sir,' advised the old man. 'Gives

338

'un summat to do. She'll only charge ten bob. Knits and sews and makes cushions. Made the hassocks for the church.'

We left the old lady chuntering soundlessly to herself, her fingers with their swollen joints working nimbly over the seats. ''Un can make us some tea soon,' said her husband. 'I'll buy 'un a new pair of boots.' He moved aft. 'Let's take a look at this steering.'

Somehow, despite his age and bulk, he managed to wedge himself below and began untangling the cables. At that stage there was little I could do to assist, so I went on deck and began to saw the timber for the cabin. Pallister came through the hatch. 'We ought to keep these two for that contract on the *Queen Mary*,' he joked. 'Is that wood good stuff?'

'You wouldn't buy it easily today,' I said. I paused in the sawing. 'We were lucky this time, but where are we going to get timber and the other stuff we need from now on?'

'We'll have to be lucky again,' he said with his usual off-hand firmness. 'I've applied for allocations of materials from the Ministry of Supply. If you've got a *bona fide* company they have to dish some out to you.'

I had begun sawing again. 'We'll need transport,' I said without stopping.

'We'll keep the old girl and the handcart,' he smiled.

'I'm serious. Can you drive? I can't.'

'Nor me. We'll get somebody to teach us.'

'Then we'll need something *to* drive,' I continued. The wood dropped with a solid clatter as I sawed through. 'Don't go bruising that timber,' came Tom's voice from below. Pallister picked up the piece and handed it to me carefully. 'We'll get something,' he said. 'Have faith, Jonesey, have faith.'

Tom called that he needed some help and I went below. Mrs Rollings was busy with a huge pair of shears, her lips moving in a soundless incantation as she worked.

The old man and I worked at opposite ends of the steering system for two hours. At twelve o'clock he stopped work and so did Mrs Rollings. They sat on the deck in the chill day and ate sandwiches and drank Tizer, a white tablecloth arranged before them. 'I got lots of tools down my old yard,' mentioned Tom over two wedges of bread and cheese. 'I might sell 'un.'

Mrs Rollings shook her head and said: 'It's they greyhounds.'

'Won't be doing that sort of job now,' the old man went on. 'And I got my own tools, like you see.'

He finished his sandwich and said we could walk to his yard if I liked. He took me along the quay and up the ascent to their cottage. He opened the side-gate and at once dogs began to bark.

'That be they,' he said.

At the end of the yard was a run and within it, behind wire netting, were two thin, curved dogs. When they saw Tom they began to howl louder. 'Wish they'd run like they holler,' he said philosophically.

'You race them?' I said 'Where?'

'Taunton, next Saturday night,' he said. 'At Newton Abbot they both come last. In two races that is. Mind, if they'd been in the same race, they'd still come last. My brother gave 'un to me. Good of him, waddn't it?'

We walked towards a lean-to shed on the other side of the yard. 'Tools been in 'ere,' he said. 'Shipwrights' tools.'

He opened the door and I walked into a warm, hay-smelling hut. It had one clogged window but the light was good enough from that and the door for me to see ranks of tools held in racks along the walls; saws of different kinds, sizes of planes, screwdrivers, hammers, chisels ranged according to width. He picked up a brace-and-bit. It was clean and turned with a touch. 'Don't reckon they'll ever make them like this again,' he said. 'The way the world is going. Everything's going to be cheap now. I don't mean in price, just cheap.'

'Tom,' I said. 'We're just starting up in this business.'

He grinned wisely. 'I know'd that,' he said. 'By the way

you go about things. That Mr Pallister, 'e don't know aft from for'ard, do 'e?'

'He looks after the books,' I explained.

'Ah, the money,' he nodded heavily. ''Ow much for the tools?'

'How much do you want?'

'I reckon if I kept them a while I'd get forty, maybe fifty pounds for them. There's a lot here. But now I got the greyhounds . . . well, how about thirty pounds?'

'Done,' I said. I had never paid thirty pounds for anything in my life. 'We'll pay you with the job.'

'Come tomorrow and they'll all be packed up for you. You can take them on the bus then.'

I glanced at him. 'You come down on the bus from Avonmouth, didn't you?' he said. 'Not much goes on in these parts that don't get around. 'Tis cash, I takes it?'

We returned to the boat and found Mrs Rollings cutting the fabric with her shears while Pallister held it in front of him. I told him I had just bought the tools. His eyebrows rose. Tom went back to the steering and I went out on deck to continue shaping the wood. Pallister followed me: 'It's all right now,' he said cautiously. 'But we don't make decisions without each other in future, is that agreed?'

'You mean the tools,' I said surprised. 'They're worth every penny, I tell you.'

'I'm sure they are,' he said, still tersely. 'But we always have to know what the other partner is doing. It's what a partnership is all about.' He went down the gangplank. 'I'll get the money from my savings book,' he called back to me. 'But don't buy anything else while I'm away.'

He stumbled off along the quay. I felt angry and foolish. I sawed into the wood fiercely. He had not asked me about stealing the fabric.

By four o'clock the steering was repaired. When Mr Phelps returned, appearing anxious even from the other end of the quay, I was standing at the wheel turning it this and that way under Tom's shouted instructions. Much of the wood had been replaced in the cabin and Mrs Rollings was tacking the upholstery material into place with small taps of a hammer as if she were striking insects.

'Does it work?' asked Phelps pointing at the wheel.

'Feels like it does,' I said. 'We'll have to take her out to make sure. We can do that first thing tomorrow.'

With only a break for a cup of tea, which Pallister made because he wanted to keep the old lady moving, Tom turned his attention to the cabin. I had already done much of the work. Now he took over and worked for another two hours, quickly and expertly. At nine o'clock we were all finished, including the varnish. Mr Phelps had gone to get something to eat. He returned, sniffed the varnish and viewed the saloon with astonishment. 'She *will* be pleased,' he breathed happily.

Blod's hushed front parlour was converted into an office. I brought in the kitchen table for a desk and Pallister arrived on a rainy evening with a filing cabinet which, he said, had been entombed for years in the cellars of his former employers. The first items to be filed were receipts for the purchase of a desk and a filing cabinet. When we were leaving Ilfracombe on the bus he had asked me for the receipt for the money paid to Tom Rollings for the tools, enclosed in two canvas bags on the seat in front of us. He took the piece of paper with the old heading: 'T Rollings. Shipwright' and deftly altered the figure of thirty pounds to read eighty pounds. 'They're worth eighty,' he said putting the slip away in his notebook.

In the file marked 'Receipts' he also clipped the amended accounts for our three nights' lodgings. With his sly smile he replaced the file in the cabinet. 'They could be historic documents one day,' he said.

The following morning a General Post Office van drew up outside and a telephone, black and upright as a nun, was placed on the desk. People looked out of their windows to see the engineer putting up the wires. 'First telephone in this street and for some distance,' said the Post Office man. He looked thoughtful. 'Nearest one is at Evans, funeral director. You'll get all the neighbours knocking at your door with their pennies in their hands wanting to phone their relatives in Swansea. They're frightened of going to the undertakers.'

Pallister pinned a notice on the front door. 'Private use of telephone, sixpence.' He regarded it sagely. 'Somebody would *have* to be dying to pay that.'

The upright telephone stood like a cowled figure. We sat watching it. When it rang we both jumped. We looked sharply at each other. Pallister picked it up. 'Pallister Jones,' he said throatily. It was only the engineers testing the line. We sat down once more and stared at it, daring it to ring. It remained silent. After twenty minutes Pallister said in his snappy way: 'All right then, if nobody is going to ring us, we'll have to bloody well ring them.' He took out his notebook and began to telephone contacts he had made on our journey around the Bristol Channel. I admired his coolness. 'Hello, Desmond Bowles please ... Oh hello, Des ... Graham Pallister here. Pallister Jones. Right, that's it. It was good to meet you. I'm just ringing to give you our new number. We've just moved to bigger offices.'

He made eight or nine calls while I watched, thinking of the cost. Then we sat down and stared at the black instrument again. The only sound was the ticking of my auntie's mantel clock. 'Let's go and have a pint,' I suggested.

He glanced at me as though I had spoiled something. But with a sigh, as though regretting the weaknesses of others, he stood and put his coat on. Then the telephone rang. We fell across the room to reach it. I got there first but handed it to him. 'Pallister Jones,' he announced sedately.

'Oh hello, Mr Deakin. You soon called back. Reminded you. Yes ... right ... of course. We can handle it. Where is she lying? Port Talbot. Well yes. Boiler scaling, deck repairs ... no, that sounds fine. I'll be over there this afternoon.'

I felt my eyes protrude. A wad of excitement and consternation hung in my stomach. He was continuing: 'Sailing Thursday ... coming to Barry and then Newport, picking up cargo. Just our speciality, of course. We can pick up on the job in each port. No delay to the ship. See you this afternoon. I've got a lunch meeting, so it will be about four-thirty. Right. Thank you. You'll be more than satisfied.'

He replaced the phone and remained slumped across the table. I sat speechless. Suddenly, together, we leapt in the air and shouted and danced about, sending the glass droplets on the mantelpiece ornaments jangling. I mimicked him. 'Sure we can handle it . . . just our speciality.' He rolled with laughter.

'But how?' I demanded ecstatically. '*How*, for God's sake, are we going to do it?'

'*Do* it. Just *do* it, boy! Listen, we've got to get a move on. We'll get on down now and get some employees. Two boiler scalers, two shipwrights and a boy.'

'And somebody who can drive,' I put in soberly. 'And *something* to drive. What are we going to do?'

'Get a man with a lorry. Or just a lorry. We'll get there if I have to drive the bloody thing myself.'

'You can't drive, neither can I.'

He looked at me straight. 'It can't be all that difficult,' he said. 'Other people do it.'

We almost raced down into the town. His leg was no handicap. If I did get ahead and looked back he would urge me: 'Go on, go on, I'm with you! I'll catch up!'

Breathlessly we arrived outside the Shipwrights' Arms. 'Stop,' said Pallister halting. 'Stand still a minute. Let's get our wind back. And our brains. We don't want to go in like it was the Relief of Mafeking.' He stood and gazed out at the docks and Barry Roads beyond. 'All right,' he said calmly at last. 'Now, nice and casual. We want two boiler scalers, a lad, and two men who know what they're doing on the deck.'

'And a driver with a lorry.'

In two hours of dodging around the town, knocking on doors and making financial inducements, we had our men, except the driver with the lorry. Pallister was getting the train to Port Talbot. 'I'll leave the lorry to you, Jonesey,' he

344

said before leaving. 'Get one whatever you do. It's not just the men, it's the tools and we'll have to pick up some materials. Our own lorry will look good.'

At five o'clock I found a small truck which had belonged to a builder. He had sold it to a man in Penarth who lent it to me for a pound for the day. He drove it himself and we parked it outside the house. Only then he revealed he could not drive it the next day because he had to go to hospital about his feet. It was getting late. I went rummaging around the town for a driver.

In those days there were far fewer people who could drive. It began to drizzle and, tired with walking, becoming despondent, I finally spoke to a twitching man in a pub and he said he would drive the vehicle for ten shillings; five shillings and five when he had done the job. Greatly relieved, I handed him two half-crowns. Going home I was passing the office of Ephraim Morris, the solicitor, and the boyish Morris was just leaving. Pallister and I had already talked of having him as our company lawyer once we could afford one.

'You've left the lights on,' I said to Morris nodding back at the loft.

'My mother clears up,' he said. 'How's the brave business venture going?'

'All right,' I said. We were walking along the dock road in the drizzle. 'Big repair and scaling job in Port Talbot tomorrow. Pallister's down there now.'

'Odd bloke,' he said. 'But clever, isn't he?'

'*I* think he is. We've set up the office, we've got a phone.'

'Want somebody to answer it?' he asked. 'When you're not there. Like a secretary, types, reliable. Not much to laugh at but she'll do the lot for a couple of quid a week.'

'Your mother?' I guessed.

'That's her. I can't stand her looking at me like she does. With you she might cheer up. And anyway . . .' He paused and his eyes slid sideways as we walked. '. . . there's a girl from Thompson Street I want to employ.'

'I'll talk to Pallister about it,' I said. 'She would be useful.

We've got to have somebody to answer the phone and type letters and so forth.'

'When will you know?' he asked, adding craftily: 'It's a matter of timing, you see . . .'

'Oh. Well. Tonight. If you give us a ring about nine, say.' I told him the number and he wrote it down.

'She could start when you like. Tomorrow even.'

'You're anxious to start training the new girl?'

'Exactly.'

He called at nine and we agreed to employ Martha Morris. She began working for us the following morning. She was there before any of the men assembled to go to Port Talbot. She sniffed around the office and began to rearrange things. She had brought a portable typewriter with her, and she set it on the desk and in a sharp, businesslike way, tried it out, like somebody tuning a piano in a place strange to them. When the men were there and Pallister was looking at his watch the telephone rang and Martha picked it up. 'Good morning, Pallister Jones,' she said with authority. She turned stiffly: 'For you, Mr Jones,' she said.

I took the instrument. My heart dropped as I listened. I put the earpiece back on its cradle. 'The driver,' I said to Pallister. 'Can't do the job. He's appearing in court. He didn't tell me that.'

Pallister gave me a hard look. 'He wasn't likely to, was he,' he grunted. 'Sod it, now who is going to drive the thing?' He turned to the four men and one boy. 'Can *anybody* drive?' They shook their heads.

'I can drive,' announced Martha firmly. 'I've never driven a lorry but I can try.'

In its first month Pallister Jones made a clear profit of sixty-seven pounds, fifteen shillings. We were jubilant. We voted ourselves an immediate salary rise to five pounds a week and we gave Martha Norris an extra pound. The downcast lady who had shifted and shuffled in and out of her son's office became the fulcrum of ours. She was concise and effective,

346

calm and clear-headed, in control and took twenty minutes for lunch, during which she picked at a sandwich, drank mint tea and read *Home Notes*, a motherly magazine. She also gave us driving lessons.

Men were eager for employment by us because we kept our wages threepence-an-hour above those of the bigger companies and the workers were paid by the job. After the completion of a contract, usually a span of no more than a few days, sometimes only one, they would troop into the office and take their pay in their hands. There was no waiting until Friday. We appointed as foreman a slow-smiling, hard, big, Cardiff West Indian called Ginger Griffiths. He was the first black man to become a foreman in all the South Wales Docks. He got a bonus of ten shillings every time a job was completed on time, and he made sure they were. He once threw a lazy painter into Penarth Dock and had to dive in to rescue him.

But there were difficulties. 'We're under-capitalised,' said Pallister. In the evenings we went for a drink at the St David's Hotel. We began to take important customers there for lunch. 'If we don't get an injection of money we'll always be in the basement,' he said. 'We'll never get beyond the minor jobs. We'll have to go to the bank and raise a loan.'

'How much?' I asked.

'As much as two thousand pounds,' he said. He saw my expression. 'Look, Jonesey, we need a yard, we need materials, we need a car when we've passed our driving tests. And we can't go on using your front room as an office. It doesn't look right.'

I fiddled with my whisky. 'The choice is to be brave,' he said. 'Or bankrupt.'

Two days later there came a telephone call from Will. I could tell he was speaking from the Millcreek telephone box because I could hear the church clock chiming. 'Davy, you know I told you I'd let you know about any timber that's going, well there's some going. A big lot of good stuff and some metal, copper and tubing and suchlike, and machine tools.'

'Where is it, Will?'

'It's down at Keyhaven, along the coast. Wartime store, but we had some heavy weather last week and the roof was just about blown off the place. They want to get it sold quick. It's Ministry stuff, and they won't go through the usual rigmarole of tenders or an auction. It's got to be sold and moved out, quicker the better.'

'Thanks, Will. How much do you think it will fetch?'

'Oh, I don't know that. It's pretty good by all accounts. Oak and elm, even some teak that came from somewhere. Someone said two or three thousand pounds.'

Pallister was at the dock superintendent's office in Cardiff. I waited for him in a café across the road. He came out and we sat in the café drinking tea. There was a girl with a flower in her hair serving there. 'We've *got* to raise the cash,' said Pallister pushing his fist into the palm of his hand. 'We can't let this slip. It's a voice from heaven. You know how hard it is to come by materials, and if they want to shift this lot in a hurry . . . I say we get down there tomorrow.'

'Where's the money coming from?'

'The bank,' he shrugged. 'That's what they're for. I'll go over right now.' He got up to pay for the teas and the girl smiled at him. 'You used to go the Saturday dances at the Orchid in Port Talbot, didn't you?' she said. She took in his suit and briefcase. 'In business, are you?'

'Shipping,' he said. 'Busy, busy.' He winked at me. We went into the street and down to the station. 'It's amazing what a clean shirt and a few bob can do for you,' he said. 'She's never said a word to me before. Except when I asked her to dance and then she said no.'

We got on the train at seven the next morning, the old seaport route; Swansea, Cardiff, Newport, Bristol and then Southampton, the same line that I had first taken years before when I joined the *Orion*. Pallister had never been to Southampton and, although we had only to change trains

348

there for Lymington where Will was to meet us, we left the station so that I could show him the view of the docks. We got to the brow of the brief hill and looked over to the port, the mesh of rigging, the colours of the funnels and the flags. 'Elder Dempster, Blue Cross, Shaw Saville,' I recited the shipping lines. Pure white smoke, curled as a shell, came from a raked yellow and black funnel and a siren boomed over the town. 'She's sailing,' I said almost to myself. Pallister was sniffing the air in the way he did, like a dog. There was no room for romance in him. 'There's money there, son,' he said. 'We've got to get some of it.'

Thoughtfully we went back to the station and boarded the local train to Lymington. The bank had half-promised the loan but they wanted to see the account books. Martha Morris was taking them in that day. 'It's all waiting there for us,' said Pallister nodding at the lined-up ships as the train trundled alongside the harbour. 'We've got to grab it, Jonesey. We've got to have daring.'

Will was waiting at Lymington with Mary, who cried as she embraced me. She went back to the village having made us promise that we would spend the night at the cottage. 'Love to,' said Pallister. 'Thanks so much.' I could sense him toting up a free lodging.

'He's got a car, this man from the Ministry,' announced Will. 'Mr Hawkings. He'll be along here in a minute.'

Hawkings, who wore a shabby bowler hat, arrived and we got into the pre-war Morris. At Keyhaven we could see the store, its damaged roof open to the uncertain sky, tarpaulins sagging inadequately.

Pallister began to tut-tut. The watchman who had told Will of the timber unlocked the door. We walked into a treasure house. There was sawn oak and elm, plank upon plank; there was some fine teak; there were sheets of tin and lead, rolled like fire hoses, paint, ropes, woodworking machinery that had never been used. 'All or nothing,' said Hawkings. 'We can't mess about with splitting it up.' In

349

twenty minutes we had bought everything for two thousand, three hundred pounds. It was worth twice the money.

'Two thousand, four hundred and twenty pounds,' mused Pallister on the returning train the next day. 'God help us if the bank decides to change its mind.'

'Two thousand, three hundred,' I corrected. 'And you gave ten pounds to Will and ten to the watchman.'

'And a hundred to Mr Hawkings,' said Pallister looking out of the window.

We left the train at Bristol and went down to the dock superintendent's office. Pallister went in alone and I walked along the breezy quays. There were ships loading and unloading in the dun afternoon. Beyond them, in a separate basin, were some smaller craft. I walked along the jetty. Tied up at the distant end was a boat that was familiar. I could see the name on her bow: *Fanny Bailey*. I had painted that there.

There was an indent in the quay wall and as I drew close I saw a green Wolsey Ten-Fourteen, clean and gleaming, parked there. When I was alongside the *Fanny Bailey* a man came up from below. 'Major Perring,' I said. 'Remember me, David Jones?'

'Good gracious,' he responded. 'You're just the chap, Mr Jones.' We shook hands. 'She hit the breakwater yesterday, sides stove in, and she's starting to leak.'

He invited me aboard and poured two tumblers of whisky. I told him of the business we had begun. Pallister arrived and I introduced them. Harry Perring poured a further Scotch. 'We can have our men down here tomorrow,' said Pallister in his confident way once he had seen the extent of the damage.'

'You operate out of Bristol as well?' said Harry Perring.

'All Bristol Channel ports,' said Pallister. 'Swansea to Ilfracombe. Eventually we plan to open in Liverpool, Southampton and other places. The idea is that repairs can go on while the vessel is still picking up cargo.'

'Sit down,' invited Perring. 'Have another drink.'

350

He had bought four former landing craft now, he said. Two of them he had intended to work on a ferry crossing over the River Severn, at a point not far from where the Severn Bridge was built years later. The road journey from South Wales into England in those days was a long detour through Gloucester. His ferry would cut the time by up to two hours. 'My business interests are elsewhere. This is only a hobby,' he smiled. 'I have an attachment to this particular hulk because I commanded her in Normandy. Not that we got very far. By the time we hit the beach there was hardly anybody left to get ashore.'

He suggested that we had dinner with him that evening. 'Perhaps we can talk business,' he said.

As we walked from the Bristol rain into the foyer of the Great Britain Hotel, Pallister muttered: 'Look like you dine here every night, Jonesey.' We had come from our lodgings in St Paul's by bus and then taken a taxi half-a-mile to the hotel. A doorman with white gloves opened the cab door.

Pallister told me to slow down and we strolled into the panelled bar. Perring was already there. A waiter in tails and a white tie that seemed to be securing his large red chin hovered. 'Any preference, sir?' he asked me after I had ordered a whisky. The top half of his body came stiffly forward causing his jowl to overhang. 'Bell's, if you please,' I murmured.

'It's astonishing how they've been able to get this sort of place near enough into shape, so soon after the war,' said Perring looking around. 'A bomb came through the roof of this hotel.'

'They came to Pallister Jones,' laughed Pallister. 'Hotel Division.'

'People want things as they once were,' said Perring smiling politely. 'They want to get back to the good old pre-war days, but how long that is going to take is another matter entirely. Good God, to think that we now have *bread* rationing. That didn't happen through the whole of the war. A

Socialist government might have seemed like a good idea in theory, but in practice . . .'

'I'm one of those who believe that the Conservatives purposely lost the election,' said Pallister looking wise. 'On the premise that any immediate government would have such a hard ride that they wouldn't sniff power for years after.'

'Could be true,' agreed Perring. 'And if you can survive now in business then you should be able to survive any time and anywhere.'

He began to ask short, careful questions about what we were doing, and went on through dinner in the glowing dining room. It was the first time I tasted asparagus soup. The beef was carved below a tureen at the table, one slice to a plate. Another was secretly added to it. There was only one piece of bread for each diner although an extra piece could be obtained on request. We drank French white wine and had brandy afterwards. Pallister told him about the purchase of the timber and other materials from Keyhaven. He whistled softly. 'That's good,' he murmured. 'That's clever.'

His own family business, from thin beginnings, had been concerned with transport. 'My grandfather began with one and a half horses,' he laughed. 'We shared one horse with someone else. But in the year before the war we had more than a hundred motor vehicles on the road. We also bought into property and banking.' He glanced from Pallister to me and back again. 'Perring's have never had any dealings with the shipping business,' he said. 'Perhaps it is time we diversified. Would Pallister Jones be interested?'

A flick of Pallister's eyes warned me to remain in my seat. 'Well,' he replied thoughtfully. 'We would naturally be interested in talking about it. We have ambitious plans, as I've already outlined, but some were in the long term.' He touched his fingers together and let his smile drift down one side of his face. 'Yes, we're interested.'

We came out of the Great Britain Hotel into the wet Bristol evening. I could hardly contain myself. 'Five *thousand* quid,' I breathed. 'Five *whole, thousand* quid.'

352

'In exchange for a seat on the board and some other considerations,' said Pallister. 'But we'll still be driving.'

'We're going to grab it, aren't we?' I asked him anxiously. 'God, it's the big opening for us.'

'Not *grab* it,' said Pallister. We were walking through the old and narrow window-hung streets, away from the hotel. 'We'll accept it, of course. We'd be mad not to. But we won't *grab* it. Perring's no fool, Jonesey. He thinks he's onto a good idea, but he'll make double sure he's right about it before he writes any cheque.'

A stationary taxi glimmered on a drizzling corner. 'Come on,' said Pallister abruptly. 'Let's treat ourselves.' I began to trot towards the cab, but his arm pulled me back. 'He'll wait,' he cautioned. 'No need to rush.'

'Kelly's Terrace, St Paul's,' he said to the taxi driver. It was our usual cheap neighbourhood. The taxi driver pulled a face and repeated: 'St Paul's.' He started the engine and then, on a thought, leaned back and announced: 'It's going to be two shillings, this time of night.'

'Kelly's Terrace, St Paul's,' Pallister told him tersely.

We sat back against the leather seats, warm and worn. A sort of joy was welling inside me. It was with Pallister too. We looked at each other in the passing light of street lamps, our grins breaking wide. Suddenly and simultaneously we emitted two great whoops of exaltation. We threw our arms about each other and kicked our legs in the air. Pallister's leg support drummed on the floor. The taxi driver applied the brakes. 'No rowdyism in my cab,' he complained.

'Do you want this fare?' demanded Pallister, leaning back regally.

'Well . . . yes . . .'

'It's Kelly's Terrace, St Paul's,' said Pallister. The man drove on muttering.

Our grins were still fixed across our faces. 'Now we won't need the loan from the bank,' I said. 'We won't have that worry on our minds.'

353

He looked at me seriously. 'We'll have that as well,' he said.

After five years Pallister Jones was among the most vigorous of the ship-repairing companies in the country. Profits, which were tight for two years, began to expand poetically towards the end of the third; business begat business; there were branches in all the ports around the Bristol Channel and at Liverpool, Glasgow, Newcastle, Tilbury and Southampton. Pallister's original scheme of contracts fulfilled while the ship took on cargo in different ports, and even while she was at sea, had given us the difference we needed.

He was quick, realistic and ruthless. He could pick a good foreman from half a mile off. Ginger Griffiths, the Cardiff-Caribbean, became the general manager throughout South Wales and when his massive black head and bunched shoulders emerged from his white car everyone redoubled their efforts. He was one of the first men to have a white car along the docks. In those days it was considered effete, open to ridicule and coal dust. But nobody ever laughed at Ginger.

Pallister, however, was one of those one-sided people who, while he could pick unerringly in his professional life, was no judge of friends or women. Two years after we established ourselves he married Rose-Marie Jenkins, the girl with the flower in her hair from the café in Cardiff. A year later she absconded with a man from Watchet, a small port in north Somerset.

'A spiv,' Pallister said when he came to tell me at my house overlooking the lake in Roath Park, Cardiff. I had sold Griff's house the year before, wanting to cut free from a place that no longer seemed to hold much for me. I poured him a long whisky. He sat thinly on the settee, his wrong leg thrust out in front of him. The man, he said, had an American chrome car, wore crepe shoes that added an inch to his height, and he had made his money on the black market in wartime and after. 'Rose-Marie knew him before she met me,' groaned Pallister. 'She said he could get *anything*; nylons, petrol, Scotch, anything. He had an inexhaustible supply of bread coupons. People like that impress her.'

We had some more drinks, both of us sitting on the settee facing the picture window which looked over the lake, its birds and its memorial to Captain Scott of the Antarctic. 'Pioneers, that's what we were, Jonesey, just like him,' said Pallister pointing out of the window. We deeply depleted the bottle and became maudlin about our struggles and achievements. 'I'm glad she's gone,' he moaned. 'Bloody glad. She was always trying to, you know . . . put me down . . . diminish me. However well I could handle business . . .' He regarded me with deadened eyes. 'And I can, can't I? You know that.'

'I know that, Pally,' I agreed.

'But when I went home, once I'd closed our front door . . .' He made the motion. 'Once that was done I was a failure.' Hurriedly he corrected himself. 'I don't mean between the sheets, I was all right at that. It was *getting* Rose-Marie between the sheets, that was the trouble. She'd do everything she could to humiliate me . . .' He began to laugh and cry at the same time. 'God, she threw my leg support out of the window once. In that hotel at Falmouth.' He began to grin slowly. 'Knocked a man off his bike.'

'It didn't!'

We began rolling around on the settee. 'It did!' he hooted, the tears streaming. 'Hit him right on the napper. Terrible trouble that caused . . .'

'You didn't tell me.'

'I wouldn't tell anyone, would I? She told her mates, I reckon, because they began laughing behind their hands . . . you know . . .'

We became friendly drunk, as we did on occasions, boasting to ourselves about what we had achieved and what we would do in the future. We were both thirty-two years old. 'What are you going to do, Jonesey? When we've made our pile,' he said.

'Go back to sea,' I told him.

At first he looked shocked but then snorted: 'In your own

yacht,' he said. He leaned over confidingly: 'Remember what we said, when we started, when we were in that crummy old lodging place, and I said to you that one day we would go to London, have a suite at the Savoy and get a lot of women in. Why don't we do that?'

'We could,' I said.

'We haven't got any women of our own to worry about. Not now. I don't care what Rose-Marie thinks. Let her go with her spiv. We could go next week. Have three women each.'

'Next week we're going to Birkenhead,' I said.

'So we are. We've got to. Bloody nuisance.'

'And then I have to stay here because Harry Perring is coming down.'

'Ah yes. The good Mr Perring.'

I glanced at him. 'He has been good.'

'To us? God, I'll say, Jonesey. He's been sodding marvellous. No interference. Takes his earnings and leaves us alone.' He was very drunk now. He lay against the back of the settee and looked through half closed eyes out of the window. It was winter and there were a lot of birds on the lake.

'Ducks,' he observed. 'When you think about it, ducks can come and go as they like. Free as . . . ducks. There's us, we can't even get to London to get those women into the Savoy.' He smiled like a ghost. 'We've had some good times with women though, haven't we? Remember that pair in Port Talbot . . . and the tubby one in Plymouth, the one who fell behind the couch . . .' We both laughed. 'And what-was-her name . . . Brenda, that one you had in London.'

'And those two secretaries in Haverfordwest,' I put in.

'Oh God . . . *those two*. I don't want to think about *those*, Jonesey. I was getting married the next day.'

'I remember. And the one you had found out . . .'

'Drunk I was. Like now. And she threatened to turn up at the church!'

I poured the last Scotch from the bottle. 'And that blonde bombshell in Antwerp who turned out to be a man.'

He began to laugh hysterically. 'She . . . he . . . said he liked my leg. Oh, that bastard! I remember . . . I remember getting into bed and wondering who the extra dick belonged to!'

We hooted at the memory. The telephone rang and I went to answer it. When I returned he was propped back, both legs extended, his calliper visible below his trouser turnup. He was studying the cold lake. 'I'd like to know something about birds,' he muttered. 'I don't know one from another.'

'That was the secretary of the new dock superintendent at Swansea on the phone,' I said. 'They're having a party tomorrow. He wants to meet everybody.'

'Any birds?' asked Pallister still searching the lake.

'Only wives.'

'And they're dragons, Welsh wives.' A taxi pulled up outside. 'Ah, here he is. I'd better go. I hate going home to a house with nobody. But I don't care once I'm inside. I'll get used to it.' He swayed as he stood. We went unsteadily towards the door. 'Rose-Marie stopped wearing that flower in her hair when we got married,' he remembered. The sharp air at the doorstep struck us. 'I told her it didn't look right on the docks. Maybe I should have let her go on wearing it. It was only a flower.'

We shook hands solemnly. 'Don't forget the Savoy,' he said. 'Ever.'

'We'll do it,' I promised. 'Next time we have to go to Tilbury. We'll do it then.'

'Good. We'll do it on the business.'

'All right. Business on the business.'

He began to go down the path. The driver came to meet him and help him. 'Leg hurting today is it, Mr Pallister?' he asked.

Pallister turned around and wagged his finger. 'Three women each,' he said.

The year before, I had been to America and tried to find Dolly. I told no one of this, not even Pallister. At times I had passed the house in Barry and looked for a moment at the porch where I had once held my girl. Once I went to the door and rang. The brass was not quite so bright. Her mother came to the door, looking old, and said: 'Oh, it's you again.' She looked at my clothes, my tie, and the car parked outside and said: 'You'd better come in.'

The room appeared as worn as she did. 'The war took it out of me,' she said. The clock had not been brought back. 'Went off forever with her, he did,' she sighed. 'Abandoned me on my own.'

She knew why I had come. 'She's in America,' she sniffed. It was not the beginning of tears but chagrin. 'Don't care about me now. And she certainly don't care about you, David Jones. Married a Yank. She sends me a Christmas card most years but that's all. And then it's late. February last time.' The card was still in its envelope despite the fact that it was early summer. As she began to take it out I took it from her and glanced at the postmark as I did so. It said: 'Leeway, NJ.' I looked at the round handwriting and smiled. 'I'd recognise her writing anywhere,' I said.

'You might not recognise her,' Mrs Powell said. 'I didn't. Tarted up. Chewing gum. Talking all Yankee. God knows what her husband does. He was in the chicken business, she said.'

'Do you know her address?' I asked.

Her face squeezed itself into suspicious lines. 'No,' she said. 'Even if I did I wouldn't let you know. It's all past. You were never any good for each other.' A touch of defeat came into her voice. 'You've got a car then.'

'Yes, the company's doing quite well.'

'What company is that?' she inquired sulkily.

'Pallister Jones,' I told her. 'Ship repairs, boiler scaling. I'm a partner.'

'Oh, dock work. Like always. Dolly always wanted something more glamorous.'

'Chickens,' I said.

I never saw her again. I read in the *Barry Herald* that she

358

had been fined for shop-lifting and she sold the house and went away after that. Even her neighbours did not know where it was although they thought it might be somewhere north.

Four months later I went to New York about a contract with an American freighter line. I had found Leeway, New Jersey on the map and on the Sunday I drove there. It was one of those wooden towns that clutches the highway like a lifeline. It scarcely extended three blocks back from the road. As it was Sunday the shops along Main Street were closed but people were coming from a white-faced and spired church, luminous against the deep autumn sky, the clergy-man shaking hands with them at the door.

'Didn't see you in the church,' said the pastor. I had joined on the line and had shaken hands with him. 'Always notice a stranger.'

'I'm sorry,' I said. 'I've only just arrived.'

'You want something then?'

'I do,' I agreed. 'I'm trying to trace someone, a lady, who lives in this town, at least she was here last Christmas. Dolly or Dorothy Powell. She's married but I don't know her married name.'

'Never came to church,' he said shaking his head. He called to the last of his parishioners walking away to lunch, 'Mrs Ligny, do you have a moment?'

The lady returned, head on one side. She was the sort who knew everybody. 'Ask her,' the pastor said. 'He wants to know whereabouts,' he told her.

'Who would it be?' She was going to treat it like a challenge.

'Unfortunately I don't know her married name, but she's British, Welsh actually, and her husband keeps chickens. I know her as Dolly Powell.'

'That one,' she said pushing her lips tightly together after saying it. 'Lived out at Treeline, five miles on. Named Gorkin. But they've gone now. They needed to.' She studied me. 'You a debt collector?'

I said I was not, thanked them and drove out to where a sign said 'Treeline', although there was no evidence of trees and there were few houses, just the brown grass of the New Jersey fall. There was a track and I took it. A man was burning leaves in the yard of the only house.

'Sure,' he said. 'They lived right here.'

He called to a boy listlessly twisting the chain of a swing. 'Herbie, get your mom, will you?'

He changed his mind. 'Come on in,' he said putting down the leaf-broom. 'Have a beer.'

I opened the wire gate. How many times had Dolly opened it? 'All their chickens died,' he said. 'My name's Albie Sweet, by the way.' I told him mine and we shook hands. 'This is Alice.' We had reached the porch and a flimsy woman drying her hands came out. 'Man's looking for the Gorkins,' he said.

'You a debt collector?' she asked. 'Maybe you can collect some for us.'

'No, no, I'm just someone from way back,' I said. They asked me into their room. I looked around seeking a sign of Dolly. 'From Wales.'

'She came from somewhere,' said the woman. 'And they went somewhere but I don't know where. We got mail for them, a whole pile of bills by the look of it. You want to take them?'

I said I would. Later, in the car, I opened them. They were all small amounts for groceries, gasoline, chicken feed. When I got back to New York I paid them all off. The things I have done for Dolly Powell.

BOOK FIVE

One

Driving from Liverpool on an icy night, nearing Hereford, the car performed a figure eight at a crossroads and ended up leaning like a drunk against a stone wall. It was some miles distant from the route that both Pallister and I normally took after business visits to Merseyside, but I had made a detour to see Harry Perring who was living in amiable and solitary retirement near Ludlow. We had spent the winter afternoon tramping across his fields, of which he was very proud, although they were only fields, and having an early dinner in his large, unsuitable house. His wife, whom I had only met once, had gone off after the war ('Joined the hordes of females doing the same thing, old chap,' he explained. 'Waited and then wished they hadn't.') and he had never remarried. On this early evening, we were alone and we talked until I left at eight-thirty.

When the car came out of its spin I was uncertain where I was. The very mishap was caused by my thinking that I had missed a junction. Everywhere was black as only a country winter night can be. It began to sleet. Cursing, I put my overcoat on and picking up my overnight bag left the car to walk back to the junction. One of the arms of the signpost said: 'Packwick 1 mile'. A place from the past. I took this direction and found myself walking along the same road I had trudged on that Christmastime morning in the first year of the war. A building appeared through the sleet, a single guttering light, the station where I had left the stifling train. What was Paula doing now? I had never attempted to contact her again. She had a child and a husband; a closed episode.

I pushed on through the windy sleet in the direction of Packwick and the Stag's Head. I half-expected to hear the clipping hooves of Billy's baker's cart behind me on the cold road.

It was just before ten o'clock and I saw the wet, yellow light ahead. The branches around the inn were rattling against its roof. I felt myself smile when I saw it. The low windows glowed. I pulled down the latch and stepped in under the crouching door.

I do not know what I expected. It was the same rosy room, empty of customers. A pale young man behind the bar said: 'You just got here in time. I was thinking of closing.'

'My car's come off the road,' I said. 'You used to have accommodation here.'

'Still do,' he replied. 'One of the rooms is aired. Gentleman didn't turn up because of the weather. It's thirty shillings bed-and-breakfast. There's a hot water bottle.'

I had a Scotch and bought him one. 'I came here during the war,' I said. 'Jeff Blewis was the landlord then. He had a daughter called Paula.'

'Not anyone I'd know,' he said. 'Been here only a couple of months myself. I just come in some nights when Mr Bannister and missus want a night off. They'll be able to tell you. The missus serves breakfast.'

He led me up the remembered curling stairs to the room where I had slept long before. It looked like the same bed. I lay there hearing the branches scratching the low window just as I had on that distant night. Twelve years had gone by now.

In the morning a bundle of a woman, beaming face, brought in a cup of tea. 'Arrived late then,' she said. 'Well, it's a nicer morning. Bit of sunshine for a change. Still bitter though.'

She said her husband would get a garage to retrieve the car and by the time I was at breakfast it was out in the yard, scoured on one side but otherwise undamaged. 'Sorry we wasn't here,' said Mrs Bannister as she served breakfast. I

364

was the only guest. There was an early fire in the flagstone bar. The landlord appeared, as rounded as his wife. 'Go to the pictures on Tuesdays,' he said.

'Every Tuesday,' confirmed Mrs Bannister. 'Mind, the plate's hot.' She put two sausages, a rasher and two eggs sitting on fried bread in front of me.

'Good or bad,' said her husband from behind the bar. 'Whatever the weather or the picture that's showing. Last night they were both lousy.'

'Did the barman tell you I had stayed here before?' I asked.

'Alfie? No. Just that you were upstairs,' Mrs Bannister said. 'He left us a note.'

She poured the tea. 'When was it?' she asked. 'Long time?'

'During the war. Nineteen-forty. Christmastime. Jeff Blewis was the landlord then.'

'Oh, yes. Well, he's been gone four years,' she said.

'Not dead,' elucidated her husband. 'Retired.'

'But then he died,' she said as if they were playing a game. 'Not long after.'

'He had a daughter, Paula, I remember,' I said. 'She used to help him here.'

Mrs Bannister looked thoughtful. 'Ah, yes. Now, she's in Hereford. I'm near sure she is. If she's still there. She used to run the teashop in the market square . . .'

'Hollyhocks,' he put in. 'Next to Burtons.'

'We used to go in there for tea when we went to the pictures in the afternoons,' she said. 'She's got a nice face. Manageress, I think.'

The past has always held a fatal attraction for me. Sometimes it is better left alone. I drove into Hereford, parked and walked into the market square, found the teashop and the moment I looked in the window I saw Paula.

There were big curled letters on the window saying: 'Hollyhocks' and some green plants inside. She was talking to a girl carrying a tray, then she turned and vanished into the back of the shop. I went in and sat at a round table in a corner, screened by a potted plant.

She had not changed very much. I watched her come from behind the cake stand, the compact figure in a blue skirt and woollen jumper. At first I could not see her face but then she turned and smiled at someone at a table out of my sight. She glanced up and briskly came across holding a tray.

'Yes, please,' she said flicking something unseen from the table top. 'Would you like . . .?'

She saw me. The tray dropped from her hand striking the table on its way down and landing on my foot. I picked it up and handed it to her. She had gone pink. 'Hello Paula,' I said.

She recovered quickly. 'David,' she said. 'Well, well . . .'

Standing up I held her fingertips and briefly kissed her on the cheek. 'I thought I would never see you again,' I said.

'I've been here,' she said oddly, a little hurt. 'Around Hereford. And you . . .'

'Mrs Marshall,' called the girl behind the counter. 'Will we have the special chocolate cake on Friday?'

To my surprise the hand that held the tray was trembling. 'Oh . . . one moment,' she answered. Then to me: 'Problems. I'll be back.' She went towards the counter and I sat watching her in profile as she assured a woman that Friday would see special chocolate cake. She returned and said to me: 'I'll get some tea. Would you like some cake or something?'

'Special chocolate cake,' I said. 'Please.'

'Stop it.' She smiled openly. 'I'm just so amazed to see you.'

She went and spoke to the assistant. The girl attempted to see me through the screen of green leaves. Paula came back. 'The tea's coming.' She said. She sat down and studied me. 'You're looking well,' she said. 'And prosperous.'

'Things are going well,' I said. 'And how are you, Mrs Marshall?'

She put her fingertips to her mouth. 'You remember. . .?' Then she realised. 'Oh, you heard Pru.' The girl appeared with a tray and a teaset. There were two slices of chocolate cake. When she had gone away Paula said: 'Being Mrs Marshall finished a long time ago. I've just got the name now.'

'And your daughter?'

She flushed. 'Yes . . . well Annie stayed with her father. She is still with him.' She looked down at the table. 'I ran away,' she whispered.

'Oh, I see.' I touched her fingers on the teapot. 'I'm sorry, I didn't mean to pry.'

'You're not prying,' she said more briskly. 'We've got a lot of catching up to do. What happened to you? You were a prisoner of war. My letters came back marked 'Unknown' and 'Gone Away' which seemed odd coming from a prison camp.' She completed pouring the tea, looked up and put her hand to her lips. 'Oh, I see . . . gone away . . . you escaped?'

'I went away,' I laughed. 'Then I was in France for a few months and then the first time I was ever in an aeroplane the damn thing crashed. Hit a deer on the runway, would you believe. In hospital, came out, worked, went into partnership in a business, ship repairs, and that's where I am now. That's the story so far.'

'What about your wife?'

'Dolly . . . well she had such a good time during the war she couldn't stop having it. The last I knew of her she was in America trying to make money out of chickens.'

'You're divorced now?'

'Years ago. When I was a prisoner.'

'That must have been awful. I wish I had kept writing to you.'

'Both of us,' I said. 'But you were married and you had a baby . . .'

'And you've never remarried? You're the marrying kind.'

'It's been work, work and work to get the business going,' I said. Her teacup was poised. 'Any chance that you would like to marry me?' I asked.

She let the cup remain for a few moments, then slowly lowered it. 'Don't joke, David,' she said.

'I'm not joking. Would you?'

Her eyes were wet. 'Of course I would,' she said. 'My God, it's been some morning.'

When we were married a week later we had known each other for ten days, including the three days of twelve years before. After the wedding I asked her about her daughter. 'I don't think I will ever see her again,' she said. 'She would not remember me.'

'You feel very guilty.'

'Of course. I had to make a choice. Who knows about choices?'

She had chosen a brush salesman, exempted from wartime service by reason of his feet and eyes. In three months he had stolen everything she had, including the ring from her marriage, and had run off to Lowestoft. 'He said the east attracted him,' she said.

We flew to Nice for our honeymoon, staying at the Excelsior. On the first evening as we walked along the Promenade des Anglais, we passed what I thought was the apartment block where Antoinette had hidden me. I pointed it out to Paula. 'You should go and ring the bell,' she said.

'I'm not sure which one,' I said. 'Things look different.'

'Did you sleep with her?'

'What sort of question is that to ask a man on his honeymoon?' I smiled. She did not answer.

We drove the next day up onto the Corniche and descended to the village where Curnow and I had been hidden by Alfred Laurent at the Hotel de la Rive after our escape from Italy. The hotel had been converted into apartments and there was little I could recognise of it, only the blue view over the Mediterranean. It was a fair winter's day, the sea bright and brittle. We walked along the cliff. Below I could see the small hook of the remembered harbour. I pointed it out to her but she said little. She was staring over the bare sea. We appeared to be running out of conversation.

It was mild enough to sit in the open air. There was a café in the street and we had a drink and looked through the lunch menu. The patron spoke some English and I told him that I had stayed in the hotel during the war. Paula went on reading the menu. He nodded benignly: 'So you were a silent guest! Monsieur Laurent had many. The Germans came into the Unoccupied Zone and they took him.'

'I think I will have a *Salade Niçoise* and some fish,' said Paula to me. She handed the menu across. 'And a good bottle of wine.'

When the patron returned with the wine he said: 'There was an Englishman who stayed. He was here all the war. He is in Nice now. He never went home.' He laughed and said: 'He was afraid of his wife.'

'Not Curnow?' I said slowly. 'Is that his name, Curnow?'

'One moment,' said the man. He went into the restaurant.

'You don't find this interesting?' I said to Paula.

Her expression altered. 'Of course,' she said. 'There is nothing like retracing footsteps.'

'*Voilà*, it is the name Curnow,' said the patron. He reappeared with his animated wife. She gave a little bow to us and then spoke rapidly to the man.

'He is in Nice, at the Hotel Belvoir,' he repeated. 'He has been there for many years. He is the chief *concièrge*. He has a coat *avec des boutons*.'

That evening while Paula was getting ready for dinner I walked to the Hotel Belvoir. I saw him at once, writing in a ledger behind a polished curved counter that was just below his chin. *Excusez-moi, monsieur*,' I murmured.

He looked up: '*Monsieur?*' he answered. His face changed. 'God strike me, it's Jonesey!'

Outside a car eased up and the driver came into the lobby. 'Stay here, sir,' he said to me. 'If you don't mind me calling you sir, Jonesey. Force of habit. I'll be straight back. *Tout de suite*.'

He fussed around the new arrivals, a young couple with much luggage. Two porters appeared and Curnow, jangling keys, his silver buttons bouncing, took them to the registration desk in the inner lobby. I was sitting in a high leather chair when he returned. 'You look as though you're used to it,' he said. He went behind his counter, stored a tip and emerged again. 'I'm trying to be,' I said. We shook hands again warmly. The long bonnet of another car appeared outside the door. 'More honeymooners,' he said.

'I'm one myself.'

'You are? *Salutations*! Your wife never came back then?'

More luggage began to pile up in the lobby. 'I'm finished at ten,' Curnow said hurriedly. 'Where are you staying?'

'The Excelsior.'

'Very good. Shall I come over there about ten-fifteen?'

'Please. You could meet Paula.'

'We could fill in a bit of history.'

Paula and I had a quiet dinner and at ten-fifteen Curnow, wearing a short, dark suit, arrived in the lobby. After introductions and one drink Paula said she was tired and would go to bed. Curnow and I sat in the bar. 'Pretty wife,' he said. 'Very reticent.'

'Two weeks ago she was leading a steady life in a teashop in Hereford,' I said. 'Now she's here – and married. Perhaps it's all been a bit dramatic for both of us.' I saw his question but I forestalled it. 'So you've been down here all the time. I can't believe it!'

'Nor me sometimes,' he nodded. 'Life's full of surprises. Last summer Captain Franklyn – remember, the camp leader in Italy – he turned up. Walked into the hotel. Recognised him at once. Just like you. He told me a few things. When we escaped, it was all planned with Colonel Maroni.'

I laughed. 'So we had the camp commandant on the escape committee.'

'Well, he had no time for the Teds, the Germans, and he needed a few escapes to justify his troops being there on duty at all. They had to *guard something*. If everything stayed peaceful, his blokes would have been hauled off to the fighting. As it happened they went off to fight anyway. Most of them against the Germans. And that prisoner who was shot, remember, the big New Zealander – the one who didn't *want* to escape. He turned out to be a risk and they had to deal with him.

'When I got out of here I thought you'd be on my heels,' I said.

'Safest place here, as it turned out,' he grinned. 'It got hairy towards the end, when the Jerries moved into the Zone, but as things went from bad to worse for them they couldn't have cared less. By the end of the war this place was being run by the French, like it more or less always was.'

I said: 'They took Monsieur Laurent away.'

'Never a word of him again. There were a lot like that. I had to lie low, naturally, hide up, but when it was all over I felt I more or less belonged here. I wrote to the wife and said I was never coming home and she wrote back, just two words: 'Good Riddance.' I worked at the de la Rive for a while, right after the war, and then I moved into Nice and here I am, a native.'

I laughed and patted his shoulder. We had another drink.

'You're doing all right now,' he approved. 'Staying at The Excelsior and you look prosperous. Everything turned out well?' He looked thoughtful. 'Was Antoinette your courier?'

'Yes. Is she still in Nice?'

'She was executed.'

'God. That's terrible.'

'Towards the end all sorts of strange things happened.'

'The Germans found out,' I said.

'The French executed her,' he said.

Our marriage lasted fourteen years. There were better times when we came to know each other more, but there were bitter quarrels and sad moments too. In the main it was two people living together by accident; and knowing it. The truth is that we never loved each other enough.

Paula had a miscarriage after two years and another a year later. After that she never became pregnant again. The business continued to build through some difficult times; not much that Pallister Jones did went awry. Much of my time was spent travelling and I was never completely glad to go home.

Paula opened a home design business with a man called Handcock, with whom I know she had an affair. The business came years too early and it failed, leaving me with the debts and Paula with the sense of failure. I was in my forties and my life was not blameless. There was a woman of twenty-three in London with whom I used to go to bed at least twice a month. Her name was Veronica and she was beautiful but beyond that uninteresting; I found our secret dinners far more trying than being at home. The boredom she inspired when dressed began to outweigh the pleasures of her naked-ness and it ended. She told me, at the spiteful end, that she had found me dull both out of bed and in it. Gratefully I went home to Paula.

I began a relationship with Adrianne Porteous who came to work with Pallister Jones in Bristol as a consultant on management handling. It continued in a hotel bedroom on most Wednesday afternoons for a year while her husband, a policeman, played rugby and, in summer, cricket.

We were careless, going to the same fringe-of-the-city hotel each time, having lunch, drinking a bottle of wine, and then repairing to a regular room for an afternoon of sex with intervals for talk and more wine from a bedside bottle. We were satisfied, undemanding of each other, each of us exactly aware of the basis for the affair. In the afternoon intervals she would tell me about her husband and her child. We always had a break at three-thirty. She would check her watch because that was when a neighbour picked up her small son from school. 'I hope she remembered,' she would say, and later she would telephone and make sure the woman had remembered. She always spoke to the boy on these occasions, asking what he had been doing in his lessons and promising that his mother would be home with him soon and that his father would be there not long after. Then she would turn with an apologetic and inviting smile and stretch on her back.

When she was talking to her son from the bed I often felt a touch of envy because she had a good home life. 'I love my husband as a husband,' she used to say. 'And you as a lover.'

On those evenings I tried to stay away from home. It was rare for Paula to ask questions but I have always been an unskilled liar, and *I* knew where I had been that afternoon even if she did not, and apparently did not require to know. Returning home I felt furtive and mean and we would have an argument about some different and unimportant matter. So I would go to the Grand and eat alone in the dining room or sit in my room with a room service tray and watch television. I would think of Adrianne with her family, effortlessly carrying off her act, and Paula alone at home, probably watching the same television programme. I do not think she had other affairs. I doubt if it meant that much to her.

But a woman is as simple and as complex as a clock. While she never questioned my whereabouts, the moment she *knew* that I was someone else's lover on a regular basis, and what was worse, was *told* about it by another woman, there was trouble.

It was an act of spite on the part of a shorthand-typist in the Bristol office, a chatty blonde with whom I had flirted mildly at a staff Christmas party. In the banal bonhomie I slipped my arm around her and she had simpered and eased her breast down so that it rested on my index finger. One evening early in the New Year she asked me if I could give her a lift home. I suspected that she had been lying in wait in the gloom outside the office. She caught me by surprise but as I was driving near her home anyway I agreed.

Nothing happened. I dropped her off at the corner of her street and thought no more about it. Her work became more slipshod and the head of her department reported that she had threatened to get him dismissed, boasting that she had influence with me. She had embroidered a fantasy onto the drive to her house that January evening and confided in anyone who cared to listen that we had been lovers from that moment, and that this gave her powers over even her department head, Mr Brewster, a Bristolian.

'That Fional,' he said using the final Bristol consonant. 'She's making trouble. It's either Fional or me that's going, Mr Jones.'

I told him that there was no need for the choice.

Fiona went. That evening she telephoned my wife and told her I went to bed at the George Hotel, close by the Avon suspension bridge, with Mrs Adrianne Porteous and that it happened on Wednesdays when Mr Porteous was playing for Bristol Police.

Paula contacted the policeman husband and they evolved a plan. He obtained a key to the room and while Adrianne Porteous and I were in naked embrace they entered. He had trained my wife in the art of silent intrusion.

The husband carried a pail of sand and Paula a smaller container of the sort of mixture used by men who paste advertisements on hoardings; thick, glutinous but swiftly spreading. We lovers were engrossed and it was a dark afternoon, the bedroom lights were out, and they entered with professional stealth.

An abrupt pulling away of the bedclothes was followed by Paula, with an eerie laugh, throwing the paste. Sergeant Porteous then flung the pail of sharp sand. We were closely entwined, trying to disengage ourselves. It struck us unerringly. The gloy mixed with the sand and slid down and between our bodies. Police Sergeant Porteous then turned on the light. We sat up in bed like bog creatures, shocked, soggy, speechless.

'It's not what you think,' I managed to say. Paula had some glue left in the bottom of her bucket and she threw it in my face.

*

374

When I returned cautiously home the following day she had left. The glutinous substance was still adhering to the crevices of my body and there was a sheen of it all over my skin. I was like a chrysalis. Pieces peeled off.

Pallister came around to the house and laughed uncontrollably. I faced him unhappily. 'I'm glad you think it's so amusing,' I said. 'It was a disgusting thing to do.'

'Would you rather he'd strangled you?' he inquired. He stopped laughing. I left him with the Scotch while I had another bath.

It was early evening. He suggested we went to the St David's Hotel. 'Like old times,' he said. 'Exclusive, we used to think it was.'

'Happy days,' I said. 'Before we were successful.'

'Shut up, Jonesey,' he admonished. 'I'm happy. I've got *three* dolls on the go at the moment. You could be the same. Why do you need a wife? What does Paula want you for? Just to sit stuck in this room together? Pack it in. Who's going to lose?'

We drove into Barry. The funfair was locked and shrouded but there was an amusement arcade and we went in there and began to play the fruit machines and the pinball tables. A man in a vicar's collar was the only other customer. Lights flashed and the tables dinged. At the end was a booth with a row of distorting mirrors.

'Come on,' urged Pallister. 'It's years since we did anything like this. After, we'll go up to the hotel and pick up some women.'

We walked into the booth and put money in the slot. A gate opened and we paraded before the rank of bent mirrors. We became fat and thin, huge-bodied, long-chinned, and spindly. The vicar followed us in and began to pose with us. We hooted at each caricature in our slightly drunken way. Then we stumbled out, still laughing. 'It was worth it,' enthused Pallister. 'You looked worse than *me* in there.' The vicar came out and smiled tentatively and went off along the grey seafront.

We went to the St David's and after our meal walked into what was now called Le Bar Cocktail. There were knots of young girls drinking rum and Coca Cola through straws. 'This is the place they come to pick up older men with a bit of money,' confided Pallister. 'Somebody a bit sophisticated, they know can buy them a decent drink. We'll be all right here.'

Music was coming from a flashing juke box which heaved massive records into place with an arm like a man lifting a heavy weight. Eager, whispering girls gathered around its glass dome, peering in as if it might tell their fortunes.

The music was blatant and the barman said it had once been worse. 'I made them fix the volume,' he said. 'Otherwise we'd have all been deaf. Look at the silly little cows now.'

Girls sitting at tables were performing jerky movements with their hands, keeping in time with the beat of the juke box. Their eyes were glazed, mesmerised by the music. 'Hand jive,' said the barman. 'We haven't got a dancing licence so they do that instead. Bloody mad.'

We accosted two girls who drank several rum and Cokes and agreed to ride in the car back to my house where we would listen to records. When I drove the Rover around to the hotel door they were impressed. Pallister had already sorted them out between us. Tracy came into the front of the car and Angie climbed into the back seat with him. He began kissing her.

At the house we poured them gin and lemons. They worked in a machine shop, fitting pieces into radio sets. Angie said: 'It's really just like doing the hand jive, isn't it, Trace?'

Tracy agreed: 'Just the same. We do it all day and we do it all night.'

We all thought this was funny. They could certainly take their drink. Pallister poured two more all round and I was beginning to feel vague. They were impressed with the size of the house and that we each had a car. Pallister kept winking at me. Their minds were solely concerned with popular music. I ventured that I liked Lonnie Donegan's 'Does Your Chewing Gum Lose Its Flavour on the Bedpost Overnight.'

Still winking, Pallister strolled to the radiogram and changed the record. 'Smooching music,' he announced in a pseudo-Hollywood voice. 'Sinatra.' He extinguished some of the lights. I began to worry that Paula might change her mind and come back that night. We stood up to dance with the girls. Tracy hung around my neck and wriggled between my knees. She had a heady, cheap smell, and her skin was soft as a damson. I was aware of Pallister and Angie leaving the room; he was muttering and she was giggling.

The record finished and I went to the radiogram. 'Put on a pile,' she suggested. 'We may be a long time.' She had taken her shoes off and she looked slim and innocent standing on our carpet. I put on six random records. I went back to her and we moved minutely in the dimness. The music was moody, Ray Coniff and his orchestra. We danced, face against face. I began to unbutton her blouse. The record changed. 'The Hallelujah Chorus' filled the room. I cursed and she went decisively to the radiogram and rejected it. Ben E King singing 'Spanish Harlem'. That was better. I got two more drinks and we swayed against each other while we drank, each of us putting the glass to the other's lips. 'You're quite sexy for your age,' she said.

She let me ease the unbuttoned blouse over her shoulders. It fell away to hang from her waist. 'It's a new bra,' she said. 'I'll do it.'

She unhooked the clip and releasing me for a moment pulled it away and dropped it to the floor. Her breasts were toy-like. 'My mum would go mad,' she said. 'Doing this with a married man.'

'How do you know I'm married?'

'Oh, come on. You're too well-kept to be single. And, this place. You don't live here on your own.'

'I do at the moment,' I said. I lied. 'I'm waiting for a divorce.'

'You're years older than me.'

'How old are you?'

'Seventeen.'

'I'm years older,' I agreed.

'I don't mind.' She rubbed the eaves of her breasts on my shirtfront. 'I've been around. I've been to bed with the Bonzo Dog Doo Dah Band.'

From her tubular waist I counted my fingers up her ribs to the underside of her breasts. 'You're turning me on,' she murmured.

'I'm on,' I told her.

Her hand went down between us and she felt through my trousers and whispered: 'So you are.'

All was destroyed in a moment by a screech from upstairs. Tracy pulled herself away. 'Angie,' she said. She called out: 'What's the matter, Ange?'

Angie appeared, dishevelled, at the door, one shoe off. 'We're *going!*' she rasped, struggling to put it on. 'And now!' She took no notice of her friend's bare bosom. 'We're not staying here, Trace.'

'What happened?' asked Tracey. She glanced at me but I knew she was on her way out.

'Him!' exclaimed Angie. 'Oooh, he's a filthy swine! What he wanted me to do! Offered *money* too. Twenty pounds.'

'Twenty pounds!' exclaimed Tracy, impressed.

'Come on,' insisted Angie. She picked up Tracy's brassière from the floor and in a motherly way began to put it on the other girl. She clipped it fiercely and began to pull the blouse up from Tracy's waist. 'I'm not leaving you here.' She began dragging the other girl towards the door. 'Not with these.'

'I'll drive you,' I offered.

'No fear. We'll get a taxi,' said Angie. They were at the front door now. 'Tell Hopalong he's a filthy pervert.'

My wife stayed away almost three months. For two weeks I heard nothing from her and then a postcard arrived from Brussels saying simply: 'I am here. Paula.' Almost every following week another card came, from Paris, Rome, from

Naples, Athens, then Madrid. I could scarcely believe it when a card arrived showing the great mosque in Istanbul. Each time the message was the same: 'I am here. Paula.'

There seemed to be no way I could find her. One lonely night I sat down with a list of all the hotels in Madrid and telephoned each one. It was a long, laborious business and with no result. She was apparently criss-crossing Europe and even into Asia Minor with no trace, and to what purpose I could only imagine.

After three months I was at home one evening, drinking Scotch and half-watching television, the house mute around me, the breakfast dishes unwashed and the bed unmade because the daily woman had given notice, saying she did not feel comfortable working for a solitary man. The telephone rang and it was Paula.

She said: 'Will you come and fetch me? I'm lonely.'

'So am I,' I said. I choked over the words. 'Where are you?'

'Dover,' she answered. 'The Cliff Garden Hotel.'

'I'll come right away,' I told her.

'No. Come tomorrow. You'll have to drive all night.'

'I don't mind.'

'No, David. Come tomorrow.'

'Of course. God, how I've missed you. Life's been so empty.'

'Well,' she answered quietly. 'We'll have to see what we can do about it.'

I was on the road by seven. It was a limpid summer morning and my heart was light. I reached Dover at three. She was sitting in the sun in the garden of the hotel, overlooking the Channel. I walked up the path towards her and I saw her start when she saw me although she remained sitting in the deck-chair. My eyes were wet. I put out my hands and took hers and lifted her from her seat. She would not kiss me then but we hugged each other.

'It's almost tea-time,' she said. She looked tired and

379

thinner. Her eyes were unsure despite her calm. 'Mrs Osborne won't mind getting it five minutes early.'

The way she said it made me say: 'How long have you been here?'

'Three months,' she answered.

She went to the french window and called: 'Mrs Osborne, could we have tea? Yes, he's here.'

We sat down by a white wooden table. The garden was elevated and there were ships in the Channel. A ferry was approaching the entrance to the harbour. 'You've been in *this* hotel ever since you left?' I said. 'What about all the postcards? Madrid, Paris, even Istanbul.'

She grinned rather than smiled. 'You got them. Good.' The tea tray arrived carried by the elderly Mrs Osborne. 'My husband,' Paula said. 'I told you I had one.' Once the old lady had gone back into the shadows of the hotel she studiously poured the tea.

'You got other people to post those cards for you then,' I said. 'I thought it was a slightly crazy journey, one end of Europe to another.'

She smiled and handed me the tea cup. 'I used to get people who stayed overnight here on their way to the continent to post them,' she said. 'I gave them the money for the card and the postage, or bought them a drink or something, and gave them the address.'

'Just one sentence! "I am here, Paula." In capitals,' I said. I grinned at her. 'Istanbul,' I said shaking my head. 'I wondered what you were doing in Istanbul, for God's sake.'

'When I first got here I had every intention of running as far as possible,' she said regarding me frankly. 'But I was frightened. I stood here and looked at the Channel and I thought "What will I do over there? Wander from place to place?" I'm not a wanderer. I'm not like you, David, so I stayed her and pretended.'

'Are you coming back?' I asked. 'Please.'

She nodded. 'Yes. I'm tired of it.'

'I've missed you,' I told her. 'I'm not cut out for living by myself.'

'Nor am I.'

We kissed sincerely for the first time in more than a year. She began to cry and I tried to comfort her. 'Let's stay until tomorrow,' I said. 'Have a little holiday.' She agreed, just nodding her head and making her tears drop into her lap.

'You can't drive back now anyway,' she said. We went from the hotel garden holding hands and we walked down to the shingle beach.

'Not many people come here,' she said. It was a fine afternoon but the seashore was empty except for three children playing in the distance and a slow man and a woman walking separate dogs. 'Everyone just passes through. Going somewhere else, over to France or back home. I felt so envious of them, going home. I must hold the record for the longest stay in Dover.' I turned her to me on the beach and hugged her. We were both crying, my wet cheek against hers. We were sorry for ourselves.

'I did one positive thing while I have been here.' She spoke as if she were unsure about telling me. 'I went to see my Annie.'

We had climbed to the promenade from the beach and we sat on a seat facing the enclosed harbour. Gulls were circling the lamp-posts. 'How did she take it?' I asked, surprised. 'You said you never would.'

'I know I did,' she said. 'But some events make you think over your life very carefully. Anyway, I'm lying in a way. I did go to see *her*, but she didn't see *me*. She wouldn't know who I was anyway. She is aware that I exist somewhere but the only mother she knows is the one married to her father.'

'What did you do?'

'I spied on her. They live in Canterbury so it was not far. I just got a bus from here. They're quite near the Cathedral and they do bed-and-breakfast. I got a room across the road; it's all small hotels and boarding houses.' She laughed quietly. 'I told the landlady I had to sleep in a room at the front of any house I stayed in. Psychological reasons. They thought I was odd but they had a room there anyway and I just sat there, near the window, and watched for Annie. She's twenty-four now and I didn't know how I would know her. She might not even be there, she could be married or away, anything. But the first time she came out of the house I knew it was her . . .' Her voice slowed and I thought she was going to weep again but she recovered. 'She looks wonderful. Fair hair. She came out on a bike. I saw her half-a-dozen times. The people in the house must have wondered what I was doing.'

'I understand,' I sighed patting her hand. 'Did you spot Tim?'

'Yes, he was there. He's one of those men who hardly seem to change at all. There was no sign of his wife though. I wondered what she was like. Women do, you know.'

I nodded and said: 'Yes, they do.'

'When I sat down and thought all about it,' she continued, 'about everything, I decided that I did not want us to split up, no matter what. David, you're all I've got.'

We kissed again. 'And you're all I've got,' I told her. I took her hand and we walked together along the breezy promenade to the hotel. We went to bed and with the setting sun glowing through the curtains we made love and slept until the evening.

That night we went to a restaurant and drank too much. We came back giggling through the town, quiet except for the stream of cars coming from the docked ferry.

We had our arms about each other's waist. 'My God, it was funny,' she said. 'You covered in sand and that gooey stuff.' She began to laugh. 'And when you sat up in bed, both of you running with all that muck, and you said . . . you said: "It's not what you think." All the goo was dangling from your upper lip like something in a horror film!' She dabbed her eyes.

'I can't believe how you got into the room. Not a sound.'

'Planning,' she said. 'Porteous isn't a policeman for nothing. Anyway, you were too occupied.'

'It was terrible,' I said. 'I'm sorry, Paula.'

'Perhaps we were all to blame, each of the four of us in our own way. There's always a reason.'

We reached the hotel. The summer night was clear, without a moon. In the harbour the lights were sharp and still. There was a taste of salt on the breeze. 'I've been drinking too much while I've been here,' she admitted. 'I was afraid it was getting a hold on me. Every night, gins, wine, liqueurs in the bar. There was always somebody to talk to.'

We slept deeply and I awoke to the sound of ships hooting, the sound of my life. She was lying against me. 'One day, I've always felt,' she murmured, 'that you'll run away to sea again.'

'Perhaps we could both do it. But I'm in too deep now. Pallister Jones marches on.'

'I find it difficult to like him,' she said.

'Pally? Well he's a strange customer. It's that leg. Ever since we were kids at school. But if it hadn't been for him none of it would have happened. He's full of laughs, bravado really. He needs somebody to look after him. Like we all do.'

'I can't think who would have him,' she said. 'It's not his leg, it's the rest of him. And he's jealous of you.'

'Nobody's been jealous of me over the past three months,' I said. We looked at each other, our faces close in the bed. 'Let's go home.'

'You're sure?'

'I'm very sure.'

Neither of us was sure. We drove home across the country. We ran out of things to say. I said this to her and she replied that it was not essential for people who were married to have to make constant conversation and I was relieved.

For the next two years we remained married. Sometimes I would lie in bed at night, eyes wide open, wondering what we were doing together, and then I would realise that she was lying awake, staring at the shadowed ceiling as well. It ended very suddenly. In fact everything did.

Both Paula and I were drinking heavily. One evening at nine o'clock I came in and found her on the floor incapable of rising. I had been drinking myself and I berated her for being down there. While I was taunting her I was pouring Scotches for myself, neat, large and quickly swallowed. Pointing accusingly at her I toppled forward and slid to the carpet and we skirmished and spat at each other down there like serpents on our bellies.

'Don't let's discuss it,' she warned the next morning. We had slept on well-separated areas of the carpet and I had risen stiffly to stagger to bed at first light, leaving her curled there. 'I don't think there is anything to say,' I replied and there was not. We were in agreement about that anyway.

On the night of the twenty-first anniversary party of Pallister Jones she was at the Park Hotel in Cardiff, where the party was held, before I had arrived. Both Pallister and I had been accepting congratulatory drinks all day. Pallister Jones had survived recessions and the business disasters of associates and had climbed back. When we reached the hotel Pallister had difficulty in reading coherently the telegram from the now infirm Harry Perring. Martha Morris, our first secretary, who had come back from retirement for the celebration, had to read it for him. There were more than a hundred people in the room. At ten o'clock Paula came to me and said she wanted to go home. We had planned to go to a restaurant where there was dancing and a cabaret.

'We're going to Carmen's,' I reminded her.

'I wish to go home. You go if you like.'

'I'll get you a taxi.'

'Don't bother. I'll get one myself.'

Carmen's was walking distance. Twenty of us were sitting at a long table and someone asked me where Paula was.

'She's gone,' I said. 'She's not very sociable tonight.'

'Pally took her,' said one of the women.

'Pally did?' I felt my heart jump. 'But he's in no fit state to . . .'

'He seemed all right.'

'Pally drives better when he's drunk,' put in someone else.

I kept watching the door for Pallister to return. After an hour I went out to the foyer and telephoned home. There was no answer. I returned to the restaurant. The cabaret had just begun and the comedian was welcoming everyone with jokes. He saw me in the doorway and made a quip about me being a long time in the toilet. I was laughing with everybody else when I saw a policeman outlined at the door with Martha Morris. I felt my face stiffen. I walked straight past the comic who leaned over me and said: 'Somebody can't take a joke. Goodnight, sir.'

'The officer says there has been an accident,' said Martha as though unwilling to take the responsibility herself. She spoke in her normal calm, office voice, and I said: 'Oh, where?' The comedian was milking more laughs behind my back. 'Drink up everybody, it's the police. We forgot to apply for the licence!'

'Perhaps we can go outside, Mr Jones,' said the policeman. Martha touched my arm and said: 'Don't worry. She's going to be all right.'

The officer was looking at his notebook as if rehearsing his lines. 'Eleven-twenty-three this evening, Cathedral Road, sir. Head-on collision with another vehicle. Mr Graham John Pallister dead on arrival at Cardiff General, Mrs Paula Jones injured, extent of injuries unknown.' He looked up. His forehead was wet with sweat. 'Cardiff General,' he said. 'Can we take you in the car?'

Martha said she would come with me. Two youths with guitars were now singing under the flashing lights of the stage within. We went to the police car. Martha said again: 'She's going to be all right.' I patted her hand gratefully. At the hospital they could tell us nothing. I sat in the casualty waiting room for two hours with Martha before she agreed to go home. She was worried about her two dogs.

It was quietly getting light outside the window before anyone came to speak to me. A nurse brought me a cup of tea and I was drinking it when a young doctor said I could go in and see her. 'But keep it short,' he said. 'Please.'

Paula was in a small room, scarcely space for the bed and a chair. The nurse came with me and repeated. 'You can't stay long, Mr Jones.' There was a light over the door. The figure in the bed was breathing deeply and I felt a surge of relief. Carefully I approached. Her face was bruised to the colour of an overripe plum. There were stitches over both eyes. They opened to slits. Her hand moved and I took hold of it. 'You're going to be all right, Paula,' I whispered, almost choking with tears. 'They say it's all right.'

'David, you must know . . . something,' she said. Her voice was grating, like a man's. It was an effort. 'I must tell you.'

'Another time,' I said. 'You've got to rest. They say . . .'

'Now,' she said. She rallied herself. 'Annie is *your* daughter,' she said. 'She can't be Tim's. He believes she is, but she isn't.' I was hunched beside her, pressing her hand.

The nurse came in to usher me out. I kissed Paula's fingers and she closed them around my hand. I went out of the hospital. The street-lights were waning against the growing day. All the hospital windows were pale yellow. Two nurses went by exchanging some secret. They had sent for a taxi and I went home and let myself into the shadows of our house. I poured a Scotch but put it aside and made a cup of tea instead. Brokenly I went upstairs, crying to myself, undressed and got into the bed we were never going to share again. She died the following afternoon. I went to the hospital and the nurse said that Paula had made her promise to deliver a message to me. It said that she was sorry.

I was afraid to go home. Down at the docks I walked aimlessly along the wharves. Outside in the Bristol Channel a ship was sounding her siren as she left for some far, far place.

*

For six months I dumbly presided over the disintegration of Pallister Jones. The entire concern seemed to fall and tumble away. Pallister, the kingpin, the frail, strong, support on which the whole company was founded, was gone and pieces simply sheered off, fell and hit the ground with explosions of dust. He had held things together with cobwebs, I discovered. His poetic accounting had deftly performed manoeuvres over the years which had given a healthy look to stitched-up balance sheets. I brought back Martha Morris, out of retirement, and together we watched, mere spectators, while one part of the business collapsed after another.

I observed it in a detached sort of way, as though I had always expected this, as though the company had given me wealth only on loan, but that this credit would at some time come to an end. It was a curious sensation. I could not even feel sorry; in fact I began to sleep better at nights. Eventually it was all finished, creditors were thankfully paid off with the help of a considerable contingency fund known apparently to only Pallister himself, which emerged during the investigations of the financial detectives. The offices were closed and their leases sold, materials were returned to the suppliers or auctioned, men were paid off. Ginger Griffiths was well enough covered to buy a property at Porthcawl which he turned into a seaside boarding house for West Indians. It was called Antigua Villa and overlooked the pebbles, the often sunless sand and the pale unwarmed sea of the Bristol Channel. People came from the West Indies to stay there.

The last office to close was at Barry, where we had started. Eight months after the funerals I locked the door there for the final time. Martha stood tearfully on the pavement and we hugged each other and walked in separate directions. I was left with my house and my car and my personal possessions. I was free.

During the sleepless hours over many nights that followed Paula's death the notion to go and see my daughter came to my mind. In the dark the desire grew in shape. I had no plan, no notion of revealing myself to her, disturbing her life and the lives of the couple she had regarded as parents. I had written briefly to Tim Marshall telling him of his former wife's death and had received a note in return which said: 'I was sorry to hear about Paula. Please accept my condolences.' That was all.

When I had finally decided upon it I put together some careful strategy. Then I drove down to Canterbury. The street was lined with bed-and-breakfast houses, some aspiring to notices saying: 'Private Hotel'. Pelham House was a large end-of-the-century villa. I drove past once, then parked the car in a town garage and walked back along the street. The driver of an almost-new Jaguar would be unlikely to seek bed-and-breakfast accommodation. Nervously I walked to the house and touched the bell. An overalled woman wearing a scarf enfolding her head like a turban answered. 'They're out till tonight,' she said. 'Up London. But I can show you the room if you like.'

It was the front room overlooking the street. From there I could see directly across to the window from which, I was sure, Paula had watched in the opposite direction. In the registration book I signed my name as Peter Griffiths of Liverpool. I left my bag in the room and returned into the city. I walked around the cathedral until five o'clock and then had some tea before returning to Pelham House. The cleaning woman was still there. There seemed to be no other guests. I had a bath and then went out to a small restaurant, returning at eight-thirty. My unknown daughter answered the door.

She was fair and opal-skinned with Paula's eyes. Despite my resolve I must have stared at her because she became flustered and said: 'Oh, you're Mr Griffiths. Please come in. We've only just got back.'

Tim Marshall was a man with wiry hair and pitted skin on his cheeks. His wife, a fussy Scotswoman, made me a cup of tea. My scenario had been carefully assembled: my name was Peter Griffiths, I was a draughtsman, Welsh-born but living in Liverpool. I was in Canterbury to deliver some drawings to a local company, Allen John and Partners, whose name I had taken from the Yellow Pages telephone directory.

Tim Marshall was pleasant, his wife chatty. It was the end of the main tourist season and they were planning a holiday in Portugal. Annie had to go out and returned at ten-thirty. We all sat in the living room having a bedtime cup of tea. I never remember feeling so strange, a man returning to somewhere he knew, even belonged, but had never been.

'Annie's the star of the drama society,' said Tim's wife Betty. 'And tomorrow is the big opening night.'

'Please, don't,' protested Annie. She turned Paula's eyes to me. Her unease had gone. 'Final pep talk from the producer tonight. We didn't dare have another rehearsal in case it all went wrong again and we'd be completely demoralised.'

'It's always all right on the night,' said Tim. He was sitting astride the edge of her chair and he touched her hair fondly.

'I wouldn't count on that,' she laughed. 'Tonight I felt that if Ken . . .' She glanced at me. 'That's our producer . . . I felt if he'd wanted to call the whole thing off, I would have been relieved.'

'You won't be like that tomorrow,' said Betty. 'And what about all the tickets you've sold?'

Annie smiled: 'We'll have an audience. It's the play I'm worried about.' I tried to see if I could detect any of myself in her, but it is difficult to recognise yourself in others. 'Are you going to be here tomorrow night, Mr Griffiths?' she asked.

'Well, I had intended to start back . . .'

She leaned eagerly. 'But you could stay, could you? Would you come?'

'Yes . . . well . . . yes. Will I be able to get a ticket?'

'You can have mine,' said Tim.

'Stop it, Daddy,' she said. She returned to me. 'I can get a ticket. It's *See How They Run*. It's very funny . . . I hope.'

'At least with a farce if anything goes wrong you can always claim it's part of the plot,' said her father. 'Don't you agree, Mr Griffiths?'

'I certainly do,' I said. I glanced at him but I could see nothing in his eyes.

I remained the next day and in the evening walked with Tim and his wife through Canterbury to the theatre. It was very strange being with them, pretending I did not know them. I felt like a spy.

It was a small theatre where the rising curtains sent out a cloud of dust which set people sneezing as far as the back of the stalls. I sat and laughed at the play with everyone else, and Annie was the exuberant star. That day, ostensibly out about my business, I had taken the train to Dover and walked along the desolate beach where Paula and I had walked on the day I had gone to her there. The windows of the Cliff Garden Hotel stared opaquely at the sallow sun. The garden was bare, the white table and chairs where we had sat at tea piled against the fence.

Now, watching Annie, laughing at the frenetics of the play, doors opening and banging, characters colliding, madly mistaking each other, mixing motives, I had deep within me a sadness that I could not explain. I had found nothing, but I felt that I had now lost everything that ever could have mattered.

There was a party after the play in a room backstage, everybody excited and chattering about the fun and success of the evening. Annie introduced me to the director. 'I'm so glad you stayed, Mr Griffiths,' she said. 'I think you were a good luck charm.'

'It was wonderful,' I said. 'What's the next production?'

'Life with Father,' she said.

As I was leaving the following morning Tim offered to drive me to the station. It was difficult to escape. 'I'm going in anyway,' he said. 'It's no trouble.'

Annie had gone to work. She had brought me a cup of tea that morning and said how glad she was that I had stayed and enjoyed the play. We shook hands solemnly while I was sitting up in bed.

Tim brought out his small car and took me to the station. 'There's a London train at fifty-five.' I thanked him and we shook hands. I had difficulty in meeting his eyes.

Elements of the previous night's farce unfolded. I did not want to board the train because my car was at the garage in the centre of Canterbury. Going into a phone box I remained there until Tim had gone, pretending to make a call under the petulant eyes of a man who genuinely needed to make one. When I thought Tim had gone I edged out of the station like a felon, only to see him talking to someone on the opposite side of the street. I dived into a coffee shop and then realised they were crossing the road to enter it. There was a back door but it went through the kitchen, and I startled the staff as I made my exit that way. Running along the backs of the shops I emerged near the garage. The man blinked at my confusion and hurry. Eventually I got in the car and drove out into the main streets, looking in the mirror, and driving as quickly as I could through the crowded town.

A week later I received a letter with a Canterbury postmark. It said simply: 'Dear Mr Jones, Thank you,' and was signed, 'Tim Marshall.' Below was a postscript: 'Allen John and Partners moved to Brighton six months ago!'

Two

The Isles of the Bingo Sea lie so lightly upon the water that they might easily be afloat. At evening each island often appears to grow another identical island below itself for there are no great currents, storms are few, and the sea is a mirror. There is a place we used to call Bingo village where you could buy fish and thin beer.

A man was living there, an American who wore the sombre clothes of a Japanese peasant. Somehow, in years, his eyes had narrowed; he had a beard like a thin white waterfall. The American had been left over from the war. He had a Japanese wife and he had never left the island except to fish since he first arrived. 'Not too long ago the only sailors in Japan were from here in the Inland Sea,' he said. 'For two hundred years, by decree of the Emperor, no man could build a boat of more than one hundred and fifty tons. The Emperor did not want the people to travel to see other places. The dream was to keep Japan to herself.'

Then Cox's Bazaar is on the Bay of Bengal, almost against the Burmese border. You can see pagodas over the trees if you travel a little south. They called it after an Englishman who set up a shop there along by the fifty-six-mile beach which they say is the longest in the world. The town is famous for cigars. Local people go there to swim in the sea and sit upon the sand, a Bangladeshi Barry Island.

Cox's Bazaar; the Isles of the Bingo Sea; Malacca; Manila; Bikini; the Coromandel coasts, both of them; Ball's Pyramid standing like a castle in the Tasman Sea; the Marianas, sitting above the world's greatest chasm, 36,000 feet deep: I saw them all; for I became a sailor once more.

On the eve of my fiftieth birthday I altered my life again. The lake house had been sold the year before, and I had bought a small place, overlooking the Bristol Channel. I put a telescope in the seaward window and I would watch the ships coming and going up the seaway, light on their white superstructures, tresses of smoke at their funnels, the smile of their bow-waves. It was a powerful telescope and I could often see the men moving on deck. In heavy weather smaller vessels fought the seas, trying to push them aside as they plodded; the large freighters, bulk carriers and container ships dipped on with massive indifference.

When the last branch office door was locked, the last debt settled, the last document signed, and the ledgers of Pallister Jones were finalised, I went to see Harry Perring, still in Shropshire. The next day I was going to Australia. He was seventy-eight and had been in poor health and he employed a housekeeper and a nurse, who did not trust each other.

'Each one thinks she's going to lose out to the other in my will,' he laughed sitting in his bed. 'That's the way to get the very best of treatment, keep the workforce uncertain of their future.'

He had lost most in the collapse of Pallister Jones but he said: 'It's the way of business. Life's like a nudist colony, David. You go in naked and you go out naked.'

I said: 'I felt very guilty about you. You, who put us on our feet at the beginning.'

He was wearing pyjamas with red stripes. His empty sleeve was tied in a knot. 'I look at myself in the mirror and I pretend I'm a footballer,' he grinned. 'A footballer in poor shape but still with an eye for goal.' He looked down at himself, studying the stripes. 'Where does it all leave you?' he asked. 'No wife, no partner . . .'

I shook my head: 'It all went very suddenly.'

'Pallister could have been a genius,' he said. 'That leg held

393

him back. I can sympathise. My arm finished me for golf. He wanted women, didn't he?'

I nodded and said. 'Poor old Pally.'

'In another five years,' mused Perring, 'he'd have probably gone suddenly off somewhere, no questions answered. Asked, *yes*, but not answered. And with a few million. Either that or he'd be doing a stretch in Wormwood Scrubs.' He began to readjust his pillows. I moved to help but he waved me away. 'I just imagine I'm a coalman,' he said throwing one pillow over his head and down to his back as if it were a sack. 'When you're in bed most of the time you have to enter a life of imagination.' He glanced up as if wondering whether to confide in me. 'Sometimes I arrange everything and pretend that the bed is the old landing craft going ashore in Normandy,' he said. 'And this time I get it *right*. Nobody even gets their feet wet. You know the crucifix, the one you found in the boat when you were re-doing it?'

I remembered. He said: 'Well, quite out of the blue, I recalled who had worn it. He was the least religious chap I've ever known: Sergeant Down, Bill Down, absolutely foul-mouthed. He won the crucifix in a poker game while we were waiting to embark to go across. There were some big poker games then because a lot of chaps felt that they had nothing to lose.'

'What happened to Sergeant Down?'

'First one to get it. Smack, right in the throat. The chap who had gambled the crucifix – shy fellow, forget his name – got off scot free. Just goes to show.'

The housekeeper brought a tray in with some tea. Following, a short, anxious pace behind, was the nurse with an extra plate of biscuits. 'These are more digestible, Mr Perring,' she said over the housekeeper's shoulder.

They both waited, daring the other to leave first. The housekeeper won in the end by a ploy of making minor adjustments to the bed. Grimacing the nurse went out. The housekeeper left after giving her employer a warm and triumphant smile.

'See what I mean,' Harry chortled. 'Silly old cows.' He bit into one biscuit and then tried one from the second plate as though to compare them. 'No difference,' he said. He handed me a cup of tea which he had poured. 'What about you then?' he asked.

'What am I going to do? I'll go back to sea.'

'It's always been in you. I've seen the look in your eyes at the docks.'

'It's all I've got. It's my profession. My family.'

'Do you know that song "The Leaving of Liverpool"?' he inquired in his strange tangental way. 'It's a good song that. I heard it on the radio the other day.'

'I said I did and added, 'But I won't be leaving Liverpool. Not for a long time. I'm flying to Australia tomorrow. I want to start again. Before it's too late.'

We shook hands as if we would see each other again and I drove south and came to the junction where that sleeting night, years before, I had skidded the car and taken the road back to Packwick and Paula. This time I had intended to by-pass the junction but I turned down it. The station was still miraculously the same. I reached the hamlet and the Stag's Head. In the yard of the inn was a coloured giant to attract children and a sign by the door said: 'Live Music Tonite'.

I had already sold or given away everything I possessed except the car, my clothes in my old sea-bag and a few personal things in a small case. I drove across country to the motorway and then to Heathrow where I stayed at one of the airport hotels. The following morning I sold the Jaguar at a garage on the old Bath Road where the man must have thought it was his lucky day because I took his first offer. 'In three hours,' I said, 'I'm clearing out for good. The car is the last of my possessions.' He paused in writing the cheque and looked as though he might reduce his bid. Instead he said: 'Just like that?'

'Just like that,' I said.

'Where are you off to for good then?'

'Australia.'

'I wish I could run away. Just dump everything. I bet a lot of people do.'

He offered to drive me to the terminal but I declined. 'You're not walking are you?' he said unbelievingly. 'Nobody ever walks.'

But I did. I wanted to walk, to feel the sea-bag on my shoulder, its rough canvas flank against my cheek. I went under the tunnel on the elevated path, causing mystified motorists to flash their lights. Once out of the tunnel I followed the footpaths around the car parks and other terminals to Terminal Three. Two-and-a-half hours later I was in the sky looking down at the toy fields, the cubes that were houses, the thin roads, a place where people lived and worked and loved others and had families and routines unquestioned by the time they were in middle life. But not me. The next day I would be fifty years of age.

They call the latitudes at the back of Australia the Roaring Forties; beyond the Bass Strait and the Southern Ocean, chill and turbulent seas that roll from the Antarctic Ocean. It was down there that we lost Robert Horncastle from whom I inherited my trunk. The air currents from the ice cap move north and east into the Tasman Sea, the gulf between Australia and New Zealand, and meet the warm breezes drifting from the Pacific at the summits of the twin mountains on Lord Howe, the most southerly coral island in the world. Anchored in the bay you can look to the peaks of Mount Gower and Mount Lidgbird, and see clouds form before your eyes.

Along the Queensland coast, among the Whitsundsays, are the inner passages of the Great Barrier Reef, coral cellars roamed by fish, and then in the north the baked brown islands that lie in the Arafura Sea and the Gulf of Carpentaria. We used to voyage around the great continent, under and up on the west to Fremantle, further north to Port Hedland, a bare place, and hot. It was in Chez Nous, Port Hedland, that I met Daniella Rankles.

I had to sail as a deckhand on the *SS Marcus Grimm*. My third officer's ticket had lapsed during my long absence ashore and it was two years before I regained it. The ship was under the British flag, picking up cargo in Australian ports and then heading north into the Pacific to discharge it. It was the dream of the crew that one day the vessel would be consigned a cargo destined for the Pacific Coast of the United States, or even for England, but invariably the dream was broken and the *Marcus Grimm* would return from Fiji or the Philippines to Australia and start the journey all over again.

Regularly a rumour went about the ship, when we were in Manila or Suva, that a secret cargo – known only to the skipper – had been taken aboard and that we had sailing orders for the Panama Canal. But, clearing the harbour, we would turn on the familiar track, due south, the trade winds at our stern, and the men – who had been so expectant – would grumble and go below.

One night we hove-to outside Apia, Western Samoa, riding at anchor for two hours, and the excited stories flew around the lower deck that this time we were certainly bound east-nor-east for Balboa, and then on to Lisbon and London! The officers' steward had heard the course being plotted. Men stood on deck, in the dark, and waited for the ship to get under way. I was not anxious to make the journey as I had only a year before travelled in the other direction, but I need not have worried. When we got under power the stars turned in a slow dance above our heads and stopped once they had reached their common positions in the sky. We were steaming south again.

It was on one of these trips that the dance hall fell down in the Philippines, when I saved Robert Horncastle's life and, I am certain, caused him to bequeath his trunk to me.

Seamen going ashore wash until they shine, smarm down their hair, put on their port clothes – stiff shirt, ugly tie and often unsuitable suit – and stroll with assumed casualness into town. You can spot a landed seaman from the length of the street; the gait, the polished face, the slicked hair and the unaccustomed tie. In every port, however, even in Harwich, there is always one place that draws the nomad mariner. There, as the door is opened, he finds himself facing a cavern of drink, music and negotiable women. Here he may lie with his arms about two or more facile girls and tell drunkenly of his love for his home and his wife. One of the girls is often picking his pockets. I am a sailor and I have been in states and places which I would not have liked Annie to know about.

The dance hall accident in the Philippines was singular because of its simultaneous destruction by forces within and without. It rains so thickly there that it is difficult to see the rain, and this was one of those seasons. We had almost reached the shore, a place called Sulu Town, before we knew for certain that the land was where the captain believed it to be. Instruments can do unaccountable things in heavy weather. When the shore appeared through the wall of rain it was as though a grey whale was appearing off the port beam. We edged into the harbour, for no pilot would come out for us, and once we were safely in I saw the skipper leaning against the wheel, like a tired lorry driver.

The taxi driver charged double to fetch us from the ship that night, although the rain had uneasily eased, and by the time we reached the dance hall it had ceased, although the next mass of jet clouds was piling up. The dance hall was cavernous, made of wood and plaster and with a tin roof. There was a dance floor sown with sawdust, for blood was spilt there, with a frightened-looking band who had a door marked Emergency Exit immediately to their rear and who kept glancing over their shoulders to ensure it was still there. The lighting was predominantly red, reducing to pink at the parameters where there were booths for the entertainment of women and the diversions of men. Champagne was local, cheap and perilous. There was a food menu but no one had ever been seen to eat.

When we arrived on that evening the place was already

thronged with men, mostly seamen; perspiring Japanese, Indonesians, Chinese, Australians. The girls sat like side-shows. We had seen steam rising from the roof as though it were on fire, and inside there was a warm fog through which the rosy lamps glimmered. The band was playing 'Home on the Range', a favourite with the Filipinos.

Although Horncastle had Hooker Collins as his old woman on board, he was not averse to the company of females when they were available, and we were sitting in one of the pink alcoves with four women; two mothers and two daughters. Several bottles of Filipino champagne were rolling emptily on the table and the mothers were suggesting opening bids for the rest of the night. The cabaret was beginning and so was the rain. They always opened with a conjuror and often these received more attention from the audience than the strippers and live sex acts which followed. The whores who worked there were, as always, delighted and mystified as the magician took rabbits from hats and asked people to pick a card from a pack and then brought down a dove, which was not inappropriate, for the rain was rattling on the tin roof as it might have rattled on the Ark.

By the end of the magic act the downpour was so deafening that the applause was drowned. The conjuror bowed and doffed his top hat just as the water began to streak through the ceiling; thin spinning columns. The next act, the first of the strippers, kept looking up at the roof, and moving to another part of the stage. A sex game involving two girls and a ping-pong ball followed but by now there was a candid air of uncertainty. Horncastle and I would have left if it had not meant being deluged outside. Electric sparks began to sizzle from the band. The lights went out. There were five or six hundred people in the dance hall and most panicked. There was a great struggling crush, screams and shouts and skirmishes. Sailors have an instinct for abandoning ship. The flimsy place began to shake, the building supports tumbled and the rain battering from the top pushed the tin roof inwards.

The mothers and their daughters had vanished in the sightless *mêlée*. Horncastle was lying across the table with a large baulk of wood across his back. Dark though it was, I could feel it and I could feel him below it. Water was cascading, the building was collapsing all around. I managed to get my arms around the timber and, slithering and staggering, I heaved it aside into the dark. As it went and crashed down I heard a cry from the floor so I may have thrown it on top of someone else. But it was no time for apologies. I picked Horncastle up under his lumpish arms and dragged him backwards. I knew there was an escape behind us because I could feel the storm sweeping in. Dragging him with me I backed towards it and fell into the open rain.

There were twenty-three fatalities in the dance hall tragedy. According to the newspaper four people drowned in the street. I picked Horncastle up and put him across my shoulder, and with the downpour beating on us I staggered two hundred yards to a hotel and toppled into the lobby. A waiter approached and asked if we would like to order a drink.

Horncastle was always grateful to me for that night and that is why he left his trunk to me when he jumped into the South Tasman Sea two trips later. His old woman, Hooker Collins, was distraught, of course, and said he would like to jump overboard also. Except he was afraid of the sea.

My life, like my travels, has always gone in circles; forever Revolving Jones. Some things return after years, and then return again. Like Mrs Tingley.

When I had regained my third officer's ticket I began to voyage up through the Pacific on the hundred thousand tonners, mainly carrying steel from Port Kembla, New South Wales, to Singapore, Hong Kong, to Yokohama, with other cargoes to San Francisco and as far as Vancouver. On my third voyage to San Francisco we had orders to dress the ship overall, to deck her out with flags and pennants, to ensure she was buffed spotless. There was a port festival.

'The owners want us to look pretty,' said the captain. 'And pretty we will look. Everything shiny and bright, all the signal flags freshly laundered. If they want us to wear funny hats, we'll do that as well. You, Jones, you're the literary man. You'll write a poem about San Francisco. That's an order.'

We went through the Golden Gate looking like a Christmas tree. Below decks I was composing a poem.

> 'Morning landfall
> Misty, cool.
> Every sailor's half a fool . . .'

Every ship in the port was decked and decorated. There were prizes and all officers were required to attend the announcement of the judging and the awards, at Fisherman's Wharf below the cross-stays of the old museum vessels.

We went ashore in our summer uniforms and sat with the row on white row of officers from other ships in chairs arranged on the quayside. There were banks of spectators in stands all around. The sun was insistent and the ceremony long with speeches. For half-an-hour I sat there before I began to notice her.

She was at the end of the first row of important guests on the platform, elderly, smart, wearing expensive clothes and a challenging hat. Her legs tucked beneath her chair were slim. I watched her. I knew her.

On the back page of the programme was a list of names under the heading: 'Sponsors and Committee Members.' Almost at the end was: Mrs Helena Tingley.'

Amazed and fascinated, I observed her. She smiled at some remark from the dignitary making the speech, and there was no doubt about that smile. Almost forty years had gone but it was her smile. I could not think what to do. I could see us now, me seventeen, book open in hand, she reaching out and drawing me towards her, to that wonderful bed. The elbow of the first officer nudged me: 'You're on, Jonesey,' he said.

Confused, looking about me over the heads as I stood, I began to move through the chairs. The microphone was echoing: 'This is the first prize for a poem with the San Francisco Harbour as its theme.' He had already announced my name. I wore a rigid smile as I walked towards the platform. All I knew was that I was walking towards Mrs Tingley. As I mounted the steps I looked directly into her face and I knew she remembered.

'Third Officer David Jones of the *Australian Crystal*, Sydney. His poem, judged the best of many entries, is called "Golden Gate Story". I won't ask him to read it now.'

Laughter floated up from the guests and spectators. I walked along the platform and accepted a certificate and a cheque. I was so confused I scarcely heard what he was saying. 'The poem will be published in Wednesday's *San Francisco Examiner*.' The jaunty band started up 'Waltzing Matilda' and I returned along the platform. She extended her hand and I stopped, and once more we were face to face. 'You are, aren't you?' she asked quietly.

'I am, Mrs Tingley,' I answered.

'Please wait later,' she whispered. 'I would love to talk with you.'

At the end of the ceremony an official came to the head of the row of chairs and asked me to follow him. 'Mrs Tingley,' he enthused. 'She's a great supporter. She just *loves* the sea and sailors.'

There was a marquee behind the platform where guests were drinking Martinis. My guide took me by the doorman and into the stuffy tent. Mrs Tingley was standing with a man. She whispered something to him and he smiled and slightly bowed and moved away. She turned to me and held out both hands. I took them.

'Davy Jones,' she said. 'And after so long.'

'It is, Mrs Tingley. I don't know what to say.'

She leaned an inch forward: 'Don't say you're going to turn me in,' she whispered with her smile.

I accepted a Martini from a tray. 'I've always felt grateful to you,' I said. 'I've always remembered.'

She regarded me seriously. 'It *is* quite amazing. To know so much of both our lives have gone by since then. It was here that the ship, the *Orion*, wasn't it, came in, here in San Francisco?'

'On the next pier,' I answered. 'When you went ashore I remember I got myself wedged in a small porthole so that I could see you down below, with your friends. But you couldn't see me.'

'And life has been good to you?' she asked. 'You look fine. Do you mind if I ask how old you are now?'

'Fifty-six,' I said. 'Now you look younger than me.'

She laughed. 'That is flattery,' she said. 'But ages do seem to catch up on each other. There seemed such a gulf between us then.' She dropped her tone conspiratorially. 'What a terrible woman I was.'

'Not at all. As I said I've always been glad.'

'It was naughty but quite romantic, wasn't it?'

I smiled at her: 'It spoiled me for other women.'

'Are you married?'

'I have been. One divorce. My second wife died.'

'I am so sorry. You live in Australia now?'

'I went there after Paula died. I wanted a fresh start. That was six years ago. I don't know if I'll stay forever.'

'When do you sail?' she asked.

'Seven this evening.'

'That's a shame. Will you be back? I have a real reason for asking.'

'Yes, I'm sure I will,' I said. 'This ship does the trip two or three times a year.'

She put her drink on a table and reached into her handbag. 'Here is my card,' she said. 'When you are due to come back please make sure you write me, or call me. There is something I do want to tell you. You thought our story finished when I left the ship here, but it didn't, Davy. Something happened that was very strange indeed. You obviously do not know. I will tell you next time we meet.'

It was four months before I returned. She lived across the Oakland Bridge towards Sacramento. After half-an-hour's drive the car, which she had sent for me, turned up a road with white stones at its edges. There was a gate which rose obediently at our approach and the road continued steeply for several hundred yards before emerging into a Spanish courtyard. The door of the low brick house opened and a maid led me in. The house was on several levels, cool and minutely furnished. She was sitting on a terrace, beside a pool, and looking out over the evening. We shook hands and then embraced warmly. 'I'm *thrilled*,' she said. 'I'm *really thrilled*. And what a Californian sunset!'

The iron landscape had turned serrated orange in the final light of the autumn day. A manservant brought me a drink. Mrs Tingley went to a bureau in the room adjoining the terrace. 'Your poem,' she said. 'Did you see it?'

'No I never did. As you know we sailed that evening.'

'It reads beautifully, Davy,' she said.

> 'Morning landfall,
> Misty, cool.
> Every sailor's half a fool . . .'

She paused. 'I've read it a dozen times.'

'That's how many times I wrote it,' I laughed. She handed the cutting from the *San Francisco Examiner* to me. The poem was in the centre of the page. I read the opening as she had and said: 'I don't think I'll take it up as a profession.'

'Perhaps when you've finished with the sea?' she suggested.

'I imagine the sea will finish with me first,' I replied. 'I was away from it for too long.'

'How was that?'

'I went into business. Marine repairs. Eventually it failed.'

She moved gracefully. 'I thought we could have dinner out here on the terrace,' she said. 'It's still warm enough.'

A table had been laid on the other side of the pool. 'It's a magnificent house,' I said.

'I live in lonely luxury,' she confided.

'You were going to tell me something, reveal something to me,' I said.

'Not yet,' she raised her hand. 'Let us have dinner. It has waited years. It can wait a few more minutes.'

She was a marvellous woman. There was no discomfort with her, no moment when I felt she did not want me to be there. We went effortlessly through the meal and sat drinking wine after it. 'Now, you want me to tell you,' she said.

'Yes, of course. I can't imagine what it is.'

'It's something that may not please you,' she warned. 'In fact it may give you a shock. But there is no reason why you should not know.' She regarded me seriously. 'You could not know,' she said. 'But your mother met my son.'

My mouth must have fallen open. She gave a grave laugh and said: 'How strange are the twists of fate.'

'But . . . my mother . . . your son . . . I don't understand.'

'Her name was Dora, wasn't it?'

'Yes . . . it was. She died in an accident during the war.'

'I know,' she said simply. She got up from the table and went to the wall of the terrace to look out at the purple night. 'You remember that you left me your address on the *Orion*,' she said.

'Yes. You asked me to write it in your book.'

'Indeed. And I sent you a Christmas card for two or three years after that. To the home of your uncle in Wales.'

'Yes.'

'Well, when the war arrived, and America entered the war, my son Oliver was drafted and then went to Europe, to England. I gave him some addresses of people I had met, in London mainly. But apparently he took a look through my address book himself and found yours, from several years before. To be truthful I had forgotten it was there.'

'And he went to my uncle's house?'

'Yes. He was stationed in that part of the country for a short time and so he went to Barry and visited your relatives. It's amazing, isn't it? He was that sort of boy, loved getting about and meeting people.'

'I can hardly believe it. And he went to the house . . .'

'You were in a war prison camp,' she said. 'He wrote and told me all about it. But while he was there, maybe on another visit, I don't know, because he was very taken with your aunt and uncle, while he was there anyway . . .'

'My mother turned up,' I whispered. 'This is so strange.'

'It becomes stranger,' she answered. She looked down into her wine glass. 'Your mother was a very lively lady, by his account. He was fascinated by her. What an amazing thing. Your mother and my son. His mother and you.'

'They . . . they were . . .'

'Lovers? I don't know. Things happened in wartime. But in any event they met up in London. She had a ride back to London from Wales in a US Army truck, so he told me in a letter.'

'And she died on a US Army motorcycle,' I said slowly.

'Driven by a friend of Oliver's. They were going to a party. And that's the story. Every bit was in his letters to me.'

'And what about your son?' I knew the answer before I asked the question.

'He was killed in Germany a month before the end of the war,' she told me looking down into her glass. The manservant came in, saw the attitudes in which we were set, bowed and still, silhouettes against the night. He was about to ask something but she looked up at him and he withdrew.

'And that's the whole amazing story,' she said quietly.

But it was not.

Port Hedland is a hot place where they mine and load steel and make salt which rises in hills like snow just inland. Daniella Rankles was sitting at the bar of Chez Nous. She was a large but beautiful girl, bangles on her wide brown forearms and her hair ringed like more bangles down her back. She wore torn denim shorts and a vest. Three empty tins of beer were on the bar in front of her, she was drinking a fourth and a fifth lay on the floor below the stool. Politely I picked it up.

She regarded me with curiosity: 'You're not from these parts,' she said.

'I live in Sydney,' I said. 'But I'm a Pom.'

'Nobody for five hundred miles around here would have picked up that tinny from the deck,' she nodded. 'Have a beer.'

The barman slid one down the counter towards me. I broke open the top and drank.

'Loading?' she inquired.

I nodded. 'Sailing on Monday for Japan.'

'You've got time to meet my brother. He's an artist.' She lifted the container of beer. 'And I don't mean with this.' She glanced aside, no more than half a look, and two more tins of beer came careering down the bar. 'He lives in a cave,' she said. 'His art is on the walls.'

'Are you from Port Hedland?'

She looked shocked, something you might have thought beyond her. 'Here? This dunny? Strewth, do I look like I come from here?'

I agreed she did not. 'Dubbo, New South Wales,' she said. 'That's where I'm from. Biggest outdoor zoo in Australia. I'm a schoolteacher.'

We went to look for her brother, but although we got to the cave it was locked. As happens in Western Australia we met other men and drank with them and then moved on. A savage sunset fell across the sea and sky and the temperature dropped to below a hundred. At midnight I went home with her to her caravan, a metal box on a concrete base. It was like climbing into a baking oven. She was incapable of getting up to the top bunk but she achieved it with my help. Twice she fell on top of me and she was not a light girl. Eventually I wedged her into the bunk and pitched into the bottom one myself. There was no air. As she shifted above me dust fell on me, lodging on my face, in my eyes and down in my throat. I fell asleep for an hour but I awoke choking and, making for the door, I tipped out into the deep, hot night.

There was a rough bench on the concrete and I sat on it and drank two more beers. Water was not only scarce but it tasted unpleasant. Her head, its cascade of hair over her face like Medusa, emerged from the caravan door. 'Couldn't take it in the van eh?' she said. 'Thick as a wallaby's pouch in there.'

She came out and sat by me on the bench. We were still wearing the same clothes as when we met twelve hours earlier. 'What do you teach?' I asked her.

'Kids,' she replied. 'English and French and anything else I can think of at the time. A broad curriculum.'

'I'd like to go for a swim,' I said. 'The sea's no good, I take it?'

'Not unless you're partial to sea snakes, sharks, octopus and stone fish,' she said. 'And the river's full of crocs. They're a protected species and they know it.' She regarded me softly in the dimness. 'Why don't I throw a few buckets of water over you?' she suggested.

We went around the other side of the caravan to a concrete area with a runaway, a drain, a standpipe and a tap. 'It's the only way to cool,' she said. 'Drop your strides.'

She turned to fill a bucket with water. 'None wasted,' she said as she ran the tap. 'It goes down the hole and back into the tank. That's why we don't use soap. It makes the tea taste bad.' She turned with the bucket. I was standing naked.

'How old are you?' she inquired casually.

'Fifty-seven,' I replied.

'You could be fifty-five,' she said. She threw the tepid water over me. It felt like a benison. Filling the bucket again she flung half of it at me, then came near and poured the rest, in small cascades, over different parts of my body, down my neck, in my face and onto my chest. 'Now my turn,' she said. 'Don't look.'

I turned my back while I filled the bucket. When I again faced her she was standing wonderfully naked, her fine breasts like twin moons, her strong legs together like a plinth. 'Right, let's have it,' she said. 'But don't throw it over my hair.'

When I had thrown both buckets I stood against her and we embraced nakedly. 'I could get my brother out of the cave,' she suggested. She kissed, her loaded breasts flattening against my chest, my hands holding her buttocks. 'It's a pleasure to meet a gentleman,' she said gently. 'Let's get in the jeep. I'll get the bastard out.'

We drove unclothed in the jeep over the gritty night road, returning to the cave where we had been that day. There was a crevice, like a rabbit hole, close to the ground. She asked me to relieve myself into this.

An echoing moan emerged as I did. 'What the hell d'you want?'

'Peter, it's me,' she called down the hole. 'I need your bed.'

'Well, you can't have my fucking bed.'

'You owe me, Peter. *You* know how much.' She looked up at me, her round face smiling like a seraph. 'He'll come out,' she forecast confidently.

The door of the cave was scraped open and a man stood in the aperture. He was wearing neat blue pyjamas. 'And where am I supposed to go?' he protested. He nodded in my direction. He made no comment on our nudity and there were no formal introductions. 'Take the jeep,' she said. 'Go and see the sun come up. Get some inspiration.' She looked hard at him. 'Then we're all square,' she said.

That decided him. 'I'll paint the sunrise,' he said. 'Everybody paints sunsets.' He took the keys from her and walked towards the jeep. 'What about his paints?' I said to Daniella.

'Don't keep taking the cares of the world on your shoulders,' she advised softly. 'He'll *see* the sunrise. He'll keep it in his mind and paint on the walls of the cave.'

The jeep started and Peter, in his pyjamas, drove away towards an orange fingernail along the eastern horizon. Like two naked cave dwellers we went into the hole in the ground. It became cool. A lamp was hanging from the roof illuminating the walls covered with animals and mountains, people in cities and ships upon the sea. 'He's very original,' I said.

'It runs in the family,' she said. She eased herself onto a bed which occupied an alcove like its own small cave. I slid on top of her. She looked around me at the paintings. 'His drawback is he can't have an exhibition without breaking his home up,' she said.

During the following night's wedding ceremony she was to give her age as thirty-three. She was certainly in her physical prime, a finely-built woman, with a doll's face and an ocean of hair. 'Your skin's beautiful,' I said as I ran my hands over her.

'There's a lot of it,' she whispered. 'It's good in here, don't you think. So private. You'd think in a country the size of Australia you could easily get privacy, but you just try.' She caught my head in her big hands and looked in my face. 'I'm ready for you now,' she said. 'And I understand you're ready for me. You're in good shape for your age.'

We lay together until the sun was coming through the cave door like a searchlight and Peter returned with the jeep.

I have regretted a good many things in my life but none more than Daniella Rankles and her aftermath. It was the incessant drinking of tinned beer that did it. The following night we went to a place off the coast thirty miles away called Brute's Island where there were three hundred men drinking beer from cans under a massive shed. Daniella was the only woman there except for an old aborigine, who went around gathering up the tins from the floor and even she left when the great bin in which she was putting them tipped up and thousands of containers cascaded across the floor.

It was searing hot. There was nothing else but dirt and scrub on the island and there did not seem to be any apparent reason for the shed. 'It's for drinking,' shrugged Daniella. 'These blokes all work in the mines and digging the steel ore out of the ground; they have to have somewhere to go for their social life.'

Most of the men were wearing only shorts and hats; there were men with guts, men with ribs, men with beards, men with moustaches, men with teeth and men with none. There was nowhere to sit and they stood for hours under the baking metal roof and drank thousands of tins of beer. There was no music. I have only a shadow of memory of what took place that night although, God knows, I have tried often enough to reconstruct it. At some point, very late, Daniella Rankles and I went through a form of marriage. A missionary was brought from somewhere and with the great drunken throng around us we were joined in some sort of matrimony. The witnesses kept falling over. Certificates were signed. Daniella cried.

I passed into unconsciousness at some point just after the ceremony because I knew nothing more until I awoke in a bed at one end of that great hot building. The floor was strewn with thousands of beer tins, the sun was cutting through the roof making the containers sparkle like the sea, and I was alone. The ship was sailing at noon and I just got there in time. We sailed out of Port Hedland and I stood on the bridge and searched the land for some sign of my bride. I was never to see her again.

In the Timor Sea we met typhoon weather. There are few more stirring sights, or quietening experiences, than being aboard a ship of 180,000 tons, long as a street, going through mighty seas and pounding winds. During the whole of the great storm I was trying to telephone the registrar at Port Hedland to find out something about my bride and my marriage.

The telephone cubicle was next to the radio cabin and while they were taking and sending storm messages, and the ship was pitching and rolling hugely, I was shouting down the phone to a clerk, far beyond the storm, who could not hear me. The radio officers watched me in amazement as I shouted on the other side of the partition. The radio cabin was perched high on the island, near the bridge, and from the thick, rain-splattered window of the telephone booth I could see the swollen sea all about us, running at us in fury, breaking over the bow, swamping the deck cargo, while the ship went like a corkscrew. I telephoned the police at Port Hedland, asked telephone inquiries for the numbers of people called Rankles in Western Australia, even contacted the school authorities in Dubbo, New South Wales, but none of them could hear me. I had to wait until Yokohama.

I had not known her long enough to miss her. I was not in love. I merely wanted to know where I stood matrimonially. Was that dim and drunken dream a reality? Where did the missionary come from, where did he go? What did I sign? Was I married?

From Yokohama I was able to make more satisfactory calls. The education authorities at Dubbo gave me the number of the school where Daniella Rankles was a teacher. This, at least, confirmed her name for I was beginning to wonder how far the fantasy stretched. I telephoned the school and the headmistress, who said they had never before had a call from Yokohama and she would tell the children and point it out on the map, told me that Daniella had not returned from leave of absence granted a month before. She was a week overdue. The Registrar of Births, Deaths and Marriages at Port Hedland said they could not answer inquiries of a private nature on the telephone and that I would have to call in, a rule not altered by the fact that I was in Japan. The Western Australia police seemed interested and asked me questions to which the constable appeared to be slowly writing down the answers. This was proving expensive and when I said I was phoning from Japan and that I would like to *ask* some questions, since *I* was making the call, his interest waned and he said also that I would have to drop in.

Finally I telephoned Chez Nous at Port Hedland and explained my predicament to the barman. He seemed unsurprised by the story.

412

'She's not been in,' he told me. 'She's gone.'

'What about her brother? The painter who lives in the cave?'

'He's never come to town anyway – never saw him – and he won't come now anyway because he's dead. Blew the cave up with him inside it. Something to do with being artistic.'

I was shocked. A Japanese man was asking me for change for the telephone. He was very persistent and finally I handed him a handful of coins. 'My God,' I said eventually to the long-distance barman. 'He blew it up! But, but . . . that could be the answer . . . Daniella may be under there with him.'

He remained calm. 'It's a possibility. She hasn't been in. There's a rumour she went to Port Moresby. That's New Guinea.'

'I know,' I said. 'I'm a ship's officer.' The Japanese man was trying to give me back my coins. I took them, for some reason thanking him with a grim smile, and then returning to the faraway barman. He was not offended at my sharpness. 'Some Poms wouldn't know where it was,' he said.

I left the telephone office not knowing whether I was a bachelor, a married man or a widower. Returning to the ship I was told we were outward bound for Sydney.

At sea the weather again deteriorated and in another whistling tempest we made our fraught passage across the Pacific. I had sleepless nights below and when I was on the bridge at night, watching the white tops of the waves fly like ghosts through the blackness, my mind was pre-occupied with whether Daniella Rankles was my wife or not, whether it was all an elaborate Australian joke, if not whether such an *al fresco* wedding was legally binding, and, indeed, whether my bride was still alive.

The situation was not one you could readily confide in others but one forenoon watch I was with the mate on the bridge. 'You've spent this trip staring at the horizon like you're expecting a mermaid,' he suggested. 'And you've run up a bill for telephone calls which is a record for this ship, and that's saying something the way the Chinese in the crew back horses.'

'I'm trying to find out if I'm married,' I said and told him the story. He did not laugh but said: 'Don't worry. In law marriages after dark are not legal.'

I felt astonishment light up my face. I could have embraced him. We went down to his pitching cabin. 'I wanted to be a lawyer,' he said. 'I've still got the books.'

They were lined behind his bunk as if they were on shelves in some judicial chambers. He checked through an index, muttered, 'Marriages,' and opened a volume. 'Don't know why I didn't go on with it,' he mused. 'It must be better than this.'

Carefully he read: 'Marriages must take place between the hours of eight in the morning and six at night, according to this,' he said. 'It doesn't mention sunset. That's unless you have a special licence or you're a Jew or a Quaker. You're not, are you?'

I said I was not. 'Does that mean that a marriage at night is not valid?'

'It still stands,' he replied. 'But it's not legal. You've committed a criminal offence.'

As soon as I could leave the ship at Sydney I flew to Port Hedland. I had tried to formulate some plan, some sequence, some attempt at logic. From the airport I went to Chez Nous.

'I phoned you from Yokohama,' I said to the barman. 'About Daniella Rankles. Have you heard anything?'

He put a beer on the counter in front of me. It was a late, hot afternoon. Three men were asleep, their heads pole-axed on a table in the corner. Heavy flies cruised. He said: 'The only thing I heard is that there was a landslide over where the cave was. The explosion weakened the rocks, they say, and a few more million tons came down. If there's anybody under there they won't be looking for them.'

'I'd hate to think of Daniella in there,' I said sombrely.

414

'Me too. Good sort. Sexy. She could get a horn on a dying hermit.'

'I think I may have married her. Out at Brute's Island.'

'You said, but don't be so sure. Those mining blokes play all sorts of unreal tricks, you know. They got nothing better to do.'

I asked him directions to the caravan and the cave and he called a taxi for me. 'Want to go sightseeing?' asked the taxi driver, who told me he was from Italy. 'Scenic views around here. Holes in the ground, mine shafts, hills of salt, dried up waterbeds, spiders, crocodiles. Just like Tuscany, where I come from.'

I said I wanted to see the cave. 'That's interesting,' he said. 'That artist, he paints the walls, then he dynamites the place around him. Kind of thing could happen in Italy. You know, romantic.'

He remained in the car while I walked to where the cave had been. There was no sign of any of it now, only a mountain of desert rock, and a trodden path leading to where the entrance had once been. Sadly I wondered if I was close to Daniella. I walked slowly back to the taxi. The Italian was leaning on the window. 'Maybe he's still under there somewhere, still painting,' he suggested. 'Nobody to disturb him.'

We bumped along the desert roads until we came to the hot and solitary place where her caravan stood. There was somebody in occupation; a few rags of washing were hanging on a rope over the concrete. I left the taxi and knocked on the tiny door. There was a shout from within but it was a long time before the door was opened by a drained-looking man wearing a beard and a pair of dangling underpants.

'Jehovah's Witness?' he asked suspiciously.

'No,' I said. 'I just wanted to ask you something?'

'Police?' he guessed again.

'No. I want to know if you know anything about Daniella Rankles who lived in this caravan?'

'No women here,' he said sturdily. 'Not for miles. That's why I came. I'm on holiday.'

He closed the door with finality. I knocked on it again and he shouted as he had done in the first instance and then opened the door. But I could think of nothing further to ask. 'Thank you,' I said.

The taxi took me back to Port Hedland. It was now evening and a pale light was glowing above the police station. A sergeant behind the desk listened to my story. 'We don't know what's under that pile of rock,' he admitted. 'Only a snake could get in there.'

'There was some rumour that Daniella might have gone to Port Moresby,' I said hopefully.

'That's worse,' he said. He was looking through the incident book. 'She's not officially been reported missing,' he said. 'And you say she could be married to you?'

'Very likely,' I said. Nothing surprised him. He filled out the form and inserted her name as Daniella Jones followed by a question mark, *neé* Rankles.

'He must have been mad to blow up that cave,' I commented.

'Environmental Authorities,' he shrugged. 'They were getting on his back. Reckoned the cave was important and they didn't want him painting things on the wall. Graffiti, they said. Turned his mind, I suppose. Broke him up.'

That night I went to Chez Nous and questioned some miners in there. It was not crowded because a string quartet from Darwin was giving a recital in a cave where the accoustics were unique. 'Not much goes on in the entertainment line round here,' said the barman. 'They'll go to anything. They'd go for flower arranging.'

None of the men present could remember being at my wedding, which did not surprise me. One stringy miner with flat eyes said he thought he might have been there but he could not be sure. 'We've had three funerals since then,' he said. Some recalled Daniella and agreed she was a good sort. Nobody had seen her since the night the cave was exploded.

As soon as the registrar's office opened the next morning I went in. The man behind the counter looked surprised. He had a broom. 'Early bird,' he said to me. 'Ain't swept the flies up yet.' Sighing, he ceased his housework and sat behind the counter. 'Birth, Marriage or Death?' he asked professionally.

'Marriage,' I said with some hesitation.

'You're not sure?'

'No, actually, I'm not.' I told him the circumstances. He became interested.

'Unusual,' he agreed. 'Let's dig out the certificate, if it's here.'

He went into another room and I could hear him pulling out the drawers of filing cabinets. 'Jones, Jones,' he recited as he came back through the door. He had a handful of certificates. 'Got a few Joneses. Ah, here. David Jones . . . that's right.'

I did not know whether to feel glad or sorry. 'Can't see the date,' he said holding the certificate up to the light. 'In fact, can't see anything else. Somebody's spilt beer over it.'

He laid the certificate on the counter. It looked like a patterned wallpaper. 'We've probably asked for another copy,' he said. 'This is no good. Can't see anybody else's name. Not even the missionary's.' He looked up at me. 'So we won't know who to ask.'

Narrowing his eyes he examined the document. 'There's more than one tinny gone over that,' he said. 'Looks like they had a game with it. Like blotting paper.'

'What am I going to do?' I asked. 'I want to know whether or not I'm married.'

'You thinking of getting spliced again?'

'Jesus, no. I only want to know.'

'You ought to take a walk down the street,' he suggested. 'Go and see Bill Harman. I'll show you.'

He came to the door and pointed down the roadway, already hard bright in the sun. The office of Harman and Wilks, Solicitors, was just opening. Bill Harman listened solidly to the story and appeared as unsurprised as the others

I had told. I said to him: 'Is it true that weddings after six o'clock in the evening are not valid?'

He was a florid man, his complexion made more flamboyant by his multi-patterned shirt. He wore shorts and knee-length socks. He stood heavily and went to a bookcase and removed a volume, blowing the dust from its edge in a sharp cloud. 'Let's see,' he said. 'It's not a thing many people ask.' He sat at the desk and read pedantically. 'What made you think that?'

'I understand it's English Law.'

'It isn't Australian Law,' he said still reading. 'Any time is good provided you have a licence.' He closed the book. 'If you get a roving registrar, he can marry you at any hour anywhere. Some people get married under water.'

'This was under beer,' I said. I related what had occurred at Brute's Island. 'All I remember is I woke up in a bed at the end of this building with millions of beer tins around me.'

'We get through a lot of it around here,' he said. 'And the certificate's unreadable. So nobody can be traced, not even the missionary. There's a few of them around and they keep moving on.'

'That sums it up,' I said.

He turned the desk fan to him then turned it back a little towards me. 'Are you thinking of getting married again?' he asked as the registrar's clerk had done.

'I've no one else to marry at the moment.'

'Unless you want to search for this lady, in New Guinea or . . . wherever she may have ended up . . . I can't see what you can do. If she's going to turn up she'll turn up. You're either married to her or not. After two years' separation you can get a divorce anyway, although she'll have to agree to that; and that, of course, poses a problem. After a few years you can apply to have her presumed dead.

He looked at me and tried to smile. 'If I were you I'd go home and forget about it,' he said.

*

It was very difficult, whatever the lawyer's advice, to go home and forget I was possibly married. I went out to the engulfed cave again and walked around it, prodding the unmoving boulders with my foot, tempted to shout her name down through the fissures. During the next few years I returned regularly. Every time the ship docked at Port Hedland I asked after her at the Chez Nous, at the police station, the registrar's and at the solicitor's office. None of them had any news. And I always went out to the cave. It was my conscience.

On my last voyage there, before I quit the sea forever – I was shipping out of Australia on my final journey home and three years after I first met Daniella Rankles – I went out to the cave. The taxi driver had to make a delivery twenty miles further down the desert road so I told him to drop me there and pick me up on the way back. There was nothing morbid about my visits. Daniella, I liked to hope, was alive and was possibly now the stalwart queen of some tribe in the Owen Stanley Mountains of New Guinea. Or perhaps she had gone to Manila or Hong Kong or Honolulu. She was the sort of person who might.

Nevertheless my conscience about the cave and whoever might be interred below it, added to a certain element of fascination, and led me to walk thoughtfully around its great covering boulders. Nothing changed from one visit to another apart from the amount of rubbish in a litter bin by the roadside on what had curiously been designated a picnic and barbeque site, rarely used it seemed, and not likely to be because of its bleakness and the hot spurts of desert wind which periodically blew dust and debris across the place.

While I was there by the unchanging pile of stones, waiting for the taxi to return, a small truck appeared and a man got out and emptied the litter bin. 'Resting?' he called to me good-naturedly. He wore a sort of dust-coloured uniform. 'Or d'you want a lift to Hedland?'

I thanked him but said the taxi was returning for me. 'Saw him ten miles back, still heading out,' he said. He lit a cigarette and dropped the packet into the bin he had just cleared. 'You've got an unusual round,' I said.

'You a Pommie?' he said. I admitted I was.

'So am I, more or less,' he said. He was dark and solid as a dwarf. 'My old man came out from Holland.' He puffed at the cigarette letting the smoke dangle in the heat. He flicked the ash carefully into the bin.

'Funny job,' he agreed. 'You're not wrong. A desert Garbo, I am. Keeps the place tidy, I suppose.' He gazed around at the red and riven landscape as if taking in the magnitude of the task. Then he turned his attention to the pyramid of rocks over the cave. 'There's two bodies under there,' he said firmly.

I was about to question it but he went on: 'Bloke called Rankles and his wife. He blew them both up.'

'I was here at the time,' I told him carefully. 'I thought they were brother and sister.'

'Don't you believe it, mate. I was here when they first turned up. Married couple, Mr and Mrs Rankles. I was a postman then, always been in the public sector, and I delivered their mail. Only place around here where I put the letters through a hole in the ground.'

Choking back my eagerness I said: 'I was certain they were brother and sister. She didn't live here when I was in Hedland.'

'Ah,' he said, a sharp light in his eye. 'You had some dealings with her then, what was her name . . .'

'Daniella,' I said. 'And he was Peter.'

'You're right. Their letters came addressed to Mr and Mrs and they were the only two people in that cave. Then she took herself off. Went. Somewhere, I don't know. Maybe they got divorced. Great looking sheila. You know, big where you would notice. Oh, yes, you knew her. The husband stayed here, trying to be a painter. Painted all the walls of the cave. How he expected to sell any, Christ knows.'

'And she used to come back to visit him from wherever she'd gone?'

420

'Torment him, more like it. Poor bastard. She used to drive him mad. She'd come up to Hedland, pick up some bloke and flaunt him around, even bring him down to this cave while her old man – or her ex-old man, if that's what he was – was here. I heard she was always bringing blokes back to sleep and kicking her husband out of bed . . .'

He saw the expression in my eyes. 'Oh . . . but then you knew her? You probably know all about that.'

'A bit,' I agreed. 'But you think they're both buried under there do you?'

'I reckon so, mate. I came past here one night, a bit late because the truck had broken down. I was here, just where we are now, clearing the garbage receptacle, and I heard them having a mother and father of a row. You couldn't help but hear because that cave is full of holes, or was, like an organ, like one of them amplifiers. Shouting out all over the desert. I just stood here, sort of a one-man-audience, on this spot. They was at it so hard that they was bawling over each other. It was deafening coming out of those holes. But I did hear her say, or shout anyway: "Go on, blow the place up then, you bastard! Go on, I dare you." Words to that effect.'

'And he did,' I said.

'You're not wrong. About a week later it went up with an almighty bang. They heard it in Hedland.'

'Did you tell the police?' I asked.

He looked shocked. 'No fear, mate. And I ain't going to now.' He looked at me strangely. 'You're something to do with it, are you? I'll deny I ever said a word. I've got this job to think about.'

I patted him on the khaki arm. 'I wouldn't say a word,' I said. 'It's been interesting that's all.'

'And you'd better not repeat it, not in Hedland,' he said. His voice modified. 'If you don't mind.'

'I'm sailing from here tonight,' I said. 'And I don't ever expect to be back.'

'Good,' he said uncompromisingly. 'Better be going. Thirty miles to do yet. Got two more receptacles to empty.'

We shook hands as though making a pact. He took a last look in the bin, picked his own cigarette packet out and threw it in the back of his truck, then climbed in and drove away, leaving me looking at the stones piled above the cave, with a pensive and sad smile upon my face.

Three

In my sixty-first year the world became much smaller. I had left the sea forever. No more sailing to Manila, Malacca, Demerara and the two Coromandel coasts; the Horse Latitudes (where they threw horses overboard to lighten becalmed ships), the Roaring Forties, the Tropic of Cancer and the shoals of Capricorn; never again the Bay of Fundy with its great tides (so great that fish nets are set thirty feet above sea level) or Richard Toll up the Senegal River. It was goodbye to Lorenco Marques, Wales in Alaska, the Outer Banks, Charlotte Amalie and the Skeleton Coast.

From that time on my voyages were confined to the swirling three minutes between one bank and the other of the River Tilly, at Llanwonno, ten miles from the town where I was born, Barry. To be captain of a ferry may not be the dream of every retired mariner, indeed many would not want to venture again on water, whatever its location, although they would not mind watching it from a safe distance. I had my doubts about the ferry myself. Its horizons were small, its excitements limited, but there was water under the bow, it had a peeping siren and I could, and often did, pretend to myself that I was casting off for Boston.

Llanwonno ferry had been running by charter since the fourteenth century when I arrived. They had a ceremony for the four hundred and fiftieth anniversary and I had my photograph taken with the Member of Parliament. I had only been back in Wales a week, standing, in fact, knee-deep in crates of bananas on Barry dock, when I heard about the vacancy. Barry had become the biggest banana port in the

423

country. Theere was no more exporting of coal. Bananas were cleaner and brighter. The ferryman had retired ('Tunnel vision,' they said) and he was not replaced easily. Men had arrived, gone backwards and forwards for a couple of days, and rightly decided they were going nowhere. But my future had gone and there were advantages: my own command, at last, and a cottage by the water. Llanwonno Council were obliged by their old charter to keep the ferry in use, even though roads, even a motorway, now took most traffic away from the town. It was too ancient to lose. People there said that the flat boat had made the same journey so many times that, like Moses, it had cut a special path through the water.

In summer the vessel which could accommodate three cars and twenty passengers ('Lifebelts available for all') made as many crossings as reasonably required but in winter, from 21 October, for some ancient reason, it tripped across three times a day, nine in the morning, noon, and four in the afternoon. One night somebody came down, lads I suppose, and painted the name 'Titanic' on the side. I did not mind. At least *my* command was still afloat, and at little risk from icebergs, but Lewis Lewis at the council insisted that it had to be obliterated and the normal word 'Ferry' re-painted. He was not a man of imagination.

People used to come just for the ride, for it was free (cars were fifty pence), staying aboard for several journeys if we did not want to break off a conversation. It was easy, undemanding, and the crossing was almost at the river mouth, so that from my bed I could hear the big ships in the night on the Bristol Channel.

The cottage was white, its penthoused windows and door so spaced as to give it a surprised expression. The roof was well-set and even Welsh winter winds scarcely displaced a tile. I bought some extra furniture and put my trunk, Robert Horncastle's trunk, with its brass-studded initials, in one corner. It is here that I have set down my loves and journeys, bringing to my mind again some of the strange things that have occurred in my roving and unsettled life. Once I went

424

down to Canterbury again but the house had changed hands. It was called 'Port Stanley' because the man had been in the Falklands. He said that Tim Marshall had died and that his wife and daughter had gone to Canada. Some truths are better not known. Often I have thought of my wives: Paula, lying for years now among the angels and stones in Cardiff; my uncertain coupling with Daniella Rankles. And Dolly, ah Dolly, my Dulcinea. I used to think of her raising Plymouth Rocks or Reds on Rhode Island. Owing bills for chicken feed.

But, in fact, she was not. One morning she was standing on the far bank of the Tilly River as I was readying to cross on the first voyage of a summer's day. She was the only passenger, standing in a breezy dress on the slipway.

I saw her at that indistinct distance from my window first. There was something about her that made me look again, about the way she was set, hands on hips, hat askew. Distant as the width of the river, she stood, summoning a suspicion in me, a growing feeling in my ageing breast. I could have taken out my binoculars and focused them on her, but such was her magnetism for me that in a sort of trance I went out of the door and walked towards the boat. She waved and, uncertainly, I waved back. First thing in the morning the old ferry was generally drowsy but today, as if eager to see for herself, the engine started second time and I went to the wheel and began crossing the river.

Oh, but that morning was something magical. The lovely air, the river like old silk from China, the trees crammed with summer, the sun on the rise, and Dolly . . . Dolly! . . . there on the far slipway.

Halfway across I was certain. Her dark glasses could not deceive me. 'Dolly,' I called, gently at first, tentatively. Then: 'It's *you*, Dolly. It's *you*!'

The breeze was blowing her dress and she was blowing kisses. She produced a big bandana and waved that. 'Davy!' she called. 'Davy Jones! You're still living!'

'And so are you!' I cried back. I had to keep wiping my eyes to see. She looked fine and slim and full of being Dolly.

425

Nearer and nearer we came. I had the old sufferer at full speed ahead. Never had the ferry crossed that river so dashingly. We were waving and shouting. 'Dolly!' 'Davy!' 'Dolly!' So excited and entranced was I that I forgot to slacken speed until it was almost too late and the ferry went crashing and sliding up the slipway, slewing around and flinging me off my feet. She ended sideways on. Dolly shouted: 'Christ almighty, you get worse!'

It mattered nothing. I stumbled over the side and we ran to each other's arms, embracing and inaccurately kissing, not caring about all the years that had flown; here, in our sixties, we were young again and still in love.

'Let me see your eyes!' I pleaded leaning back from her, my arms about her waist. She felt like a girl pressed to me. 'Your lovely eyes.'

'One's gone,' she said stoically as she took off the dark glasses. Her left eye was absent. 'A chicken had it.'

'I came to look for you in America, years ago,' I said. What, after years, mattered an eye? And it was the only missing bit of her. 'But you'd gone.'

'We were always gone,' she affirmed. 'Chicken feed is expensive.' The ferry had almost refloated but I got her to help me push it into the deeper water. Then I handed her aboard like Cleopatra mounting her barge.

'I knew you were here,' she said earnestly. She sat down and we began the return voyage. 'I saw you in the *Barry Herald*.'

'Anniversary of the founding of the ferry,' I said. 'With the Member of Parliament.'

'You're *always* in the *Barry Herald*,' she said.

'Have you come back?' I asked her.

'From where? To where?' she asked. 'I've been sitting twiddling my thumbs in Cardiff for three months, but I didn't know you were here on this thing. Not till I saw it in the paper.'

She stood up and we embraced romantically and oblivious of everything, even the approach of the bank. The ferry struck

426

it even more resoundingly than it had struck the slipway on the other side. We were thrown off our feet into the bottom boards. We lay there, the breath knocked from us. 'You're going to wreck this, and me!' she said sounding just like her old self. 'I've brought you something to drink. We could start now, while we're gassing.'

Her voice was only touched with Welsh. It had a gravel American sound. Her skin was fair and tanned, her hair still good and her figure slim. She had been sizing me up too. 'You look in good shape, Davy,' she approved. 'Although *your* eyesight's not too good. Hitting the bank.'

'It was you!' I laughed as I helped her ashore. 'It was your fault.'

'Go on, blame me. Start an argument.' She laughed and we put our arms around each other's waist as we walked towards the cottage. 'Are you married?' she asked. 'Any women?'

'No, not now,' I said. 'There was never another like you.'

Someone was calling from the distant bank. 'Customers,' I sighed.

'Tell them it's broke,' she said. She did not wait for me. She waved her arms across each other and shouted: 'No good! Kaputt!' The people, a group of three, remained disappointed on the distant bank. 'Have a drink first,' she said. 'Then we'll go back together.' I led her into the cottage. She looked about her. 'Or maybe I'll stay and tidy this place up a bit.'

'You're staying?' I said in delight and dread.

'If you want me to,' she answered. 'I haven't got anywhere else to go.'

She took from her long canvas bag a bottle. 'Wild Turkey,' she said. 'American juice.'

We had a glass each. I choked on the fiery liquid. There were more people on the far bank now, some of them waving. 'I'll have to go,' I said. 'They want to come across. There's a charter that the ferry must be kept going.'

'Charter farter,' she said. 'Same old Davy. Always trying to please.'

427

'Never mind,' I said. 'We've found each other again.'

'Yes,' she agreed pouring herself another glass of the clear whisky. 'We'll be together for a long time. Or even longer.'

Before the day was out she was running the ferry, wearing my ripe old cap and a blue jersey and jeans borrowed from a girl of twenty at a holiday cottage along the river. She left me at the wheel and strode up and down the deck, chatting to the passengers, chivvying the cars along an inch or so, calling 'All Aboard!' and 'All Ashore!' in her all-American voice at each bank, and giving a potted history of the region to passengers, many of whom had lived there all their lives. At the end of the day she informed me that the car fares were too cheap and foot passengers should be charged, despite Llanwonno's ancient ferry charter which forbade it.

In the evening she told me why she had left her husband and a thousand unpaid-for chickens in Nebraska. 'We'd got to the point,' she said, 'when we were getting at each other, arguing over nothing, trying to raise cash, *blaming each other for getting old*. I felt it was time to quit.'

'You were married to him a long time,' I said and laughed. 'Longer than you and me.'

She grimaced. 'That wasn't difficult. I'm not a woman who can be *left* to herself, Davy. That was the trouble with you and me. Grimshaw and I were hardly ever out of each other's sight. We had some tough times. I've lived on sardines and apples. And eggs of course. Sometimes just on eggs. Yuk, you get to hate them. And hens.'

We went to the Bombay Curry House in Llanwonno and afterwards the Turk's Head. We rolled down the path to the cottage, singing, our arms twined around each other. 'That's one thing you've always done better than me, Davy,' she said. 'Sing.'

There was a misty moon, making ruffled shadows on the river. The ferry was tied up below the house. 'Come on,' she said nudging me. 'Let's do it again.'

'What?'

'Davy, you know. Go out in the Channel.'

Shocked, I said: 'We can't do that. On the ferry, you mean?'

'Well, we can't walk. Come on. Let's. She must get fed up with just sailing backwards and forwards all the time. How old is she anyway?'

We were now outside the cottage on the slipway. More to distract her from the scheme than anything, I calculated the ferry's age. 'She's about thirty years old,' I said.

She started counting on her fingers. She was going to tell me how far the vessel had totalled in half-a-mile journeys, but she gave it up. 'Never could calculate,' she shrugged. 'That was one of the drawbacks with the eggs.' She smiled at me in the opaque moonlight. She looked resolute in her dark glasses. 'Come on,' she encouraged again. 'Let's give her a treat.'

In vain I argued. After ten minutes we were walking down to the ferry, at my insistence carrying life jackets. 'I bet you've never even tried to turn the wheel,' she said. 'I bet you don't know if it *will* turn.'

I sighed. 'It turns to starboard,' I said. 'I know.' One of the car ramps which were at each end of the flat craft had once become jammed and I had needed to turn her in the river so that the cars could disembark. It had, however, been difficult. I had promised myself that I would practise turning her around in midstream, perhaps on quiet days, but I had never done it. Dolly hurried ahead and climbed aboard.

'Dolly,' I said remaining on the slipway. 'This might be dangerous.'

'It *was* last time,' she recalled. 'But we were saved, weren't we?'

I clambered aboard. I made her wear her life jacket. As I was tying the tapes for her she kissed me on the cheek. 'We can't sleep together until I'm divorced,' she whispered.

'I can wait,' I told her. 'It's you I want.'

'You're sixty odd,' she said. 'Can you still . . .'

'I'm a bit out of practice.'

'I've had plenty of that,' she said with a sort of sadness.

429

She brightened: 'But if we're staying together for the rest of our lives then there'll be time for both of us.' She tugged my sleeve and kissed me again. 'You're a bit like this tub, not sure if it can make it. Let's give her a try, come on.'

I was still doubtful. The ferry had lights, although they had never been used in my time. We had always finished before dark. I turned the switch. She went first to one side and then the other. 'Green,' she announced at the starboard bow. 'Red,' from the port.

'Are you *sure* you want to do this, Doll?' I said. 'I could lose my job. And the cottage.' Within twelve hours of our being reunited both were at risk.

'We'll keep chickens,' she said. 'I know about chickens.' She produced another bottle of Wild Turkey and I thought I needed it. We both had a drink. It was warm and encouraging. 'All right,' I said. 'Let's see if she'll go.'

I backed the boat out into the river. Retired water birds complained at the intrusion. The engine sounded loud, much louder than I had ever heard it before. Lewis Lewis, of Llanwonno council, lived on the river edge of the town.

'The town clerk lives across there,' I said to Dolly. 'I hope he won't hear us.'

'No talking then,' she replied decisively. The engine throbbed and I tried to turn her in midstream. I got the wheel over but it would not go back and the ferry began to describe moonlit circles in the luminous river. Round and around we went. Dolly was laughing and swigging at the bottle. 'Give her some of this,' she advised happily. 'That should straighten her out.'

As though responding to the promise, the ferry at last answered to the wheel. We headed towards the sea and the moon watched us go. Our bow cut a silken track in the surface. Owls hooted over the water and coots and ducks stirred among the reeds.

We were passing the bottle between us. Dolly said she would take the wheel. 'There's something ahead,' she called at once. 'Something big.'

'It's the Bristol Channel,' I said a little drunkenly.

'Ah, so it is,' she enthused. 'I remember it now.'

Forty-seven years and more had gone since that first escapade, two foolish and frightened children in an open boat far out at night. Now, as we left the entrance to the Tilly River and sailed easily out into the fringe waters of the sea, an inebriated peace came over us. We sat in the stern, my one hand on the wheel, the other around her waist. She fed me sips from her glass of Wild Turkey. The moon remained unsure but the Channel waves were like a rolled-out bale of best, thick velvet. On shore there were points of light and the night shoulders of the hills.

'Oh, Davy,' she whispered. 'I should have sailed with you long ago. When we were first married, I should have gone with you then.'

'You would have been torpedoed,' I reminded her.

'We could have clung to each other in the water.' She shifted in my hold. 'Let's pretend you're taking me on a voyage through the whole world. Show me the places. Point them out. What's that over there?'

'It's Rio de Janeiro,' I said looking towards Barry Island. 'See the statue of Christ on the mountain?'

'That's the Maison de Danse,' she said. 'We used to go there, didn't we? Why is it called that? Not the Maison, Rio?'

'The River of the first of January,' I said. 'That's when it was discovered. Like Natal in South Africa, named after Christmas Day. And Santa Espirito is an island in the Pacific named after the Holy Ghost.'

'There's a bank called that,' she said practically. 'The same name. In Italy. I tried to borrow some money there once but they wouldn't. They weren't very Christian I must say. What's that, Davy, over there?'

'Capri,' I announced. Sully Island lay on the port beam. 'And that, see the lights, that is the magic city of the Angels.'

'New York,' she guessed.

'Los Angeles,' I murmured. 'Sometimes known as Cardiff.'

431

'Don't spoil it, Davy,' she said. 'Although I *do* like Cardiff.' She turned and pointed behind us. 'And what's that?'

I looked aft. 'That's a fog bank,' I said, my heart dropping. 'And that's the way back.' I began to turn the wheel.

She giggled. 'We might sail right past Llanwonno . . .'

'More than likely,' I said.

'And end up in Rio. Then we could really see Jesus on His mountain.'

'Dolly,' I warned. 'This is not funny. We're going to be out here all night.'

'Again,' she said, her mood swiftly altered, her voice tart: 'Well I hope you're more use than last time.'

We advanced on the fog and it advanced on us. When the first skein drifted over she complained of its coldness.

'It's hard to get warm fog in the Bristol Channel,' I said. I was edging through the outskirts but I did not believe I would ever find the river mouth. 'Why don't you turn the thing around again and go to Cardiff?' she demanded. 'It wasn't foggy there. We could see the lights.'

'What will Lewis Lewis say if Llanwonno ferry is docked in Cardiff tomorrow morning?' I asked.

'Not so much as he'd say if she was in Rio.' She shivered. I could scarcely see the bow. 'Davy, I'm cold,' she said. As I did years before I wrapped her up, I gave her my life jacket as extra warmth and put her below a canvas sheet. 'This always seems to happen,' she moaned. 'We're fated.'

We were in the deepest fog now. It was like snow, like being in deep drifts, and silent as snow too. The compass on the ferry had not been used – or needed – for years and was stuck firmly on south-south-east. There were no batteries in the torch. Somewhere ahead was the mouth of the river but also somewhere were the pointed rocks and their attendant currents. Dolly began to cry. 'You'll never change, Davy Jones,' she complained. 'I should have listened to my mam.'

Whatever retort I might have made to this was forgotten because with a great, regretful bellow a ship came through the fog. It was almost as it had been all those years before, the soaring sharpness of the bow, its eye of red light, the massive wave and wash. Dolly screamed as I flung the wheel to starboard. 'I'm going to die!' she shouted.

'*We're* going to die, you selfish cow!' I shouted at her. 'You should have stayed with your chickens!'

The ferry, after years of sedate, short passages, seemed shocked and affronted by the wash of the big ship. She heaved and lay over on her side then went back again in time to take the next wave inboard. It fell like a waterfall on Dolly, sending her shrieking and sprawling to the bottom boards. The ship never saw the ferry. It steamed by at slow ahead but not slow enough for us. Its fog horn said goodbye and it slipped into the obscurity. The ferry continued to pitch and rock but the waves decreased and she finally settled. I picked Dolly up from the deck. She was shivering. I gave her my jersey and began shivering myself. 'Why did you *have* to be a sailor?' she complained. 'Anything but a sailor.'

'How about a chicken farmer?' I shouted at her.

'You're so cruel,' she sobbed. She was turning around trying to find somewhere to sit. 'Look! A light, Davy. It's a light.'

For all I knew it could have been someone's front room, Lewis Lewis even. But then I realised it was the buoy marking the entrance to the Tilly River. 'We're saved, Dolly!' I exclaimed. 'We're saved!'

'And I saved us,' she replied still shivering. 'I saw the light.'

It was not quite so. We entered the wide mouth of the river but the fog seemed even thicker there, as if it had become wedged in the estuary. The ferry was a foot deep in slopping water. Dolly had her feet up on the seats. Her teeth were chattering. Somehow we turned, drifted, into one of the numerous side-channels of the Tilly and I knew nothing of it until I saw the bank coming through the fog. Quickly I threw the wheel over and we skimmed the mud. Then we struck something with a blow that toppled both of us into the swishing sea-water at the bottom of the boat. Too late, I realised where we were, what was ahead. I cut the engine but we still had enough way to send us nosing under a wooden footbridge across the inlet. There we stuck.

'We're under the bridge on the Rene inlet,' I said picking myself up.

'I don't need a guided tour,' she wailed as I helped her from the bottom of the boat. 'Get me out of here.'

Over the foggy mudbanks we scraped and scrambled ashore. Across two fields full of fog and cows we went. Visibility was nil. Dolly walked immediately into a cow and her howl sent the entire herd on the rampage, mooing and prancing about in the unknown. She was crying and staggering and I was trying to hold her up. We eventually found a stile and then the faint blush of a light came through the fog; a house.

There was no one in but they had left the light on and the door was open. Soaking and muddy, Dolly sat on the settee in the sitting room, water dribbling from her clothes onto the carpet. I found some coats in a closet and put them around us and I lit the gas fire. There was half a bottle of Scotch in a cupboard and I poured two stiff glasses. She drank it as if she were thirsty. She took her dark glasses off to clean them and she looked at me with one eye. 'What a mess we are, Davy,' she said.

'I've got to go back,' I said to her. 'I've got to get that boat from under the bridge.'

'Why? Why?' she demanded. 'It's safe as houses there.'

'The tide is almost in,' I explained. 'And the Tilly is tidal. It's going to shove the ferry up and up under the bridge. The whole lot could go.'

'You're like Sinbad or Popeye,' she complained inaptly since she was still wiping her glasses. 'Go on, then, rescue your boat.' She looked around. 'Have they got any more Scotch?' We found a bottle of sherry and I left her with that. Once more I stumbled and staggered across the fields, setting the cows stamping again, and reached the bank of the inlet.

Feeling my way along the slippery side, trying to pierce the white fog, I eventually found my ferry. The tide was almost at its height. The vessel was jammed like a wedge, trapped below the bridge. Bridge and boat were groaning woodenly in their predicament. After ten minutes, during which there was nothing I could do, there was a great crack. And another. The bridge split crossways at its middle. The two parts raised themselves up like arms in the fog. The ferry shrugged and backed away with the release of the pressure, pulling one section of the bridge down onto its deck. The other followed. I heard myself sob. It was less than twenty-four hours since Dolly Powell had come back into my life.

I tied the ferry up and found the field again. The cows shifted moodily around me in the undiminished fog. I located the stile and then saw the blur of the lit window of the house. There were more lights there now and voices and *music*.

I reached the door, exhausted. It was open, I pushed it and hung onto the doorpost. Dolly, in fresh clothes, rosy cheeked, full of Scotch, excited and acting, was at the centre of a group of laughing people, all with drinks, all listening spellbound. I must have seemed like an apparition when I came through the door, soaking, weary and weak-kneed. Everyone turned.

'Davy!' exclaimed Dolly. 'These are my friends! I've been telling them how I saved us, Davy, I'll be in the *Barry Herald* again, maybe even the *Western Mail*!'

She changed my life, as I always knew she would. The cottage had fresh curtains, carpets, furniture, a television set and video, and a microwave; a new, red, front door, a dog and a cat, and there was talk of a mongoose. We drank a lot of wine and ate unsuitable foods. Three times we went to the 'Bondage' disco, successor to the Maison de Danse at Barry, and every Friday and Saturday night we spent in the pub and came home laughing, disputing, and arms about each other.

It was amazing that I was still in command of the ferry at all. But Dolly had gone to Lewis Lewis and told him how I had courageously saved the boat when the engine ('a disgrace') failed during a test voyage and the fog came down. They did not even mention the cost of the bridge. They decided that, after all those years, a new ferry was in order, and that there was a clause in the charter which could be roughly interpreted to mean that fares could be introduced for foot passengers. Dolly collected the fares while I captained the boat. In the evenings in summertime we often took it out fishing, sometimes alone and at others with a group who paid five pounds a head for the trip. Lewis Lewis said nothing and the council were quietly pleased that Llanwonno had at last got itself on the front page not only of the *Barry Herald* but the *Western Mail* as well.

Dolly bought a hundred hens and a cockerel and started a chicken farm behind the cottage. Some of the hens used to travel to and fro on the ferry because Dolly thought the fresh air and the journey might be good for them. They became quite famous and their picture was in the *Daily Mirror*.

After two years we were married again. It had to be at the registrar's office but we were blessed afterwards at St David's, Barry Dock. 'Better luck this time,' said the vicar. Dolly's divorce had come through without argument from America and, in response to a careful inquiry I made in a letter to Harman and Wilks, Solicitors of Port Hedland, Western Australia, I was told that during new mining operations the buried cave had been uncovered and that two skeletons had been found, identified as Mr and Mrs Peter Rankles. As we walked from the church, under the smiles of a lot of new friends, I touched the pew where my mother told me I had been conceived. That was one story not finished.

That winter I had pneumonia and Dolly saved my life, I swear, by getting into the bed and holding me. Then *she* got pneumonia and I did the same for her. On one dark, low,

January afternoon, while I was holding her, the ferry abandoned, she croaked: 'Remember Tosh, Davy?'

'How could I forget,' I answered.

'Well, I shoved him. I just gave him a push up there and over he went. Don't tell anybody.' I promised.

When we were recovered in the spring, she produced a letter. 'It came when you were on your deathbed,' she explained. 'So I didn't show it to you.'

It was from a lawyer in San Francisco. Mrs Tingley had died six months before, leaving me a thousand dollars 'to buy a first edition'. She had written me a note with which was enclosed an old letter. Her note said: 'This was the one letter, from my son Oliver, which I did not show you that night when we dined so happily.' The letter, yellowing now, was written in 1943. It was full of enthusiasm about Dora, my mother. 'She's amazing,' said the long dead soldier. 'She is so full of fun and stories. She's a great one for wine and champagne. Last night she told me that her son believes his father was a soldier she met on the last night of the Great War in 1918. She had even told her sister, Blodwen, the one I met, that it was a *German* soldier! Can you believe that! And all the time her son's father is really his *uncle*, Blodwen's husband. But don't tell anybody!'

I was astonished but relieved. I had never felt even half-German and Griff had always been a good father to me.

Sometimes Dolly goes off. She finds it hard to change. She went away for three weeks once with a man who promised to take her to Egypt but did not, and just before our wedding she disappeared with a company director who had come to fish in the estuary. He had his own boat and a big car. 'It was the Mercedes that tempted me, Davy,' she wept afterwards. 'And he was so romantic. He said he didn't notice my eye was missing.'

We cried together in bed and she swore she would never do it again. She said she was getting too old for that sort of thing anyway. 'I missed you and our red front door,' she said.

It would never surprise me if she did, though, for I know Dolly. But she would come back. We would lie again of nights, as we do now, as we should have done all through our lives. While she sleeps I often listen to the ships. I hold her and I love her. She belongs to me.